ALSO BY CHRISTINE LEMMON

NOVELS
Sanibel Scribbles
Portion of the Sea
Sand in My Eyes

GIFT BOOK
Whisper from the Ocean

Steps
to the
Beach

A Novel

CHRISTINE
LEMMON

Penmark
Publishing

Penmark
Publishing

Published by Penmark Publishing
Printed in the United States
First edition November 2022

The Library of Congress has cataloged the trade paperback edition as follows:
Author: Lemmon, Christine.
Title: Steps to the Beach: a novel / Christine Lemmon
ISBN 978-0-9837987-3-6 (trade paperback)
ISBN 978-0-9712874-9-5 (ebook)

Cover design by Kristen Ingebretson
Internal design by Danna Mathias Steele

For to be idle is to become a stranger unto the seasons,
and to step out of life's procession,
that marches in majesty and proud submission
towards the infinite.

—Kahlil Gibran, *The Prophet*

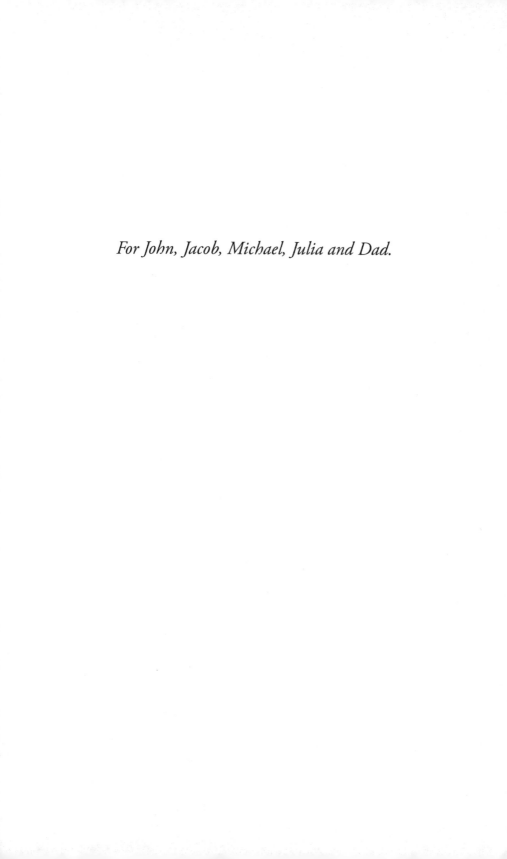

For John, Jacob, Michael, Julia and Dad.

ONE

"**I**s it on the beach?"

That was the question burning in the minds of every person attending our going-away barbecue. I didn't blame them for asking. It sounded too good to be true. What more could anyone want than to live mere steps from the beach? It wasn't mere steps to any old beach, but to a beach on an island my mother once took my brother and me to when we were kids. He and I came back with great tans. She came back a new person for reasons we never understood, other than it was an extra special island—its beaches known the world over for their seashells!

"Mere steps away," I'd answered again and again, and didn't mean to rub things in. It was August, and Michigan's temperatures were plummeting. The leaves were changing, falling prematurely, and the entire neighborhood was crammed into my small backyard, shivering, huddling closer than we liked for whatever bit of body heat we could muster.

"Back when I turned fifty," Fran said, puffs of her breath floating in the air, "I cut my hair short and colored it red. Wish I did something fun...bought a house on an island, like you, Adele!"

"Your hair was fun. I liked your red hair."

"No, Joe told me I looked like a clown. I changed it back the next day." She reached over to the buffet table, dipped her finger into the giant bowl of potato salad, then popped it in her mouth for a taste. "What was I thinking?"

I had no idea what she was thinking. Fran was a nurse, like me, and should have known better. People got sick from sticking fingers into food like that.

"Seriously," she said through chattering teeth, "why didn't I do something outlandish, like you?"

"Don't be so hard on yourself, Fran." Mrs. Pessimistic, my neighbor of twenty years tried to be nice, but there was the usual look of irritation on her face, which she couldn't help. Three decades as a customer service manager at a major superstore deepened the frown lines between her brows, making even her resting face irritable. "Coloring your hair was outlandish enough. I'd be scared out of my wits if I were Adele." She crossed her arms and looked at me. "Who in their right mind buys a house online, sight unseen?"

"Aw," Fran said on my behalf, "I get everything online—" She pulled a pickle from the crudité platter and touched it to her nose. Then, with a dissatisfied look, returned it "—toilet paper, dental floss, an LED bow tie for Joe, lip balm…where else can you find pickle lip balm? I'm a huge fan of online shopping."

"Oh, I know you are," Mrs. P said irritably. "Those trucks are always coming down our road. I hear them backing out of your driveway late at night. I'll bet you return half of what they bring you."

"No, just the light-up bow. Joe refused to wear it, and the slow flashing mode didn't work. Other than that, I'm not a big returner. I do my due diligence…read the reviews before I buy."

"Well, bow ties are one thing," said Mrs. P, who dealt with returners every day. She sounded ready to scold Fran for smelling, then returning the pickle to the platter. Instead, she looked at me. "What if you get all the way to Florida, and don't like the house you bought online?"

I was a pro at imagining worst-case scenarios, thanks to my years working in the emergency room, my sensitivity to events happening in the news, and my kids emerging into adulthood in a very scary world. Catastrophizing was a habit I was trying to break. But that particular what-if caught me off guard. Not liking the house that I bought in Florida hadn't once crossed my mind, and I didn't want it to then.

"Uh oh, excuse me," I said, giving in to an irresistible urge to escape. "I better go help Mallory with those candles before the yard catches fire."

I rushed over to where my youngest daughter, a professional events planner, new to her career, and the one responsible for whipping together the surprise farewell party, was lighting coconut-shaped candles that a troublemaker of a breeze kept blowing out. "I didn't plan for it to be this cold, Mom. The weather guy lied. What do you think—should I move the luau inside?"

"Nah, keep it outside." I took the lighter from her hand, giving it a try. Mallory didn't need to know my reasons. The frigid temps helped with my hot flashes. But mostly, keeping festivities outdoors during the chilling preview of winter's imminent arrival might shush people up. Yup, have them biting their lips rather than telling me how off the deep end I was for having bought a house online. I didn't want to hear it. I wanted to be nothing but excited about moving on a whim to a tropical island. Not only was Sanibel known for its shells, but it was a birder's paradise. And I loved birds as much as I did shells!

"You've invited a tough and hardy group." I handed the lighter back. "Don't think twice about the weather. They'll endure."

"You like the yard, Mom? Are you glad I had the party here, and not at a restaurant?"

"Do I like the yard?" I repeated with a gust of emotion. "No, sweetheart, I don't like the yard. I *love* the yard. I will forever love this yard!"

Even though I was leaving it, how could I not love the yard where my babies learned to crawl, and as kids, climbed their first tree? Where they built snowmen in the winters, and pranced through sprinklers in the summers? I looked over at the tiki hut, and the flip flop balloon bouquet. Mallory did a brilliant job decorating it for our good-bye finale. Pink tinsel flamingoes dangled from the branches of the crabapple tree, and hibiscus paper lanterns were strung along the fence separating our yard from Mrs. P.'s. Giant beach balls were flying overhead, like at a Jimmy Buffett concert, and friends were keeping warm while having fun.

I only wished that Mallory could have decorated the drooping branches of the weeping willow. It looked sad, like it knew we were leaving and was remembering when the kids sat in its branches and played under its shade. The willow and my kids grew up in the yard together, and I didn't want to think about leaving them behind—the yard, the willow, and my four young-adult kids.

I turned my face from the tree. "Where's your sister? She was out here putting these Hawaiian leis on all of us, then disappeared. I haven't seen her since."

Mallory rolled her eyes. "In the house with *you know who*…breaking up again."

Lucy and her boyfriend were always breaking up, then making up, and since Lucy was a theater actress, the break-ups and make-ups were dramatic, to say the least. I let out a grunt and was about to go into the house to pull them out when Fran's husband Joe came over.

"Vacationing in Florida is one thing. Living there? No thanks. All that red—"

The word "red" had Mallory automatically pulling a squirt bottle filled with water from her apron pocket. Apparently, she had written on the invitations there was to be no talk of politics, and if anyone mentioned so much as one word about anything controversial, she was going to squirt them with water, like she did to her naughty cats.

"—red tide," Joe insisted, but it was too late. He wiped his face. "I was talking about harmful algal blooms in the water, that's all. Florida can be a wild place to live…humidity, hurricanes, sinkholes, aggressive iguanas—"

"Heard about those on the news," my Aunt Nora said in passing. "They drop from the trees when the temperatures lower." She pointed her finger at me. "You people better be careful there!"

Refusing to let anyone obliterate my excitement, I let out a fake laugh, then headed for the house to get Lucy.

"None of my business," our neighbor from two doors down was murmuring to another, "but I don't know how they're doing it. We just put our four through college, and we're lucky if we get to go to the movies. Even then, we don't buy popcorn, if you know what I mean. Judi pops it at home, puts it in her purse."

My heart skipped a beat. There was no denying, life was ridiculously expensive. I hadn't been to the movies in years, and wanted to share that with him—tell him I understood. But then I heard my husband's voice above all others in the yard. Peter and I were like two Canadian geese, mated most of our lives. I was good at distinguishing his voice, especially when he was hissing about things that I didn't want him hissing about. I cocked my ear in his direction.

"I mean sure," he was confiding to the guys at the grill, "we talked about one day moving south of the Mason–Dixon line. I just figured in our nineties, not now."

"Couldn't she have bought a hot tub instead?" Tom, who lived across the street, seemed unusually contemplative for having five leis around his neck. "We could have partied in your yard every night."

"Or what about a cruise?" Mr. P added.

"Nope, tried that." Peter shook his head from side to side. "Way back for our twentieth, I suggested a cruise. Adele didn't want to spend the money, or take time off, or leave the kids and her mother." An exaggerated expression overtook his face as he flipped a steak. "And I sure wasn't going to bring them along!"

"Hmm, but she'll buy a house on an island just like that." Mr. P's eyes were suspicious, as if we had won the lottery and were keeping it a secret. "You two are rather young for that…the taking off to Florida thing. Hope you don't mind watching shuffleboard. They won't let you play you know…you're too young."

I felt my nostrils flaring…and fire coming off them. Did I really need to march on over and defend myself? Couldn't they tell by the premature wrinkles on my forehead that life in general, along with weathering one too many Midwestern winters without a vacation, had me feeling decades older than I was? Maybe I didn't qualify for early bird discounts, but I sure craved the warmth and therapeutic benefits that came from living closer to the sun as much as any senior.

I took a few steps toward them, then crouched behind the giant ter-racotta pot with the baby crabapple tree in it—a unique going-away gift from Mrs. P, who had been wanting one for her own yard, and probably knew I wasn't able to bring it to Florida with me.

"So, Peter," Mr. P's eyes were piecing together clues, "is there a side business we should know about…and if so, are you hiring? I need to get my wife out of customer service."

Peter glanced around but didn't see me hiding behind the pot, ready to jump out and protect my secret. I had insisted he never mention the word to anyone. *Inheritance.* It wasn't a bad word, but a word that made me uneasy. I was that kid using my hard-earned lemonade stand money for everything non-essential, like nail polish, ice cream, and even a can of pink paint, once. What girl didn't want a pretty bedroom! Respectfully so, I was raised to work hard and save up for things that I wanted, even putting myself through college, waiting tables.

I taught my own kids, too, not to expect anything for free. Well, except the groceries I still bought for them, and kitchen appliances, as needed. And their cell phone bills I helped out with, and car insurance, which I fully covered. But we weren't able to pay their college in full, and they were going to have to work for years like Peter and I had in paying off our student loans.

Inheritance. It was just enough to buy the place on the island, although we had to sell our home in Michigan, and have a garage sale, to make ends meet. The snowbird thing wasn't an option. But such details were ours, and I didn't appreciate all the beating around the bush nosiness. It was my mother's hard-earned money…money she saved, not me. And she could have spent it on herself. But she didn't. She saved it, as if her savings—and all that she had sacrificed for my brother and I—were her greatest life achievement. I swallowed hard. What daughter didn't want to see her mother living out her golden years financially carefree, traveling, pampering herself, or going to the movies and ordering not just popcorn, but peanut M&Ms too!

"To tell you the truth, I didn't think she'd do it." Peter's voice was louder than the pineapple sizzling on the grill, "I mean, sure, she mentioned more than once how she wished she could quit her job…become a beach bum instead. Then one night," his voice turned like a master storyteller around a campfire, "she was going on and on about this place she found online."

"Let me guess," Tom said, "you told her, 'Fine dear, whatever makes you happy.'"

Peter hesitated, as if letting the song that was playing in the background inspire him. "Well, she claims, I told her, 'Ooo that's where I wanna go, let's get away from it all. What are you waiting for…buy now!'"

"You didn't say that, did you?"

"Of course not, I was asleep. I had fallen asleep, and she heard what she wanted to hear in my snores. Adele does that, puts words to my snores—that's what really happened."

All eyes were on him, poor Peter. I stood up from my hiding spot and took several steps closer.

"What threw me the most," he went on, "she's a practical person. Other than splurging on the kids...over-the-top Easter baskets, stuff like that...there's no history of reckless spending. You guys know Adele. She's no prima donna. We're talking a woman who refuses all fuss for her birthdays. Our anniversaries come and go, and she's happy with a frozen pizza at home, in her pajamas...as long as I make it."

"Seems out of character for her to have done this." Mr. P rubbed his chin. "But there's a lesson in this, gentlemen. If we don't insist on little fusses along the way, look what happens. When opportunity presents, they tally up their losses and make up for it in some extravagant way."

"If you really want to know what I think." Peter turned the flames up so high, his face was glowing red. "It was either a hormonal stunt, or a momentary lapse of reasoning on her part, an illogical, spur-of-the-moment, impulsive click of the mouse, and boom. We own a house on an island and we're moving to Florida! What more can I say?"

"Looks like you won't be around for hunting season."

"Shuffleboard is year-round," Mr. P added optimistically. "As soon as you're old enough, you can play that."

"Pickleball," a neighbor I hardly knew suggested. "You should try pickleball."

Enough already. I charged over, ready to give my husband a goose egg, and become that creepy wife gone mad from his embellished story. But when he saw me—when all of them saw me coming at him like an aggressive, angry goose spreading its wings—they backed away.

"What on earth, Peter?" I stepped up to him. "The birds do it. They do it all the time. Nothing illogical about it. It's a natural instinct thing, a matter of survival."

"Um." Peter glanced at his support group, to see if they were as spooked by his wife's melodramatic side as he was. "What do you mean, honey...the birds do what?"

"Head south in the fall. And it's perfectly logical. No one questions them!"

I stormed away, when really, I could have said more, but why bother? Using Mom's money not for bills, but for something extraordinary—flapping my wings south, before it was too late, because who knew what the winter of my life had in store for me, wouldn't have made sense to the guys at the grill. But it might once they left the grill and experienced just how cold the night had become.

I was about to go chit-chat, and perhaps vent to my brother when the wind picked up. Balloons popped, and Mrs. P screamed so exceptionally that she could have made a living selling her voice as a stock sound effect for horror movies. Mr. P hollered for her to calm down, and my twenty-two-year-old twin boys, who had grown up with Mrs. P scorning them from her side of the fence, came sprinting out of the house to join in on the excitement.

Charlie pulled two *Bon Voyage* signs from the dirt, handing one to his brother. Mrs. P screamed again, even though she had seen them with sticks in their hands thousands of times before. They loved the audience, and like two knights in combat, went at it, engaging in a sword fight with the decorative signs.

"At least they're not inside playing video games," I said to her judgmental eyes, when truth be told, they had been playing all evening, and only her screams brought them out.

"Brownie highs," she snarled. "That's what those boys of yours… men…no, dueling dragons are on. I saw them out my window, before the party started, hiding beneath the willow tree, brownie platter in hand just like when they were two. But that's not my problem. I need to watch out or I'll get hurt."

Far more dangerous than my dueling sons, the enormous tropical balloon bouquet broke loose and whipped through the air. It departed our yard and headed into another neighbor's. I chased it, and when I caught it, two popped in my face. The blow deafened my hearing, although I still heard Mrs. P's screaming.

I should have stopped the boys the moment they pulled the signs from the dirt. But weren't my days of scolding, putting them in time-outs, stopping them from doing impish things supposed to have ended? I staggered back into the yard, where Charlie was on the offensive, showing off his footwork to a circle of female spectators, while Henry was displacing his adversary's blows with counterstrikes. Peter was rooting them on.

"Gladiators…I've lived next to gladiators all these years," Mrs. P remarked with a gleam in her eye. She was going to miss the excitement those look-a-like boys growing up next door had brought into her life. I had caught her crying from her window the day they left for college.

I was going to miss them, too, but they hadn't seemed bothered when I told them the news. "Cool, hope you guys have fun," Henry said, as if we were going on a cruise. "Don't stress," Charlie assured me. "You can still buy us food…online, delivered to our door. We'll download the app for you, Ma. We know you love buying us food."

Mallory took the half-popped balloon bouquet from my arms and handed me a paper plate. I went to the food table, filling my plate with everything but the potato salad Fran had stuck her finger in. Should we have gone on a cruise after all—seven nights, departing from Miami? Oh well, it was too late to reverse all that I had set into motion. I sank down onto the chair next to Peter. No sooner had I taken my first nibble of grilled pineapple when the barrage of questions started up again.

"So, is Peter quitting his job?"

"Nope, working remote…flying back as needed."

"What about you?" Missy asked in her notorious sing-song tone. She was top on my list of very difficult people in my life. I had worked with her one too many years, and wasn't going to miss her. "You don't have to work at all anymore?"

"I can't imagine not working," Fran said warmly. "I'm jealous, but happy. You know I'm happy for you!"

Mrs. P cleared her throat, then placed her hand on Fran's arm, to comfort her. "It might feel like *Fantasy Island* when they first arrive. But after about a week, I guarantee, it'll feel more like *Gilligan's Island*. They'll be wishing to return."

"So, what are you planning to do," Missy said across the table, publicly challengingly me "with all your free time…lounge around in a life of leisure?"

The yard went quiet, even the voices at other tables. Every person at my farewell fiasco wanted to know what I was going to do with my free time on an island. I looked at Peter, hoping after all our years of marriage, he'd feel my stare and know. I needed for him to jump in and say something good.

TWO

Sure enough, Peter put his fork down. "Let me tell you about Adele." He gave me a wink. "She loves birds, and she loves shells. We'll start with that. I imagine she'll spend time looking for birds and shells." But then, a foreshadowing grin overtook his face...letting me know one of his not-so-funny one-liners was coming. "And who knows, maybe like Sally, she'll sell seashells down by the seashore."

I laughed with the audience, but when the laughter ended, all eyes were still on me. They wanted a better answer. I pressed my lips together, and the word lollygag came to mind. But did I really want to tell anyone I was going to lollygag for the first time in my life?

Peter clanked his plastic fork against his plastic cup, and when he got no attention for it, he pushed his chair away from the table, and stood up. "You've probably all heard this story before." He put his hand on my shoulder. "Adele and I met freshman year of college, in the library. She was so beautiful, I kept walking by. I probably walked by a thousand times, but she didn't notice. You know why?"

"Why?"

"She had her nose in a book, that's why."

"F. Scott Fitzgerald," I added with a smile. "I was enthralled by his writing."

"One of many," Peter remarked. "Every night, around the same time, I'd go to the library just to see her enthralled, lost in whatever novel she happened to be reading. Finally, I knocked on the book she had up to her face, and introduced myself. She made it clear she was far more interested in Fitzgerald than me. But to answer Missy's question...what is she going to do now that she's no longer working?"

He better not say it…lollygag…lollygag for the first time in her life.

"Well," Peter paused, prolonging the suspense, "Adele is finally going to write that first novel she's always wanted to write. A life dream interrupted and put on hold…but not given up."

I'd rather he said lollygag. If he was still sitting, I'd have kicked him under the table for spilling out my most intimate ambition. Didn't he know that not all dreams were meant to go public? At least not until the dreamer emerged from lollygag mode and was taking measurable steps forward in the direction of the dream. I put my hands to my cheeks, hot as the cinnamon candies Mallory had out in bowls.

"Yep, this is her chance. No more excuses." Peter patted me on the back. "She's at last going to do it…crank out that novel."

Crank out a novel? It took Margarette Mitchell ten years to write *Gone with the Wind* and J.R.R. Tolkien sixteen to write *The Lord of the Rings*. It was going to take the rest of my life on Earth just to figure out whatever it was I wanted to write.

"What title do you have in mind? We'll watch for it."

"Lollygag," I said, even though I had no intentions of writing anything called, *Lollygag*. I just wanted the spotlight off my life aspiration made prematurely public.

"Show us the house…the place where you'll write your first novel!"

That prompted Mallory to continue with her order of the events. She handed me a framed description—printed right from the Internet—of the house I fell in love with online. I kissed my daughter on the cheek, then read it out loud for all to hear.

Mere steps to the beach! Three bedroom, two bath, lightly furnished piling home with vintage chandeliers in every room. Nestled among canopy palms on just under an acre, pick fresh fruit from your own backyard—orange, grapefruit, key lime, Meyer lemon, lychee nut, carambola, and papaya. Motivated seller looking for just the right buyer—a do-it-yourself enthusiast. Add your own touches, make it your home. TLC needed. For sale "as is."

The moment I finished reading, Mallory wheeled out a screen, and with a few clicks of her techno-savvy fingers, the house I fell in love with online appeared—a much larger and close-up view of it than I had on my laptop in the wee hours, when I couldn't find my reading glasses, and my fingers hit *PURCHASE*.

"Oh my," someone gasped. "For real?"

"No, it must be a joke," another whispered. "They're having fun with us."

"What's the return policy?" Mrs. P asked.

"Sweetie." Fran looked at me sympathetically.

Without thinking, I reached over to Peter's plate and took the last of his potato salad…comfort food.

"How long was this thing on the market for?" Missy asked.

"Six minutes," Peter answered, then paused, as if he wanted to count the gasps because they were on his side.

"If I waited a minute longer," I said, chewing, "it would have been gone. Things go fast in Florida. I had to be quick."

"A real fixer-upper, alright," Mr. P, whose hearing aid was malfunctioning, shouted. "Hope you've got handyman skills under that belt of yours, Peter."

"Yeah, I've got a pretty decent set of tools," Peter nodded.

As they continued to react like a bunch of kids watching a scary movie, I scanned their faces for one person who maybe saw things differently. I pinned my brother, Luke, with my powerful stare. I needed his encouragement, one vote of confidence.

"Why you looking at me like that, sis?" He put his cup down. "Still not liking my ponytail?"

His shoulder-length hair, slicked back and tied at the nape of his neck, surprised me at first, but he wore it well. My brother, the archeologist who eloped with a woman from Australia, the two of them and their six cats living on the other side of the globe, returning to Michigan once every couple of years to visit—his hair had nothing to do with why I was staring at him. Despite the geographic distance between us, Luke had known me the longest.

Come on, Luke, give a shout-out to your lil sis, tell them who I am at the core of my being!

Most everyone knew I was that grown daughter, trying with all her might the last couple of years to pick up my mother's scattered thoughts, glue together the pieces of her memories, and revive Finley Child into the vivacious, intellectual, opinionated woman she once was. But only Luke knew me when I was little, how even then I was drawn to certain challenges...projects that needed tender loving care. He witnessed me bringing home injured and malnourished mutts, going to extremes, trying with all my heart to rehabilitate them.

"You know that dollhouse of yours as a kid?"

I nodded. My most beloved childhood item, I had bought it at a yard sale with my lemonade money.

"That thing was in shambles, hardly worth two bucks." Luke popped the last of his coconut brownie into his mouth. "I don't know if you remember, Sis, but it was so rundown, we all tried talking you out of it." He wiped crumbs off his face. "Everyone but Mom, that is."

I swallowed hard, then pushed my plate aside. "I forgot about that. Mom supported me buying it, didn't she?"

A look of bewilderment overtook his face. "You two must have seen what none of us did."

"What...what do you think we saw?"

He put his hands up. "Potential. You saw the little house's potential. And Mom, she believed in you...that you had it in you, to fix it up."

Mrs. P leaned forward in her chair. "But did she? Did she fix up the dollhouse, or try returning it to the garage sale she bought it from?"

Luke was a laid-back individual, and even a personality like Mrs. P's didn't stand a chance at riling him. "I call it like it is. My sister did a fine job fixing it up, like she'll do with that place." He pointed to the screen, then looked at me and winked.

I wanted to jump up, throw my arms around him for pulling that piece of relevant history out of his memory. I had indeed refurbished the dollhouse. I painted its roof light blue, glued back together its broken gingerbread trim, added a trio of window boxes filled with tiny plastic flowers, and redid its interior. My, all the years of made-up dramas brought to life in it, and the extravagant parties I threw on its wrap-around porch overlooking the sea. It was only a poster of the sea hanging on my bedroom wall, but Luke knew. He knew that all my life I'd lived with a coastal dream house in the back of my mind.

"She'd pack up Barbie and Ken," Luke was telling Fran next to him, "travel them in their plastic convertible across America. They went from a corner in my closet," he glanced at me and smiled, "all the way to the beach house in her room."

My archeologist brother reaching into my past like that, unearthing those forgotten artifacts, meant the world to me. And to think, I judged Luke's work to be no more than playing in the dirt. But his excavating my mind right then and there at my backyard barbecue was monumental.

It was the boost of confidence I needed, reminding me who I was as a child and what drove me as an adult to take on a distressed house without even seeing it. I looked at the smiling sun centerpiece, then stood up from the table and clapped my hands to silence the crowd. Kind enough to attend my farewell celebration, they deserved a speech from the guest of honor.

"I'd like to circle back…try and answer what I think you want to know." I looked at their faces. Some had blue lips. Others, red noses. I paused, concentrating on where I wanted my words to go and where not to go. "Most of us would agree…I don't think anyone here would disagree…our world, and our country, they're not at all well. We're talking critical condition, overtaken by unrest, and more intense by the day, it seems. Who isn't deeply affected…all the human suffering…one disturbing trauma after the next? In our own homeland, the nauseating—" when Mallory pulled her spray bottle from her pocket, I rerouted my words, even though I had no intention of going wherever she thought I was going, "—strife, let's leave it at that! But where am I going with this?"

I put my hands to my mouth and exhaled a couple of warm breaths into them. "I'm a worrywart, that's where I'm going with all of this. And I'm trying not to be. It's not good for me, and who does it help? A few minutes each day, I try not to think about stuff…for my own well-being. I close my eyes and go somewhere…visualize a better place. And always, it's a beach. I'm always on a beach when I close my eyes. Maybe you all have happy places, too…where you go to get away from it all, even just a few minutes each day."

"Nope, haven't had a Happy Meal in years," Mr. P shouted from the farthest table.

"We're returning that hearing aid of yours tomorrow," Mrs. P snapped. "It's not working."

"I know what you mean, Adele," Fran said tenderly. "I go to the Amazon."

Some thought she meant the river in South America that flows through Peru, Columbia, and Brazil, but Fran's happy place was the other Amazon, the one that drains not two-fifths of the continent, but her finances.

I held my hand up because there was one more thing I wanted to say. "Retreating inward, going to some imaginary beach in my mind has its benefits. It's relaxing. It calms my breathing. But you know what?"

"What?" someone asked.

"I'm tired of pretending, tired of visualizing a never-never land. I wanna go somewhere real…open my eyes and still be there. I don't mean bury my head in the sand to current events. But find a little corner of the world, some spot I can go to, some place that I love, if that makes sense. When I landed upon that unpretentious shack mere steps to the beach," I glanced over my shoulder at the big screen, "I was more than ready…ready to turn one of my childhood notions of how I imagined life to be, into a reality. And what's wrong with that?"

Except for the raffia table skirt flapping in the breeze, there was an awkward silence. Probably, I went overboard with my wording, as I often tended to do. I started around the table, gathering up plates, stacking them in my hands. Maybe it was careless of me, what I said in my impromptu speech. What if I inspired people to quit their jobs, sell their homes, and embark on selfish, foolhardy pursuits of their happy places?

"One more thing," the responsible side in me added. "The imaginary places we think up in our minds are wonderful, too. And way more practical."

"Oh, stop," Mrs. P scolded. "You can't take back what you said. I won't let you." She clapped. Fran joined her, and so did the others. I gave a quick bow.

Later that night, after the guests left and the house was quiet, I opened the door of Mom's old room and went in, plopping myself down on the floor by the box filled with photos. I didn't expect to come across a picture of me and Mom with my dollhouse right away.

"Thank you." I touched Mom's face in the picture. "Thank you for letting me buy it, and for believing in me." There was so much I wished I could tell my mom, share with her the one big thing I was struggling with, and ask her what she thought. "Do you mind how I spent your money?"

I could have used it on practical things…paid off the kids' student loans, helped them with car repairs or rent. Or invested in gold and silver, like Luke was doing with his half. I could have helped someone other than myself…funded a shelter for women in need.

I looked into Mom's sparkling eyes. "Are you okay with what I did? Was it a selfish, irresponsible, impulsive purchase? Or is the place on Sanibel a bargain that has you applauding me from Heaven? Oh, Mama, I wish I knew!"

But only time would tell. I picked up another picture that Mom took of me in the middle-school play. Even as I had struggled to remember my lines, there she was—*woo-hooing* in the front row, jumping up from her seat, giving me a standing ovation. I never imagined that years later, the same quick-witted woman with a contagious laugh would be waking up confused, heading out the front door into darkness, and wandering alone through the empty streets with no friendly faces to call out her name, or tell her she was going the wrong way.

When police found Mom sitting on a park bench in the middle of a snowy night, she didn't recognize their uniforms, or understand they were there to help her. And she didn't recognize me…that I was her daughter, and she was my mom. Of all the plots, the dramas I had put my dolls through, I could never have imagined putting them through that. I never fathomed a mom—anyone's mom—forgetting who she was, her roles in life.

But when it happened to mine, all I could do was encourage her, be there for her as she had always been for me. It was why I applauded her any time she recalled my name, recognized my kids, or remembered that the strange man in the house wasn't an intruder but my husband, my college sweetheart.

There were too many pictures to sort through in a single night. When I heard a suitcase rolling down the hallway, I gathered the ones I found of my brother, put them in a bag, and got up from the floor.

"Here, I want you to have these," I said to Luke, who was standing alone in the dimly lit front hall, ready to catch a red-eye back to Australia. "They're pictures of you and Mom."

"Thank you so much." His tone was formal. He was trying to keep it from turning into a mushy good-bye. I wanted to change the formality, throw him a light punch, tickle and tease him as I used to do, to lighten the mood. But all of that would make me cry.

I went to the blinds and peeked out. It was pitch-black. The streetlights were out, and there were no signs of his ride. It didn't seem right for Luke to be walking out my front door, into darkness. But Mom had. She had wandered right out my front door, not knowing where she was going.

I turned from the window and faced my brother. "Having you here was the highlight of my party!"

"I wish I could have been around more," he said, monotone, which wasn't like him at all. I liked better when his voice fluctuated up and down, like the price of gold, as he told me stories over the phone of his wild adventures halfway around the world. "Wish I could have helped more with Mom." His hands clutched the bag of photos.

"I wish I could have done more, too." I wiped the corner of my eyes.

"No, you did a lot."

"Yeah, but all the research in the world, the medications and homeopathic remedies…all my efforts, Luke, they weren't enough. They weren't enough to restore our Finley Child back to her glory days."

Light from an arriving car lit up the hallway. Luke unzipped a corner of his suitcase and tucked the bag of photos inside. "You were there for her, Sis." He wiped his eyes with his arm. "You gave her what she needed…tender loving care. Isn't that what mothers want most?"

I held my pinky to my mouth and bit at my nail—a childhood habit. "It can happen to us, Luke." I sniffled. "It runs in the family."

With that, my brother took me in his arms and squeezed me tight. "Then set sail, Addie," he whispered into my ear. "You hear me? Set sail here and now, like a pirate…before it's too late." It was his usual tone of voice, the one I loved. It went up and down like the billows of the sea. "Go off to that island and claim your treasures…whatever treasures life has yet to offer!" He kissed me on the cheek and headed for the door. "That's what Mom would have wanted. She'd want that for you!"

"What about you?" I asked. "Are you happy in Australia? What if things get crazy there, too…where will you go?"

"Meh, don't worry about me. I'll go to the moon…the bright side of the moon, if I have to, Sis." And with that, he went out the door into the darkness.

THREE

The drive from Michigan to Florida should have taken no more than twenty hours. But I came down with the flu in Kentucky, and after spending several nights lethargic as a zombie at a roadside dive, Peter came down with it in Tennessee, where we stayed more nights. I didn't want to blame Fran for having stuck her finger in the potato salad at our going-away party, but sure enough, I called and she had just gotten over it herself.

Blame it on not feeling well, nothing out my window was pretty, and even as we drove across the sunshine state, its brightness was nauseating. But when Peter drove onto the three-mile Causeway Bridge leading out to the barrier island off Florida's Gulf Coast, it was like the trillions of cells in my body were reacting on my behalf, converting my road trip fatigue into zestfulness.

As we crossed the first stretch of bridge that went high over the water, a mammoth pelican glided along, escorting our car. When the bridge brought us water-level, out from the glistening turquoise came dolphins— one, two, three of them—leaping mid-air. I didn't know where to put my eyes. The island I visited as a kid, the place that revitalized my mother, was looming before us, more beautiful than I remembered.

Unrolling my window, I looked up at the seamless blue sky. "Maybe there's a hole up there, a crack, a tear."

"What do you mean?" Peter asked.

"Look around." I pointed toward Sanibel. "A piece of paradise right there in front of us! There's got to be a crack in the floor of Heaven, where it all fell out from. And where Mom is peeking through at us, smiling."

"Um," Peter said, as he always did when I slipped into what he called my overly dramatic way with words. "I think we've gone too long without a vacation."

I couldn't help but word things dramatically. I was doing it…no longer closing my eyes and pretending, but moving to a real happy place. "They say Disney World is the happiest place on Earth," I told Peter. "But I'm not sure, never been there. All I know is this is breathtaking, and crossing the bridge alone is making me happy. No wonder Mom left here a new person."

"You told me," Peter said, "but tell me again. How'd your mother manage a whole month here?"

I had told him before but he often tuned me out, so I was used to telling him things twice. "Her book club sisters. A couple years after Daddy died, they chipped in and bought us flights. One of the clubbies owned a second home, a condo on Sanibel. We stayed with her. I don't even remember her name, isn't that awful?"

"How old was she?"

"Old, much older than Mom…passed away decades ago. I wished I remembered where the condo was." I sighed. "I do remember some things. I remember Mom taking off for a couple hours alone each day."

"To where?"

"I have no idea. Her friend would take us to the beach, then Mom would meet up with us later. It worries me that I don't remember more."

"It was a long time ago," Peter said. "No big deal."

But it was to me. I rummaged through my purse for sunglasses and my mind for answers, wishing I had listened more, sounded more interested when Mom talked about what was going on in her life. If only I had asked more questions, like where was she going, what was she doing with her couple of hours of private time each day?

"She probably told me, and I tuned her out," I told Peter.

"You were a kid, Adele. I wouldn't beat myself up over it if I were you."

Peter was right. I was young when we spent the month on Sanibel, and in that selfish phase of life, engulfed in all-consuming girlhood melodrama. From the part in my hair not lining up, to my brother imitating me, pushing my buttons, to the salt water burning my eyes, there were countless battles engaging me every moment of the trip. Mom probably needed private time to get away from me. I just wished that when I finally left the all-about-me-phase, I had played catch-up with Mom about her life, and all the details I missed along the way.

Peter hung his arm out the window. "Didn't you say your mother was on the brink…that's why they all chipped in to send her here?"

"Overwhelmed," I said, in fairness to Mom. Maybe once I had said she was "on the brink" because exaggerating was a habit of mine. But Mom was never on the brink that I knew of, just overloaded with responsibility and in need of a refresher, as was any mother, let alone a widowed mother, working full-time, trying to keep up.

When the bridge brought us through another strip of low-lying beach plopped right there in the midst of the bay, Peter and I acted like kids in a candy shop all goo-goo-eyed over palm tree lollipops, white sugary sand, and salt water, blue as taffy.

"Hey, watch where you're going, or they'll be reeling us in," I snapped when Peter's eyes left the bridge and were on a fishing boat far out in the bay. "You like what you're seeing, though, don't you?"

Unable to drive, talk, and take in such beauty all at the same time, he slowed to five miles per hour. "I'm not going to lie, I'm glad we didn't wait till we were ninety. We still have our eyesight. For that reason alone, let me pull over a second, take all this in."

I was thrilled when he veered off the road, parking at the water's edge beneath an Australian pine. I knew it was an Australian pine thanks to my beloved straw bag filled with Sanibel Island nature books. Mom's friend— the one we stayed with for that month—had gifted me the woven tote as a souvenir, which I never got rid of. All through the years, I kept it on display in my house. And once in a while, I'd pull out a book, meander through its pages, and learn a thing or two about the trees, shells, or birds living on the island I once visited.

Even on our trip down, I had kept the book-filled tote in the backseat of the minivan. While Peter took his turn with the flu, I spent my seventy-two hours in the roadside dive submerged in nature facts, and fascinated by everything from Australian pines (which some wanted removed), to the zoology of shells.

Beneath the Australian pine, Peter turned the car off, and stared straight ahead at the bay. I liked the look in his eyes. It validated further how good he was with the geographic rerouting of our lives. Then again, we were still on the bridge.

"Let's keep going. I think we should see our house."

"Meh," Peter said, kicking off his sneakers. He got out of the van and went straight to two palms at the water's edge. "What you don't realize about me," he announced, "I could care less about a house. All I need is a hammock, right here, between these two palms. I'm a pretty simple guy."

My shoes took way too long to untie, but once they were off, I hopped out of the van, which felt more like a Pegasus. It didn't have wings, but it had carried me from my place of fantasy, across the highway of my worries, to taking steps…real steps in fine-grained powdery sand, all the way out to Peter, who was already ankle-deep in the warm bay water.

"Four, five, six—" I counted when bursting forth in front of us were too many dolphins to keep up with "—seven!"

"Nine," Peter corrected. "You missed two over there."

I smiled at my husband, whose clear blue eyes matched the water. His tawny hair was a mess, and his face weathered and worn. He hadn't shaved once on the entire trip down and might never shave again. Already I was picturing him in our Christmas card photo months from then with a ponytail, like my brother's, and a beard. The greeting would come from a talking parrot on Peter's shoulder:

All is merry. All is bright.
Warm, loving thoughts
from our new island life,
which fits us just right.
No returning for us in sight.

Add a fishing pole to Peter's hand, and he would have lived happily ever after on the Causeway Bridge. But there was a house with our name on it, waiting for us on the island. With wet, sandy feet we climbed aboard the mythical creature. As it took us the rest of the way over the bridge, Peter and I were communicating better than we had in years, through sounds and whistles, like happy dolphins, oohing and awing with delight.

"Left," I insisted seconds after we drove onto the island and came to a four-way stop. "Go left!"

"Why left when my phone is telling me right?"

"Your phone is correct, but the lighthouse is to the left, and I want to see it. It's the beach where I remember spending all of our time."

As we turned, then headed east with our windows open, I caught wind of something special going on. I didn't mention it to Peter, but I sensed a spirit of restoration in the air, that all of creation seemed a part of.

Red-bellied woodpeckers were hammering on aluminum roofs and into hollowed trees, snowbirds were freshening their winter homes, and merchants, in the wake of summer tourism, were painting, cleaning, and fixing-up shop before the fast-approaching winter season. City workers were trimming overgrown vegetation near power lines and resurfacing the streets.

People and nature were working toward common goals—renewal, repair, refurbishment. Or perhaps fighting against common foes—against the harsh and deteriorating effects of time and weather. Maybe I was hypersensitive, having gone through a monster storm with Mom, but I wanted to be a part of it—that something special going on.

When we rounded Sanibel's easternmost tip with the lighthouse standing as I remembered on its four iron legs, I couldn't contain myself. Poor Peter hadn't even stopped the car, when I jumped out, skittering onto the beach, to where a group of volunteers were hustling about, removing litter and debris from the sand.

"Life is a tug-o-war," I said to Peter when he joined me minutes later. "Don't you think?"

"What do you mean?"

"One big, never-ending game of tug-o-war. And you know what?"

"What?"

I put my hands together and held them at my lips. "I want to be an active participant…on the side of restoration…be a part of what I'm seeing, don't you?"

"Um," he said. "You want to volunteer…pick up litter? I'm sure you can sign up for it, if that's what you want."

I walked over to a piece of driftwood the size of a loveseat and sat down. Of course I wanted to pick up litter…do my part in caring for the planet. But more than that, I wanted to believe that the spirit of restoration was stronger than the spirit of deterioration. And live my life hopeful and passionate, an active participant on the winning side.

I didn't tell that to Peter, though. I didn't want him squelching my moment, calling me dramatic. But after witnessing the ravishing effects Alzheimer's had on my mother, watching it chip away at her mind, fade her memories, strip her of the comforts of familiarity, I had every right to be dramatic! The storm affected me, too. It took Mom and left me behind. And loved ones left behind had a right to their dramatic thoughts, and to join forces with whatever hope was out there in the doom-and-gloom world.

From my driftwood bench, I took a deep breath in and let the collective efforts of the litter-picker-uppers, the singing birds, the refreshing breeze, the swaying trees, and the sand between my toes minister to me in the most unexpected ways. I felt a tugging on my insides, as if my heart, soul, and mind were responding to a recruitment-like call. Recruiting me for what? I wasn't sure but couldn't wait to find out.

I got up from the driftwood, then picked up a plastic bag from the sand. "Look at me, I'm already joining in, making Earth a less-littered place." I stuck the baggie in my pocket, then followed Peter to the car.

"Now, if we come to another beach…" he started to say once we were driving again.

"Oh, we will alright. Fifteen miles of beaches on this island, how can we not?"

"Well, we're not going to stop. It's time we get there…get to where we're going."

But then we did stop. Not for a beach; but for a large turtle crossing Periwinkle Way.

"Great," Peter said, as if late for work and the turtle was a train he had to wait for. "What do you think, should I get out and hurry it along?"

"What on earth, Peter, why would you want to hurry Mr. Turtle along?"

"It's hardly moving, that's why."

"It's not like you're late for work." I put my sandy feet up on the dashboard. "And listen to our backseat. I don't hear any hungry, bickering kids who need to use the bathroom, do you? No one is asking if we're almost there yet."

The moment I said that, I missed our kids. I loved them all grown up, but missed the little people they once were. Their noses would have been pushed to the window with delight over a turtle crossing the road. I wished we could have done what we were doing with them, taken them along on our ride to the happy place.

"It's not moving. Let me get out."

"Don't you dare. Seriously, Peter! What's the rush when life has done nothing but speed on by? Turtle speed sounds nice to me, but we have to relax. We're not used to relaxing, that's all."

"Fine. Why's the turtle crossing the road?" he asked. "And don't say it's on a sacred mission to slow us down so we can appreciate the moment. There's another reason."

"I don't know any other reason. You tell me."

"It's crossing so Florida's senior drivers can take their afternoon naps."

I gave him the robust laugh he deserved. Funny-man Peter was brilliant like that, a true comedic genius at times. Still, I couldn't help it. I glanced over my shoulder at the empty back seat and sighed.

"What?" he asked.

"I'm missing the kids."

"Take a nap. I'll tell you when it gets to the other side."

"I'm too young for a nap. Did I goof things up…moving us away like this? Are we doing it wrong, Peter? Was it supposed to have been the kids who moved away from us? I feel selfish, or like we've abandoned them, and it's not a good feeling at all. What if there's a war…a civil war, a world war?"

"How'd you go from missing the kids to 'what if there's a war?'"

"Oh, gee," I said sarcastically. "Could it be you keeping the news on for the last eighteen hours of our ride?"

"Want my advice?"

"I don't know."

"Don't think so much." By then, the turtle had made it halfway across. "That's your biggest problem. You think too much."

"No such thing," I insisted. "No such thing as thinking too much. I love thinking. One can never think too much!"

I just wanted to think pleasant thoughts…make the most of the time the turtle was giving me, and think wonderful things. I didn't want to drive my husband crazy like I had mile after mile in Atlanta traffic, exhausting us both with my worries for the kids.

Peter didn't get it. Just as pieces of land were zoned differently, so were our brains. His was roped off into organized areas where thoughts stayed put. My brain had acres upon acres of fenceless open pasture where my worries ran wild, and my *should-haves* flocked together with my *could-haves*, and my anxiety over the shaken-up world my kids were inheriting bred out of control with my imagination, producing nothing but litters of unwanted *what-if* scenarios in my brain.

"Oh, my little sugar plum," Mom used to say when my overactive imagination first started kicking in, "stop thinking so doom and gloom… go outside and look at the birds. They don't worry, neither should you."

I shouldn't worry, but did anyway. And to break the habit, I often tried humming instead.

"A 'Rocky' song, Adele? You think humming 'Eye of the Tiger' is going to speed the turtle up?"

"It just did," I declared with a laugh as the turtle reached the grass.

We drove the rest of Periwinkle Way, passing quaint shops and places to eat, then turned onto another road. Seconds later, our car came to a screeching halt.

"I don't believe this," Peter said. In the middle of the road stood a tall, elegant egret, nonchalantly looking at us. "How does anyone get anywhere on this island?"

Its neck was shaped like a perfect letter S, and I took it as another hint. The word "slow down" started with S. Then again, so did the word "silly." And it was silly of me to be looking receptively at a turtle, an egret, and who knew what next—as if they were teaching props, all with life lessons or reminders.

"Should I honk?"

"If you honk, Peter, I'm getting out of the van and walking the rest of the way. Of course, you shouldn't honk. I'll bet they ticket people who honk at birds here."

Whether Peter appreciated it or not, over sixty percent of the island was protected and preserved as a wildlife habitat. Sanibel was a sanctuary island where birds had rights and honking at them was unacceptable.

"Well, someone ought to teach that bird basic fear…how to run from cars." Peter put his hand out the window and snapped his fingers. But he was no good at snapping, and the long-legged creature stepped even closer to the front of our van, staring at us head-on.

"What a dummy," Peter said.

"And what a meanie you are…calling the egret a dummy. It's no dummy." I loved birds, and if I had to be anything other than a person, I'd have wanted to be a bird. "Don't you wish you were a bird, Peter?"

"Depends if I live here, or in Michigan, and what season it is. A turkey up north in November? No thanks. How about you? Why would you want to be a bird?"

"They don't worry. Not a care in the world…what they wear, what they eat. They don't drive themselves crazy when their little ones fly the nest."

He looked at the bird standing in the way of our van, then at me. "Why not make it easy on yourself…be a person who doesn't worry?"

I rolled my eyes. The world was shaken up, and so was our nation, causing trauma in the minds of many. I didn't want to be a person who worried, but couldn't help it. My mind went there, and being a mother compounded my worries tenfold. I didn't want anything to happen to anyone I loved, but knew personally that worst-case scenarios sometimes really did happen. My daddy died when I was little.

"I have a feeling you're going to feel like your old self again in no time," Peter said.

By then, the egret had stepped to the side, allowing us to continue. What had Peter meant by that…which old me? The girl he fell in love with, the one in the library with her nose in the books, reading not just Fitzgerald, but Thoreau, Emerson, and Whitman, all the while self-reflecting, and exploring her feelings and emotions? The egret took flight. Who even was I then? I wasn't a transcendentalist. I never found answers to life's mysteries in me, or in nature. I did not believe God and nature were the same. Rather, I was raised to believe, and did believe in the One who created nature. God was the source of everything that existed. But that old college me went wandering past the outskirts of my childhood indoctrination…and hadn't found my way back.

"You know?" I said to Peter.

"What?"

"I don't want to feel like my old self."

"Why not?"

"I don't know. I'd rather feel like a new me instead."

"Um, okay, sure. How are you going to do that…focus on self-improvement rather than things that wear you down?"

"No, I don't know. I'm not sure."

But if it happened to Mom—if her time on Sanibel had her feeling like a new person, then it could do the same for me. Was it the sun, the beaches, or getting away from the hassles of everyday life? I had a feeling it was more than all of that. There was something bigger going on behind the scenes in Mom's life that had her leaving Sanibel and returning home, feeling like a new person again.

FOUR

As Peter drove into the late afternoon sun, I kept my head out the window, inhaling Florida's air until he tugged on my sleeve, pulling me in.

"I'm smelling sea salt in the air, Peter. You know what that means?"

"You wish you had chocolate to go with it?"

I let out a whoop of laughter, "No, it means we're getting closer to one of my wildest dreams coming true…living mere steps to the beach! That's what sea salt in the air means."

"Why do you think I pulled you back in?" Peter made a turn onto an unassuming road covered by a canopy of arching tree branches with dangling moss and vines, and bits of sun reaching through. "I think this might just be our road."

"Are you sure it's even a road?" It looked to me like a trail one might stumble upon while hiking through a tropical jungle.

"I didn't see a sign, but according to my phone, it's the road, alright."

"Your phone is always right," I said. "So yes, I think it's safe to declare it our road."

It was a gravel road, and bumpy. Peter slowed to turtle speed, and since our tires were making loud crunching sounds, I pushed my upper body out the window, to see what we were driving over. "No," I declared, "no way!"

"What…tell me it's not a flat tire?"

"Nope, bits and pieces of miniature chalky white seashells." By then I was hanging so far out of the van I tried reaching the shells with my fingertips. Some were chopped as if they had gone through a food processor, others intact. "We're driving over shells, Peter. Not only do we live mere steps to the beach, but our road is made of shells!"

"Okay, but I'd get my body back in the car if I were you," he said, as another car was heading toward us on the narrow stretch.

I did as he suggested, and when Peter drove to the side, letting the other car go by, the outstretched branches of an exotic tree came barging in through my open window, right onto my lap. "Sea grape leaves," I yoo-hooed, then grabbed onto one of the round, waxy, leather-like leaves I had seen and read about in my nature books. My imagination went wild. "They're like lily pads only stronger, memo-pads I can write on, salad plates we can eat on. I can put stamps on them and send them to the kids, like postcards!"

"You can do all that and more. But right now," Peter said once the oncoming car had made it past us, "I need for you to let go of those leaves, or the whole tree will be coming with us. And we don't want that."

Soon, there were openings on both sides of the road—long driveways revealing glimpses of concealed houses tucked way back. After passing seven or eight driveways, we came to a house at the end of the road that, unlike the others, was too big to hide. It had a curved, thatched roof poking out from the treetops.

"Japanese meets Western modernism?" Peter held his foot on the break as we stared open-mouthed at the unique house sticking out from treetops. "I'm not so sure what to think of it. Looks like something from the South Pacific, not Florida."

"Not the typical beach house," I agreed, "but imagine the views—neighbors with the Gulf of Mexico! I wonder who lives there. Don't you wonder what sort of an eccentric character lives there?"

"Rich," Peter said. "Rich lives there. And look at Rich's mailbox!"

The stained glass and intricate carvings of maple leaves alone were impressive, and the mailbox was large enough to be a house...for a dog. A spoiled standard poodle could have fit comfortably in it.

"You write that bestseller, honey, and we'll have a mailbox that nice."

I shook my head, annoyed at him for putting pressure on my writing. I already felt guilty not working, but didn't need income expectations put on my writing. All I wanted was to write for the joy of it, like when I was young, and played with my Barbie dolls and dollhouse. I did so way longer than most girls cared to admit...into my teens.

I loved the entire process of naming them, picking out their clothes, having them say what I wanted them to say, behave how I wanted them to behave, all the while acting out the juicy dramatic plots I created for them. There were always problems. Life in the dollhouse wasn't perfect, but I solved the problems I created, played things through to resolution phase before closing the doors of my dollhouse each night.

Only when Luke barged in, interrupting my imagination, did I drop my dolls and no longer feel like playing. I had a feeling writing was going to be similar, and I didn't need Peter bugging me. What I needed was care-free privacy in which to play around with ideas, figure out what I wanted to write, then go about picking my characters, plots, themes, and wording of things. I was sure of the setting, though. It was going to take place on an island.

"Um," Peter said when we reached the end of the road and still hadn't come to our house. "Did we miss it?"

That worried me, too, but I put my worries on hold, enthralled instead by the dead-end in front of us. It wasn't an ordinary dead-end, but a mammoth wall of towering pines, Cuban Laurels, and sea grape trees that together formed an arch. The arch was as triumphant as the Arc de Triomf, in Barcelona, Spain. I had seen pictures and knew from my reading it was built as an entrance to the World Fair.

"Look at that arch, Peter!"

"What arch?"

"Right there in front of us."

"Um, the opening in the trees?"

To Peter, it was an opening in the trees. But to me it was a gateway, a majestic entrance to my happy place: a beach, another beach! But different from all the other beaches, it was our beach—our very own beach at the end of our road. I put my hand on the door, ready to jump out.

"You sound like you're hyperventilating, Adele. Please don't jump out."

"You think I'm going to jump out?"

"Yes, I do. But if we don't find this house of ours…"

"I want to find it as badly as you do, Peter. But please, don't squash my excitement. I won't jump out, but give me a second, to take it all in!"

I stuck my face out the window and with squinting eyes, peered through the hole in the trees, and down the long chamber-like trail leading to the beach, as if looking through a kaleidoscope. With the slightest tilt of my head, green leaf patterns shifted, bits of blue from the sea shimmered, and fragments of reflected sunlight at the end flashed around us. If only I had a pen and paper, to put down in words what the peephole view of the sea was doing to my insides. It was shaking them up, refreshing my world view, and bringing into focus sure and eternal things I hadn't thought about in ages, reminding me that reality was both material and spiritual.

I didn't always see life in its most dazzling and colorful form, but with a few slight adjustments, and shifting here or there, its brilliancy was always there, waiting to be appreciated. The sneak peek of the beach at the end of our road was like a preview. There was more to life…infinite possibilities…and already, ideas in my head were launching full force ahead like a high-speed ferry en route to somewhere exciting.

I hoped it was the house. Never mind what it looked like in pictures. I wasn't photogenic, either. As long as it had a roof and four walls, the basic comforts, I was going to be thrilled. I didn't need extravagance…just a place to relax, write, and make the old me better. That, or bring out a new me…I didn't know which.

As Peter put his foot on the gas, I let that sneak peek of the beach at the end of our road remind me that no matter how far the currents of reality may have taken us from the way we imagined life to be, fragments of our water-logged dreams and aspirations were still out there, not far in front of us, bobbing up and down, waiting to be reclaimed.

"Really, Adele…Christmas carols? A few months early to be humming Christmas carols, isn't it?"

At least it was 'Carol of the Bells'. I always hummed 'Carol of the Bells' when I felt in my bones something dazzling around the corner.

Peter turned the van around, then drove up and down the road two more times, watching for our street number without success.

"Where is it, did we miss it?" His tone was nothing like his tone on the bridge. "You haven't heard in the news about a scam, have you?

'Warning—don't buy tropical island beach houses for sale by owners over the Internet. Too good to be true. The houses don't exist.'"

I didn't answer, but longed to hear his other tone of voice again. My Ken doll always had a laid-back voice, even when under pressure, I gave him the sweetest, most laid-back male voice I could make.

"What if there's no house, Adele, and the whole thing is a scam, what then?"

What if my dolls were unable to find the dream home they bought online, what then? I'd reach into my pile of dolls and bring out another doll to help them. "Stop the car," I said when I spotted a landscaper working high up in the branches of a tree. "Maybe he knows."

"Who?"

I pointed upward.

"You mean God?"

"No, you nut. The guy working high up in that gumbo-limbo tree. Stop the car and let me ask him." I put my head out the window once again, far as it would go, and made a mental note to trade the van in for a convertible. "Excuse me. Excuse me, sir."

The man, dressed in camouflage matching the tree, turned and looked down at me.

"Hi," I said. "Do you know this road?"

He opened his mouth and chuckled, although it came out more like the *hoot, hoot, hoot* of an owl. But then, a knowing look took over his face, like there was no one better in the universe I could have asked. He slid down the ladder with ease, then patted the tree trunk, as if letting it know he'd be right back.

"Do I know this road?" As he stepped up to our van, I saw his cheeks and forehead were reddish-brown, like the bark of a tree, and his skin old and peeling. "I guess you can say I know the road. I know its trees, and the birds in its trees. I've been working here longer than the two of you have been alive, why do you ask?"

I glanced with relief at Peter, then back out the window at the man. "We've driven up and down, but we're not seeing it…the house we bought online…and it's making us kind of nervous."

Peter cleared his throat and I regretted having disclosed my impulsive shopping incident to yet another person on the planet. The old man didn't seem to judge me for it, and without even asking its street number, he nodded in the most reassuring way.

"Sure, the little pilings home, the only house recently sold on this road." His voice was strong, but his body small in comparison to the trees that stood behind him. "It's back that way," he pointed, "almost to the end…right before the mansion, look closely and you'll see an opening in the trees. Don't look for your mailbox, though. It blew away in a storm and no one bothered to replace it. But the osprey nest is still there." The old man pulled his gloves off. "You'll be glad to know, they just returned."

"Who?"

"The ospreys."

I looked at Peter, to see if he looked glad—glad to hear that the ospreys had returned. But no, he didn't look glad. There were probably other things he needed to hear from the old man in order to be glad—like, '*Congratulations on your purchase, it's a charming house. You're a fortunate couple to own such a place. Wish I had bought it first.*'

Instead, the old man wiped his brow with his sleeve. "One day you'll miss those birds when they're gone. You won't believe how quiet the street gets. But they return. Every year they return to the same nest they abandoned in the spring. It's right outside your front door, you know."

By then, Peter was leaning over, almost in my lap, but not saying a word. He had a miserable look on his face.

"So, tell me," I said, trying to make up for Peter's sourness. "It's a good thing to have their nest right outside our front door?"

"I think so. They serve as reminders." The man shrugged his shoulders. "But not everybody wants to be reminded."

"I do," I said right away. "Reminded of what?"

"Well, if the ospreys can do it," the old man's eyes were large and unblinking like the eyes of an owl, "then so can you!"

"Do what?"

"Fix up that disarrayed nest of theirs. If they can fix up their nest after leaving it all winter, then you can fix up that house of yours, which by the way, has been abandoned longer than a winter, you know."

I bit my lip, having no idea of its history.

"But unlike the ospreys," the wise man's eyes turned cautionary, "you cannot do it yourself. You're going to need help."

Upon hearing that, Peter returned to his driver's seat, and in an eerily calm manner stared straight ahead, hands gripping the wheel, like the captain of a ship that was headed for an iceberg.

"Nah," I said. "We're planning to do it all ourselves. Is it really that bad?" By then I was whispering, not wanting Peter to hear. But the man had age lines on his face that were deep as trenches, and surely, he had lived through it all—epidemics and depressions, hurricanes and wars. If he said it was bad, then it was bad.

"Let's put it this way." He scratched his chin in hesitation. "Get ready for its flaws, its brokenness, and the things wrong with it to pop right out, smacking you in the face. But when that happens, think about all it has been through, and pray."

"Pray?" I asked. "You mean pray for the house?"

"No, just pray. Pray for compassion."

"Say good-bye now, Adele." Peter nudged my arm.

"I'm sure all it needs is TLC," I told the man who spent too much time up in the trees. "That's what the description claimed."

Hoot, hoot, hoot, the old guy chuckled. "TLC makes the world a better place, but it's not enough." He rested his hand on our van. "You said you're doing everything yourselves, but when you realize you can't, well, I know a handyman…a real jack-of-all-trades, works with his father. Funny, I was talking to him right before you came down the road. A while back, they did work for me, which saved me."

"Tell him so long, Adele." Peter put the van into drive.

"Thank you." I waved.

"Cry out for help," the old guy called out. "The ospreys will remind you. They're always crying out. You'll know what I mean soon enough." *Hoot, hoot, hoot.*

After that, all the way down the road, Peter let out one extended sigh after the next, and soon his sighs joined together, forming an expressive song. It wasn't an uplifting song, but the kind belonging at the start of a suspenseful thriller.

I didn't say anything to interrupt his sigh-filled song. Life in general, mixed with moving, was stressful enough, and the sudden onslaught of moans and groans was his way of expressing his rightful frustration. Once we found our driveway, it would turn into a celebratory occasion and he would stop with the sounds, and hum along with me instead.

"You think that's it?" I pointed to an inconspicuous break in the trees, right before the mansion. "You think that's our driveway?"

"It looks more like an alligator step-through. It's hardly big enough for a car to go through, let alone our van. Better not be our driveway!"

We both knew that it was. Peter glanced into the rearview mirror, then into each side mirror, then with a surge of enthusiasm, and the face of a boy playing bulldozer, plowed full force ahead through the crack in the trees.

Horrible sounds were made as whatever we were driving over scratched away at the poor underbelly of the van, which we needed to keep after all, and not trade in for a convertible. It did a fine job paving the way, snapping branches as it went. When a few got caught on the window, blocking Peter's view, he put the windshield wipers on, and the branches were gone. As old as the van was, I was older, and the bumpy ride hard on me. I was used to body parts drooping down, although it was nice to know they still had it in them to bounce up.

Once we made it through the trees, we came upon a winding half-gravel, half-shell pathway covered with puddles. Several of the puddles were filled with water too murky to be rain, and I worried they were swamps instead.

When we came to a giant puddle—or sinkhole—with no room to go around, Peter stepped full force on the gas, giving me no time to close my window. As we blew through it, the mucky water splashed my arm and face. I was busy wiping it out of my eyes when he slammed on the breaks.

"What?" I said, my eyes sealed shut from the muck. "What now?"

"Well, let me start by telling you what it's not. It's not a turtle, or a bird, or an old man dropped from a tree," Peter said with an ornery voice. "And it's not a gator, although I'm sure there's one nearby, watching us."

Enough of his games. I opened one eye, to see what he was talking about and there it was, standing on its slender stilt legs, peeking out from the voluptuous branches of banyan, palm, and rubber trees—the 1,200 square-foot solitary structure I fell in love with online. Despite the muck on my eyelashes, I opened my other eye, too.

I could have bought a brand-new convertible, or gone for a manicure (I went the day before our wedding, and ever since, longed for a second). I could have treated my kids to a bunch of dinners, redecorated their apartments, redone our entire Michigan home, turned it into a Midwestern dream home. That would have revived the old me, or had me feeling like a new person.

I could have splurged at the grocery store, for once not caring about the prices. Rather than spending however long it took in the yogurt aisle alone, doing the mental math, then going with the brand that gave more cups of yogurt for our hard-earned buck, I could have gone with the yogurt that looked good.

But no, what did I do? I squandered Mom's savings, her leftover money from life in pursuit of a real—not imaginary—happy place?

I let my bottom lip protrude, then closed my eyes, to see if it was still there—the palace by the sea, that place in my imagination. It was indeed, and I wanted to stay there, but knew I had to open my eyes to the reality in front of me, and the husband beside me.

All that time, the two of us had been sitting there like characters in an old silent film, staring at the horror in front of us, saying nothing, but reacting with melodramatic facial expressions. The silence broke when my neck cracked in three places as I turned to look at him. If I had leftover change, I would have announced—surprise, we're spending our first night at a resort, my treat! There was nothing left over, though, and no options left but to live—or try to live—happily ever after in the despicable shack in front of us.

"Say something, please," I said to Peter, who sat gripping the wheel with straight, stiff arms, ready to high tail us out of there. "I feel like we're in one of those silent horror films. I know you can talk, though, and sighs don't count. Words…I need words, one after the next until they form a sentence, and better yet, a paragraph."

He let go of the wheel. "You think you overpaid for this? They would have given it to you for free. Did you ask? They would have paid you to take it."

His sarcasm at a time like that made me want to take my ring off and throw it at him.

Overly observant Peter noticed right away. "You're fidgeting with your ring. Trying to get it off?" he asked. "We could sell it. We're going to need all the money we can get just to fix this place up!"

"We wouldn't get much for it," I said. "It's not even a diamond."

The moment I said that, I felt bad. When my diamond fell out years earlier, and he surprised me with a cubic zirconia, to replace it, I was excited. I never thought twice about the
beautiful, affordable fake.

I wanted to apologize, but he was already out of the van, standing in the tall weeds that were up to his knees. I got out, too, and once more was about to apologize when he climbed up and sat on the hood of the van, which he always yelled at the kids for doing. I stood there huffing and puffing, hoping to blow the place down until he reached his hand out.

I took it and let him help pull me up. "I'm sorry," I told him.

"Listen." He squeezed my hand. "I don't mean to be mean…working my way through an initial processing phase in my mind, that's all."

I leaned into him, and awful as it was, when a branch poked at my head, a part of me wanted to laugh. At least we weren't sitting around on the boring old couch, watching TV. I was about to say that to Peter, but the look on his face told me there were things he was preparing to say. That, or he was about to get sick.

"Are you okay? You don't look good," I said.

He licked his lips, as he did when preparing to give a monologue. "I don't look good? Hmm, I wonder why?" His eyes turning distant, he stared straight ahead, as if he were on stage, talking to an audience and not me. "I don't look well because my home is one tropical storm away from falling down. Because it reminds me of a tree house, a boy's clubhouse… the kind I'd set stink bombs off in as a kid. No need to worry about girls coming around…other than you, no girl in her right mind would go near the place. Hey, whatever you do…don't sneeze, or it'll fall down." By then, his voice had turned arrogant, like a world-renowned comedian putting everyone in stitches, but me. "Do you happen to know any stick figures?"

"Peter," I tried to stop him.

"Yeah, you….do you happen to know any stick figures? A single line for their torsos, arms, legs, and a circle for a head."

"I know what stick figures are." I rolled my eyes, even though I had no right to be annoyed with him. The situation we were in was one hundred percent my fault. "No, I don't know any stick figures, why do you ask?"

"It's the perfect house for a stick figure…it's made of sticks." He was hardly taking breaths in between and pushing himself into hyperventilation mode. "Remember that mailbox we drove by…next door? I hear our neighbor is renting it out…an annual lease. I'll go see if it's available."

Peter's one-liners went on and on. If we needed to, we could have sold tickets. People could have brought their own chairs, sat under the clouds at our outdoor comedy club…the van our stage. We were a comedic couple together, but I wasn't thinking straight. I felt like both crying and laughing at the same time.

"I miss my old neighbor," Peter went on, resorting to humor as his coping mechanism. "It's a small world, so I'll call her Mrs. Pessimistic. She was miserable, but I think we'd be best friends right now. Don't they always say misery loves company?"

Hearing that made me miss Mrs. P, and the life we walked away from. I turned and looked over at the mansion poking out from the trees. If it was all just me playing with dolls, I'd have a great neighbor of a doll living next door. When my dolls moved from the shoebox into the eyesore dollhouse that I bought at the garage sale, I made sure to give them an upbeat neighbor…one who threw parties and invited them over all the time, while their own house was being worked on. The parties were so big I had to buy more dolls.

When Peter's song and dance ended, he hopped off the hood and grabbed my hand, pulling me off, too. It was sweet of him to pull me off when he could have left me there. That simple gesture meant a lot to me—Peter was trying to forgive me. It inspired me to adjust my view of things ever so slightly, and remain hopeful and optimistic, no matter what.

"You know," I said as we trekked through the field of weeds toward the house "it kind of looks like an old, abandoned church, or a dilapidated chapel stripped of its glory, don't you think?"

Peter squinted his eyes, trying to see what I was seeing. But just as kaleidoscopes differed with regard to the materials in them—some having glitter and pearls, and others geometric shapes and small rods—so differed the insides of Peter and me. He shook his head, wanting to see, trying to see, but unable to see what I was seeing. Even with the late afternoon sunlight bouncing off the tin roof, Peter couldn't see a single beautiful thing about the house.

I didn't know if I was born with it, or if life circumstances contributed. I was filled with bits of stubborn determination, sprinkles of grandiosity, specks of dreamer dust, and slivers of hope. And when shaken up by life's circumstances, all those things together altered my view, helping me see things in my own unique way.

"We can do it," I chanted beneath my breath as we approached. "No matter how bad things are, we can do it. We can bring the place back to life. We can!"

Whether he believed my chant or not, my view of things was enough to get us started. Peter was filled with his own wonderful materials that I didn't have, and too many times to count in our marriage, we had relied on his perspective to get us through.

It was my turn to be optimistic.

FIVE

Back and forth through the sky, the ospreys flew with driftwood, sea-weed, and frizz from the cabbage palms dangling from their beaks. What handy materials for fixing up their nest piled high on top of a broken-down tree trunk outside our front door.

"If the birds can do it, so can we," I said to Peter as we went up and down the rotting, wobbly steps of the pilings home, toting bags of supplies, tools, and new pairs of flip flops from the back of our van into our own simple roost. Ravished by a hurricane, let go, boarded up, then abandoned by its prior owner and left vacant for a year, the house was in critical condition.

It was ninety degrees outside and Peter's face was flaming red, like the crest of a woodpecker, and he was driving me crazy whistling that Led Zeppelin song, 'Stairway to Heaven.' I wanted him to focus on not hyperventilating in the extreme heat, and to whistle a more relevant song. The tall flight of porch steps wasn't leading to Heaven, or anyplace like it.

I was in no better shape than he, struggling to catch my breath. It wasn't just houses that needed repair. People weathered storms and needed fixing, too. Peter and I did, and with every trip from the van to upstairs, I found myself relating to the house's dull exterior and its worn-out windows. Surely, it must have endured its share of gossiping bystanders, gawking at its rundown condition while doing nothing to lend a hand. People back home had been casting *poor thing* glances at me, too. I saw it in their eyes, even at my farewell barbecue, they wondered about my unkempt hair, extra twenty pounds, and circles beneath my eyes.

"Fine, just fine. How about you?" I rattled off whenever someone asked. I wasn't going to give an honest tour of my interior...of me bawling my eyes out over my mother's deterioration, or moaning about how tired work left me, or crabbing about my messy house, or sobbing about my kids growing up, wishing I had spent more quality time with them, back when they wanted to spend time with me. It was easier to say, "Fine. I'm doing fine, thank you."

"Wait, listen!" Peter said, stopping midway up the porch steps, with me following a couple of steps behind him. "Do you hear that?"

Sure enough, through the trees and coming from the mansion's yard next door were the sounds of commotion—car doors opening and closing, people talking, although I couldn't hear what they were saying. "It's a party," I said. "Mansions have parties all the time!"

"They're celebrating us, that we're here." Peter's voice sounded like Eeyore from *Winnie the Pooh*. "'Someone bought the place and will bulldoze it down, build from scratch!'"

"Oh, come on, no more sarcasm. Let's keep positive."

But as I went up the steps behind him—muffled, explosive sounds coming from his mouth—it was hard to stay positive when my most relevant work experience—fixing up that dollhouse as a kid—was proving inadequate. I didn't like Peter going from funny man one moment to Mr. Sarcastic the next, but also didn't blame him. The splinter-causing, scratched-up knotty pine floors, musty-smelling, bug-infested shag carpet, outdated wallpaper, dry rot on the windows, darkened interior, cockroaches and legions of ghost ants, not to mention all the carpentry, plumbing, landscaping, and air conditioning work needed was wreaking havoc on both our moods.

Every time I stepped into the dark, depressing hideaway, I feared we didn't have all that was needed to make the place new. Some people didn't have green thumbs, and others couldn't cook to save their lives. Peter and I lacked fixer-upper skills. When the shower rack broke back in our Michigan home, it stayed broken for years. And when the doorknob on the boys' door fell off, we figured great, they can't lock their door on us anymore. We only fixed the broken cabinet in our master bath when the listing agent insisted. And we hired an expert to do it for us.

As for other things—keeping our bodies in shape, and even our marriage—no wonder we were both ready to collapse. We were never the athletic couple waking early Saturday mornings, training for marathons, triathlons, or even assistant coaching the sports that our kids played. I was always wearing workout leggings and sneakers, but never working out. I wore them because they were comfortable, and they stretched along with me as I grew. Also, I could fall into bed wearing them at night, and wake the next morning already dressed.

"What on earth was I thinking?" I said to Peter as we dropped the last of our stuff onto the kitchen floor. "That by moving to an island we'd have a shot at turning our run-down, middle-aged bodies, neglected marriage, and abandoned inner selves into more?"

"What happened to being positive? Peter said with beads of sweat dripping from his eyebrows, down his cheeks, and right into his mouth.

"The swing of the pendulum," was all I said. "Your turn to be positive."

"Okay. Well, here's my advice. We do the bare minimum. Strip the place bare, redress things, throw paint on everything. Then I go fishing, you go to the beach, and we call it a day."

Beneath the low-lying kitchen ceiling, I took a step toward him, ready to give my husband a hug for having flaunted such a youthful trait at a time like that—the *no big deal* look on his face and nonchalant confidence that no matter the mess we got ourselves into everything was going to be okay. It was exactly what I needed, and the trait my younger self had admired most about him, way back when. But as I approached him, he stopped, dropped, and rolled onto the kitchen floor. It wasn't courtship behavior. I looked around to see if the house was on fire. It wasn't that, either.

"No," he groaned, grabbing his lower back. "Another one…another pinched nerve!"

My, how the storms, and the daily rains, too, all had their way with things, wearing and tearing down houses, bodies, and bird nests. I slid down next to him on the splintery kitchen floor. Nothing in life was simple—not for us, the ospreys, or for anyone.

"Speaking of stick figures," I said as I rubbed his back. "I bet you wish you were one."

"No. I'm glad I'm not. Why?"

"Life would be simpler, that's all. You wouldn't get pinched nerves, and we could scribble ourselves a house with pencil on paper…live simple and happy."

I wasn't serious. I was trying not to be so serious. Often, I was too serious. I didn't want to be a stick figure. Being an elaborately complex person, wrapped in flesh, and filled with a heart, soul, and mind was a gift. But even then, we stood vulnerable to being erased. I had witnessed it with my own two eyes—an eraser in the hands of an evil monster, erasing parts of Mom, her memories, and parts of her that I had always assumed were in permanent ink.

"Hand me a shoe, will you please?" Peter asked when a cockroach we had been watching disappeared beneath the refrigerator, and a second one came strutting out from under the oven.

I crawled over to his feet, untied both his shoes, yanked them off, and handed one to him. He threw it at the bug, but missed by a long shot, and when the bug picked up speed, he whipped the other shoe. That time, he hit the bug, but like an indestructible war tank, it kept going.

"Give me your flip flop," he insisted when at top speed, a third cockroach emerged from under the oven, following the same path the others had taken. It was like a timed arcade game, and even though they were a brand-new pair of flip flops, I wanted Peter to score a point.

But he didn't. He missed all four times and with no shoes left to throw, the two of us sat sulking like a couple of kids winning nothing at the carnival. I began to worry, and how could I not? The heavily armored bugs occupying the kitchen were like enemy soldiers, chasing my peace of mind away, overtaking my thoughts. Who knew how many more were lurking under the oven, waiting to come out en masse at night, and then what—crawl into our ears and noses while we slept?

Other than worrying, if there was another weakness I could have chosen for the long haul, a less consuming one, I would have. But did we choose our weaknesses in life, or were we assigned them? Regardless, no matter what I tried—remembering the birds of the air, even—nothing seemed to stop my heavily weighing thoughts from marching forward.

Would I ever find in myself whatever was needed to wage war with the cockroaches and my worries, to fix my broken dreams, revive my interior and exterior self, and secure the loose spots in my marriage? Would brand-new sledgehammers be enough to remove the drop ceiling and knock out a short wall in the claustrophobic kitchen? And would walking the beach remove my fatigue, knock out my weariness? I felt it all the time. The weariness washed in over the years with the storms of life—settling, damaging the surface of things, while never fully washing back out again.

Like a mummy, Peter stiffly turned his body to face me, then reached over, and took my hand. "You're quiet. That means you're overthinking. What are you overthinking now?"

"I don't want cockroaches climbing into my ears when I sleep, that's all." I rested my head on his shoulder.

"Your imagination is doing you in again. You wonder why you're exhausted all the time."

"I can't help it. We're wired differently. I'm wired to worry."

"What are you talking about?" he said, like I was a cuckoo bird singing a ridiculous song. "You're not wired to worry. You choose to worry. Even if you were wired to worry, wires can be deactivated."

"Creepy, Peter. I don't want anything in me deactivated."

"You know what I mean. 'Oh no, the sky might fall.' And guess what? The sky never falls. You're a bundle of nerves, and seriously, you think too much. That's your problem. Stop thinking so much."

"Never. I will never stop thinking!" I let go of his hand, got up from the floor, and went to the window. The same brush fire that swept through Mom's mind—the uncontrolled burn that destroyed her memory—could be headed my way next.

Mom's diagnosis had been the starting whistle within me. If my mind was a muscle, rather than run, I was going to think, think, think so my mind stayed strong. I had no choice but to make thinking my sport, although I had to better train my thoughts to run in beautiful places, and not round and round the same old track of worries.

"If I could be you," Peter went on, "I'd round up all the stuff in my head, and herd it onto paper…do something productive with it, turn it into a book. That's what I would do, but I'm not you, and there's not a whole lot going on in this head of mine." A moment later, "Then again, I could write a bestselling joke book. I do have a lot of funny stuff in me."

I gave him the laugh he deserved, but knew if ever he wrote such a book, I would be the subject of his jokes. We didn't try, but on occasion, the two of us were funny together.

"Remember the last suggestion you gave me," I said, still staring out the window.

"I've given too many to remember."

"You told me to visualize myself throwing my worries into boxes, taping the boxes shut, then loading them onto the worry truck."

"Yeah, that's right. I told you to wave good-bye to the truck. How'd that work for you?"

"The truck driver went on strike—a replacement driver did eventually come, but the truck ran out of gas in our driveway, and with the price of gas, the driver refused to fill it up, and before I knew it, my worries spilled out. Our road had to be shut down, and Fran's toilet paper that she bought online couldn't be delivered, which provoked more worries. She and Mrs. P got in a fight when Fran knocked on her door late at night to borrow toilet paper."

"Um, okay. Why don't you try my idea…put them all into a book!"

All that time, I had been looking out the window, trying to spot a bird, but maybe the birds were on the beach. As I was about to give up, I saw not a bird, but something better. Hiding behind bushes, hanging between two royal palms: a major prop in the dreams Peter had for his life.

"You'll never guess what I see," I announced in an ecstatic tone, wanting to cheer him up.

"What?" he asked with a blank expression.

"I'm not telling." I turned from the window. "You have to see it for yourself. Give me your hand, I'll help you up."

Once he was up, I gave him an aspirin, then a bottle of water. We slipped into our new flip flops, and right before we headed out the door, I reached into my woven tote and pulled out my favorite Sanibel Island bird book.

"Whatever you do," I said as we rounded the house to where the surprise was, "don't go jumping up and down, or act crazy, not with that nerve of yours under pressure like it is."

He obeyed and with little fanfare, fell flat-bodied onto the hammock. Without shaking it, I settled down next to him. I didn't ask, but was sure he felt what I did, the tall weeds poking through the soft cotton rope, scratching at his back.

I closed my eyes, not wanting to look at the yard. It needed more than a lawnmower…a tractor, perhaps, to plow through the weeds. I wanted to relax and enjoy my back scratch, but all I could hear was our fixer-upper crying out for help.

I opened my eyes, then opened my bird book, focusing on that instead.

"Trees, shells, cockroaches—what are you reading about now?" Peter asked.

I tilted the page, letting him see the snowy egret elegantly standing on long, thin legs at the water's edge. "A stylish bird. Look at its yellow feet. They look more like golden slippers, don't you think? I hope it's going somewhere special…sunset on the beach. With feet like that, it's got to be going somewhere special."

"Hm." His eyes closed. "Good for you…that books take you somewhere special."

"If you happen to hear a harsh and raucous call," I said, "don't be alarmed. Just know it's a snowy egret."

A few seconds later, from his mouth came a high, clear series of piping calls lasting several seconds, as if he was being silly, pretending to be a snowy egret, even though he sounded more like a woodpecker. He was snoring.

Back home, I'd snarl at his first snores of the night, then retreat into Mom's room to sleep on the cot. I used to feel guilty flying off to my own spot in the middle of the night, and when I told Fran about it, she advised against it. She bought me earplugs, the kind the hunters used, and she used too, but I didn't like having things in my ears. When I mentioned it to Mrs. P out in the yard, she told me Mr. P snored, and it was the reason for her droopy, bulldog-like eyes. After that, I decided Peter and I were better off roosting in different branches of the tree. I didn't want drooping eyes.

Wuk, wuk…cuk, cuk. Peter's snores changed into what sounded like an angry woodpecker. *Wuk, wuk…cuk, cuk.*

I wasn't going to nudge him awake, not with his pinched nerve. But there went my peaceful time reading, or hopes of falling into a cat nap of my own. When the rhythm changed and the sounds from his mouth grew more resonant, I eased my body out of the hammock without waking him or causing him to fall.

Determined to experience the amazing intricacies of life on the sanctuary island and get to know the native trees and wide variety of birds I was reading about—to be a part of it, and for it to be a part of me—I went for a walk.

I wanted the worriless, happy-go-lucky state of mind that the whistling birds possessed, but all the way down our road, my mind was noisy as a heronry—*Gators. Hurricane season. Frogs, my deathly fear of frogs! House on rotting stilt legs. I don't want my memories to rot! My girls, my boys, and the rampant wickedness all around them in the world…the motherlode of all my worries! What if there was a world war, and they all got drafted. My kids, how I miss them, and wish they could still come over with their dirty laundry, then leave with it clean, and with rolls of toilet paper, boxes of spaghetti from my pantry, and other random things.*

What was I thinking, moving so far away? My kids still need me. The girls are a year older, and more mature…sometimes. But the boys…they aren't even men yet. Boy-men, that's what they are, half boy, half man, still in transition. And didn't boy-men still need their mothers at least fifty percent of the time? Maybe not. Maybe I was the one stalling their transition…doing too much for them. Or, did I not do enough? Frog, frogs, frogs!

From World War Three to frogs, my worries were all over the place, a disorganized mess. But who trained their worries to line up in an orderly manner? I looked up into the trees for the old man landscaper, wishing he was up there, whispering words of wisdom down to me, telling me what I already knew, that my worries were as unproductive as the decaying palm fronds, and served no purpose. Still, hard as I tried to let go of them, my worries refused to drop.

When I reached the end of the road, I kept going, walking right under the majestic arc of trees, into a vibrant green tunnel of leaf-laden overarching branches, a place so beautiful maybe worries were forbidden. And then, right there in front of me was a bird, and not any old bird, but a special one.

"I love your golden slippers," I said softly to the long-legged creature, white as snow. "Did you buy them online?"

The snowy egret did what I knew it would do. It opened its slim black beak and let out a few croaks, followed by a rasping sound.

"Wait my golden-slippered friend," I called out when it hopped away. "Don't go…not yet. I'm not done looking at you."

It stopped, then turned and took two steps back toward me.

I crouched down and held still, hoping to forever capture in my mind the moment when I first saw—not on the pages of a book, but right there in front of me—a real, living, breathing bird with golden slippers.

"I have an invitation," I whispered, "for you and for all your feathery friends."

Be my guests, won't you? Please, Snowy Egret, wear your golden slippers, dance your graceful dance in the shallows of my mind. You too, Little Blue Heron—you stealthy stalker, you! And Pelican, go ahead and make a big splash wherever you can in the pond of my memories. Lurch along faster, Reddy Egret, before it's too late. I hope I get to see you, so you, along with all the others can make yourselves at home in that area of my mind where the memories live.

I ask of you this. Don't let anything chase you out!

Should my mind erode, and my words for things no longer make it out into the world, but stay perched on the tip of my tongue, and my thoughts be washed away…won't you please stay? Whatever the tide brings in, stay put as a memory in my mind, so I always have something beautiful to look at, no matter what.

Good thing Peter wasn't with me. He would have told me I was being dramatic, as usual. But how could I not be? I wished I could have asked Mom—when you were in the midst of the storm, did you have any company, even one beautiful guest of a memory residing in your mind?

The snowy egret turned and took off down the trail. I could have followed it to the beach, but it didn't feel right going all the way to the beach at the end of our road for the first time without Peter. It was like we had tickets to a grand show, and I wasn't going to sneak out and see it without him.

On my walk back, as I passed the luxurious-looking mailbox and the mansion poking out from the treetops, I couldn't help but imagine who might be living there.

"Hello, child," I heard.

I turned and saw at my heels a woman with an enormous bun on her head.

"I am so sorry, child." She looked no more than a decade older than me and didn't need to call me "child." "I did not mean to startle you."

"It's okay," I replied with a curious smile.

"I saw you go by. I have been waiting around ever since, and did not want to miss you. Are you the one?"

"I don't know. Who do you mean?"

Her eyes smiled warmly at me. "The one who bought the…the…the fixer-upper?"

"Oh, yeah, that's me, alright. I'm the one, the proud owner of the eye-sore." I wanted to ask, *who are you? Are you the one who lives in the mansion, blocking my view of the Gulf of Mexico?* "I'm Adele. And you…I'm guessing you're my neighbor?"

"No, no, no, child," She shook her head. "I am not *her!*" Her face looked relieved—relieved not to be *her,* and I could tell from her eyes she had a lot to say about *her.* "I am Marita. I work for her. I cook, and clean, and do pretty much everything…more and more each day." She studied my face with her giant eyes, determining whether I was trustworthy. "Only God knows," she looked up at the sky, then back at me, "if I'll still have my job tomorrow. Pray for me," she insisted, without bothering to ask whether I was a praying woman or not. "Pray for me, please! And pray for *her,* too." She tilted her head toward the mansion.

"Uh oh, why? What's wrong?"

"Fine, if you really want to know," Marita said, like I had been begging it out of her. "One by one, she is letting us all go…the person who tidies her house, her part-time handyman, her landscaper. Things are not good, but that is all I will say." She shook her head in a flustered manner, then handed me a small, glittery gold bag. "This is why I chased you down. It is for you…from her. Welcome child, welcome."

I took the bag, peeked inside, and let my mouth drop open. My neighbor and I shared a fetish for sea grape leaves. The bag was filled with them, enormous and round like the ones I took hold of when the branches came in through our car window to greet me when we first arrived. But the ones in the bag were dried and pressed, with handwritten words on them in black ink.

Marita pointed up to the top of the mansion poking out from the treetops. "She sees your place from that window of hers, and it drives her crazy, the condition it's in. She's been staying up late writing on the fallen sea grape leaves collected from this road. She likes to help…needs to doing something. She…your neighbor…was a reputable interior designer at one time, and has written advice on each leaf, to help you get started."

I needed to be pinched. It felt like a dream. Already I was imagining the two of us out leaf gathering together, me picking her interior designer brain. "When can I meet her?"

Marita looked at me with knowing eyes. "She isn't in the mood for people. It's a dark time for her."

"The world is dark," I said automatically. "It's dark for a lot of people right now…all kinds of depressing things happening. I watch the news and long for the days when my kids were all tucked into their beds at night, down the hall from me. Of course, they don't want that. If anything, they want space from me. They call me Nervous Nellie, and I'm sick of it. I don't want to be her anymore. I'm exhausted. Why do you think I up and moved to this island?"

"Why?" Her eyes were concerned.

"I was tired of closing my eyes, going to an imagined utopia. I was ready to live in a real near-perfect place."

"Child," she said, like it was common sense and I should have known, "no such near-perfect place exists…on Earth, or in your mind, because your mind isn't perfect." She closed her eyes, muttered a few words I couldn't hear, then reopened her eyes and looked at me intently. "Right here." She tapped on her chest, where her heart was. "Not your mind, but here in your heart. Here is that place…not of happiness…but of peace and joy and love, where the best of you is brought out."

"Aw," was all I said, but her message was profound and I wanted to give it more thought. "Thank you for sharing that. It's worth thinking about."

She pulled the clips from her hair, reworking it all into another fabulously sloppy bun on top of her head. "I must go. I have things to finish before I leave for the night."

"I wish I could thank my neighbor for these leaves. Let me know whenever it's good for her!"

"There will never be a good time," Marita whispered miserably. "But I will tell her, and we shall see. Bye-bye." And with that, she turned and hurried off.

As I went down my driveway, strange noises—what I assumed were bellowing gators—spooked the life out of me, and even though the water in the potholes was shallow, I kept watch for gator eyes. When the bellowing grew louder, I worried about Peter and forced my legs into a sprint all the way back to the hammock.

But there he was, sound asleep still, with a dreamworld look on his face, mouth wide open. The noises were coming from him. With the gift bag dangling from my wrist like a bracelet, I took hold of the hammock with both my hands, pulling it toward me like a swing at the playground. Peter's eyes opened wide.

"No underdog," he said right away, as if I was capable of doing such a thing. "Pinched nerve, remember?"

I returned the hammock to its resting position. "You won't believe," I announced cheerfully. "Our neighbor is an interior designer! I didn't get to meet her, but I met a nice woman who works for her. Look what she gave us...a bag full of interior design advice to help us get started."

With a cynical look on his face, Peter sat up and put his feet to the ground. "I'd watch out, if I were you. Remember what happened to Mrs. P? She bumped into that lawyer friend of hers at the grocery store. They got talking in the produce aisle, and a week later, she got a seven-hundred-dollar bill in the mail...for legal services, which she had thought was just small talk."

Of course I remembered what happened to Mrs. P. Every time she shared that story, her left eye produced a bitter tear, and her brows pushed closer together, and they never went back. "Nah, that won't happen," I insisted.

"My point is," Peter went on, "nothing is for free. Be careful. Don't ask questions or she'll write up an invoice and drop it in our mailbox, that's all I'm saying."

I didn't like when Peter took something exciting and turned it into a negative reality. As we headed up the porch steps and into the house, I didn't bother telling him more about Marita. But she was right. The go-to happy place in my mind was never perfect. It was as good as my limited imagination allowed, and even then, pain, sorrow, and worries always broke into it. There were no perfect, nor even near-perfect places on Earth, either. And it got me thinking about a different place...that place in my heart...which I hadn't thought of in a while.

SIX

INTERIOR DESIGN TIDBITS

* * *

Imagine the potential hidden within the flaws.

* * *

Give that house of yours a name.
Every house deserves a name.

The next morning I woke to the chirp of cardinals coming in through the opened windows. *Purdy, purdy, purdy...whoit, whoit, whoit,* they sang. But my mind heard *wheat, wheat, wheat.*

Mallory liked wheat, not white bread, all those mornings I woke before the sun to make their school lunches. She liked wheat with no crust, ham and Swiss, mustard, no pickles, and a light squeeze of mayo. Lucy, on the other hand, liked white bread *with* crust, turkey and cheddar, no mustard, mayo instead, and extra pickles...or was it no pickles?

"Hey, Peter," I called out without opening my eyes. If I opened my eyes, the sandwich-making factory in my mind would have shut down, and I didn't want it shutting down yet. "Who was it that liked all the pickles on their sandwich...Lucy or Mallory?"

"Um," Peter whispered from right next to me. "I think you're dreaming. You're talking in your sleep."

"I'm not dreaming. I'm awake and trying to remember. It bothers me that I can't remember which of my daughters liked pickles, and which one didn't. That's not something I should be forgetting ...not after making their school lunches every morning, twelve years in a row!"

"Relax, you don't have it. You don't have Alzheimer's, Adele. Stop with the memory games so early in the morning. And besides," he touched his

53

toes to mine, "the kids can make their own sandwiches now. You have other things to think about than who liked pickles, and who didn't."

Peter was right. I wiggled my toes back at his. I did have other things to think about. For starters, it was demolition day in the kitchen, but more exciting than that, it had been ages since Peter and I woke up together in the same bed. Our toes hadn't touched in years, and there was a reunion going on under the sheet.

"Hey," I said when Peter's feet left the bed. "Where are you going?"

"Where am I going? Our windows are open. Don't you feel it? It's like a sauna in here. No, a furnace. What were you thinking?"

I didn't want to tell him why I had opened the windows in the middle of the night. We were getting along, and I didn't want to ruin things, or make him feel bad.

"Help me to understand," he said with the same tone he used on the boys whenever they acted brainlessly. "It's ninety-four degrees outside, not to mention the humidity. If we didn't have mold before, we have it now!"

I looked up at the slanted ceiling. Should I tell him I was doing what our neighbor suggested in one of her interior design tidbits? Imagining the potential hidden within the flaws. And there were flaws alright, not just in the house and in our marriage, but everywhere in the world. The whole wide world was flawed, or so it seemed, but instead of my limited mind trying to imagine the potential of the world, it was best to start small, imagining the potential in my own life first.

Our nights on the island had the potential of being greater than our not-so-great nights in Michigan had been, and I wanted to stay put next to my husband on the generations-old iron bed and paper-thin mattress that came with the lightly furnished place.

Peter was getting all huffy puffy, struggling to shut the third stubborn window. I didn't like when he got huffy, especially when I was in a good mood. "You were snoring. That's why I opened the windows."

"Um," he looked at me and scratched his head, "you were planning to throw me out?"

I had to laugh. "No, you nut! I wanted to stay next to you...wake up in bed next to you for the first time in years. To block out your snoring, I opened the windows to a super loud chorus of breeding frogs. Their croaks were louder than your snores, and better than a sound machine."

"Aren't you afraid of frogs?"

"I am."

His eyes softened. He gave up trying to shut the windows and sat down on the edge of the bed. "Is that why you were snuggling so close?"

I nodded, then sat up and put my arm around him.

"I guess it's no big deal if they're stuck open a crack. And by the way," he gave me a grin, "you snore, too."

"No, I don't."

"Yes, you do. But don't worry. It doesn't bother me." He closed his eyes and ran his hands through his full head of tawny hair.

I was about to invite his toes back to the reunion, but then my cell phone rang. It was Aunt Nora, my mother's older sister—older by fifteen years. She never called, and I couldn't stop my reactive mind from going to the what-ifs. What if there was an emergency, and she fell, and couldn't get up, couldn't think straight, and didn't know who else to call?

"Aunt Nora, everything okay?" My heart was pounding.

"I'm sending you a gift," she shouted into the phone, hard of hearing. "Came across it in my attic, felt you should have it...especially with everything happening in the world...and knowing how worked up you get. It's special."

"What is it?"

"If I tell you, it won't be a surprise. But remember when your mother moved in with you? I took a bunch of her stuff, since you people didn't have room. Well, I got around to going through it all and found this something special that I think you'll want. You need it, but I think you'll want it, too. Watch for it. It should be there any day now. Can you hear me?"

"Loud and clear, Aunt Nora. You're on speaker."

"Well, I can hardly hear you. I guess I'll say good-bye now. Always look up...watch out for the falling iguanas! Bye-bye." She ended the call.

My mind skipped right over the falling iguana thing and went instead to the greatest possibility of all, that it was a novel, or better yet, all the novels from my long-lost literary collection. All through high school and college, I read each of my all-time favorite novels three times. What happened to the beloved collection once I got married? It remained a mystery. Likely sold at a yard sale.

After coffee, Peter and I picked up our matching sledgehammers and got to work stripping and gutting the inefficient kitchen. For days on end, we pounded in sync with the pileated woodpeckers in the mornings, and the torrential rain beating down on the tin roof in the evenings. We couldn't wait for our little house on stilts to reach its full potential.

"Imagine the splinters on the floors filed down," I said to Peter, "the faucets no longer leaking, the hot water working, and the toilet seats no longer falling off when we sit down."

"Like you, I look forward to all of that. But our expectations could be higher."

Peter was right, so while in the midst of ripping out a drop ceiling, I allowed myself to imagine even greater potential. While standing on a can of paint, on top of a chair, I let myself go there, dreaming of the day when our kids came visiting with the loves of their lives, one of them proposing at sunset, another getting married on the beach—our beach!

Oh, and the entire gang from our farewell barbecue there for the wedding, and right before boarding the plane back to Michigan, Mrs. P saying, "I take back all the stuff I said behind your back. I was wrong. You're not mad as a hatter. You're all there, and brilliant, buying this family retreat! Let me know if another one goes up for sale. Maybe family would start visiting me. And you and I could be neighbors again."

"What's so funny?" Peter broke into my daydream.

"Oh, the fun family potential this place has, that's all. Imagine our grandchildren…over the bridge and through the mangrove to Grandma Adele's they'll come…fishing with you and building sandcastles with me!"

Sweeping renovating scraps off the floor, he shook his head, like I was silly. "I don't have an imagination like you. But whatever makes you happy."

I looked over at the wall where I had thumbtacked a couple of the sea grape leaves. "So, what should we call this place? Our mystery neighbor claims every home deserves a name."

"I know what to call the place." Peter held the broom still. "How about *The Great Eyesore*." He licked his lips. "Or, *Disaster Waiting to Happen. Crab Shack. Old Shed, Barracks, Crazy People's Kennel*."

"Wow," I remarked. "Your imagination is bigger than you realize!"

"*Lean-to*," he continued in his comedic tone of voice. "*Flophouse, Crash Pad, Hostel, House of Cards, Pigpen.*" He looked around at the protective tarp that was hanging all over the place, covering the cabinets and spread across the floor. "*Peter and Adele's Circus Royale.*"

I hooted and hollered, liking that name the best. I tossed a piece of ceiling scrap down at him for fun, even though the top of his head was already covered with fallen sawdust.

"I don't know about you," he said as he tied shut the world's largest bag of scraps, "but I'm calling it quits, done for the night."

"Oh, come on, don't desert me now! We've been warming up all day. The show is just starting…the drop ceiling about to drop. You don't want to miss the drop ceiling dropping, do you?"

Even as the rain picked up intensity and was coming down like a drum roll on the tin roof, Peter dragged the bag of scraps toward the exit, his shoulders slouching like a worn-out clown. He opened the front door to a burst of thunder as I had never heard before and a few seconds later, death-defying lightning had him running back inside with a package in his hands—a package for me.

"My something special from Aunt Nora! Oh, no. Is it ruined?"

"Nope. Delivery person left it in a safe spot on the porch."

"Hand it to me."

"How about I open it for you? You falling, breaking your neck is the last thing our circus show needs right now."

"Oh, please. Hand it up. I want to be the one who opens it. I'm not going to fall." I bent at the knees, reached my hands down, and took hold of the something special.

"Fitzgerald? You think I'll be competing with Fitzgerald again, or Thoreau?"

"Neither." I turned it in my hands, "Too heavy. But it's definitely a hardcover." I went about untying the outer twine. "I hope it's not Moby Dick. I'm not at all in the mood for hopeless pursuits. Maybe it's Jane Austen." Any of my old Austen books would have had me leaping off the can of paint, twirling through midair. And if it wasn't Jane Austen, but Virginia Woolf instead, I'd end up doing a *triple* somersault. "*Ta-dah,*" I sang as I let go of the twine, which fell through the air, landing on Peter's head.

Next, I tore through the thick, stubborn outer packaging, hoping it wasn't *To the Lighthouse*. It was the last book I read in my college literature class before switching majors and bidding farewell to my pursuit of a writing degree, surrendering to a more practical pursuit—nursing.

The brown postal wrap came loose and fell to the ground, but there was more to unwrap. Aunt Nora had covered it in dazzling glittery white paper, tied with a fancy golden ribbon.

"Open it, will you?"

"I'm trying," I told Peter as I worked on a knot in the ribbon. Good thing there was tissue paper. I was going to cry a hundred tears if it ended up being *One Hundred Years of Solitude*—the last novel I started reading, but never finished. Halfway through it, science in the form of a home pregnancy test detected the presence of human chorionic gonadotropin. In other words, I was pregnant.

No offense, Gabriel Garcia. But how could I have gone on reading your tragicomedy of humankind when I was going through my own, minus the comedy! The positive sign, then shelving Garcia's book in the middle of reading, marked the end of an era for me, in which I forfeited all leisure reading, and all selfish pursuits.

After an initial dark solitude of my own, I emerged, and while Peter and I figured out a wedding, we also finished college, and I landed my first job at the hospital before Lucy was born.

"I sure hope it's not *Utopia* by Sir Thomas Moore." I let the ribbon fall through the air.

"Why not?" Peter sounded only slightly amused by my impassioned silliness.

"I'm rethinking utopia, that's all." I still hadn't told him about Marita, and what she had said out on our road. But also, why read about a fictional island society in the Atlantic Ocean when I was living on a real island in the Gulf of Mexico!

"*The Ignorant Fool's Guide to Fixing Up a Dive* would be nice," Peter murmured. "Maybe it's that."

I shook my head, aware that he couldn't help his one-liners from slipping out, although he probably did hope it was that. But after years of digesting nothing but lean medical journals and articles on cognitive decay, I wanted it to be a novel...and to read for pure joy.

As I tore the tissue off, I peeked down at Peter who was looking up at me with the eyes of a fisherman, curious to see the catch I was reeling in. "What's your bet, Peter, what's it going to be—a white whale, or magnificent marlin?"

"I don't care if it's Hemingway. I don't care if it's Moby Dick. Will I have to drive ninety miles per hour, swerving around turtles, or will a helicopter come get you when you fall...that's all that's going through my mind right now. Hurry up, will you? Get this show on the road, Adele."

The moment he said that, the ringleader in the sky sent forth another startling, thundering drum roll, causing our tent stakes to shake. "One Mississippi" later, and the world outside *Peter and Adele's Circus Royale* flashed with lightning. The lights under the big top flickered, then went out. Sure enough, I lost my balance and crashed down onto the sawdust-coated floor.

Peter's hands found their way in record speed and braced my shoulders. "Are you okay!" His voice was frantic. "Are you hurt?"

If I had fallen on my arm, the show would have ended differently, but I landed on my cushioned bottom and was about to reassure Peter when there came another loud burst of thunder. With it, the book—that must have been teetering all that time on the edge of the counter—came flopping down weightily onto my lap.

"A light," I said.

"You see a light? There's no light. What kind of a light do you see?"

"No, you nut. I don't see a light. I need a light. Get me your cell phone, or that flashlight under the sink!" I touched the spine of the book to my nose and sniffed. Amazing. It smelled amazing, as did all old books.

"I'm trying my best to find this flashlight."

"It's okay. I'm content sitting here, smelling its spine."

"Are you sure you didn't hit that head of yours, honey?"

"My head is fine, Peter."

A second later, towering over me, he aimed the light on the book in my hands. "So, what book is it?"

It wasn't any of the books from my beloved collection. And of all the recommendations from friends, titles I had compiled throughout the years, hoping to one day read, it wasn't any of those, either. "It's the record of the relationship between God and humans," I said.

"Huh?"

"The Bible, Peter. It's a Bible."

He let out a quick roar of laughter. "Wait a minute, you mean, *The Holy Bible?*"

"Yes, the *Holy Bible*. Which other Bible is there?"

By then, he was aiming the light up his chin, showcasing his face. On it was a grin so big that even his gums were showing, and then the one-liners came. "Sounds like the perfect beach read! I hear it's going to be a nice day tomorrow. See you on the beach with your book! Keep your nose in it, and you won't need sunscreen. I was wrong about Fitzgerald, Thoreau. Looks like I'll be competing with Jesus now."

"Stop with the wisecracks, Peter."

"I'm sorry. But you should see your pout."

"Take that back! I'm not pouting."

"Yes, you are. But it's okay. You were excited, expecting something else. I get it. I know what that's like."

Okay, sure, in fairness to my pout, it wasn't the something special I had in mind. And even though it was the world's most talked about, influential writing ever, reading any book thousands of pages long would blow me off course, put me on a distant, remote island of procrastination in which I'd never get around to doing any of the things I wanted to do…lollygag, search for shells, look for birds, and write my own something special.

But despite all of that, neither Peter, nor the greatest know-it-all on Earth had any idea what was going on within me, beyond the layers of my pouting flesh, and deeper than the shallows of my mind.

There was a fluttering…a certain fluttering in my heart, which I hadn't felt in years.

I put the Word of God to my chest and held it there.

The fluttering continued. My heart and my flesh were having a spat, bickering like siblings back and forth. A part of me wanted to open the book in my lap, and another part of me wanted to shelve it, pretend it never arrived. If my heart had its way, my lips would have surrendered, declaring right then and there a personal read-a-thon…an all-I-can-read Biblical feast. But my flesh was saying, "No, thank you."

The house was pitch black, and there was one flashlight. Peter slid down onto the floor next to me. He didn't want to climb into bed until we checked it for bugs. "I'm sorry I laughed."

"It's fine." I wasn't going to tell him what was going on within me. I didn't need him getting in the middle of what was happening between my heart and my flesh. "Why don't we sit here until the lights go on. It feels good to sit."

We were quiet after that, and the rain stopped. A silence overtook the house. I felt like a tightrope walker, whose focus had been off, and whose toes weren't pointed in any one direction. I wanted to believe the ringleader was there, whispering to me, "You can do it, one line at a time. I am here with you."

"Me?"

"Yes, you…the most spectacularly loved you that ever was…flawed and imperfect, but loved. Stay in my Word and walk in my will for your life, so full of potential."

I didn't hear that, but wanted to. I wanted to believe in a hidden potential for my life.

"Peter," I said, breaking the silence. "This place needs a more genuine name."

"Fine by me, what do you have in mind?

"Hidden Potential. Let's call it, Hidden Potential."

"It's hidden alright," Peter remarked. "And we're not finding it tonight.

SEVEN

I took the flashlight from Peter's hand, and there on the kitchen floor around midnight, I sided with my heart. I opened the great big book of truth about life and eternity.

"Oh, wow," I gasped.

"What, everything okay?"

I read out loud what was written on the inside cover. "This Bible belongs to Finley Child."

"Aw, that's nice…your mom's Bible." He gathered the excess tarp, bunched it like a pillow, then rolled down onto his back next to me on the floor.

I propped up the flashlight, then fingered through the pages, remembering the walks I used to take with Mom, and how on those walks she loved to talk about God. Mom was always talking about God. She took Luke and me to church most Sundays, and before tuck-in time at night, had us kneeling beside our beds to pray. I used to pray a lot back then, and my, how lovely it was between God and me!

It was like riding a triple-decker ferry—prayer powering me up and down the rivers of childhood. Sometimes I stood praising God, the Father, from the sunny upper deck, and other times I sat listening to the narrated tours on the crowded middle deck. I also cried my eyes out to the Son, Jesus, in the deep, enclosed lower cabin. But when Daddy died, I stopped cranking out prayers, and into my teens declared the Word of God no more than a lecture to be endured at church…when Mom still had the energy to drag us there.

Leafing through the pages, I came to a passage highlighted in yellow and encircled in a red heart. "Mom must have liked Psalm eighty-four, one through four."

"Read it," Peter said with a yawn from his pile of tarp.

"Okay." I first read what Mom had scribbled in the margin. "'The words of King David.'" Then, I read the passage.

"'How lovely is your dwelling place, O Lord Almighty! My soul yearns, even faints, for the courts of the Lord; my heart and my flesh cry out for the living God. Even the sparrow has found a home, and the swallow a nest for herself, where she may have her young—a place near your altar, O Lord Almighty, my King and my God. Blessed are those who dwell in your house; they are ever praising you.'"

Sleepy-bird Peter said nothing in response. But the words reached my heart like a ferry reaches its landing. King David knew of a special place. He had been there before, and was longing to return. His special place was with the Lord Almighty, His King. God's presence was his go-to place, his real—not imaginary—special place!

Why or how after such a long stretch of time did King David's words make their way across the straits of apathy, docking at the pier of my mind, unloading their goods into my heart? Maybe the ferry conductor was at work. I wiped a tear from my eye. It was a single tear, but my insides were experiencing a flash flood of emotion, trying to recall the last time my soul yearned for, cried out to, or praised the living, breathing God.

All through the years, I held onto the word—Christian. I wore it like an old, faded t-shirt hidden under my sweater, a souvenir from having gone somewhere real and special. Peter wore it, too, like a label handed down from his parents, grandparents, and great-grandparents. But just because a person was handed a label to wear didn't mean they knew the designer behind that label.

"You think all the stuff happening in the world…natural disasters, wars, and rumors of wars…means we're getting closer?"

"You mean closer to the end?" Peter mumbled. "No, there's always been that stuff. I don't think that at all. I wouldn't catastrophize like that, thinking it's the end of the world. What's really on your mind?"

I hesitated. "Do you feel close to God? Do you ever pray?"

"All the time," he said, surprising me. "I'm always praying that God takes care of you, the kids, and me. I pray that He takes care of Himself, too, because if anything happens to Him, we're all in trouble. I pray He makes me a better person, but if He can't, it's okay. I like who I am. I even prayed when I was on the hammock…asked Him why the alligators made it onto the arc. Did we need alligators on Earth?"

"Peter, I'm not finding you funny."

"Okay, I'm sorry. All kidding aside, I do pray, I really do. I pray for our finances, and for the kids to be well-off, and for God to relocate Lucy's boyfriend—to the Antarctic. I prayed for your mother, which I hope He heard! My most recent prayer? Please, God, no toxic mold in this house… praying the reports come back good."

I cringed. His prayers were like mine—a Christmas list for Santa, wishes for the Genie, a to-do list for the Miracle Maker. "Why do you think it is…that we don't pray more intimately, or for bigger things… world peace…human suffering to end?"

"I don't know." He was quiet for a moment, then repositioned himself, resting his hands behind his head. "I can only speak for myself. I guess my relationship with God is sort of like the relationship I had with my great-grandfather."

"How so?" I turned the flashlight off. "What do you mean?"

"Just that I never spent time alone with him, didn't know him personally. We lived so far away…it never seemed like he was a part of my life, that's all. He sent me ten bucks every year for my birthday, which I appreciated."

"Did you read the cards?"

"Nope, just took the goods. I'm not a big reader, you know that. But when Great-Grandpops got sick, my folks drove us all the way up to Mackinaw to see him."

"That must have been quite the reunion!" I had heard Peter's story before, but hadn't heard it in the context of Peter's relationship with God.

"Thirty-six grandkids from fourteen states…all of us showing up one Sunday at the foot of his bed." Peter chuckled. "The old guy knew each of us better than any of us knew him. You should have seen all our pictures taped to his walls. He knew everything about me…my baseball season, my wins, my losses, my good and bad grades. But did I know him?" Peter was quiet for a second. "I knew about him. My parents told me stories… the same infamous stories over and over again."

"So, you sort of knew him," I said, still connecting it to God. "You knew his characteristics, from the stories your parents told you."

"Sure, I knew things about him. He was creative...turned planks of wood into a table just as Grandma pulled the Thanksgiving turkey from the oven one year. And compassionate...gave a homeless person the coat off his back. Oh, and slow to anger...didn't yell when my dad stole a pack of gum."

"Yikes. I would have yelled if our kids stole a pack of gum."

"Well, as the story goes, he first went into my dad's room and told him he loved him. Then, made him go into the dime store, apologize to the owner, and pay it back tenfold. A week later, he bought him a pack of gum."

Peter got up from his pile of tarp, then moved next to me with his back against the cabinet. "So, there we all were, crowded around his deathbed, my mom and her sisters crying."

"Did you cry?"

"Nope, I hid behind my older cousins...chimed in with the group as we all celebrated Great-Grandpop's final jokes. No doubt, he deserved to be praised for the man that he was." Peter's voice turned regretful. "I don't get why I never reached out to him. It was always my parents picking up the phone, talking to him. I never did."

I leaned my head on his shoulder. "He was old and far away. You figured he couldn't hear. And besides, your parents kept him informed... filled him in on everything going on in your life."

"Yup." By then, a cloud must have moved. The moon appeared out the kitchen window. In the slightly lit room, Peter stared up at the disarrayed ceiling. "My parents, they were always praying for me...filling God in on everything in my life. Who knows why I don't pray more? Maybe I figured their prayers were enough."

I heard it in his voice, he was grateful for the prayers. And maybe more than once, the prayers of his parents were the buoyancy that kept him afloat. Still, it was bothering him—why had he never taken the opportunity to spend an intimate moment alone with Great-Grandpops, or with God? Why had he not made the effort—away from the group—to reach out himself?

I wanted to tell him it was no big deal, but that wasn't the case. It was a huge deal. "You know—" I rubbed my fingers across the distressed pinewood floor "—nowhere have I heard that God has grandchildren. He has children—sons and daughters."

He was quiet after that, and who knew if he was thinking about it or not, but I was. As a kid, I asked Jesus into my heart. According to the Bible, I became a child of God, but not just that, a beloved child of God. I didn't become His granddaughter.

I used to like being called a beloved child of God, just like I liked it when Mom called me her *little sugar plum.* But then I grew up and became her big sugar plum, so why did I never grow up as God's daughter, maturing in my knowledge of Him, and getting to know and love Him more deeply?

The lights were still out and the kitchen dark except for the moon shining in through the window. Peter and I were all alone, like two mariners in distress sitting on a makeshift raft on the high seas of life. We had let go of our steering poles, lost our navigational equipment long ago, but there was a fervor within me...a fervor for just the right wind, currents, grace of God to show up, and get us where we needed to be.

"I don't know about you, but I sure am wondering, where is He?"

After a long, ominous moment, "Who?" Peter mumbled.

The Coast Guard of our souls, I thought but didn't say. And why, when we first drifted away, didn't He come to get us—children, fallen overboard—and tow us back to safety?

"You think He called off the search?"

"Who?" Peter mumbled again.

"God. Where is God?"

Trying hard not to slip into sleep, Peter took hold of my hand, and squeezed it. "You're asking the wrong person. I told you about my lackluster prayer life, and how I hardly knew my own grandfather. What about you...your prayer life?"

It had been forever since Peter and I had a good, in-depth talk about anything other than finances, kids, or the work we were doing on the house. "You really want to hear about my prayer life?"

"Wouldn't have asked if I didn't." He let go of my hand and stretched back down onto the exposed wooden floor, the pile of tarp as his pillow.

"Okay, it's more like prayerlessness." I laid down, too, resting my head on his chest. "When I switched to nursing, my science professor told us that radio messages sent from Earth might never reach the distant regions of space. And even if the universe went on forever, then space may expand faster than light can traverse it."

"Okay, but what's that have to do with praying?"

"Nothing," I admitted. "But those distant regions of space are taken to exist. And they're believed to be part of reality as much as we are. It's just that we can never interact with them."

"You're not sure how to interact with God, is that what you're trying to say?"

"Yeah, or that it feels like He's so far away. I prayed fine as a kid, but to be honest, if I were to pray now, it would seem like I'm writing a message, putting it into a bottle. Who knows if my prayer would even arrive—into the ears of God—or end up stranded on a faraway island of lost-at-sea prayers?"

"Um," Peter said, then paused.

I gave him a moment to think it through, but then he let out a snore. I set the flashlight up like a lantern, and perused through the Bible's pages. Mom had scribbled her thoughts in the margins and tucked pieces of scratch paper covered with her handwriting all throughout the Old and New Testaments. I pulled out a yellow piece of paper tucked within the pages of Galatians, and after unfolding it, let out a squeal.

Mom's long-lost lemon bar recipe! The lemon bars were an all-time family favorite, the dessert Mom made for every occasion, and finding the recipe had my insides rejoicing. There was even a blob spilled on the paper. I put it to my nose and sniffed. Sure enough—lemon!

I closed my eyes, and sniffled. When Alzheimer's shut down her ability to make the infamous bars, I asked for the recipe, but it was too late.

"C'mon, Mom. You can do it. They're lemon bars…let's start with lemons. We know that much, right?"

"Sugar…plums," she had said.

I didn't want to upset her by telling her there were no sugar plums in lemon bars. *"Okay, sure…sugar and plums. What else?"*

"Patience."

"Your bars require patience? Is that what you mean? Okay, but what about lemons? How many lemons do I use if I want to make your bars?"

"Whatever you find in the branches. The Branch of Righteousness."

"Mom, we're talking lemon bars, not Jesus. You've switched to talking Jesus again, but it's your lemon bar recipe that I want."

I gave up after that, but went into the bathroom to sob. The disease that took possession of Mom had shut down her ability to live, bake, and share her greatest recipe with me.

"Peter, wake up…you won't believe what I found in this Bible!"

"Um, let me guess."

I didn't want to hear his one-liner guesses. "Mom's lemon bar recipe," I said right away.

"Your mother's recipe is in the Bible? I didn't know they ate lemon bars in biblical times. No wonder her bars were so heavenly!"

"No, you nut. The recipe isn't *in* the Bible. Mom wrote it out, then put it in the pages of her Bible, like we used to do with fall leaves. We'd press them into that giant hardcover dictionary to preserve them."

"I see, okay. But hey, if you're going to keep calling me a nut all the time, could you at least switch it up…call me different kinds of nuts?"

"Go back to sleep, almond. Sorry I woke you."

If we hadn't found a cockroach in our bed the night before, I would have encouraged him to get up from the floor, go to the real bed. All I cared about was finding more of Mom's long-lost recipes—her French silk pie, perhaps. I reached for a pile of scraps, a cushion for me to sit on, and it was then that I spotted it…a white folder with a golden heart drawn onto it. Auntie must have packaged the folder in with the Bible, and I didn't see it fall out.

"No way!" I gasped.

"What now?"

"Prayers…an entire folder filled with what looks like prayers, or letters Mom wrote to God!"

"I wouldn't read them if I were you."

"Oh, please, Peter. You have such a superb ability to weave in and out of sleep during select conversations. Why on earth should I not read these?" I pulled one out.

"Um, Lucy or Mallory snooping through your stuff…just saying, how would you feel? You want your daughters reading your letters to God?"

"I've never written any letters to God. How should I know?"

"Fine, but if you want my opinion, you've stumbled upon private property. Reading them would be like…trespassing, that's all."

I needed Peter to fall back asleep, so I didn't reply. I wanted to believe that from His headquarters in Heaven, God went about coordinating the logistics of the global courier delivery system on Earth, working behind the scenes through people like Aunt Nora, so Mom's Bible and the folder with her letters express-shipped right into my hands.

Better yet, maybe it was in invitation—inviting me to return to that someplace special, that real someplace special I went to as a kid, when I sat in the presence of the Lord, God Almighty.

Whether Peter was asleep or not, I went ahead and started to read the first letter out loud, "'To the One who loves me and knows me more than anyone else, here I am, my Dear God, sitting on this bench overlooking the Gulf of Mexico—'" I stopped reading.

"What's wrong?"

"Mom wrote these letters while here…on Sanibel!"

"For what it's worth, I still don't think you should read them."

I turned the flashlight off, and while waiting for Peter to drift off, I played a game of truth and dare with myself, picking dare—daring to believe that what I had in my hand was like a royal treasury washed ashore, and meant for me.

EIGHT

* * *

"Jesus replied, 'If anyone loves me, he will obey
my teaching. My Father will love him, and we will
come to him and make our home with him.'"
—John 14:23

* * *

"Submit yourselves, then, to God. Resist the devil, and he
will flee from you. Come near to God and he will come
near to you. Wash your hands, you sinners, and purify
your hearts, you double-minded. Grieve, mourn and wail.
Change your laughter to mourning and your joy to gloom.
Humble yourself before the Lord, and he will lift you up."
—James 4:7–10

To the One who loves me and knows me more than anyone else,

*Here I am, my dear God, sitting on this bench overlooking the Gulf of Mexico.
When I glance over my shoulder to the left, I see the tip top of Sanibel's historic
lighthouse poking out at me from the trees.*

*I still can't believe they've done this—my book club sisters, all of them chip-
ping in, sending me and the kids to this island for a month to stay with our oldest
clubby, a snowbird who owns a condo here! I tried telling them it was too big of
a gift, but they insisted, saying they recognized the zest in me fizzling out, along
with my oomph, my pizzaz, the sparkle in my eyes, and the bounce to my step.
After years of organizing and hosting our meetings, I canceled four in a row.*

*When I hold my pen still and watch the prancing birds, I crave to be
refreshed, to return home with a renewed verve of my own. I'm not sure what*

happened to my verve. All I know is it got up and went, and I've been finding it hard to open my eyes in the morning.

I'm worn out from the move. Unable to keep the house on one income alone, I downgraded into a small, yard-less, two-bedroom rental. The kids don't like it and when they're not happy, it wears on me. Add to all of that the pace of life…working, mothering, social demands…and there's never a quiet moment. My days are noisy as a heronry, and I long to be reclusive—reclusive as a mangrove cuckoo. Or to burrow, like the ghost crabs burrowing in the sand near my toes.

My friend—the one we're staying with—insists I go off on my own two hours each day. I hope she didn't hear me crying in the wee hours. I was grieving, mourning, wailing from my heart because I've lost sight of You in my crazy, hectic life, and miss You. I miss the days when I walked and talked with You daily.

But here I am now, like a bird gone south for a season, getting away from it all. I don't want to get away from You, though. There's no need for me to be walking around distant, like Eve, in the Garden of Eden, after she outright defied You. I can sit here long as I like, dwelling in Your presence. You are accessible, and made a way for me to be with You. Whereas all that's separating me from the water right now is a patch of scruffy beach plants and sand, all that was separating me from You was my sin. But Jesus cleared the way. The only thing getting in the way now is me. I seem to get caught up in the weeds of my busy, hectic life…and I forget to include You.

So I'll be perching myself in special spots around Sanibel for two hours each day, to rest in Your presence, like I used to do, and acknowledge You— God Almighty, the God that I love. You desire that. You desire for me to walk and talk with You, and rest in Your presence.

Our book club already voted on its list of titles for the upcoming year. This morning, however, I've decided to withdraw and spend my free-time reading the Bible instead, as I've done before, off and on all throughout my life. The club can run without me, but I can't run without You. I can't go another inch running on fumes, without refueling, filling myself with Your Word on a daily basis. I've been longing to get back into the Bible again, and to reacquaint myself with You, my favorite author—the author of Life, the author and perfecter of Faith, the author of Salvation!

71

I keep turning to peek at the lighthouse behind me. It reminds me that Your loving eye is always on me. I didn't need to go off to an island. I could have veered off from the craziness of each day, gone to my dark, messy closet to sit in the light of Your presence. But here I am anyway in the most beautiful place I've ever seen. I feel washed ashore, like I'm catching my breath after being pulled from the overwhelming turbulence of life, from one thing after the next coming at me so fast I was gulping for air and no longer catching glimpse of Your presence.

Sitting here alone with You—the One who made me in the first place—I can be me. I don't have to be anyone but me, and already, I'm shedding myself of the plumage that the world had me dressing up in each day. Good thing I have on my oversized don't-look-at-me sunglasses. My emotions are for You. I don't need anyone walking by, seeing the tears in my eyes as I sit here remembering what I loved about You from the start... Your presence, Your ever-presence!

When I lost my teddy bear as a child, I searched and searched, then gave up the search, crying into the wee hours. My mother prayed with me, and told me You were there, that even though I had lost my teddy bear, I would never lose You. I would never have to go searching for Your whereabouts.

How could I have forgotten that, when all throughout the Bible, You've made clear and specific the unique places You put Your presence on Earth. In the Old Testament days, You put it in a tent, then in a moveable tabernacle, and after that, in a temple—Solomon's temple. You did this to interact with Your people. But You are omnipresent, in all places at all times, so those weren't the only places You were present on Earth. They were the places You were especially present, manifesting Your presence to your people back then.

I'm glad I dusted off my Bible, brought it with me for this month. Reading into the wee hours last night, I was overwhelmed by emotion over Your details in putting together the tabernacle. You were so particular about it, and no wonder—You filled it with Your Presence, Your Glory. I know (from studying it in the past) that as I continue my reading of the Old Testament, the temple will replace the tabernacle, but even then, the temple gets destroyed, then rebuilt, and in the New Testament, Jesus (the greatest manifestation of Your presence on Earth) teaches there at the temple.

But then, once Jesus is crucified, there's no more tent, nor tabernacle, nor temple. There's us—the body of Christ, and You fill us with Your Glory. I couldn't find my teddy bear that night, but as a child of God, Your glory was in me! It's what I've loved about You from the start, that You're not far away. You're right here with me, and it humbles me and comforts me that Your Spirit makes His home in us. We are temples of the Holy Spirit.

My, the lively discussion, even debate, that topic alone—we are temples of the Holy Spirit—would spark among my bibliophile sisterhood! I love when that happens, when our discussions turn heated and reach excitable levels. Then again, we've read a myriad of genres—romances, mysteries, thrillers— but the Bible has never come up.

I wonder if they'd be interested. It would take a year for us as a group to read through it together, and we'd have to put all other titles on hold. But what would they say if I told them we could have You, the author of the world's most influential book, present at our discussions!

For now, I'll focus on writing You these letters. I'll share my thoughts with You as I read through Your Word, in which You share Your thoughts with me. And who knows, maybe one day I'll turn these letters to You into a devotional for others to read. The only problem: I'm a voracious reader. There aren't enough hours in the day for voracious readers to also be writers. I'd have to partner with more of a writer than me in order for it to ever happen. Who? I have no idea. I'll put that in Your hands.

All I know is You designed me with purpose—to bring glory to You—and also, to walk through my life in Your presence. I feel so loved by all that You've done—sending Your only begotten Son into this world to die for my sins, so I could be made right with You. And when Jesus rose from the dead, went back up into Heaven until His return, You didn't leave us here on the Earth alone and without You. You house in us the Holy Spirit. And if You cared about the particulars of that physical tabernacle, and later, the temple, no doubt You care about us—our interior, our exterior, and every detail of our being. We are walking temples of the Holy Spirit.

It was You who first loved me—before I loved You. You loved me "as is" but saw my potential, and went to work in me. What a beautiful thing when You, God of the Universe, is at work in someone. But even though I declared long ago that Jesus is Lord, and have always believed in my heart that You raised Him from the dead, in recent years I've neglected to appreciate that most perfect work You did in me.

When King David found himself in the wilderness, far away from the tabernacle—the place of Your presence back then—his soul hungered, his flesh was consumed with a desire to return, and he mournfully cried:

"How lovely is your dwelling place, O Lord, Almighty! My soul yearns, even faints, for the courts of the Lord; my heart and my flesh cry out for the living God."

Reading it struck a chord in me. My heart, soul, and flesh have been out of tune, longing to dance in Your presence again, and walk in sync with Your will. I didn't need to go off to an island (although I'm glad to be here). I didn't need to go anywhere. You put Your Spirit in me. You made me a dwelling place for the Holy Spirit.

When David became king, he built a marvelous palace, but was bothered that the Ark of the Covenant remained in a tent. He swore an oath to You that he would not enter his own house or go to bed until he found a dwelling place on Earth for You. He then went about drafting plans for the temple.

Although David was given the idea for the temple, and went forth making plans to build it, it was his son, Solomon who took the baton from his father, and had it built.

As a mother, I've wanted to build my kids up into God-fearing, God-loving people. I helped paved the way, helped with preliminary preparations. We'd walk and talk and I'd tell them Bible stories about You. And I brought them to church. It was like I was buying the land, and collecting the building materials for them to become temples of the Holy Spirit. But they had to take the baton…which they did. They went straight to Jesus themselves. That, I couldn't do for them. Through Jesus alone we become righteous before You. I am just their mother.

I hardly talk about You to them anymore. My sugar plum has entered this stage where she no longer likes anything mother likes. And loves whatever mother can't stand. I don't want her to stop liking You just because I like You, so I try not to say too much. I do still manage to get us all up and out the door to church once a month.

Trust me, it's hard. She doesn't want to go. You know how gung-ho in love she was with her daddy, and so was I. She misses her father, and our big house, and the way things used to be. I miss all of that, too—the best days of my life, when my kids were little, and my husband alive, and all of us going on bike rides and playing in the yard.

The kids don't want to hear it, but I do. I need the reminder, need to hear it, read it in Your Word that I am Your daughter! I may be living in a rundown rental, but You've made Your home with me. I'm still Your princess. I can dance right now in the courts of the Lord. Your kingdom is here and now, although I look forward to my dream home in Heaven!

Still, when will it end—the stage my sugar plum is in, where she refuses to hear a single word of encouragement that her mama tries to say? Even Luke rolls his eyes if I try talking virtues. Do I dare even mention how I'm spending my two hours alone each day—reconnecting with You? They wouldn't want to hear it. All they care about is surfing…catching the big waves. I've tried telling them a thousand times, but they have to learn on their own…there are no waves here. And no surfing, either.

Oh well, they both looked thrilled when I said good-bye to them this morning. Speaking of which, uh oh, my time is up.

Love,
Finley (Your daughter with sand between her toes, the one who doesn't have to search for Your whereabouts…all she has to search for are seashells)

NINE

INTERIOR DESIGN TIDBIT

* * *

Think back to what you loved about your house in the first place.
Was it the enormous yard, the view out the
windows, the charming architecture?

God's presence—that's what Mom loved way back then. She loved His ever-presence in her life!

We made it to bed, but I tossed and turned as things I read in her letter repeated in my mind like an internal tracking system indicating how far I had wandered, yet how close God was all along. I wanted to appreciate His presence in my life, too!

The next morning, Peter got up before me, and later returned with two café lattes and a bakery bag. I sat up and stuck my nose in the bag. The everything bagels sure smelled good, but my insides were starving for more. More than positive thinking, dreaming of wonderful things, and living in a beautiful place, the spiritual side of me was hungering for the Word of God, and for Truth. My cravings were strong—to love Him like I did as a child, but to know Him more intimately, and appreciate His presence.

I didn't mention any of that to Peter, though. I didn't want him thinking I was spiritually dramatic. "I've got an idea." I closed the bag and climbed out of bed.

"Uh oh."

"No, a good idea…bagels on the beach."

"Not a good idea at all. It's a great idea." He kissed me on the cheek. "And by the way, happy anniversary! I was going to get you a card, but—"

I put my hand up. "Shush, I didn't get you one, either. Neither of us should be spending five dollars each on mass-produced cards created by writers paid to be mushy." I went into the closet and put on a t-shirt with short leggings, then came out looking for my flip flops. "If you add up all the money that we've spent on store-bought cards through the years, we could have bought a boat with it instead."

Peter looked relieved as always on our anniversary, glad he didn't have to make a big fuss. His face was relaxed as he watched me brush through my hair.

"It's finally growing," I said. "I know you like it long."

"I like it however you happen to wear it."

"Aw, that's nice of you, but I won't chop it off again. Or, if I do, I'll go to a salon. I won't do it myself."

He knew, though, why I had chopped it to my chin. Washing, drying, and combing through Mom's hair became time-consuming enough, and I wasn't going to cut hers short. Mom's hair was forever long, and she wore it in a golden braid down her back with wispy strands of strawberry blonde sticking out near her face. Even when it tangled into a rebellious mess, and took me an hour to untangle, I refused to cut Mom's hair. Losing her thoughts, her memories, and her independence was already too much.

"So, do we dare do the math?" I asked Peter as I pulled my own hair into a short, perky ponytail. "How many years has it been?"

"I knew you were going to ask me that," he said like the unprepared kid in class, clueless when called on. "Can I borrow a calculator?"

"Very funny, Mr. Class Clown. But it shouldn't be too difficult. All we have to do is take last year's number, and add one year."

"Yeah, but what was last year's number?"

I stepped up to him and dabbed sunscreen on his nose and cheeks, then rubbed it in. "I don't remember last year's number…maybe after my coffee."

Content beyond words to spend our anniversary having bagels on the beach, I followed him out the front door. But midway down the porch steps, he stopped. "For the record, I did try getting you flowers, but the flower shop was closed. I'll swing by again later. Get you some then."

"Oh, shush." I looked over at the royal poinciana tree shading the bottom porch step, and the fuzzy white blooms of the twinberry shrub lining our drive, and the hot pink bougainvillea already growing around our new mailbox. "I have all the flowers a person could wish for right here in this yard. Don't stress yourself, Peter."

"How about perfume?" he said as we reached the driveway.

"Why on earth would I want you spending money on perfume when I've got the fragrance of the ylang-ylang?"

"The what?"

I pulled him over to the thirty-foot tree blooming at the edge of our yard, near the road. "Can you smell it? It's the scent that Coco Chanel went looking for, the very scent she deemed fit for her Chanel No. 5."

Peter put his nose in the air and whiffed. "For real?"

"Yep, for real." I walked under the cascading, yellowy-green flowers, curled like ribbons. "I read all about this tree. There's one at the Edison and Ford Winter Estates, over in town. I never imagined having one in my own sweet yard."

"Okay, so no card, no flowers, no perfume. But still, I've got to get you something. Point me in the right direction, and we'll call it a day."

"A power washer would be nice!" I pointed toward the filthy front porch screens.

It was then we heard his cell phone ringing from up in the house, and with different ring tones for each of the kids, we knew by Al Jolson's song, "Give My Regards to Broadway", that it was Lucy. Since she was our oldest, her age did the math for us, and it was an interesting story problem. We tied the knot three months before she was born.

"Tell her again what I told her yesterday," I said to Peter as he hurried up the steps. "Not to let that narcissistic boyfriend close the curtain on her dreams. Let her hear it from you."

The situation drove me crazy, and I was overbearing at times, telling my daughter what she should do. I couldn't help it. I encouraged my girls to chase after their dreams—not boys. But all week long, Lucy had been calling, telling me she was thinking of turning down a leading role— singing and dancing her heart out for a huge show in Chicago, playing at Navy Pier's 500-seat courtyard-style theater. And all because she didn't want to move three hours away from her on-again, off-again drama-king boyfriend.

I sat down on the bottom porch step, nibbling on my bagel while watching a female cardinal chase a male through the branches of a tree. The more she hopped toward him, the more he hopped away. She even followed him to another tree.

"What...he's taking a job in Indianapolis, so now you want to go there instead?" Peter's voice from up in the house was loud and getting more intense. "I've said it before, and I'll say it again. Stop chasing after him. Chase after better things."

The flirtatious female went after the male with her wings, as he tried to flee.

"What does he have to offer? I forget what you even liked about him in the first place."

In a twist of events, the male redbird took to the offense, flying after the female, landing next to her on the same branch. He took her beak in his, ready to feed her.

"Okay," Peter was saying. "I get that. You loved that he loved...or so he said he loved...you."

The bird drama alone had me on the edge of my porch seat. Then, sure enough, the truth became obvious...Don Juan cardinal didn't have a worm in his beak to give her.

I jumped up, ready to shoo Ms. Cardinal away—for her own good, and to a different yard. But first, I tossed her seeds from my bagel. He gobbled them up before her, then took off, leaving the pale red-tinged beauty standing there alone, wings quivering.

"He wants to break up again? Don't be upset," Peter was saying to our daughter. "You should be doing the happy dance. Enjoy your season alone!"

Don Juan cardinal returned to the stage for an encore, landing on my van, pushing its beak into the side mirror, flirting with the bird it saw... which was itself. It was in love with itself.

"I'm glad you're seeing that, and yes. I'd have to agree. I think it's pretty safe to say he's in love with himself."

A few seconds later, the porch door slammed shut and Peter came down the steps.

"How many steps to the beach do we live?" he asked me.

"Huh?"

He reached into the bag and pulled out his bagel. "Lucy wants to know exactly how many steps to the beach we live. Oh, and she heard on the news about a tropical storm headed our way…nothing big and scary, just a lot of rain."

"Hold off on buying me a power washer," I told him. "Mother Nature will wash the screens for us."

As Peter stood there eating his bagel, I glanced around our flood-zoned yard, and at our house on stilts. "Will you still love me if we wake up on a houseboat?"

"Sure, I'll love you even more." He popped the last piece of bagel into his mouth. "You know I want a boat."

"Aw, see why I don't like store-bought cards? We have our way of saying things."

But really, I didn't know how to put into words what I loved about Peter way back when. It had to do with how he loved Lucy, before she was even born. I didn't want to go there, didn't want to tear up. But whether he knew it or not, that's what I loved most about him early on, and as the months and years progressed, I appreciated it even more, how before even seeing or holding her, he loved that life in me, the one we produced to-gether…planned, or not planned. She was my Lucy, and I couldn't imagine my life without her.

"I told Lucy we'd count for her," Peter said.

"Huh?"

"The exact number of steps to the beach that we live."

Funny. It wasn't the floor-to-ceiling windows in the great room, the original, wide-planked Dutch door in the laundry room, 1930s bathtub in the master bedroom, farm sink in the kitchen, built-in shelves in the hallway, or even the vintage chandeliers that had me falling in love with our house when I first saw it online. Mere steps to the beach—that's what did it. That's what I loved about the place, so early on.

"Mere isn't good enough?" I asked. "It is for me!"

"You know our Lucy. She wants to know the exact number of steps. I told her we were headed there now and would count."

"You mean, count our steps?"

"Yup," he took my hands and pulled me up from the step. "One."

I stepped along with him. "Two," we said at that same time. "Three, four, five, six."

But soon enough, we struggled. It was tricky, walking, counting, and trying to carry on a conversation all at the same time. "Twenty-one...why don't we...twenty-two...give her...twenty-three...an estimated guess... twenty-four," Peter said as we reached the road.

"Twenty-five...the crazy things we do for our kids." I shook my head, wanting to finish what we started. "Twenty-six. We're getting close to how many years we've been married. Twenty-eight."

"You skipped a number." Peter took a step backward.

"No, I didn't."

"Yes, you did. Twenty-seven. You never said twenty-seven."

I let out a flustered sigh, mixed with a laugh. "Then we'll have to start over. It's not like we have anything else to do...other than working on the house. Oh, and your work reports."

"That were due yesterday," Peter said.

I took his arm and pulled him back to the bottom porch step where we started. But first, I wanted to tell him, "Remember when I was doing my internship at the hospital in Chicago and you came to see me?"

"Um, yes."

"We were walking along Michigan Ave., and there in front of us was that old couple walking arm-in-arm, all hunched over. Remember we slowed, didn't want to pass them by, they were so cute."

"They were like a hundred."

"Yup, and he was holding her elbow as they walked...holding her up."

"I remember."

"That was one of the moments I knew for sure...I wanted to be walking with you at that age."

Peter took my hand. "Don't ever buy me a card again. That was card enough."

Hand-in-hand, we started over again, taking a step.

"One," we said together. "Two, three, four."

Peter stopped counting around the one-hundred mark, but I kept going all the way down the crunchy seashell road, under the arc in the trees, and along the tunnel-like path to the beach. It reminded me of an old commercial I loved as a kid—how many licks does it take to get to the Tootsie Roll center?

"Five hundred and seventy-six," I shouted when our toes touched the white sand. It was more than "mere," but still, what more could anyone want than to live five hundred and seventy-six steps from the beach!

As Peter texted Lucy, I stretched my arms up, then hung my head back, staring up at the sky, pink and blue like cotton candy, and with clouds fluffy as marshmallows. I didn't expect a gust of words to blow through my mind, but like a sudden breeze on a breezeless day, they did, the words of King David, blowing through my mind.

My soul yearns, even faints, for the courts of the Lord; my heart and my flesh cry out for the living God.

Like the wings of that cardinal, my arms quivered. I was tired from chasing after this, chasing after that. There I was, living mere steps to the beach, but living my life far from the One who wanted closeness.

Peter stepped ankle-deep out into the water, and I stayed put on the beach. I had taken steps as a child, ones leading me into the presence of the Holy One. First, I got down on my knees each night and asked Jesus to forgive me for white lying, for cheating, for being mean to my brother. Second, I told Him how much I loved Him as God's only begotten Son, who died for my sins. Third. I called Him my Lord. Mom always told me to call Him my Lord.

Peter waved at me, and I waved back. But if only he knew—blame it on reading the letter Mom wrote—that I, too, wanted to renew my relationship with the One I ignored for so long. I didn't want to go another day living like I was His granddaughter, or His neighbor, or a friend of a friend living down the road from Him. I didn't want to socialize and talk about Him in a once-a-week country club setting…packing my calendar with spiritual-themed social activities.

I wanted more. Like I did as a child, licking away the lollipop, I wanted to reach and taste for myself God's delicious truths, and the fullness of Christ embedded within…within me!

I slipped my flip flops off and walked out into the water. Should I bring it all up, mention to Peter how famished I was for the Word of God, and could hardly wait to read more? The two of us were brought up practicing religion on different courts. Like how tennis was played on clay, grass, hard courts, sand, or even removable carpet courts, Christianity seemed to be served from a variety of surfaces. And each surface had characteristics of its own that affected practicing style. The church Peter's family attended was on one side of the net, and the one Mom had taken us to was on the other. Both served Christ, but the rules and fundamentals differed.

If only it was simpler, like panning for gold and mining for gems. But panning for God, mining for Truth seemed…whether God meant for it or not…to be more complex.

"Penny for your thoughts," Peter said as we shuffled our feet across the warm floor of the Gulf of Mexico. "Or if you prefer, credit card for your thoughts."

He knew me well, especially when I was quiet. I was holding in a lot of good thoughts, but wasn't sure if I wanted to dispense them, and didn't know how to put them into normal-sounding words. I didn't want him thinking I was a nut…a coconut.

But after years of pulling back—spiritually living at low tide—desire was pumping through my veins again. And I wanted to believe it was the Creator of gravity pulling on my insides, grabbing me closer, sort of like the moon did to things of the Earth.

"Alright, if you really want to know, I'm wondering."

"Wondering what?"

"Do I care more about the number of steps to the beach that I'm living, or how close I'm living to God?"

Peter shrugged his shoulders, like it was a no-brainer. "Doesn't have to be an either-or," he said. "Why not care about both? You can have both. Live close to the beach, and to God."

"Oh, I agree," I said right away. "Nothing wrong with both. But for so long now, I've been wanting one without even thinking of the other, that's my point."

Peter shook his head. "I take it you read your mother's prayer last night?"

I stopped walking. "Yup, and you know what?"

"What?"

"I know my mom. She wanted me to find it, read it. Otherwise, she would have burned it, or tossed it into a shredding machine."

"When do I get my lemon bars?"

I splashed him with water for caring more about lemon bars than what my mother had to say in her letter. When Peter's cell phone rang and it was his boss, he gave me a wink, then headed toward the beach.

I stayed ankle-deep in the water and when a conch shell washed up around my toes, I reached down and picked it up, holding it to my ear, listening for wisdom or something bigger than myself. The shell had nothing to say to me, but I heard my own yearning for the Lord echoing forth from the deepest, most intricate corridors of my being.

I returned the shell where it belonged, not far from where a white ibis was probing the water with its bright red-orange beak. I had seen pictures of that type of a bird in the books, and wanted to see it up close and personal, with my own two eyes. I took a step toward it, but it took a step back. I took two steps toward it, and it took two steps back. The bird and I played a few more rounds of our game until it skipped several yards away, then flew off, sporting its black wing tip in flight.

I didn't know why even the ibis had me thinking about God, but it did. Unlike the ibis, though, God wanted to be near me as I wanted to be near Him.

Come near to God and He will come near to You.

From the beach, Peter, with the cell phone still to his ear, mimed to me that he had to hurry back, and I nodded, then blew him a kiss. A couple of minutes later, I came out of the water and started on the five hundred and seventy-six steps back to the house. But my mind was thinking about other steps, those laid-out steps I had taken as a child, that brought me to a special place.

Confess with your mouth that Jesus is Lord. Believe in your heart that God raised Him from the dead.

"Confess, one. Believe, two," I mumbled beneath my breath, shaking my head that the Creator of the universe and His morsels of truth were more reachable than the cookies in the fragile jar, way up on top of the fridge.

The One known for opening and closing doors could have kept His perfect Son out of reach, high up in Heaven. But He loved me so much— loved the whole world—that He put the Bread of Life down on my level, within reach. He wanted to be close. And not just close, but closer and closer and closer.

Submit yourselves, then, to God. Three. *Resist the devil.* Four. *Come near to God.* Five. *Wash your hands, you sinners.* Six. *Purify your hearts.* Seven. *Grieve, mourn and wail.* Eight, nine, ten. *Change your laughter to mourning, and your joy to gloom.* Eleven. *Humble yourselves before the Lord.* Twelve. *Obey His teachings.* Thirteen.

The church had done a fine job, teaching me special steps…steps leading to a closer relationship, and to walking in sync with God. No wonder I didn't feel close. I must have felt more like skipping. It wasn't the Almighty who skipped away. It was me. I was like the ibis.

When I got home, Peter was still on the phone and I could tell by his face that he was overwhelmed. I patted him on the back. "You okay?" I whispered.

"Lemon bars," he said. "Make me those lemon bars, and I'll be fine."

TEN

Finley's Meyer Lemon Bar Recipe

Notes: I'm writing this recipe out for my sugar plum, who will surely make them herself one day.

If you happen to have a Meyer lemon tree growing in your yard, by all means, use Meyer lemons! But you can use regular lemons, too.

The recipe is a personal reminder. Rather than living like an unproductive tree that bears no fruit, I want to live productively, bringing glory to the One who deserves all glory.

"And this I pray, that your love may abound still more and more in real knowledge and all discernment, so that you may approve the things that are excellent, in order to be sincere and blameless until the day of Christ; having been filled with the fruit of righteousness which comes through Jesus Christ, to the glory and praise of God."

—Philippians 1:9–11

Ingredients:
  Crust
- *2 cups all-purpose flour*
- *2 teaspoons sea salt*
- *½ cup confectioners' sugar*
- *½ teaspoon baking powder*

- *1 cup unsalted butter, kept cold (try substituting coconut oil in solid form)*
- *½ teaspoon vanilla extract*
- *4 teaspoons lemon zest (none of the bitter, white pith)*

Lemon filling
- *4 large eggs*
- *2 large egg yolk*
- *1 ½ cups white sugar (try substituting honey)*
- *4 tablespoons all-purpose flour*
- *½ teaspoon baking powder (optional—makes bars tall and chewy)*
- *½ cup freshly squeezed lemon juice, plus more if you like (I used the juice from six lemons; but grated nearly 12)*
- *4 tablespoons freshly grated lemon zest (again, no pith)*
- *2 teaspoons confectioners' sugar, or to taste*
- *Patience*

Glaze
- *½ cup confectioners' sugar*
- *8 tablespoons lemon juice*

Use a 9 x 13 pan.

Preheat oven to 350 degrees. Generously oil or butter a 9 x 13 pan, or if you prefer, line the pan with aluminum foil or parchment paper and spray with cooking spray.

CRUST. Mix flour, sea salt, confectioners' sugar, and baking powder with spoon. Put all in food processor and add cold chunks of butter, vanilla, and lemon zest. Pulse until crumbly, like sand, and do not overmix.

Moisten your fingers with water, and without overworking it, gently press dough into bottom of prepared pan.

Use a fork to prick holes all over the crust. Freeze 15 minutes.

Bake crust only until edges are barely golden brown. Peek at it frequently. Maybe 18 minutes.

FILLING. Beat eggs and egg yolk together in a bowl about 2 minutes. Whisk in white sugar, flour, and baking powder until smooth. Roll lemons on counter before you slice, then squeeze out juice. Add lemon juice and lemon zest to filling mixture, then whisk for 2 minutes. Pour lemon filling over crust.

Bake on center rack until custard is set and top has a thin white sugary crust, 25 minutes or less (if crust looks as if it's burning, cover with foil as needed). As it bakes, prepare the glaze while savoring the aroma of lemon filling the kitchen.

Remove pan from oven. Drizzle glaze over the warm top. Let cool before cutting into bars. When cool, dip knife into hot water, run around the edge, and cut into 16 squares. Dust with a teaspoon of confectioners' sugar.

Refrigerate. Bars taste better the second day.

Once you put them in fridge, do something golden while the bars are resting. My golden thing is to get down on my knees and pray 10 minutes for fruit in my life, but you can do whatever you think special.

ELEVEN

INTERIOR DESIGN TIDBIT

* * *

Ask around if anyone remembers
what your house looked like
in its glory days.

The next morning, still in my pajamas, I slipped my feet into a pair of yellow rubber boots that came with the house. On a deadline to complete his reports, Peter was out on the front porch, which was shaded by the branches of banyan and rubber trees, and except for the loud singing birds, made a wonderful office for anyone working remote, as long as they only worked mornings, before the blazing sun.

But even then, it was going to be where we hung out all day because all through the night the power went on and off, until three-thirty in the morning when it stayed off. The place was so hot that even the lizards and cockroaches were fleeing in mass exodus from closets and cabinets, escaping through holes in the screens.

It had been a rough night for Peter, and I didn't want to bother him at work. En route to the door, I winked over at him.

"Um, where are you going in your pajamas...and those boots?" he asked from the aged wicker chair, that was peeling with paint.

"Fruit...looking for fruit in our trees, so I can make you those lemon bars."

Living in a run-down dive was turning out to be the greatest appetite control plan ever. With the kitchen still ripped apart and the old appliances nasty, we were both shedding pounds, and nibbling on pretty much what the birds ate. But after reading Mom's recipe, I woke with my mouth watering. I wanted lemon bars, too.

"Be careful," Peter said as I went out the door. "I'd be careful in that part of the yard, if I were you."

From a distance, it looked more like the forest where the huntsman met up with Snow White. But as I went down the porch steps, I muttered beneath my breath an exciting promise I knew by heart: "Pick fresh fruit from your own backyard—orange, grapefruit, key lime, Meyer lemon, lychee nut, carambola, and papaya."

After making my way through the field of waist-high weeds, I climbed over a mound of fallen, decaying branches piled high like a bunch of bones. When I arrived at the row of tropical fruit trees, I went first to the carambola tree, tall enough for me to walk under. While perusing its branches for starfruit, I peered over at the multi-million dollar, seven-thousand-square-foot mansion blocking our view of the Gulf of Mexico. Might Lady Gatsby be throwing any parties?

Peter and I could bring lemon bars and a platter of our yard-grown carambola, which I'd cut in cross-sections to form perfect stars. We could introduce ourselves as the owners of the dilapidated dive next door, and ask around, "Does anyone remember what our place looked like back in its glory days?"

Worn out from the night before, the years before, and from life itself, I would have loved to return to my glory days, that time in my life when I felt my best, looked my best, lived my best. If I got around to meeting her, I'd tell her I appreciated her interior design tidbits. But did she happen to have tips for me…returning me to my glory days?

"Here, right here, children! This is where you find your glory," old Ms. Viola used to passionately shout in her nine o'clock Sunday school class, her hand on her heart when she did so. "He lives in you and you live in Him. He is Your glory, and you are His."

I hadn't thought of her in years!

I left the fruitless carambola tree, and went next to a lychee tree, grabbing onto a branch, giving it a good shake. Nothing fell out—not a single piece of edible anything. Oh well, other than going through the hassle of drying it out, turning it into a nut for Peter to eat, I wouldn't know what to do with such a delicacy if I had one.

"When you got the Holy Spirit inside of you," Ms. Viola would yell as she lined us up single file and marched us from the chapel to her classroom, "you should expect special fruit produced within."

As I left the fruitless lychee tree behind, I tried to remember what those special fruits were…love, peace, joy, kindness, goodness, gentleness, self-control. Did I have them in me?

"Let the fruit of the spirit satisfy you," she used to tell us. "Let it satisfy all your cravings because this world never will."

When a mature-looking tree, ten feet tall, with shiny dark leaves, caught my eye, I rushed over, searching like a fool through its branches for anything resembling a deep-yellow cross between a lemon and a mandarin…in other words, a Meyer lemon. But there was not a single lemon anywhere in the tree.

No wonder Mom's recipe called for patience. Everything good in life required it. It took patience waiting for trees to mature, fruit to appear and then ripen, and patience fixing up a neglected property, and one's own neglected self. Reaching up, I pulled off one of the shiny, dark green leaves, convincing myself that a fruitless tree was a good thing. At least it gave me something to look forward to.

Still, I let out a sigh, wishing Mrs. P was my neighbor and I could crab with her from my yard. She lived for moments like that. I'd confess to her my buyer's remorse, tell her there wasn't even fruit in my yard. She'd inform me of my customer rights and return policy, then gift me another potted crabapple tree, like she did last time I crabbed about my stressful job.

I glanced over at the eyesore house. From where I stood, it resembled a rotten piece of fruit dipped in white chocolate, then dropped in dirt. On the outside, it needed painting, but on the inside, every nook and cranny was crying out for revival. And so was every nook and cranny of me.

Why on earth were things so let go? The house, the yard, the upside-down world, and I—a temple of the Holy Spirit—we were all a hot mess, and so let go. The current condition of it all overwhelmed me, and wasn't what I pictured. Didn't everyone have pictures of the way things were supposed to be? Pictures that our parents, great teachers, or people of influence put within us like precious keepsakes in a hope chest.

"Now listen carefully." Ms. Viola used to point her finger at us, warning us of troubles that were out there—scary troubles in the world. We weren't sure what kinds of troubles she was talking about, but she knew, had experienced many of them already, and survived. "As you make your way through life, you've got to ride as God's children on the float of His presence. That's right, walk in step with His Word, and march to the Spirit of Him within!" Her eyes were big when she talked of such things. They were always big. "And whatever you do…" She looked at each and every one of us, her eyes leaving no one out. "Do not fall, children. You hear me? In the parade of life, do not fall away from the Lord."

If only I had raised my hand, daring to ask, "But what if we do fall away, Ms. Viola, then what?"

My, how quickly it happened, my falling away. And how the pictures faded—the pictures I had of the holy, merciful One and me, and pictures of the way things were supposed to be. It was after the pictures faded that I sketched my own version of God…a distant, abstract being high up in the endless sky, way beyond the clouds, and perhaps in another galaxy, far, far away. Others around me were also sketching, sketching their own manmade versions of who they thought God should be.

I left the section of our yard with the fruitless trees, telling myself it was for the better. Unless Mom listed ghost ants and sawdust in her recipe, it was better I waited until the kitchen was redone. But then, a tantalizing object glistening in the morning sun, dangling like an ornament on a Christmas tree, caught my eye. I turned in its direction, and my mouth dry as a desert watered.

"A mango," I clapped, "a mango!"

But there was one problem—

It was in my neighbor's yard, not mine.

I looked around for the woman who lived there, but didn't see her. All I saw were multitudes of Julia butterflies, fluttering around the vines of the lavender passionflower plant, wanting nothing to do with the mango. And the warblers…they were hovering around a golden dewdrop shrub, feasting on insects. Neither butterflies nor birds cared the least bit about the mango.

I inched my foot to the edge of her yard, then stretched my arm over the property line until my fingertips touched the mango, ripe as an avocado. Twisting it ever-so-slightly, it came loose, and was mine.

Like a squirrel with its nut, I hurried over the heap of branches, through the field of weeds, and alongside our house to a garden hose that was near the stone terrace area. Although covered in green fungus, weeds growing from the cracks, the terrace had great potential, and ideas were buzzing through my brain. After clearing it all out and repairing what was broken, I'd furnish it with weather-resistant chaise lounges, and lay stepping-stones leading from the bottom porch step. Oh, and then sit there in the mornings, eating my mangoes...or her mangoes...or store-bought mangoes, whatever.

Picking up a garden knife that just so happened to be sticking out of the dirt, I wiped it on my pajamas, then peeled the mango, and sliced it into wedges. All the while, I refused to fret about an allergic reaction I experienced years ago—nothing horrific, a bout of itchiness around my mouth after tasting mango ice cream. I didn't want that worry to ruin my moment and convinced myself I had long since outgrown the allergy.

I pushed the fruit's succulent, aromatic flesh into my mouth. Oh, it tasted like paradise. I shivered, then closed my eyes, hoping to see more pictures stored deep within me by old Ms. Viola.

"If you do fall from the float, if you fall from God's presence," she told us one Sunday morning, "cry—cry out to the Lord with all your heart and He will pick you up! Listen to me, children, don't be silent. Wail, grieve, mourn, cry out to your Father when you realize you've fallen!"

As I devoured the juiciest mango ever, I tried coming up with a name I could blame—of who shoved me off the float. But that wasn't how it happened. No one pushed me. Early on in the parade route of life, I inched my own way over to the edge of God's presence, dangling first a foot, and then my entire self. With my feet dragging, I held on for a while, but then opened my fingers and let go.

I was to blame for the distance I felt—the distance between us.

And the sudden itchiness overtaking my hands and lips, I was to blame for that, too.

I dropped what was left of the mango, which wasn't much, and wiped my mouth on my pajama sleeve.

TWELVE

INTERIOR DESIGN TIDBIT

* * *

*Realize your incompetency and call for
help. But don't just call anyone.
Call only the most reputable, experienced designer!*

There was no hiding the rash forming on my hands, and no fig leaves in the yard to cover up the reality that I was like Eve in the Garden of Eden. A descendent of hers, I got handed down the "eating fruit I wasn't supposed to eat" trait. And perhaps my every-once-in-a-blue-moon impulsivity—wanting a piece of paradise for myself, purchasing it despite my husband's resistance—came from her, too. Shouldn't I have learned a thing or two from the infamous Eve story told to me as a child—to make different mistakes than she?

When I heard the noise of a sledgehammer coming from the open windows, I was glad Peter's reports were done and he was back working on the house. I didn't want him finding me outside with a rash, then looking at me like I was brainless for having eaten fruit I was allergic to. I already knew I shouldn't have eaten the mango.

Turning the garden hose on, I waited for the smell of sulfur to go away, and for the hot, rust-colored water to turn clear, and cool. "Watch out for that serpent," Ms. Viola had warned as I left her classroom my last day of Sunday school. "Watch out for that Father of Lies, showing up in disguise, slithering into your own backyard. I've seen him, child. I've seen the devil. Don't let this world trick you into thinking he doesn't exist."

I put the hose water to my mouth and doused my itching face, trying to recall if there was such a time when Satan found me in the garden, and slithered in. Nothing came to mind, so I tried remembering instead when it was that my heart began to harden, my faith crack, my identity as God's child crumble, and a sense of greater purpose for my life rot.

Was it back when Mom tried making me read the Bible and it seemed so boring that I assumed the One worthy of all praise was boring, too? Or when my daddy died, and I blamed the everlasting Father for not being a superhero, and stopping death in the world? Was it in college, when learning new things, I pushed the old aside? Or into adulthood, when the rat race of daily life had me caught up in the weeds?

If there was a serpent, like old Ms. Viola taught me there was, it slithered unnoticed into all the various seasons of my life, producing in me a nonchalance toward the One so mindful of me. And caused me to forget that reality was both material and spiritual. Regardless, I blamed myself for the broken connection, for cutting the wires, and for the seemingly earth-to-sky distance between God and me. It was me who tossed all things God-related into one big pile, like laundry that I'd get around to one day.

The hose water tasted like fish. After spitting it out, I turned the water off, then stood drying in the late morning sun like an anhinga with its wings spread and feathers fanned open. I wasn't at peace like an anhinga, though. My eyes were watering, and my nostrils twitching. My lips, tongue, and throat burning.

I hung my neck back. The osprey was flying through the sky, carrying a fish. But then, it let go...it let go of the fish! It returned to its huge stick nest outside our front door, and let out a succession of cries for having let go of something so special. It must have known that I was watching. All the while it continued crying out in higher and higher pitches, it kept peering over at me with its yellow eyes.

I blinked, then looked away at the morning glories that were like white tissues in my yard. I wanted to pull one off the branches and use it to wipe my eyes. The raptor and I were crying together, both of us hungry, yet both having let go of the very thing we were hungering for. It was hungry for fish. I was hungering for God.

No more excuses. I dropped to my knees. "It's me," I cried out to the living, breathing One who never let me go. *Your daughter, Your princess, the one You formed in my mother's womb!*

I was crying out much the way I had to my mom back when she forgot who I was. That illness could sneak in from nowhere and rob my mother of her most precious earthly identity—who she was to me—and this cursed and fallen world could turn me unresponsive to my God-given titles of identity; that ancient evil in disguise was still at work in the modern world, rendering people blind to their true identities and their potential as children of God, and who we were to each other—sisters and brothers in Christ; and that many didn't recognize Jesus as the Son of God, Savior of the world, was reason enough for me to sob.

The osprey's cries and my cries strung together, like a series of intense chirps, rising in intensity and falling away, until we both let out wavering squeals before quieting down.

I wiped my eyes with my pajama sleeve, and looked up at the bird. "Do you think our cries were heard? I know they were. Our cries were heard!"

It was then that a strange feeling passed over me—the kind one gets when they know someone is watching. My face turned hot. Other than God and the bird, I didn't want anyone catching me in my pajamas and the yellow boots, having a spiritual meltdown in my yard. But like it or not, there was indeed a set of eyes watching me.

I got up from the dirt, trying not to look, but I did, and sure enough, she was there in her mansion, in that highest window of hers, looking down at me.

Oh, no, what if she saw me stealing her mango? And saw me on my knees crying in the dirt? I could be honest…tell her there were no signs of fruit in my yard when I really wanted fruit. And let her know I was doing what she suggested in her interior design tidbit—realizing my incompetency and crying out not just to the most reputable designer, but the One who designed me into being!

When from the corner of my eyes, I saw she was still there, I should have waved. But it was too late—Lady Gatsby closed her blinds.

THIRTEEN

Get yourself a fully stocked toolbox, one that's easy to grip, easy to open, and portable. Be sure it's from a reputable manufacturer!

More than a toolbox, we needed a fully stocked medicine box. When I told Peter about the mango I shouldn't have eaten—and he saw me covered in hives—he rushed to the local pharmacy and back. Since the power in Hidden Potential was still going on and off—mostly off—I kept myself on the porch, pacing like a rabid caged animal, frantic for the antihistamine to work. It felt like a button was pressed, launching from my nose a series of long-ranging sneezes, one after the next, loud and powerful enough to have been around the world.

"Nothing contagious," I said, scratching my throat as the electrician, after coming up the porch steps, stood staring through the screen at me. "I can't ever eat a mango again."

"Sorry to hear that. I thought it was the heat. Newcomers to Florida get all worked up over their power going out. They panic in the heat. I'll never forget the lady next door." He tilted his head her way. "She was throwing a party…hundreds of people…when her power went out. What upset her the most was her chocolate fountain not working."

Wow, she *was* a socialite. That meant she knew the island locals and already told them all about me. Invitations had gone out—movie night at the mansion, featuring The Mango Thief. Come watch the surveillance tape, starring the hyper-dramatic and peculiar woman in pajamas and yellow boots, crying in the dirt!

I wanted to know everything—what kind of fruit did she have with the chocolate fountain—but then Peter came and escorted the electrician away, rescuing him from my warty-faced presences and nosiness.

Later, the two stood talking down in the driveway. "Well, after taking a good look around," the electrician said, "It's not the ospreys. They didn't do it."

It sounded like that mystery-solving board game, Clue, and if it weren't for my wheezing and coughing, I would have jumped right in. Who on earth would have suspected the ospreys of such a thing!

But then I heard the electrician telling Peter that ospreys built their nests on whatever the highest structure happened to be, wreaking havoc on electricity—even up and down our own road a few years back—until conservation people went around putting platforms all over the island for them to build on instead.

"So, it's not the ospreys. And rest assured…it's not your wires. People get all freaked out thinking their wires are dead, but yours are fine. Your house is well-wired—most homes are."

"Okay, so if it's not the ospreys, and it's not the wires," Peter said, and I could tell from his voice he wanted the process of elimination to end and the mystery to be solved. "What's to blame?"

"Well," the electrician said, "it could be the seasonal torrents and gusty winds. They can wreak havoc on electrical circuits. Or," his tone was wishy-washy, "it might just be your foundation. You are living on shells, you know."

Peter didn't reply.

"I'm serious. Take a shovel, dig no more than a couple feet and you'll see conch, scallops, clam shells, perfectly intact."

I pushed my nose to the screen, to better see Peter, who looked like he was about to dig his own grave.

"I'm not a hundred percent sure it's your foundation. I'll have my brother come out. He's an electrician, too, and can help troubleshoot whatever is going on here. How's tomorrow?"

Tomorrow! Bending at the waist, I tried to calm down, but felt like a firecracker ready to go off, unable to wait until tomorrow for our house to cool down. Fortunately, I didn't have to wait that long. The power came back on less than an hour later, and around the time the air kicked in, so did the antihistamine. The master bathroom cooled first, and I claimed it as my own personal space to decompress.

"Are you alive in there?" Peter knocked on the chamber door.

"Yup, I'm alive."

"What are you doing?"

"Sitting here thinking."

"Uh oh…thinking about what?"

"If it's driving you crazy, and you still want to get me something, even though our anniversary is over, I thought of something."

"Let me guess…a new foundation for our house?"

"Nope."

"A fully stocked toolbox, like she wrote on the latest leaf you tacked to the wall?"

"Nope," I said again, then opened the bathroom door, and pointed to the wobbly throne where I had been sitting. "A brand spanking new toilet seat…that's what I want more than anything in the world right now!"

He looked at me like I was a spoiled queen, wanting a new throne. But I could take it no more—balancing my rump on the urine-stained, rusty-bolted toilet with the broken lid. I tried convincing myself it was building character in me, but already had more than enough character from all my other life experiences. It was one more thing…pushing me over the edge, plunging me into the abyss.

With a constipated look on his face—from holding in the nasty things he wanted to say—Peter marched over to the bed, sat down, and opened his work laptop. "I want you to buy yourself a new toilet seat."

"I can wait…no big deal."

"I'm sorry for acting like a nincompoop. I'm not upset. I'm over-whelmed. It's been a tough day for us both."

I went over and plopped down onto my back next to him, staring up at the dusty wrought-iron faux coral chandelier.

"Please don't eat a mango ever again!"

"I won't."

"Good, and I mean it. I want you to buy yourself a new toilet seat. Splurge. Pick out something nice for yourself."

He should have cracked a smile after that, but didn't.

"What's going on. What's up with work?"

"I have to show up for a meeting, be there in person…tomorrow. If I don't, I could lose my biggest account. I just found out, and booked myself a flight, a red-eye."

Even though going back and forth as needed was part of the plan, I didn't expect it so soon. "I don't want you to go."

"I don't want to go," he said. "Promise you won't eat another mango when I'm gone?"

"Don't ever ask me that again."

"I won't. But are you going to be okay here alone?"

"Of course, I will. I'll miss you, but I'll keep busy."

When Peter left to go get us takeout for dinner, I wrote out a to-do list of things that would keep me productive while he was away: clean the chandeliers; strip the wallpaper; shop for a toilet seat; go next door and meet our mystery neighbor; and last but not least, start writing my novel!

I also wanted to lollygag, but wasn't going to put that on the list.

While waiting for Peter to return with the food, the lights inside began flickering, and soon, the power in Hidden Potential went out again. My hunger from before returned. I pulled the Bible out from under the bed and took it outside, along with Mom's folder containing her letters to God.

I perched myself halfway down the splintery wooden porch steps, beneath the twisted branches of the sea grape tree. There, I opened the Bible, as if opening a well-stocked toolbox, fully equipped to troubleshoot my spiritual glitches, and power outages within. I didn't want my love to flicker, or my relationship with the Godhead three-in-one to be an on-again, off-again thing. I added Bible reading, even a few verses each day, to my list of things to do.

Then, with just enough sunlight left for reading, I pulled out the next letter Mom wrote, with a parking citation stapled to it, a *meter expired* violation. While writing to the One who held time itself in His hands, Mom must have lost track of time at the Lighthouse Beach.

FOURTEEN

* * *

"Everyone who hears these words of mine and puts them into
practice is like a wise man who built his house on the rock."
—Matthew 7:24

To the One whose presence is living in me,

Here I am again, enjoying my two hours alone, this time reclining on a comfortable piece of driftwood washed ashore. My, what a Designer You are! The best furniture makers in the world couldn't make a loveseat more beautiful. As You already know, my Father, I'm lounging at the beach near Sanibel's fishing pier, hiding beneath my wide-brimmed floppy yellow hat, sipping iced coffee, and nibbling away on organic Truth—feasting on Your Word like a mourning dove on seeds.

My mornings here are lovely, so different than back home, where I'm running around like a lunatic, getting the kids off to school and myself off to work. I'm making the most of my time—before Luke and Adele wake up—foraging like a bird, not for fish but for the spiritual nourishment scattered throughout the pages of the Old and New Testaments. How fulfilling I'm finding it, reading my way through Second Chronicles, where although You shared Your vision for the temple and handed Your plans over to King David, it was his son Solomon who was having it built and furnished.

When I think about myself as a temple of the Holy Spirit—through Jesus alone Your Spirit dwells in me—I can't imagine the care and design You put into making such a thing happen. You designed us to love and worship You intimately from our insides out.

While the temple was being built, Solomon brought in craftsmen with all different skills. Some were skilled to work in gold, silver, bronze, and iron. And others in purple, crimson, and blue yarn, as well as fine linen, and all kinds of engraving. He even had cedar and pine logs brought in from Lebanon. Although the people followed the detailed specifications You provided them, down to every last dimension, they used their creativity, engineering, and scientific abilities to make the temple all that it could be—to bring glory to You on Earth.

It's hard to wrap my mind around, but gets me thinking about myself as a temple of the Holy Spirit.

> "You are the temple. Not a temple made of stone but it's us.
> The Holy Spirit dwells in us."
> —1 Corinthians 3:16

My name is in Your book of clients, so to speak. When I welcomed Christ into the private residence of my heart, You did Your work in me and I was transformed. Love, mercy, and grace are constants in Your design vocabulary.

You brought Jesus into the chaotic, disorderly world—all the building material we need is found in Him—and Your specifications have always been clear. Christ is our foundation, our precious living cornerstone picked by You, our Master Builder.

> "So this is what the Sovereign Lord says: "See, I lay a stone
> in Zion, a tested stone, a precious cornerstone for a sure
> foundation; the one who trusts will never be dismayed."
> —Isaiah 28:16

You laid out plans for and cared about the particulars of the Old Testament temple—design and specification both inside and out—and no doubt You have laid out plans for me, and for all Your temples of the Holy Spirit walking around in the modern world today. Your eye for detail is impeccable. You care about our insides, our outsides, and every intricate detail of our being. And what an eclectic style You have, making each of us unique, yet infusing us with the Holy Spirit, turning us functional for Your purposes. You truly are the most acclaimed and rightfully exalted interior designer!

I brewed my coffee strong this morning, and before sunrise let my eyes make their slow but steady trek, and my heart its pilgrimage along the *richly descriptive, scenic, sacred passages of Old Testament scripture, arriving at Solomon's temple. The temple was adorned with precious stones, and I imagined myself stepping foot into its main hall paneled with pine, covered in gold, and carved with palm trees, cherubim, and open flowers.*

Surely, the beauty of the temple, and its atmosphere inspired awe and respect for You. I pray that the atmosphere in me—a temple of the Holy Spirit—is also pleasant and pleasing, an ambience of praise toward You.

> *"Search me, O God, and know my heart; test*
> *me and know my anxious thoughts.*
> *See if there is any offensive way in me, and*
> *lead me in the way everlasting."*
> *—Psalm 139: 23–24*

I've always loved history. Reading it brings it to life for me, and I felt like I was there, walking toward that part of the temple where the imported cedar boards from floor to ceiling formed an inner sanctuary. It was Solomon who prepared the inner sanctuary. He overlaid it with pure gold and set the Ark of the Covenant there. I imagine myself stepping up to the curtain, wanting to peek behind it, into the Most Holy Place, also called the Inner House, and the Holy of Holies.

"Step back," a man in the temple—in my daydream, of course—stops me. "You can't go near there! Only the high priest can enter the Holy of Holies to meet up with God, and only once a year."

"I respect that. But there were reasons for it then, and not anymore," I muttered beneath my breath. Should I tell him the good news—what happened in the New Testament, and how the Holy of Holies is in those who accept Christ?

"Who are you?" he demands. "What are you doing here?"

"I'm just a person strolling around, touring Solomon's temple." And since I'm a person living in New Testament times, I go further. "Would you believe I'm a temple?" I say humbly and with New Testament truths lighting up within me.

The man squints. "You don't look like a temple."

"Oh, but I am," I say softly, "a walking temple of the Holy Spirit—not made of cedar logs, but made of bones, and not paneled with pine, but paneled with flesh. Not covered in gold, but covered in the blood of Christ. Not

adorned with palms, but mercy and grace." I nod my head. "It's true. Designed by the one and only master architect Himself, my interior and exterior are impeccably crafted and sustained by God's strength alone to repent of my sins, and withstand the storms of life. And from here into Eternity, bring glory to the name above all names."

"Ludicrous," he insists. "You're a person. A person can't be a temple."

"You're smart and educated," I say respectfully. "Surely, you know that scriptures are filled with prophecies of the coming day when God's Spirit is available to anyone who calls on the Lord—when He puts His Spirit in humans, in their hearts. Well, guess what? I'm living in those times. Rather than putting His Spirit in a place built of cedar logs, He breathes His Spirit into flesh and blood. Any person who believes and confesses can be a temple of the Holy Spirit. And together—all of us who believe and confess—make up the temple of God."

> "Consequently, you are no longer foreigners and aliens, but fellow
> citizens with God's people and members of God's household,
> built on the foundation of the apostles and prophets, with
> Christ Jesus himself as the chief cornerstone. In him the whole
> building is joined together and rises to become a holy temple
> in the Lord. And in him you too are being built together to
> become a dwelling in which God lives by his Spirit."
> —Ephesians 2:19–22

Thank you, my God, for giving me my mind—as zany as it is, at times—and my affinity for reading, and now writing You these letters. Adele is always telling me she wants to be a writer when she grows up. As You know, I wanted to be one, too. But life doesn't always go the way we planned. If we're patient and trusting, though, in the end, we often find it went better than we had planned. I do pray that one day she is given the opportunity to use the talents You've gifted her with.

Although I've learned it before, I took it for granted. Now, I'm overwhelmed by what I'm reading, that me and all Christ's followers are like stones in Your temple. You shape each of us to be used for Your purpose. And Christ— He is Your chosen cornerstone, holding us all together. When a person declares with their mouth that Jesus is Lord, and believes in their heart You raised Him from the dead—You put Your Spirit right into them.

With seventy thousand men as carriers, eighty thousand stonecutters in the hills, and thirty-six hundred as foremen over them, it took Solomon and His crew seven years to build that enormous and magnificent temple.

I think of all those people that You've sent into my life, for the purpose of carving, forming, influencing, and building me up in one way or another, according to Your plan. But even with Your crew of helpers—my mother and father, teachers, pastors, friends who are believers—it has taken me way longer than seven years to fully surrender to Your blueprint for my life. I am a temple of the Holy Spirit, but parts of me are still under construction, far from being done. In fact, areas of my life are a complete mess. Thank You for being so patient, and helping me to remember that I am Your work-in-progress for the duration of my life here on Earth.

Your plan, Your love, and Your ever-presence overwhelm me. Teach me to walk in holiness and bring glory to You. Help me to grow spiritually, but never forget that all and any spiritual growth must always start and end with Jesus—the first stone installed and laid into my foundation. Christ is the starting point upon which everything else in my life must align. Otherwise, I fall out of alignment with Your edifying Word, and deviate from Your plan.

I don't want to be like the tower of Babel, whose foundation was weak, self-made, and built upon personal accomplishments. I read about this Babylonian tower in the book of Genesis, chapter eleven—how with man-made bricks the people constructed it to draw attention to and build a name for themselves, and to show the world how great they were rather than bringing glory to You.

> *"For no one can lay any foundation other than the one already laid, which is Jesus Christ. If any man builds on this foundation using gold, silver, costly stones, wood, hay or straw, his work will be shown for what it is, because the Day will bring it to light. It will be revealed with fire, and the fire will test the quality of each man's work."*
> *—1 Corinthians 3:11–13*

I don't believe there's anything wrong with personal accomplishment. You, my God, are great, and Your Spirit dwells within me, so how can I not want to accomplish great things? Ambition is good and I can't imagine a world without it, a world filled with ambition-less people.

Whether I use my skills to achieve something large, magnificent, and seen by others, or something small, intricate, seen only by You, may I do so to the best of my ability, and for Your glory. Solomon's temple was built to Your glory high up on a hill, in the center of the nation. Help me put You at the center of my life, and all of us together put You at the center of our nation. What an honor it would be, any opportunity to bring glory to You, and to make Your name great here on Earth!

> "The temple I am going to build will be great, because
> our God is greater than all other gods."
> —2 Chronicles 2:5

Thank You, Beginning and the End, and everything in between. You would never ticket me for parking too long in Your presence. But uh oh, I better get going, or they'll be giving me an earthly ticket real soon. Bye-bye for now.

Love,
Finley (glad to be a member of Your household)

FIFTEEN

INTERIOR DESIGN TIDBIT

* * *

*Does your house feel dark? Try simple things first. Wipe
clean the fixtures, then replace the bulbs with new.*

There on the porch step, holding Mom's letter to God, I closed my eyes. During our month on Sanibel, Mom tried talking to me. She told me I was a temple of the Holy Spirit, but I rolled my eyes and shut my ears to it, taking it to mean, "Can't do this, can't do that—there goes all my fun!" That's why she stopped talking about Him, and started writing those letters instead.

Peter returned with a box of crackers and a quart of hot Florida Grouper Chowder from a local restaurant, and the two of us went up into the house where the power happened to be on again. Just like I was tired of sitting on the wobbly commode, he was tired of, and too big for the delicate, wobbly bistro table set that came with the place. I wanted our dinner to be special, so I pulled an old nautical-print tablecloth from the walk-in pantry, and spread it across the hardwood floor of the great room. In front of the enormous floor-to-ceiling windows, and with nothing but a view of banyan tree branches, we sat down to picnic.

The chowder was chock full of potatoes, onion, and grouper, and with just the right amount of clam juice and heavy cream. Peter put his bowl to his mouth, sipping until it was empty. "Very good," he said.

"What's the matter?" I asked.

"What do you mean? I said it was good."

"Yeah, but I can tell by your voice…you seem down."

"I don't feel like going, that's all."

"Well, I wish you didn't have to. I like you here."

I loved having him there and was cherishing our time, the two of us alone in our house on stilts. We were still bickering here and there, but also talking and listening to each other more than we had in the past quarter of a century. Even if we weren't in the same room, there were signs of his being there—breadcrumbs on the counter where he buttered his bagel, steam on the mirror after his shower, freshly picked hibiscus in a mason jar beside our bed. I didn't see him picking the hibiscus, but knew they were from him.

Who needed furniture? I liked sitting together on the floor, where we stayed put until long after the sun had set, and the anticipated tropical rain was beating down, and crossing a power washer off our list of things we needed to buy.

"I see now why this place came with all those pillar candles in the pantry," Peter said when the lights flickered, and two seconds later, our power-challenged house went dark again. "So thoughtful of the former owners to leave so many. Want me to go light some?"

"Nah, leave it dark."

"Okay but why?"

"I don't know," I said with a laugh. "It hides the dirt and imperfections, all the work that needs doing. We can sit here in the dark, tricking ourselves into thinking everything is perfect."

We pushed our empty chowder bowls aside, then rolled down onto our backs on the floor. Like two kids on the ground watching fireworks, we oohed and awed at the lightning show out the window, and listened to the rain. We both heard different things from the rain. Peter heard it power washing our screens. I heard it tap dancing on the roof.

"I've been thinking," I said.

"Good or bad?"

"Good, but do you have to ask that?"

"With you, yes. But I'm sorry, go ahead with what you were thinking."

"Well, I've been thinking about things I don't usually think about, like what do I want most from God?"

"Longevity would be nice. How about electricity for the house?"

"No, seriously." I hesitated. No matter how I said it, it was going to sound dramatic. "I want to know Him, and love Him, and appreciate His presence—that's what I want. Do you ever want that kind of more…and whatever else God has for us?"

"It's worth thinking about," he said, and maybe would have said more but our roof was like a Broadway stage, and the rain was hitting down hard, like a thousand Billy Elliots tap dancing across it. We were both quiet, enjoying the performance, until it ended.

"Hmm," Peter said, but with a note of reflection in his voice he didn't usually use when saying, "hmm." He had already been considering, wondering about God's "kind of more."

Sure enough, around three in the morning, I got a text from him as his second flight was about to take off—

Been thinking about what you said. Does sound nice. Love you, talk soon.

I tried to text back, but it failed to go through and our inability to communicate made me lonely. Without him present, the house was dark and every sound louder than ever. Even the toilet seat made me more nervous than usual as it wobbled like an old dock ready to collapse. What would I do then? There'd be no Peter to pull me out.

I climbed into bed, fired up my laptop, and set sail on an expedition, traveling the Internet, searching the world over for a new and comfortable seat for my poor buttocks. A couple of hours later, my eyes landed on a good-looking, acrylic seat decorated with seashells, but not too gaudy or childish. I did my diligence, reading the reviews. A few were graphically detailed and should been censored, but overall, the toilet seat testimonies convinced me. Fifty-one dollars plus free shipping—I hit the BUY button and couldn't wait for the two-day delivery.

When I tried to fall asleep, a light hit me smack on my face. It was coming from next door, from that same high up window from which she had watched me in the yard. Didn't she know about Sanibel's Dark Skies Ordinance? Then again, that referred to outdoor house lights. Only certain types were allowed, and they had to shine downward. It's why the stars were so visible in the skies above Sanibel.

Propping pillows around my face like a fort, I wanted to sleep, but when I heard sirens screaming their way in the distance, and coyotes from nearby preserves howling along, I climbed out of bed, then looked out the windows, all of which were still opened a crack. The starry flowers from the Carissa shrub alongside the house were sending bursts of intense jasmine and gardenia-like fragrance into my bedroom, and I stood there breathing it in.

The light from her window was bright and high up. I worried for the newly hatched sea turtles on the beach. In order to make their way to the water, they needed to follow the moonlight reflecting on its surface. What if they followed her light instead? What was she even doing awake at such an hour—searching the Internet like me? Everyone was searching, it seemed. But in their search for the water, I didn't want the loggerhead sea turtles to be fooled into not recognizing the right light. Someone needed to report her, but it wasn't going to be me.

It was then I remembered what Marita had said to me on the road. *Pray for her.*

I would have rather reported her for that light. And besides, how was I to pray for a person I didn't know…not to mention my praying muscles were so out of shape.

Pray for her. Pray for her. Pray for her.

It was like a chant, beating along with my heart and it wouldn't stop. So, I prayed for my neighbor in the mansion next door…that she'd hang curtains on that window of hers. And I prayed for Marita who I met on the road… that I'd see her again, and learn more about the darkness my neighbor was in.

The sirens were still going. I prayed for the ambulance driver, and the person in distress. I prayed for the howling coyotes, and for the rabbits running from the coyotes. And for the newly hatched sea turtles down on the beach, that they would see the light of the moon reflecting on the water, and not be misled. After praying an unusually long time for the turtles, I worried that maybe I didn't pray enough for my neighbor, so I circled back, praying she'd see the light of Christ in the darkness, and follow it and not the artificial, disorienting lights that the world puts out.

At first my prayers were simple and storybook level, but soon they matured, and my praying picked up momentum, like a kite going with the wind. It felt so nice I didn't want to stop.

SIXTEEN

*   *   *

"This is the message we have heard from him and declare
to you: God is light; in him there is no darkness at all."
—1 John 1:5

*   *   *

"When Jesus spoke again to the people, he said, 'I am
the light of the world. Whoever follows me will never
walk in darkness, but will have the light of life.'"
—John 8:12

*   *   *

"But you are a chosen people, a royal priesthood, a
holy nation, a people belonging to God, that you
may declare the praises of him who called you out
of darkness and into his wonderful light."
—1 Peter 2:9

To the One who knows all the problems of the world, and how they'll turn out,

Here I am, this time at the end of Dixie Beach Boulevard, sitting on a gray marble bench tucked within an alcove of trees, and looking out at the bridge and the bay. The bridge looks like it's doing splits over the bay, with one foot in the City of Palms, and the other here on the island. I love the bay. It's where fresh water from the river meets up with salt water from the sea, and mixes so well. I also love Your Word, and when I read from it, Truth from it flows into me, creating a special inlet where You and I meet up.

I got out here around dusk, when it was still light enough to see the purple morning glories at the foot of the bench, and to read an informational sign on why we should restore eastern oysters. Oyster reefs stabilize shorelines from storms, and they're important nourishment for fish and other animals.

Restoration is good, especially when it comes to a restored relationship with You! I sit here after dark (with a flashlight), and I can't help but think how I need You. I need You to stabilize me in the ups and the downs, and the storms of life. And I need Your Word, too. It's the food my soul consumes best.

Adele is too young to realize, but she gets her dramatic side from me. I enjoy my dramatic thoughts, and life would be boring without them. Back home, I don't have time to sit around thinking. But here on the island, waking two hours before the kids, with no obligations, then having two more hours to myself each day, I'm enjoying the random thoughts moving unobstructed through my mind. They're like bits of dust and rock, and I don't want them falling into the atmosphere like meteorites and burning up. I want to appreciate them, like spiritual meteor showers, turning my eyes upward. In other words, thank you for giving me a mind in which to think with!

Biblical truth is enlightening, and when I read it, I feel You awakening my mind. It's like one exhilarating "aha" moment after the next. However, You did not send Your Son into the world to bring illumination to our darkened minds. You sent Him to pull us from darkness and into the light of eternal life.

I hope my kids know (I'll be sure to tell them) all the so-called lightbulb moments in their brains will never be enough to pull them from darkness and save them from death. They can grow up having so-called enlightened minds, but how far will that take them if they're not connected to You? You, Jesus, are the life eternal, and our personal connection to it!

Whether reading from the Old Testament or the New, I keep coming across the foundational truth that You are light. Even in Exodus, chapters thirty-three and thirty-four, when Moses was on the mountain, You appeared to him as light. And when he came down from the mountain, his face was radiant from the reflection of Your light. Again and again, You've manifested yourself as light—leading the Israelites by a cloud of light by day and a pillar of fire by night.

But the most brilliant manifestation of Your light here on Earth was Jesus coming as the light of the world! Thank You for calling me out of darkness and into Your light.

Finley (a person who has always loved lamps, but knows they don't sell the lamp of the Lord at any of the stores)

P.S. "The lamp of the Lord searches the Spirit of a man; it searches out his inmost being."–Proverbs 20:27

SEVENTEEN

Interior Design Tidbits

* * *

A well-lit house is vital. Lighting is what brings life to each room.

* * *

*Lighting serves many purposes, and needs to
vary its intensity according to the activities going
on. Let lighting do all it's meant to do.*

* * *

*The choices you make concerning lighting, will make or break
your interior. Give lighting the attention it deserves!*

When I woke the next morning, Hidden Potential was neither dark nor bright, but in between, sort of like my love for God had become—neither dark, nor bright, just somewhere in between. It was an overcast day, which explained why the house was dim, but had I closed the blinds on the light of Christ all through the years?

After brewing my coffee, I went around turning on and assessing every light fixture in the house, from the burlap lantern in the hall, to the copper drum in the spare room, to the seashell chandelier in the great room. I couldn't blame the overcast day. They were all so covered in cobwebs and layers of gunky dust, no wonder the house was dim!

The light fixtures were vintage, installed when the house was young, and it got me thinking about the indoctrination of my younger self.

"You're letting your Bible get dusty, Adele," Mom used to say, but at least I'd known where it was—up in my closet with all the other things I once loved, but didn't want out, including my raggedy old stuffed animals.

I stood in the center of the great room, staring up at the most beautiful chandelier of them all, at its hundreds of miniature white seashells coated in dusty gunk. I had let the dust of apathy fall on God's Word inside me, and I missed when the Bible stories and memorized verses used to glisten from within.

I filled a bucket with cleaning solution, dipped a cloth in, and stepped up onto a chair. While working on the elaborate arm of the chandelier, I prayed for the outstretched arm of God to be at work in me. But He already was. He saw me on my knees in the yard, and heard me crying out from beneath the rubble of my childhood Christianity, and already the electrician of my soul—Light Himself—was responding. And I felt my internal wires—my love for the One whose love never failed me—reactivating.

It seems like I forgot all about the work You did on the cross for me, the work You did within me. Forgive me please, for making light of it, for putting everything else before You and taking it for granted, that labor of Love you did for me. Your workmanship is perfect and complete, still intact.

I don't want to go on loving You nonchalantly. I want to love You back as You have loved me—even though it seems impossible for me to love You nearly as You have loved me. I want to know You more, too, through Your Word, and already from having read those scripture verses, I'm remembering who You are—the Light that never diminishes. Your promises are ever-bright. Your love never grows dim, and Your life-giving power never runs out.

May Your Word glisten within me, and my love for You grow brighter and more intense.

Well into wiping dust from the chandelier and tears from my eyes, I decided it was good that Peter was gone. I didn't want him overhearing my dramatic prayers from another room. But if there was ever a time to be dramatic, wasn't it while praying? I wasn't praying to a boring God, but to the One and only God who brought Light into the World, before even Thomas Edison brought his light to the world. And I was putting everything, including my dull, dim, lackluster love, into His troubleshooting hands, into the hands of the One whose passion was restoring power to those without, and bringing people out of darkness and into Light.

When I finished cleaning each and every bulb, I stepped down from the chair, and flipped the light switch on. Sure enough, the chandelier as a whole, glistened more brightly with each of its bulbs wiped clean.

I picked up a pen, and Peter would be pleased—I wrote. It wasn't the start of a novel, but of me sharing my thoughts with the One who knew me before my own mom.

A well-lit house is vital, and lighting is what brings life to each room. Please be my Light, my all-purpose Light…my comforting ambient and back-ground Light, too. May the Light of Christ evenly distribute throughout my interior, and bounce off my inner walls, bringing me joy. Whatever is needed, please do Your thing in me—be the Light that searches me, bringing attention to the areas within me dimmed by sin!

There was so much pouring from my heart onto paper that I worried my heart might drain, leaving me with nothing left to ever write again. I scribbled away until the power in the house went out again, then I dropped my pen and went out, too.

I left in my van, following directions on my phone to Dixie Beach Boulevard. Sure enough, at the end of the long road, and tucked within a patch of trees overlooking the bay, was the marble bench where Mom had sat writing her finite thoughts in a letter to the infinite One.

I sat down, staring out at the same view Mom once saw of the Causeway Bridge doing splits across the bay. If she was there with me, I'd have thanked her for her prayers, and shared with her the impact they were having. I'd also tell her she was right. I did get my dramatic side from her. But it was more fun to be dramatic, than unimpressed, bored, or unaffected.

Mom described the random thoughts moving through her mind to be like spiritual meteor showers, but my thoughts were so high-watt, I couldn't sit. In need of a walk, I got up from the bench and wandered a few yards to where Dixie Beach Boulevard curved narrowly onto Woodring Road. With the crystal-clear bay on one side, and a thick mangrove forest of short trees and shrubs crawling across the brackish water on the other, the road was so enchanting, it belonged in a storybook.

There was no one else on the road, just a woman in the distance walking her dog toward me. It looked like a mutt, which I loved. I used to take in stray mutts when I was young, always with the goal of feeding, caring for, and finding them homes. I'd bathe and groom them, then stroll around the neighborhood asking if anyone wanted them. Mom strolled along, too, when there was something on her mind that she wanted to tell me.

"Have you ever heard of a man named Saul?" she'd said once as we were walking around the block.

"You mean the old man with big eyes who moved in three doors down from us last week?"

"No," Mom hooted with laughter. "I'm talking about Saul—the well-educated, religious guy from the book of Acts. I was up before the sun, reading about him this morning. He had all kinds of spiritual training…knew the facts, stories, prophecies."

"Cool," I probably said, even though I didn't think anything biblical was cool back then.

"Sugar plum." She stopped walking, took hold of my elbow, and looked at me, her brilliant blue eyes sparkling with passion. "Saul had so much in his brain, but he didn't have Light. He didn't have Light because He hadn't connected to the source of power. He outright rejected Jesus. Do you know what that means?"

As I walked along, staring at the intricate mangrove forest to my left, I understood the intricacies of what Mom had been trying to teach me. Even if a person had light-carrying fixtures installed within them—biblical knowledge, memorized scripture verses, once-heard church sermons stored in their brains—it didn't mean they had Light.

That day on our walk, while I was gagging, picking up the package my pooch left on the lawn, Mom went on telling me what she wanted me to know.

"Saul believed Jesus was a threat to Judaism. He persecuted followers of Christ."

"Horrible," I probably said as I tied shut the stinky bag.

"Yes, but then Saul was walking along a road," Mom said like it was monumentally relevant, breaking news she had just read in the *Wall Street Journal*, "and he encountered for himself the Living Christ, the One everyone had been talking about, the One he was so against."

"Uh oh."

"No, it was good. After his personal encounter with Christ, everything about Saul changed, even his name. Saul became Paul. He was so filled with Christ's illuminating power that He went on to share the good news with others still walking in darkness. Not to mention, he wrote over half of the New Testament!"

Although I hadn't appreciated the story then, the grown-up me walking along Woodring Road was amazed. Interesting how a Bible story I seldom thought about came to mind, its details glistening clearly. But wait a minute, what was the name of the road Saul was walking along when it happened—when he met up personally with the Living Christ?

I racked my brain, trying to recall. "Damascus," I blurted out, startling the mangrove crabs. "Saul was on the road to Damascus when he bumped into Christ and everything about him changed."

What road am I on? Oh, Jesus, I don't even remember what road our old church was on. But all these years later here I am, walking along Woodring Road talking to You, the Living Christ. I don't remember the road, but I remember that time in my life when, with pouty lips, little girl me declared You as my Lord, and believed in my big pink heart that God raised You from the dead. And even if I didn't understand the intricacies then, I understood one thing—it was all out of love. The One, with holy, righteous plans, loved me. He loved me and the world so much. And I loved that God loved me and the world so much. May my love for You, whose blood was shed for me, and who made me whole, grow brighter and brighter, and may I finally in my life give you the glory and praise that is Yours!

Thank you for Mom, Ms. Viola, and all the others who taught me—instilled in me Your Truths like beautiful vintage, light-carrying fixtures, still intact. But even that wouldn't be enough without Your Spirit in me, and I thank You because Your Spirit is in me. The work You did on the cross is still perfect and complete, even though I'm a work in progress.

If the road didn't end, I would have kept going, could have gone on longer walking and talking with the One whose love for me never went out. I turned and headed back. Were people in the houses overlooking the bay watching me through their windows, talking up a storm? "What a lunatic!" they'd declare, "Talking to herself." But really, I was talking to the

One whose love for me never went out. Just as human-made generators fizzled out, Me, Myself, and I was fizzling out, exhausted from years of acting like a superpower, relying on myself.

When almost back to the van, the bright orange, red, and purple berries of a dwarf umbrella shrub caught my eyes. I picked up one of its still buttery-yellow branches that had broken off and was down in the dirt, and took it with me.

EIGHTEEN

Interior Design Tidbits

* * *

Let there be an element of surprise in every room.

* * *

Bring something from the outdoors in.
A colorful, fragrance-filled flower,
or a single branch from
the yard will do.

I put the branch from the dwarf umbrella shrub in a vase and filled it with water. My neighbor was right. Bringing a single branch in from outside was indeed a lovely thing. And so was bringing the Branch of Righteousness, the living Christ, into my daily life.

There was nothing lovely, though, about the temperature inside Hidden Potential. The power was back on, but the air conditioning was going bonkers, blowing full blast, turning the place frigid as a walk-in freezer. Having survived one too many bone-chilling Midwestern winters, I didn't have it in me to shiver through a single hour in a house.

After fiddling with the thermostat, I hurried into my closet, slipping into my old lime green sweatsuit. Lucy and Mallory tried convincing me that velvet sweatsuits had no right coming to Florida. But like comfort food, there was comfort clothing. I wore the thing every winter for fifteen years, and always when I had the flu. A few minutes after zipping myself into the wearable, velvet blankie, I felt a scratching at the nape of my neck, and a second later, a tickle around my armpit. I flew out onto the front porch, jumping up and down, screaming, shaking my jacket, and trying to get it unzipped when out dropped one of my worst fears—a creamy white f...f...frog with giant eyes! The thing was six inches long, and when it landed smack on my bare foot, I let out a blood-curdling scream, loud enough to be heard next door, and all the way in Key West, even Cuba.

Like an emergency response hero, a man came rushing up the porch steps. All I could do was point at the warty-skinned amphibian with striped legs hopping from my foot, up my pant leg, clinging to it.

"N...n...noooooo," I wailed as I fled into the house, sprinting in circles like my daughters did during their high-velocity workouts, and Peter when he passed a gallstone. The creature lost its grip and fell to the ground, but fast as Spider Man, it darted across the floor and up the great room wall, disappearing into a vent.

"I don't care about electricity right now," I said as he tried handing me his card. "Tell me you're good at catching f...frogs!"

"We all have our things. Me, I don't do crowds. You won't see me at Disney World. I went once...made my way through thousands of people...waited ninety minutes in line with my kids for the Peter Pan ride. So much for Never-Land. My kids were all grown up by the time we got on the ride. I hate crowds."

I didn't know if he was joking and I should laugh or if I should turn it into a support session for us both. I was still trying to catch my breath. I didn't reply.

"Hate to say what I'm about to say," his eyes turned grave, "but I don't think that was an innocent Florida-native tree frog."

"It could be Kermit, for all I care," I said at an accelerated rate, my words in pace with my heartbeat. "A frog is frog." It had been a green frog, way back when Luke put his pet frog in my dollhouse, a boy prank, and when I opened it, the thing jumped out at me, landed smack on my face, attaching itself to my nose. I couldn't help that I still went hysterical so many years later, every time I came in contact with a frog.

"I'm sure you saw the extra-large pads on its toes?" He looked back and forth at me and the vent the frog had disappeared into. "I may be wrong, but I think it's the kind of frog you don't want...prolific breeders, and it's not unheard of for entire properties to be invaded by them. They wreak havoc on electrical boxes. But let me go look around and see what I see before we get all carried away."

My mouth was dry and my knees wobbling as I followed him outside, then stood waiting in my driveway. Blame it on my fight-or-flight response working overtime, the velvet sweatsuit, and perhaps that midlife thing, but I was sweating profusely.

"Good news is," he said after taking a good look around. "I didn't see frogs."

"What about our power outages?"

"Well, I untangled a few things wrapped around your wires, but other than that, didn't see any major issues. Sometimes untangling things is all that's needed. Let's see how it goes from here on out."

I should have asked questions. Peter would have asked all kinds of questions. But I was still in recovery mode, and all I could do was stand there waving good riddance.

"I'd still be on the lookout, though," he had the audacity to tell me as he hung his head out the window of his truck. "There's always the chance Lone Ranger could have a partner. They like swimming in toilets, just so you know."

There went all my toilet seat excitement. With a fugitive creature on the loose, and maybe two, I didn't dare step foot in my house. Back when I found the frog in my dollhouse, I'd packed up my dolls and pounded on my friend's door. Since my mother forbid me from ever going inside their house to play, my friend brought her dollhouse outside and we played under a tree. She had the nicest dollhouse and the best-dressed dolls, even though her own clothes were hand-me-downs and her house wasn't nice. But at least she had a faraway aunt who loved to send her the best of the best doll stuff.

I could either sit on the porch steps and start writing my novel, or go next door to meet our neighbor. I looked over at the tippy top of her fortress. Great, that window of hers was open again, and she probably heard me screaming! But wasn't she the one who claimed there ought to be an element of surprise in every room? And come to think it, the one who suggested bringing something from the outdoors in?

Well, go figure how the f…f…frog got in!

"Surprise, surprise, Ms. Interior Design Guru," I muttered beneath my breath as I headed her way, "here I come, the owner of the dilapidated dive next door, the frog-phobic, blood-curdling screamer, and the mango thief who kneels in the dirt and sobs out loud with the osprey. Ready or not, here I come!"

I would have liked to have gone up into my house and changed into a more island-appropriate outfit, but with the frog in the vent, I didn't dare. Oh well; I trekked up her mammoth pyramid-shaped steps lined with potted bonsai. Was her heart as big as her house? Mansions had guest rooms, and maybe she'd take me in.

I reached the top of her steps; her front door was the size of a billboard. I tried not to worry about what Marita had told me, about there never being a good time to meet her. I knocked on the door, and when no one answered, I pounded it with my fists.

"What do you want?" said a deep, raspy voice over the intercom.

"Oh, um, I'm your new neighbor."

There was a pause, and then, "Oh, for crying out loud. Aren't you a brave soul, a real daredevil! No offense, but that's a woozy of a place. Will I hear bulldozers anytime soon?"

"No. I have no intentions of knocking it down."

"That was a trick question. And good for you, only a coward would knock the place down!"

Then, what sounded like news turned up real loud, crackling in the background—breaking news. And probably, it was horrific. News was always horrific. I didn't regret leaving our television behind, even though heartbreaking news still broke into our lives daily through the radio in the van, or when I pulled it up on my cell phone.

"Sorry about that," the raspy voice said, after turning it down. "What brings you over. Let me guess, you need to borrow almond milk, kale, m—"

"Oh, no," I cut her off before she said what I feared she was about to say, which was mango. "I don't need to borrow anything, just came by to thank you."

There was a moment of silence. "Thank me for what?"

If she opened the door, I could have told her face-to-face how her interior design tidbits were inspiring me, getting me to think not just about my house, but in a roundabout way, reflect on the infrastructure of my being. But it was too hard to say all of that through a closed door. "I appreciate those interior design tips you sent over."

There was an awkward silence. "You have no idea what that means to me." Her voice cracked. "What good am I? I feel like I help no one. The world is a mess."

"I agree," I said right away. "It's a hot mess."

"Yeah, but what am I doing? Nothing. I haven't helped anybody in so long. Thank you for telling me that. You made my day. I swear, you did."

Probably because I had just been thinking of her, my neighbor's raspy voice and the words she used reminded me of that friend who grew up two doors down from me, the one whose house my mom never allowed me to go into. I didn't just like her for her dollhouse. We were good friends, and even went to the same college together, although we lost touch after graduation. Her name was Vivienne Watts.

"I usually have people over...well, I used to. But you're more than welcome, even though I bet you've got a ton of stuff to do," she said, sounding like that long-lost friend of mine. "How can you not have a ton to do, with a house like that? But hey, if you need a quick break, you're more than welcome to come in for a second. No hurt feelings if you can't. I get it. You can swing by another time, if that works better for you."

"Now is perfect," I said. It was the invitation I wished for, to escape my frog-infested shack.

"On one condition," she said then.

By then, I had already slipped off my flip flops. "Oh?"

"No politics. We don't talk politics. I don't want to know who you voted for, or who you plan to vote for next."

"Of course not," I said, relieved by her request.

"Swear you won't go there with me?"

"I have no desire," I assured her, and little did she know, I didn't have the energy, either. I was still pulling myself together in the aftermath of my mother's recent loss. Her run against such a destructive opponent wasn't a quick, overnight thing. I was like her campaign manager who for years ran alongside her, pouring everything I had into her fight against forgetfulness, protesting to the doctors on her behalf—yet still, she lost.

And every day since, I was anxious enough...who was the disease going to be running against next? It wasn't a choice. The disease picked who it wanted to go up against, and given my family history, I seemed a likely candidate.

"Alright then," she said. "As long as we keep it to things we have in common, my door is unlocked."

Relieved, but hoping for things in common, I pushed open her enormous red door, then stepped into what looked like the lobby of a four-star resort, both ancient and contemporary-themed at the same time. My mouth dropped open at its magnificence, at its soaring ceilings, enormous stone fireplace, wooden floors, and an entire glass wall overlooking the irresistible Gulf of Mexico. I wanted to check right in and never check out.

"Bear with me," she called down from an unseeable loft. "I'm a real slow poke these days."

She could have taken as long as she liked, for all I cared. I took a few steps across the floor, then stopped. I took a few more and stopped again. Barefoot, I crossed the entire great room, listening to the peculiar creaking sound of the wood, singing with every step I took.

"Have you been to Japan?" she asked from above.

Nope, didn't have that in common, and I wasn't going to tell her that Michigan, Sanibel, and Chicago were the only places I had ever gone in the world. "Would Orlando's Japan at Epcot have counted? We almost went there when I was a kid, but then didn't."

"Hilarious," she roared at my unintentional funniness, "you are hilarious! And just so you know, my floor is supposed to creak like that. I kid you not, I designed it that way, so each plank pleasantly creaks with every footstep. Yeah, I'm wacky."

Well, I was wacky, too. We had that in common. At least Peter liked to tell me I was, although not always in the most complimentary tone. I took a few more steps and sure enough, the floorboards creaked pleasantly. She was brilliant, not wacky. The floors alone were too much even for my wacky mind to wrap itself around.

"I have a fascination with temples," she said nonchalantly, and still hadn't come down. "Can you tell? Look around. I can't help it, I love temples…love everything about them."

Goosebumps covered my arms. The all-sufficient One did not put His spirit in temples made of cedar logs, but made of bones. He didn't put His presence in buildings paneled with pine, but in those paneled with flesh. His temples weren't structures coated in gold, but people coated in the blood of Christ, and they weren't adorned with palms, but with mercy and grace.

It overwhelmed me that the One who loved the world so much sent His eternally begotten Son to take on our sins and die for me. And I was a temple of the Holy Spirit.

"What is it that you like so much about temples?" I said up to her, wherever she was, wondering if we shared all of that in common.

"Nothing to do with God. It's not a God thing," she remarked right away, and again, sounded so much like that old friend of mine whom, truth be told, I parted ways with for personal reasons. "I go wild over their architectural and aesthetic design. My floors, they were inspired by a creative trip I took to the Chion-in Temple in Japan. There, the *uguisu-bari*, or nightingale floors, as they were called, once alerted monks to intruders."

I didn't know how to respond, and feared we had nothing in common. I had never gone to Japan, then come home, inspired to do my floors. Mrs. P's kitchen floors were nice, and I once came home telling Peter we should put in laminate floors, like hers. But that was different.

"You have no idea," she said, "the endless nights I paced those floors following my third divorce!"

Did she say third? I swallowed hard, hoping there wasn't a fourth.

"My third, he was a great, great guy. I swear, I'm not exaggerating. I was a fool for doing what I did."

"What did you do?"

"Gave him the boot once the debates began."

"The debates?"

"Yeah, we got along great until the debates, then we started bickering over everything. But don't get me started."

"Okay, I won't." I took a few more steps across the creaking floor, while looking up at the loft. Why was she taking so long?

"That floor used to make happy-sounding creaks," she said. "You wouldn't believe all the fun we used to have on that floor, all the dancing, laughing, chit-chatting people who came to my parties. I miss those days, another era, back before we all looked suspiciously at each other...you know, who are the cuckoo birds that lost their minds, and who are the wise owls? The last party I threw here, I kid you not, it was like a heronry."

"A heronry of birds?"

"A rowdy fiasco of big mouths."

She was going where we agreed not to go, and to stop her, I stepped up to a wall with miniature gold leaves painted across it. "What's with the leaves on this wall...did you paint them yourself?"

"The Shwedagon Pagoda, the Golden Temple in Myanmar," she said in a more pleasant tone, that of a museum curator. "Pilgrims saved for years to buy small packets of gold leaves to stick to the temple walls. But I'll bore you to death with my temple fetish. Here I come, at last, making my way down. You must be thinking I'm a wackadoo, a total wackadoo!"

Yes, but if she wondered if I thought she was a wackadoo, then maybe she didn't think I was a wackadoo in my lime green velvet sweatsuit, or even in my pajamas and rubber boots the other day, stealing fruit from her yard, and crying out loud on my knees in the dirt, along with the osprey.

I crossed the room and waited at the foot of a spiral staircase. But then a golden door on a nearby mahogany wall opened instead, revealing a hidden elevator. When its doors opened, I blinked. Although I read once that humans blinked fifteen thousand times a day, I blinked fifteen thousand times in that moment alone when I saw who it was rolling out of the elevator in a wheelchair—Vivienne Watts, the friend with the dollhouse nicer than mine, and who went to the same college as me, and whom I parted ways with after graduation. She wasn't in a wheelchair when I knew her.

Then again, maybe it wasn't her. Didn't we all have look-a-likes out there in the world? Her enormous blue eyes moved like a counterfeit detector machine, scanning me up and down, determining whether I was the genuine thing, too—her childhood-through-college friend who right after graduation stopped reciprocating, stopped even responding to the postcards she kept sending from all over the world.

"Ring some chimes," she said, "so I know I'm not dreaming."

"Viv, it is you," I gasped after her bottom jaw dropped, displaying for me the giant, validating gap between her two front teeth.

"No way, crazy, I can't believe it," we both belted out in unison, like the chorus of a song. Then came shock, and it was hard to even talk. All we could do was shake our heads, and cover our faces with our hands.

"I see you kept your gap!" From the time we first played Barbies together all the way until we celebrated our twenty-first birthdays together, every time she complained insecurely about the gap between her two front teeth, I'd tell her, "Don't ever get it filled! Only so many people in existence have gaps like that…and it gives you an eccentric, creative flair."

"You're to blame," she said with a grin, "for why I never got it filled in. You told me I looked like Madonna. You're the reason still today, people stare, ask me what happened. And kids ask me how I lost my front tooth."

I stood there shaking my head, smiling. Even though I was to blame for us losing touch, there was so much I missed about our old friendship. "Where do we begin? How are you?"

She gave me a look, like she felt sorry for me for having asked. "How do I even answer? Character…I guess I can start with that. It's gone. I kid you not, my character is gone, despite the gap. No character left in me."

"I don't believe that," I said.

"Well, I'm not lying. Life has put me through its fair share of character-building experiences, but also keeps putting me through storms. And the storms just keep on knocking the character right out of me. Maybe it's true for homes…older homes have more character. But me?" She shook her head. "The older I get, well, I'm not feeling so full of character."

I related more than she knew, but once we acquired that kind of character, I believed it stayed in us, like a permanent feature. "Your character is hidden, or dulled, and needs to be refreshed, that's all. We could all use refreshing, right?"

When she tapped her fingers on the armrest of her wheelchair, I wanted to ask why she was in the chair, but unless she brought it up, it seemed too early in our reunion.

A giant grin took over her face. "This is crazy. What are the odds?"

"I know, we should buy lotto tickets." Then again, only one of us needed to win the lotto, and it was me. I steered the conversation back to something we had in common. "Sanibel," I said, "of all the places in the world, the country, and in Florida, how on earth did you end up on this same island as me in the Gulf of Mexico?"

"Meh." She waved me off with her hand, like she didn't feel like telling me. Or it was a long story…a story in and of itself. Whatever the case, it was only a matter of time before the details of what brought Vivienne Watts to Sanibel slipped out. Blame it on the gap between her two front teeth…words slipped right out of her. It was what I loved most about her. She said what she thought, unfiltered. And she didn't just talk about shallow things. She dove right in, going deep in conversation, and not caring what people standing around the shallow end thought of her.

NINETEEN

INTERIOR DESIGN TIDBITS

* * *

*Journal or write down details regarding the
work you're doing on your house.
Take before and after pictures, too.
You'll want to look back one day
and remember.*

She lived in a mansion on an island. She should have had a top-of-the-line, state-of-the-art wheelchair, but it was a bare bones, basic chair. And she used her own two hands to wheel it across the room, where she then took her time parking it, like it was the Jaguar I saw in her driveway, backing up twice, rolling forward until there were equal spaces on both sides, between two armchairs.

Content with her parking job, she clasped her hands together, fingers forming a steeple, closed her eyes, then took a deep breath in, preparing to say something sacred.

"I don't believe in coincidences." She opened her eyes and looked at me. "There's a better chance of getting struck by lightning, and yeah, yeah, yeah, I know we're living in the lightning capital of the world, but still! There's a reason for this. There has to be a reason. Sit down, make yourself at home!"

I sat down across from her on a red velvet sofa, and in a state of mirrored astonishment, we allowed our eyes their quick appraisals. The uncombed, dirty blonde hair she kept in college was silky-straight and shoulder-length. I shook my head, impressed by her meticulous outer appearance, despite what she had told me about her inner character being gone. And maybe I was hypersensitive, imagining a hint of sympathy in her eyes, as if in an ever-so-subtle way, she was giving her condolences for my not aging as well as she.

I didn't mean to give her a *no fair* look, but it wasn't fair. We were the same age and there wasn't a single age line on her face. There were four on my forehead alone, and a fifth forming…getting deeper by the day!

She was never the beat-around-the-bush type with me, and I didn't want to be with her. "What's your secret?" I came right out and asked. "Did you go to St. Augustine and dunk yourself in Ponce de León's Fountain of Youth?"

She gave it the quick laugh it deserved, but then shook off my question, like it went without saying there were options out there for reducing the lines on one's face.

"Aw, man," she said when her cell phone beeped. "Give me a sec. Let me reply to this doggone text."

Even as I sat there processing how well she had aged, and how I had neglected certain parts of myself, I refused to let my thoughts throw a poor-me pity party. I enjoyed my fair share of facials, and on a routine basis all through the years, three a week, every week. And I loved them. I loved my macaroni facials—I closed my eyes, held my face over the kitchen sink, and let the steam from the noodles draining in the colander do its thing!

Oh, and my daily dishwasher facial, too—opening it after the cycle ran through, letting the steam from the drying dishes hit me in the face. It did nothing to prevent wrinkles but it sure was relaxing. I always stood there for a second, closed my eyes, and pretended I was at a spa.

Viv looked up from her phone and caught me staring. "What, is my lipstick too bright? I'd ask if I had some on my front tooth, but we both know I don't."

I shook my head apologetically. Her vibrant orange lipstick was perfectly in place, and I wasn't judging it. If I lived in a castle overlooking the sea, I'd wear vibrant orange lipstick, too.

"Question," she said then, and I knew what was coming. Viv was notorious for asking questions…not small talk questions, but life's big, monumental questions. She was also a listener, listened intently to the answers given, as if through someone else's answer she might solve the mysteries within her self. "Did you want to see me again? Do you mind that our paths crossed?"

Before answering, I remembered the series of postcards she had sent to me after graduation—all of her doing whatever she wanted to do, backpacking through Peru on one trip, then India, China, and Japan on another, chasing adventures, and searching. Viv was always searching…for something bigger, greater than herself. Back when I knew her, that was her passion, searching for a higher being, and the source of life itself.

While she was embarking on one personal quest after the next, sending me postcards from distant lands, all I cared about was the whereabouts of missing pacifiers in mine and Peter's one-bedroom apartment. I hardly had time to shower, let alone hunt down reasons for my existence, or play hide-and-seek with God—who wasn't even hiding. In the land of diapers, a colic-stricken baby, and working the hospital night shift, I had no time to read, let alone acknowledge her postcards.

"You were walking your way through remote parts of Southeast Asia," I said. "And I was going no farther than the grocery store, which was right next to the hospital where I worked. So, no, I never thought we'd cross paths again," I answered, even though her question was whether I wanted to cross paths again.

"Do you remember our favorite quote?"

"*Solvitur ambulando*," I said right away. "It is solved by walking. That, according to St. Augustine."

But what answers to life was she forming in her head for having asked me that? Walking had always been her thing. It was our thing together. Maybe she was about to share with me the reason for the chair. But she didn't, and I didn't ask. I wasn't as good at asking big questions. I just wanted to break the bittersweet look on her face.

"So, what about California? That was your dream, to live in San Francisco."

"Home sweet home for me," she gasped. "Loved it there." She swallowed hard. "Florida, it's a detour for me. But isn't that life? We take impulsive turns. We get lost, and sometimes it's hard to find our way back to where we want to be. How about you? I know nothing. You dropped off the face of the planet. All I know is you went ahead and had the baby, and not long after, another baby, right?"

"Yep, two baby girls, then twin boys after that."

She covered her ears with her hands, and shook her head, like she couldn't believe it. "Oh, for crying out loud." She looked me straight in the eyes. "So, was it meant to be?" she asked point blank. "Your life having those babies, your life with kids, was it meant to be?"

There she went with another one of her questions. Viv was still Viv, getting right to the core of it, asking what sounded like simple questions but weren't. She expected big and meaningful answers, and often, I felt pinned to the wall until I replied.

I gave her a giant nod, a gross understatement for my life with kids. "Yes, it was meant to be. All four of them, meant to be. Can't imagine my life without them."

"You look great," she said.

"Oh, please!" I looked down at my lime green sweatsuit. There was a giant piece of lint, which I tried to pick off before she saw. But it was pink, from the old shag carpeting in the girls' bedroom. I didn't want to litter her singing floors with my lint, so I stuffed it in my pocket. "You don't have to be so nice," I said. "I look a mess. The last two decades of my life have felt like a rollercoaster ride."

"What do you mean?"

Oh my goodness, how was I to even put it into words? All the commotion when I first heard that extra heartbeat within me had been a warm-up for what came next…my heart taking off on a beautiful, unpredictable, all-encompassing, exhilarating ride through motherhood that had my heart doing things I never knew hearts were capable of doing—shaking, aching, resonating, quivering, tingling, and synchronizing with the hearts of my kids.

"Thrilling ups and terrifying downs," I said. "In other words, parenting. But here I am…the ride hasn't ended. But it's slower now, and I'm doing what I can to reclaim parts of me that fell out along the way."

"Like what? What have you lost?"

"Oh, where do I begin? My physical energy…dreams I had for myself. You know, things I wanted to do, but never got around to. It's going to take time."

She rolled her enormous, Bette Davis eyes. "I'm not saying it to be nice. You look great…an active participant, not standing on the sidelines watching everyone else live, but out there doing whatever you have to do, getting your hands dirty. That's what makes a person look great."

I brushed the wispy strands of hair off my face and tucked them behind my ears. "I didn't even take a shower this morning," I confessed.

"*Ha*," she wailed. "You've got to love serendipity…no formal attire required. It catches you as you are, that's the thrill of serendipity."

Easy for her to say in her an ankle-length white maxi dress with a peacock-colored sequined shawl draping her shoulders. Oh, and the orange lipstick.

"I'm going to tell you something crazy," she warned. "Are you ready?"

"Yeah, what?"

"I haven't laughed in ages."

"No." I didn't want to believe it.

"It's true. I kid you not, I don't laugh at all anymore."

"I heard you a second ago. You laughed a second ago."

"Okay, well that was rare. Seriously, I'm not lying, I hardly ever laugh. But," she put her finger in the air, as if getting to her main point, "I did laugh the other day, and would you believe it was all because I was remembering you and me…our infamous moment in dance class?"

"Oh, no," I wailed. "Dance 101, freshman elective."

"Yep, I was cracking up…you and me, we tried so hard, but couldn't do it. Even Marita heard me laughing, and she came running in all flipped out, thinking something was wrong."

"You didn't tell her, did you?"

"I didn't tell her what you did, what happened to you, no." Viv tapped the arm of her wheelchair. "But I swear, if I wasn't in this chair, I'd do it. I'd do it right now, right here…*a weight on right foot, left pointing back, arms in second, walking forward—*"

I couldn't stand there all formal and doing nothing, not when Viv made her voice sound like our distinguished dance instructor. It pushed a silly button in me. As she continued rattling off commands, I got up from the red velvet couch.

"*Tres leading left, demi-plie and pique,*" she continued, calling out the dance commands.

I did my best attempted version of it across the creaky, squeaky floor for no other reason than Vivienne Watts was that once-in-a-lifetime friend who brought out the outlandishness in me. We were always either dancing carelessly, laughing hysterically, or walking our way across campus together, deeply discussing, and on occasion bawling our eyes out over life's let downs.

"Don't you love doing things you're lousy at?" she said as I fell out of my attempted demi-plie and pique.

"Are you saying I'm lousy at ballet?"

"Lousier than ever! And isn't it fun…doing things you're lousy at? It's like taking a break from taking ourselves too seriously, when we do whatever we're lousy at."

"I should start singing."

"In the privacy of your own home, you should sing…sing at the top of your lungs. You should do what you're lousy at…and not hold back. You know why?"

"Why?"

"Because you can, that's why. No other reason, than you can."

Taking hold of my foot, I pulled it back, stretching my calf. Viv was still Viv, my zany friend who said zany stuff, but that zany stuff had a way of profoundly sinking in. But what did all of that mean to her? Would she ever be able to clumsily leap through the air with her toes not pointed, ever again? As I opened my mouth to request the story behind the wheelchair, she clicked a remote control and music went on.

"You like this song?" she asked.

"Never heard it."

"You never heard this Lana Del Rey song? I used to sing it to my second husband—a real woozy of a guy." She straightened her posture, took a breath, then sang lousily along with the eerie-sounding song. "'Will you still love me when I'm no longer young and beautiful?'" Her voice echoed throughout the room with its soaring ceilings. "'Will you still love me when I got nothing but my aching soul?'" With a simple click, she turned the music off, then wheeled over, and with her back to me, stared out the glass wall at the Gulf.

"I won't bore you with the details, but long story short, husband number two ditched me for a woman half my age. Don't ask. I don't feel like talking about it."

Still standing, staring out at the unfathomable Gulf of Mexico, I put my hands on my hips, then gasped with disgust at the woozy of a guy who did that to my friend. "I'm sorry you went through that, Viv."

When she looked my way, her nose was pink as a cherry blossom and she was biting her lip. I thought she changed her mind and wanted to talk about it after all, but then she shrugged it off with her hand, like it was no big deal. "Enough…enough about me, or I'll turn into a crybaby on you. I'm so tired of being a crybaby. It's the most unproductive thing in the world to be, don't you think?"

I was about to tell her there was nothing wrong with crying, then remembered she had seen me from her window, crying in the dirt. "We all have our moments. And no, I don't think all cries are unproductive." Crying out to the One who knows what was best for me was the most productive cry I'd ever had. The One who hears all cries, and who takes our tears and exchanges them for joy, heard me, loved me, and cared about every drop that fell from my eye. It was way better than crying into my pillow all alone.

She blotted the corner of her eye with her pinky. What did Marita mean when she told me Viv was in a dark place? How did she end up on Sanibel, of all places? And if husband number three was so great, then what happened to him? The history of our friendship warranted plopping ourselves down for hours with comfort snacks, tissues, and cozy blankies, gabbing away like we used to in college on those cold, Midwestern nights when temperatures were below freezing and our favorite activity—power walking across campus—wasn't an option.

She must have been craving that, too. "Can you stay for a while, or do you have to go? I don't want to hold you prisoner when I'm sure there's a thousand things you want to do today."

Peter was gone, and the tree frogs didn't care what time I came home. Sure, I wanted to strip the wallpaper. But meeting my neighbor, and my neighbor being a long-lost old friend, was like killing two birds with one stone. It was the stuff stories were made of, and I wanted to write my novel.

"I'd love to stay!" I told her. I'd stay for a slumber party, too, if she asked. It could be like a staycation, lounging around in her beautiful mansion, chit-chatting and catching up.

"Sit tight then. Let me quickly go call my lawyer so he doesn't come. I'm not in the mood for another seven-hundred-and-fifty-dollar meeting." Her hands gripped the wheels of her chair, and with impressive force, she was off—propelling herself with ease across the great room. With the Gulf out the enormous window, she looked like a professional rower racing across the water. Was it going to be a lifetime sport for her, or would she walk again, and do all of the things she was lousy at but loved to do?

Before rounding the corner, she came to a halt. "Feel free to snoop through my portfolio, if you want," she said with a pant. "If you like interior design."

"Oh, where is it?"

"Right there in front of you on the handmade Oriental table. You'll see I even put St. Augustine's quote on the cover."

I picked up the three-ring binder, then sank back into the red velvet sofa, closing my eyes for a moment, remembering why we declared it our favorite quote.

It is solved by walking. At the end of the semester, as soon as Dance 101 ended and we needed a form of exercise, we switched to walking instead. We always said, though, St. Augustine should have added two more words, so it read: *It is solved by walking and talking.* Walking and talking across campus together three nights a week became our thing, and we were both better at it than we had been at putting one step in front of the other and stressing about *right, left, demi-plie, straight left onto left demi-pointe (heel elevated).*

It was while walking and talking with Viv that I caught glimpse of how tough things really were for her in that house she grew up in. One fall day as we walked from the library to our dorm, she had shared with me how Sundays in her home were reserved for her father's poker and drinking, and Mondays were spent cleaning up after Sundays.

"Why did *you* have to be the one to clean it all up?"

"Well, if I didn't, our kitchen would go on stinking of dirty ashtrays," she'd said, "And the corner of the living room, near the poker table, would wreak of urine."

I opened the interior design portfolio I had been holding in my lap. Knowing how ashamed she had been by her own detestable living quarters growing up, I couldn't help but gasp at the pictures of beautiful homes she had transformed throughout the years. Her work was stunning, particularly coming from someone who never dared to invite a single friend into her house to play. But even if she had, our mothers wouldn't have allowed us to go in.

"You never had a single friend over…ever?" I'd asked once.

"I'd rather show them the inside of a dumpster!"

One night, as we were wandering around campus, walking and talking as usual, I came up with an idea. "You're artistic, creative. Even your chalk art on the sidewalk," I said, "It was better than all of ours. Why not become an interior designer? Do for others' homes what you wished you could have done for your own!"

The moment I said that, she stopped walking and grabbed my arm. "Why didn't I think of that myself?" She looked up at the flurries coming down from the sky, and when she looked back at me, there were snowflakes on her lashes. "I'll do it. That's exactly what I'll do…graduate, travel the world with you as we've planned, then move somewhere fun and far, far away like California. And there, I'll work as an interior designer." She blinked away tears. "It is solved by walking and talking. We just planned my life out tonight."

I flipped through her portfolio, admiring page after page of brilliant interior designs—private residences in Carmel-by-the-Sea, Big Sur, Pacific Coast Highway, as well as lobbies of famous San Francisco hotels, and luxury condo buildings in the Golden Gate Park area. "Wow," I mumbled again and again. Her work astounded me, and I could have spent hours looking through it had the front door not opened, and Marita walked in.

Dangling from her arms were several canvas bags with carrots, celery, and kale poking out. But when she saw me, she came over, as if the bags on her arms were merely bracelets, and bent down to kiss me on the cheek. "What a surprise, I'm so glad to see you here!"

"Hi," I said, like the girl next door who'd come over to play.

"You have no idea how happy I am to see you here! A house is not a house without friends. It is a solitary confinement cell, without friends. But God knows," she glanced up at the cathedral ceiling, then back at me, "God knows how I have been praying for her, for something extra special to happen in her life!"

I didn't want to wait. I wanted to tell her right away the very special thing—that Viv and I were friends, long-lost friends—but Marita was a talker, and didn't give me the chance.

"Oh, how I love that girl. I love her like a daughter, but she does not listen." Even with the weight of the bags on her arms, her hands gestured along as she talked. "If only she would stop listening to nothing but news all day and all night, *aye, aye, aye.* It is good to be informed, and do what one can to help, but all she does is get all worked up when maybe," she held onto her words, holding me in suspense, "she should also start looking at the issues inside her. The issues inside her need attention, too."

"Well," I said on Viv's behalf, "we all have our issues. I have mine. And who knows? The interior issues are harder to think about. We have to be ready. Sometimes it's easier to keep ourselves preoccupied with all the stuff happening out there."

"Yes, yes, of course," she nodded. "But whether our focus is on issues happening in the world, or issues inside us, we cannot go on thinking we can solve everything ourselves. I wish there was a day…one big day, where everybody that wanted to would get down on their knees humbly before God, and bring all issues to Him."

She didn't give me the chance to talk. I wanted to tell her I had done that myself, but had more issues in me, and planned on doing it again… regularly.

"Vivi looks at me like I am nonsense," she went on, "any time I talk like that to her, she thinks I'm nonsense."

Before letting our conversation go further, in good conscience, I needed to tell her the special thing—that Viv and I were friends. I opened my mouth, about to announce it, but once again, her words beat mine out.

"She is a stubborn girl. If she could have fixed it by now…what needs fixing inside of her…she would have. But she can't. And she won't ask for help."

I leaned forward on the sofa, and in a low voice asked what I shouldn't have behind my friend's back. "What exactly is her issue, what's going on?"

Marita stooped over, putting her face close to mine. "Her heart," she whispered "where most of our issues originate. Vivi does not think she is good enough—good enough to be loved."

"Married three times?"

"Yes, yes, but husband number three was a good man, a good, good man. Oh, how he loved her, and did everything right, but still, she accused him of not loving her. I am not one to eavesdrop, but I heard things. And do you blame me for that? I did something productive, at least, with the things that I heard. I brought them to God in prayer. Praying for her is all I can do." Even with the bags of produce still on her arms, Marita managed to raise a hand and shake a finger in the air. "Do you know what her third husband told her one day...what that good man said to her?"

"What?" I whispered, on the edge of the red velvet sofa.

Marita's eyes flashed around the house. "He told her he was giving up...walking away. Never mind he was a retired pediatric heart surgeon."

"He was?"

"Yes, but he could not fix the glitches in his own wife's heart...tried everything, but nothing was enough. She refused to believe...refused to believe that she was loved."

"So, she let him go?"

"Kicked him out, like she does everyone good in her life." Marita closed her eyes and bit her lip, then opened her eyes. "And now, she has no one left but me, her driver, her physical therapist, and her lawyer—we are the only ones left in her life. Thankfully for me," she stood upright and lifted her arms with the bags, "her juicing habits alone are enough to keep me employed. She won't even go to Sanibel's Farmer's Market. It was her favorite thing to do. But now I do that for her. She doesn't go anywhere."

I felt guilty listening to details behind Viv's back, but I wanted to know. "Next year?" I put the words out there like bait. "Maybe next year she'll be walking around the Farmer's Market again?"

Marita shrugged her shoulders. "Anything is possible." But then, her eyes locked with mine and they seemed to say, *if only you knew!*

It reminded me of the news Marita needed to know. "I need to tell you," I said, "but don't worry, everything you shared with me will stay a secret. I can tell you care about her, so I won't say a thing, or cause any trouble. I'm not like that. There's enough drama in the world. I don't like to add drama to anyone's lives."

"What is it? What do you need to tell me?"

"Viv and I know each other. Believe it or not, we're friends, long-lost friends."

Her eyes looked worried, and whether it was the weight of my announcement, or the heavy bags of produce, she dropped to her knees.

"Everything you told me, you said out of love," I said right away, then gave her a wink and reassuring smile. "I said it once, and I'll say it again, I'm not one to cause trouble."

A look of relief spread across her face, and there on her knees, she closed her eyes and muttered something I did not hear. She then opened her eyes and looked at me point blank. "You, child," she said, "you are it. You are the answer to my prayers!"

"Huh?"

"God knows. He knows how I have been praying. And it's you. She needs you...a friend who cares enough to speak truth into her life." Marita's face went into deep concentration. "Wait a minute," she said. "I caught Vivi laughing the other day. She would not tell me why but told me she was remembering a moment with an old friend."

I nodded. "Yeah, she told me that."

Her mouth dropped open, but not for long. "Won't you, please? Before she comes back, tell me the funny moment that made her laugh! That girl never laughs...nothing makes her laugh anymore. It will make my day knowing what made her laugh."

I wasn't sure I wanted to share it. Then again, it happened to be one of those moments that I never wanted to forget, and since Marita was kind enough to ask about it, give me the floor to relive it, it was hard to pass up.

"Okay," I said to Marita as I stood up from the sofa. "I'll tell you exactly what had her laughing." I pulled off my sweatsuit jacket and tied it around my waist, even though all I had on underneath was a pink tank top, showing off my flabby arms. "It was our first day of dance class."

"You and Vivi were dancers?"

"Well, we weren't Rockettes. If I had shorts on, you'd see why." I took the bags off Marita's poor arms, put them on mine instead, then managed to take hold of her elbow, guiding her up. As we headed for the kitchen, I stopped for a second, putting my foot in the air, toes pointed, but then stumbled from the weight of the bags.

"The dance class we took…a mix between modern and ballet…was to fulfill our college's physical education requirement. We thought it was a beginner's class…failed to read the full description, that really, it was a prerequisite for dance majors. In other words, we ended up in a class of serious dancers. And let me tell you, neither of us were ever girls dressed in pink tutus, going to ballet. We thought it would be a silly movement class of sorts, and way better than the weightlifting option early Monday mornings."

By then, we had entered Viv's kitchen, which was modern with industrial-style cabinets, silver appliances, and an enormous gray stone table with silver chairs. Marita helped me raise my arms high enough to reach the light-colored wooden counter, where together we tipped the bags over. When she rubbed her lower back, I pulled out a silver chair and ushered for her to sit down. The space was large enough to hold a dance class, and I couldn't resist. I took my position center floor.

"Viv and I were each standing like this." I showed her, standing unparallel first, with my head erect. "It was during warm-ups, as the dance instructor called out commands, '*Look to the left, back to the front, then to the right, making sure your eyes see at each side. You should be looking at the back of the head of the person next to you. If you see a face next to you, you are doing it all wrong,*' that Viv and I found ourselves face-to-face when we weren't supposed to be face-to-face."

"*Aye, aye, aye,* you silly girls!" Marita declared, but then covered her mouth at the sound of Viv's wheelchair rolling across the singing floors. There was no time to scatter. Like a warrior oarsman, Viv rounded the corner and entered the kitchen with great speed. No more than a foot away from me, she came to an abrupt halt, then looked back and forth at Marita in her front row seat, and me center stage in my awkward pose.

It was obvious she had been crying. Her nose was red as a tomato and her mascara smeared like war paint under her eyes. "I think I already know, but what are you doing?" she asked, then took a deep breath to refill her lungs.

"I was about to relive our infamous moment in dance class," I said, nervous it would upset her. "Tell Marita what you said super-loud to everybody…when we were the only ones doing it wrong, facing the wrong way."

Viv proved then she was still Viv. She rolled her chair a couple of inches closer to me, taking her place on the stage, then cleared her throat dramatically. "It's either you or me, for crying out loud, one of us ding-dongs is facing the wrong way!"

Marita let out a shriek of laughter. "What next? Did you girls figure it out?"

"Oh, no. We weren't capable, and besides, there was this overwhelming urge in my gut to erupt with laughter. I tried to contain it, but it imploded."

"And the pressure she was feeling—" Viv began.

"Oh, no," I stopped her immediately. "We don't need to tell that part."

"It found another avenue of escape," she blurted out, having no regard for my unwillingness to tell that part.

"Viv!"

"Stop, it's the best part! Your nostrils made that super-loud snorting noise, which sent me off balance and falling out of my pose."

"*Aye, aye, aye,* what was everyone else in the class doing?"

"They were all in perfect position, as ballerina majors should be, but every eyeball in that room was focused on us."

"Yeah, even their buns were perfect. But Viv and I…we were the ones who invented the sloppy buns so popular around the world today. But don't clap yet. That's not the end of our story." I pointed at Viv. "You, after I snorted, you were trying not to laugh…shaking, then you made that honking noise, followed by a quack, remember?"

"That's nothing compared to what you did next."

"Let's keep that our secret!"

But with a gleam in her eye, Viv kept going. "So, there we were, not just laughing—but snorting like pigs and quacking like ducks. With their perfect buns, they were staring at us like we were a couple of bozos, I kid you not."

"Which made us laugh harder," I added, "tears pouring down our cheeks."

"Tears?" Viv said in an incriminating tone. "You had more than tears coming out."

I shook my head. After all those years, I still couldn't go there, to what happened next.

By then Marita's hands covered her face, and although Viv stopped there, for sure Marita was filling in the blanks and probably imagining the embarrassing finale that gave me recurrent college nightmares for years afterward—not of running through empty halls looking for my classes, but peeing in my leotard in dance class.

When Marita removed her hands from her face, she asked, "What about your dance instructor? What did she do?"

"Ms. Dafferina," I said. "Before teaching at our college, she had taught forty years at the…can't remember the name of the place."

"The Julliard School of Dance," Viv said.

"That's right…so she was the real deal and we thought for sure we were in trouble."

"Remember what Ms. Dafferina did?" Viv put her hand in the air. "She snapped her fingers like this, and strutted on over. 'If this is what my class does to you ladies,' she said, 'then pat yourselves on the back. Showing emotion through natural movement is what this class is all about.'"

"Did you do that?" Marita said, "Did you pat yourselves on the back?"

"We sure did," I nodded. "In fact, patting ourselves on the back became our private joke. After that, we'd pat ourselves on the back every time we did anything less than perfect, which was pretty much every moment of the day, everything we did. I still do it, do you?" I looked at Viv.

"Are you kidding? A hundred times a day, I kid you not!"

With that, the two of us reached our hands back and patted ourselves on the back. Marita got up from her seat and gave us a standing ovation.

"You have made my day, girls. Thank you for making my day!"

Despite all the fun we had, I saw it in Viv's eyes, she was hiding something. Her emotional pain, like a backdrop, was always there. She had told me so on one of our walks, that even when cast into a new role—college kid away for the first time from a dysfunctional household—her backdrop stayed the same.

"Okay, so I've got bummer news," she announced. "My lawyer, he's already on his way, which means I need a raincheck. And *boo hoo*, I was looking forward to catching up."

"Aw," I said, unable to hide my disappointment that our reunion was cut short. "When can I come over again?"

She thought for a second. "How about Thursday? We can sit on my wrap-around deck, watch the sun drop into the water. I don't care what time you come over...before sunset."

"Four days from now is perfect. Gives me something to look forward to," I said. "I have to strip wallpaper from just about every wall in the house. Lucky me, right?"

She let out a groan. "All I can say is good luck. It's the most lonesome, tedious task in the universe; I've known people who went mad two days into it. I hope you're not doing it alone...hope you have somebody helping you."

I shook my head. "Peter is out of town."

"Peter...the same Peter you married back in college?" Her mouth dropped open.

"Yeah, same Peter. Why?"

"I'm blown away...had no idea people it was even possible that people stayed together that long. I want to hear all about it...your life with Peter. But for now, I have to scoot...get myself upstairs, prepare for this meeting. Hate to rush off like this, but he'll be here soon." And with that, she left the kitchen.

Marita was putting the fresh produce away. I didn't want to end up in another talking-behind-Viv's-back session, so I left the kitchen and headed for the mammoth red door.

"You can do it," she said at my heels. "You are the answer to my prayers."

I pretended I didn't hear, but when I opened the door, she had caught up with me.

"Tell her, please," she said, waving a bundle of kale in my face. "Tell her how much God loves her!"

I gave her a look—I didn't like kale, but also, praying for someone was one thing. Preaching another. I wasn't the type to blurt out God stuff. And even though the profound reality of His love had been overwhelming me, I wasn't going to start acting like John the Baptist, a voice calling out from the wilderness, preparing people's hearts to accept Jesus.

"She needs to hear it," she continued as I went down the pyramid steps, "how very much God loves her!"

Well, sure, couldn't everyone stand to hear how much God loved them, and wouldn't the world be a better place if they knew? But there were already people—trained professionals—out there doing just that, wording things right, and not goofing things up.

"We'll see," was all I said when I reached the bottom step. "We'll see. Bye."

I hummed as I walked the bonsai-dotted walkway, and by the time I crossed over into my yard, I was already a couple of rounds into, 'It's a Small World After All.' I wanted to stop humming and call Peter instead, but he might not like how small the world was. Of all its people, Vivienne Watts—eccentric to me, unusual to him—wasn't his first choice for a neighbor.

I wasn't one hundred percent sure how I felt about it either. The turtle and the birds reminded me of good things. But seeing Viv catapulted me back to specific moments in my life I hadn't thought of in years, and reminded me of a certain something I didn't like about myself.

I went to my bedroom and opened Mom's folder, pulling out another one of her letters to God, which happened to be written on the back of a general store flyer.

TWENTY

"The Lord does not look at the things man looks at. Man looks
at the outward appearance, but the Lord looks at the heart."
—1 Samuel 16:7

To the One who doesn't look at things others look at, but looks at my heart,

*Here I am on this bench outside Bailey's General Store, enjoying the house
sparrows flitting about the rafters. The birds are singing their hearts out, performing on a grand stage.*

*Back in the store, I had an embarrassing moment. I was praying to You,
but didn't realize I said a couple of things out loud until a woman in the produce aisle asked if I was talking to her. "Oops," I told her with a laugh, "I was
talking to Jesus but didn't realize I was doing so out loud."*

*"You'd be better off talking to a basil plant," she said, like I was mad as a
hatter, then walked away.*

*I wish we could put on special glasses, see the angels around us, or peek
into Heaven, and see Your face. It's hard for some to believe in things they
cannot see. I pray for the woman in the produce aisle. Who knows the darkness
she's in? You know her heart. May she come to know how much You love her.*

*You love us so much, You made a way—are the way, Jesus—out of dark-
ness. But not everyone knows the difference between Darkness and Light.
Darkness condemns and Light forgives. Darkness destroys and Light rebuilds.
Darkness cancels, Light restores. Darkness tries beating us into unrecognizable
nothingness, squashing the life right out of us. If it weren't for Light, we'd slip
right through the gutter into eternal damnation. Darkness hates, and Light*

loves. Light does its thing in our hearts, and helps us onto our feet again so we go out into the world with altered steps.

I can't look at the sun without squinting or hurting my eyes. I can't look at the work of salvation—that major life-and-death work You did on the cross, and did in me—without lowering my head in humility. Your love is so bright, I'm overwhelmed. I close my eyes and praise You.

That particular work You did in me is perfect and complete, but I am not perfect at all. Just as buildings need routine maintenance and often, major repairs, walking temples of the Holy Spirit do, too. I love when You're at work in me. It's a beautiful sound, a peaceful sound—more beautiful, even, than the song of the birds, and the sound of the tree branches waltzing in the breeze, and way better even than the raindrops dancing on the roof. I love the sound of You at work in me, a temple of the Holy Spirit.

When I forget that You're always present, when I ignore You, I only hear me. And I don't want to go on only hearing me. I don't want to listen to me crying myself to sleep, missing the old days when my husband was alive, and we were living in the big house, all of us laughing, playing in the yard.

Everyone loves a home, wants a home, and I hurt for the homeless. I don't want to be upset over the rundown house we're living in. But the resentment is there. It's in me. It started small, when I found out there was no insurance money, no plan for me and the kids. From there, everything turned into a matter of financial survival. I've been trying to keep up, giving the kids the basics when I want to give them more. My double shifts at work aren't enough, and they drain me. I stopped coming to You, and that's when it started to grow. The resentment in me (over my circumstances), grew. Combined with my regrets (I was ignorant and should have looked over our finances myself), it has taken up space in me, leaving me no room for joy.

But You specialize in things like this, in removing resentment. I need Your help, clearing mine out. If my heart is like a private nook where You and I meet up…a Holy of Holies, like in Solomon's temple…then together let's clear out that section where I've been hoarding bitterness.

Help me, counsel me, clear out the junk in me, so there will be more space for joy and worship and to think beautiful thoughts. I long for an atmosphere of peace in my daily life.

I believe this is what You want for me. As I sit alone with You, I believe it's the idea You've been running by me. How can I not trust and surrender to the plans You propose? You're my Designer, my interior designer, and You know me so well.

Love,
Finley

"For you created my inmost being; you knit me together in my mother's womb. I will praise you because I am fearfully and wonderfully made; your works are wonderful, I know that full well. My frame was not hidden from you when I was made in that secret place, when I was woven together in the depths of the Earth. Your eyes saw my unformed body; all the days ordained for me were written in your book before one of them came to be."
—Psalm 139:13-16

TWENTY-ONE

* * *

Keep a close-knit relationship with your designer every step of the way, and not just when you first start working together, but for the duration, start to finish. And if you're satisfied, write reviews or tell others about Your designer.

* * *

Don't be fooled. When it comes to floors, there are laminate options that give the look and feel of wood for a fraction of the cost but there's nothing like the real thing.

I started in the great room spraying two parts vinegar, one part water across a section of the wall. As I waited for the solution to soak into the vinyl on paper backing, my mind went to that certain something I didn't like about myself. I didn't want to think about it, but it was like a hornet in my house that kept bothering me.

To swat away the thought, I started to hum. But early on in rolling the scoring tool in circular motions across the saturated section of the wall, my humming went from 'Bridge over Troubled Water,' by Simon and Garfunkel, to 'Desperado' by the Eagles. When 'The Sounds of Silence' was next on my hum list, I banned myself from humming, and let myself think instead. I declared the next few days my wallpaper strip-a-thon, think-a-thon, and refused to be another person Viv knew gone mad in the process.

That thing I didn't like about myself was like a splinter that had settled under the skin but was surfacing. It needed to come out. The pressure Marita was putting on me, and the discomfort associated with it, was irritating.

Why did some talk about God in normal-sounding conversational manner, yet others, like me, found it awkward to mention His name?

I didn't care that I hadn't a singing voice, but where was my voice for the Creator of Love, the Giver of Love, the Source of Love itself? Even back in college, any time Viv had mentioned her search for a higher being, and her quest to discover the meaning of life, I acted like I had a bout of laryngitis. I had so many opportunities back then to tell my friend about the One who saved a wretch like me, and whose resurrection was living in me, and whose arms were wide open. But instead, I entered silent mode, as if a mute button was pushed on me every time the topic came up.

As I rolled the perforating tool around the wall, excuses for my lack of voice rolled through my mind. I was no poster child for Christianity. A believer, yes, but walking in sync with Christ…no. And if I talked about Him, I would have been called a fake. Holding a banner, flaunting whatever I happened to be passionate about high over my head for others to see, was never my thing. Regardless, I respected the people who were out there in the world using their voices for this and for that.

Although Christianity was like a precious gem collection given to me as a child, throughout the years, I misplaced the gems. Whenever I did spot bits and pieces of God's Truths here or there, they looked dull to me. But no wonder they looked dull. I wasn't tumbling those gems, wasn't studying or reading God's Word, or stepping foot into a church, or even talking to the living, breathing One who was with me all along. So why should any of the pieces in the Christianity collection have sparkled, or been something brilliant that I wanted to show and tell to a friend?

Hours into my wallpaper strip-a-thon, think-a-thon, I took one of the fallen scraps, and settled down onto the wooden floor with a pen. Before one sang in front of others, they practiced in private, warming up behind closed doors, learning, making mistakes, and getting to know and love what they were singing before belting it out for anyone else to hear.

Oh, dear God, having an interior designer help me with my house is a luxury, but working with You is a necessity. I don't need an interior designer telling me the hideous wallpaper in Hidden Potential needs to come down, but in me—a walking temple of the Holy Spirit—I need Your help in recognizing which of my thought patterns are uncomplimentary to the Spirit within.

May Your Truths and Your Love, permeate my stubborn spots, saturate the surrounding tissues of my heart, and make me sensitive to the things You care about. And may the words I read in the Bible function like perforating tools, roughening the surfaces of my nonporous mind.

I sit here on this wooden floor...just as there're laminate options that give the look and feel of wood for a fraction of the cost of the real thing, there are also fake options when it comes to righteousness. And those fake options might give the look and feel of the real thing, but there're life and death differences between choosing fake versus real righteousness.

Jesus,
The work You did,
on those two planks of wood
is the one and only
perfect and complete work
with eternal guarantee,
warranting the stamp of authenticity.
There's no greater validation that I am loved
than Your saving stamp of love in my heart.
If anyone else tries to offer such a thing,
it's not real.
The only authentic choice is you, Jesus.
Thank You!

I got up from the floor, tucking the piece of wallpaper scrap on which I'd scribbled into a three-ring binder. I didn't want Peter to find it and judge me as overly dramatic.

After that, I continued for hours spraying, praying, reading from the Bible on breaks in between, then waiting, and perforating more sodden wall. I wrestled not just with wallpaper, but with Truth. A lot of what I read in the Word didn't match up with current popular trends in the world. But even as the wallpaper came down, there was no pulling Truth down.

"Truth is truth," I said out loud in my quiet house. "It always has been and will forever be its own unchangeable thing." I had hidden the parts I didn't like, covered them up under layer upon layer of my own opinions, the opinions of others, and self-proclaimed expertise. But none of that changed Truth in any way.

I wanted Truth to do its thing in me. Like peeling away at the bruised skin on a fruit, I wanted the Word of God to work through my fleshly parts and reach my core. If from the heart we penned our life themes and plotted our steps, and from the heart our passions bubbled and our voices flowed forth, erupting into the world, then I wanted God's Word to do its thing in my heart.

When another nice scrap fell to the floor, I picked up my pen once more.

Thank You for making my heart new so long ago, but every day that it beats in this offbeat world, I feel like it's weakening, and even skipping a beat, too. Help me live closer to You, so I can hear Your heartbeat, and synchronize mine with Yours. I'm tired of marching to the beat of this out of tune with Your world. I'd rather march to the beat of Your heart.

By early evening, my back was aching, but I showed no signs of madness that I knew of, so I kept at it. The solution soaking into the walls was working well, dissolving the adhesive in several spots. The paper was dropping from the walls like meat off a bone. But in other spots, it wasn't so easy. And stripping Hidden Potential of its old, outdated paper was becoming more daunting than I had imagined. Nothing about the rescue mission of this distressed property was simple—it should have been demolished, after all, sold as a piece of land instead.

"Curious," I said out loud to the One who was for me and not against me, the One who was capable of doing all things, "have You ever found certain tasks in me more daunting than You imagined...to where You regretted saving me in the first place?"

But then, each *drip...drip...drip* of the leaking kitchen faucet came out like the word *no...no...no!*

I put the scoring tool down and picked up my pen.

Take hold of my thoughts! What Jesus went through on the cross for me was daunting, but without regret. You don't regret me. You knit me together in my mother's womb, and even before the first stitch, You knew the person You were knitting. From womb to eternity, You desire a close-knit relationship with me, with all of us, and You keep a close watch on Your work, making no mistakes. You never lose count of a single stitch, and You don't drop what You're knitting.

Even when I get caught up in the snags of the world, You set me free and mend the holes. Your love is too great to understand, but the fullest expression of it is Christ. The more I know Him, the more I know Your love.

I put my pen down and picked up a red permanent marker. If Viv could write her interior design tidbits on leaves, and Mom her letters to God on the back of a general store flyer, then I could scribble out the loyalties of my heart not just on wallpaper scraps, but on the wall itself. It was going to get painted over soon enough.

> *There's no greater display of love
> than the work of salvation Jesus did for me.
> It's the only perfect and complete thing in me.
> Everything else about me is imperfect.
> But I'm glad to be
> a work-in-progress
> for the duration of my life on Earth.*

If Viv owned binoculars, and saw me through that tippy top window of hers writing graffiti on the walls, surely, she'd add me to her list of people going off the deep end from wallpaper removal. But I was expressing what I needed to express, taking what I felt about the One whose nature was love, displaying it outside of me.

I was also following Viv's advice, working not just with a highly re-garded designer, but with the Father, Son, and Spirit—restoration special-ists known the world over for transforming ordinary into extraordinary and dark into light. People all over the world were talking, raving about the One whose name was synonymous with love, and His restorative work in their lives. I wanted to give testimony as well. No task was too daunt-ing. Loving and saving even the ones the world deemed unsalvageable was His specialty, His passion.

Later that night, I climbed into bed with my laptop, ready to write, and also call Peter. I needed to tell him who our neighbor was.

"No," he groaned as if it was one more flabbergasting flaw associated with the house. "I don't believe it. Are you kidding me? In a house that nice? She couldn't even afford deodorant or shampoo."

"No, she could afford it," I said. "Those two months she went with-out...she did so for world peace, remember?"

"Um, yeah, sort of. But I never understood how her greasy hair helped the world."

"Me neither, but she had good intentions."

"Call it what you like," Peter said. "What I want to know is, how did she end up in a mansion? Someone who didn't even own clothes...stole all of yours."

"Borrowed," I said in her defense. "She'd borrow my clothes, then lose or ruin them in an artistic frenzy or social project. Once, she gave my little black dress to a homeless woman."

Peter let out a sigh. "If what you're telling me is true, if this is not a premature April Fool's Day thing...half a year early...if Vivienne Watts is our neighbor, please, I urge you...right this moment, buy a lock for your closet. And hide our shampoo!"

"Oh, I don't think she'd like our cheap shampoo. Trust me, I'm sure she uses the best products. She looks young as ever, and her clothes are gorgeous."

By then, she had turned her bright light off, but the television was on, and the room flickering. If I wanted, I could have figured out which news network she was watching.

"You still there?" Peter asked.

"Yeah, but she needs to turn her television off. The lights...the way they hit our house...it lights up our bedroom."

"Alright, so obviously, this is for real. No joke. Why don't you do us a favor...buy blinds, or better yet, those total-block-out shades, or even hurricane shutters...all three!"

Peter and I talked a good hour after that, and I helped him out of his state of shock by giving him a detailed rundown of my visit to Viv's. I even told him about Marita, and the lofty expectation she put on me.

"Well, I think you're making too much of it," he advised. "Keep it to no more than three simple words...God loves you...then call it a day. I wouldn't make it bigger than that."

If only he knew that just as Viv's interior design tidbits were inspiring me with the house, the Bible was filled with interior *divine* tidbits relevant to everything within me, and I was passionate about it. "You make everything sound so undramatic, Peter."

"Better to be undramatic than a zealot, right? Don't let this Marita person, or Viv, for that matter, turn you into a zealot."

"Oh, no, that I'm not."

"Good, but you know what I mean—her gung-ho fasting, sitting there in the cafeteria, watching us all eat, claiming she was bringing awareness to world hunger. Yeah, right. Making us feel guilty for eating lunch… that's what she was doing. Oh, and spending the weekend on that street corner, posing as a homeless person in order to experience for herself how they got treated. Wearing t-shirts and shorts in snowstorms, to launch her campus conversations for the climate. Her refusal to kill bugs…catching them in your dorm room, setting them free outside. I could go on and on, but I won't. You get my drift."

"Yes, but I forget, why'd she let the spiders out?"

"Oh, who knows? Every spider life mattered. Just promise me this, if she wants you to join a cause, don't. Plain and simple, don't. And don't let her become all-encompassing, which she can be. You know that. Please, for the sake of me, don't let her swallow you up. Focus on your own stuff—the house, your writing, us. As for the whole God thing, well, she's been around the entire world, searching, and still hasn't found the higher being she went looking for. You know why? Some prefer the search, that's why."

When Peter's monologue ended, we said good-night and ended our call. I hung a sheet over the window, but when I climbed into bed, the sheet wasn't thick enough. The lights from her television went through it. I hung a blanket instead, and if that didn't work, I was going to color the glass with black permanent marker. Blame it on my hours stripping wallpaper, I was a hot mess.

TWENTY-TWO

* * *

*Carve out a sanctuary—your own secret spot, away from it all,
where you can leave your worries behind. It can be a papasan
chair with a cozy blanket, a corner in your bedroom closet, a
sheepskin rug on the floor. Make it your safe haven—where
you block out the noise and distractions of the world.*

* * *

*Don't be afraid of change.
Every change you make,
you'll wish you had made sooner!*

There was no need to carve out a spot in my house. I had an entire beach, and could pick out my own patch of sand away from it all. I went there early in the morning, packing the Bible in my bag. It wasn't the typical beach read, but it was self-care for my soul, which I needed.

All throughout the wallpaper removal, I had been memorizing verses, which was good for the brain. But also, it was like wallpapering my mind with fresh patterns of Truth complementary to the Lamp of the Lord within me.

I was most excited to read the New Testament—God's greatest display of love, Jesus entering the world scene. But I started instead at the very beginning, moving turtle-slow through the Garden of Eden. A voracious reader, I could have read fast, but chose to graze on the details and appreciate how, in unmatched creativity, the One who thought me up gave everything, even the birds skittering along the shore, their distinguishing characteristics.

From the beginning, the landscaper of that Garden, and of my soul, wanted to walk and talk and have a personal relationship with His people. But also—having nothing to do with my opinion of things—He drew right-from-wrong lines in the sand. The same One who put fruit trees in Eden made it clear which one wasn't to be eaten from.

"Because I said so," I warned my kids when they were young, "no other reason than I'm your mother, and I said so!"

"Yes, Mom," Mallory would reply with fear in her eyes, whereas Lucy usually rolled her eyes, then stormed away. The boys, they ignored me, and because of that, I was forced to take more drastic measures in letting them know how serious I was.

They struggled to understand that I had rules because I loved and wanted to protect them. They thought I was mean and unfun.

I rolled onto my back in the sand, closed my eyes, and could almost hear the chaos of four little monkeys jumping on the bed. One fell off and bumped his head. They knew they weren't supposed to be jumping on the bed, but they were exercising their free will. They had no idea, even in their rebellion, the depths of my love when I heard Charlie's voice whimpering my name, and his footsteps, along with the others, pitter-pattering through the house in search of Mama. They disobeyed me, but even after their fall, they came crying to me for help. And what a beautiful thing when they experienced firsthand my love for them, no matter what.

"I've been more like Eve," I muttered beneath my breath. "Instead of running to You when I've done wrong, I've tried hiding from You." I opened my eyes and sat up. Really, there was no such thing as hiding from God. Even if I got up and ran behind the trunk of a palm tree, He knew where I was. And even if I pressed my lips shut, locking up the private moments of my life, He knew them anyway. He knew every word in my diary, and read my thoughts between the lines.

I wished I had gone running to Jesus sooner…with everything in my life. It was never too late to start, but Viv was right. The changes I was making, I wished I had made sooner.

After the beach, I finished the last of the wallpaper removal. As I went down my driveway en route to Viv's house, I couldn't wait to tell her… celebrate with someone! But what about God's love…would it even come up, and would she want to hear? Her experiences with love had been different from mine. From early on, my parents told me how much they loved me. Their love lifted me gracefully through the air like a ballerina at ease. My father was a tender man and funny. He played checkers, took me on daddy/daughter date nights, read stories, and tucked me in each night. He was so kind-hearted that when his car hit a deer on a country road one day, he pulled over, got into the ditch, and held the creature in his arms until it died.

Love, for Viv, was never a drama-free joy. Her dad was nothing like mine. On one of our walks and talks across campus, she told me he'd take her to a bar every Sunday called Harry's and set her up on a high-top table. "Here kid, I bought you a burger." Then, he'd go join his buddies who were downing shots. He wasn't a warm and fuzzy teddy bear of a daddy, like mine, but more of a grizzly bear. And when not hibernating from drunkenness, he was angry and mean.

Viv didn't call him daddy for long. Ron was a roofer, smoked three packs a day—Lucky Strikes—and in the car, he'd puff away with the windows rolled up.

"Daddy, the smoke is burning my eyes. Roll the windows down."

"For crying out loud, whatever doesn't kill you makes you stronger, baby."

Viv's mother had issues of her own. She was passive-aggressive and critical. Rather than protecting Viv, she blamed her…blamed her very existence, pitting Viv's younger brother against her. She worked in a factory and did odd jobs here and there. One day she didn't come home, but left a note. She left Viv behind, but took the brother, and he grew up to be just like the father.

Although I had walked countless miles with Viv, I'd never worn her shoes. I didn't know what it felt like to feel unloved and uncared for.

Reaching the end of my driveway, I turned onto the road and saw Marita viciously pulling mail from Viv's box.

"Is everything okay?"

She looked at me with breaking news on her face. "No, everything is not okay, not good at all. I should not be telling you this, but the reason for that chair—" She shook her head like she didn't like what she was about to tell me. "Vivi drank too much—not one, not two, but three martinis. Lychee martinis." She tilted her head toward my property.

"Lychee from my trees?"

"Yes, but that is not all. After three lychee martinis, she climbed onto her golf cart."

"Uh oh."

"Yes, yes, and almost hit a man."

"Almost…you mean she didn't hit him?"

"No, but the poor old man, he was out taking a walk at night, and when she came full speed at him, he had no choice but to run straight into a swamp. Vivi swerved, crashing into a cabbage palm. The cart tipped over and landed on her legs. Thank goodness the man was not hurt, but still, his family is slapping her with lawsuits, robbing her of every penny. There were gators in that swamp. They didn't go after him, but still, the poor man has been suffering post-traumatic stress ever since."

My mouth dropped open. I wanted to borrow a machete and chop down that lychee tree in my yard—one more thing wrong with my property! Then again, it wasn't the lychee tree's fault any more than it had been the Tree of the Knowledge of Good and Evil's fault that day in the Garden of Eden. Eve—it was her fault, and Viv's fault, too.

"There is more!"

"How," I gasped. "How could there be more?"

"She is angry at herself. So angry, it had gotten her down. She is no longer working, or bringing in money. She is missing mortgage payments… facing foreclosure. The banks, they are calling every day now, writing too." She lifted her hands with the envelopes. "Late notices, and of course, late fees. I should not be telling you this. Pretend you do not know!"

It was too much to wrap my mind around. "What about a grace period? Isn't there a grace period?"

"Yes, yes, there is always a grace period. But one thing about grace periods…they end. All grace periods end." She blinked her eyes at me intently. "Do you know what this means?"

"Viv and I won't be neighbors for long," I said with a strange mix of emotions.

Marita looked at me like I had missed the main point. "You must tell her while you still have the chance!"

I knew what she meant. She wanted me to tell Viv about the Love and Grace of God. I gave her a wishy-washy shrug of the shoulders. After all I had gone through alone in my house removing wallpaper, I still wasn't sure how to share such a thing...wording it right with anyone.

Marita slipped the mail into her apron. Overlooking my wishy-washiness, she hooked arms with me in solidarity...leading me in a march toward the fortress in front of us, as if we were two comrades embarking on a sacred endeavor.

As we stormed up Viv's pyramid steps, I wondered—how hard could it be to tell my friend "you're loved...loved by God, and with a love beyond your wildest imagination," a free and unmerited love, unfailing, never-stopping...an eternal love. I rehearsed such words in my mind, but why did I need to rehearse?

TWENTY-THREE

INTERIOR DESIGN TIDBIT

* * *

What's calling out to you? Your junk drawer in need of cleaning?
The floor in your bathroom begging to be redone?
Whatever is calling to you, focus there next.

Viv's back was to us when we walked in, and her wheelchair parked up close to a wall. She was sketching the Golden Gate Bridge on the wall with charcoal. When she glanced over her shoulders to say hello, it was obvious from her smeared mascara that she had been crying again.

Marita rushed over, and handed her a tissue. "What is wrong, precious? I think I know but tell me. What now?"

"Life stinks, that's what wrong." Viv's lips curved downward into a pout. "It stinks as bad as Alcatraz during seagull nesting season, don't you think?"

I had never been to Alcatraz and didn't know what seagull nesting season smelled like. But I had experienced my own fair share of reeking moments, and knew that misery liked company. "I totally agree. Life can be tough. It can be so tough!"

If there were preachers in the room, they'd have told us right then and there that Jesus never promised things to be easy. He promised other amazing things, but never that life on Earth was going to be easy. In fact, it was going to stink at times. But there were no preachers present, and despite Marita casting me a pressuring look, a well-intended message like that coming from my mouth would have come out wrong.

Once the black was gone from under Viv's eyes, Marita took a step back, propping her hands on her hips. "Do yourself a favor, go without your makeup. Why bother if you plan to keep crying every day?"

"Oh, for crying out loud. I don't plan to cry! Who plans to cry?" Viv's enormous eyes flashed about. "Do you, Mar…do you wake up every morning and say, 'today I plan to cry'?"

"*Aye, aye, aye*, child. I will go into the kitchen now and get my stuff done. You girls talk."

I went over to the table with Viv's portfolio since I didn't get to compliment it the other day. "This, by the way, is amazing, Viv. I can't believe all the work you've done, and you did it in California, where you always wanted to live!"

"Don't get me started. I'm homesick…homesick for northern California. I'm not a Floridian. No offense to Florida, but it's true. I'm a fish out of water here." She turned her back and continued sketching on the wall. "You should have seen my former house, built right smack into the hill on the top of Lombard Street, overlooking the Bay. Getting down Lombard Street now in this chair would be a nightmare. But man, did I love that house, I'm not going to lie."

With the beach out her windows, it was hard to imagine a house nicer than the one she was in. "Must have been a very nice house!"

"You have no idea," she said miserably. "Too bad Mr. Dingbat got it."

"Mr. Who?"

"My second husband." She shook her head, like she wished she hadn't brought him up, and didn't want to talk about him. "A nasty fight, that's all I'll say. I lost. I lost a sweet house, and I can't get over my anger, my grief. I swear, I'm like those dog people—the ones who like dogs better than people, only I like my homes. I like them better than people. People can be pretty rotten. At least, I attract the rotten ones. It's hard not to. There's so many in this world, don't you agree?"

"I won't argue with that, but there's refreshing people, too. Lots of refreshing people in the world."

I walked over to a console and ran my fingers across a drum decorated with fish, birds, and flowers in concentric bands like ripples in a pond. "I'm sorry you lost that home." I couldn't tell her that I knew she was on the brink of losing her current home, too. "I'm really sorry, Viv. I am!"

"You should have seen it. It reminded me of Tiger's Nest Monastery."

"Tiger's Nest what?"

"Tiger's Nest Monastery, perched high on the edge of a three-thousand-foot cliff in Bhutan's Paro Valley. Of all the places I've gone, if I could blink my eyes, that's where I'd be." She sniffled. "Obviously, I'm not in a happy place right now. But oh well, it is what it is, right?"

I picked up an ancient-looking bronze bell with intricate carvings. "You sure did travel the world…went to all these cool places, did all these things you wanted to do."

She tucked the charcoal behind her ear and turned her chair around. "That's a Tibetan prayer bell. Go ahead, ring it. I ring it every day, I do. I sit here ringing it with my eyes closed."

"Why?"

"I don't know. I don't like what I see when my eyes are open."

"Yeah, the news?"

She made a face and nodded. "I try so hard. I close my eyes and try to see what I want to see."

"And what's that?"

"I don't know, a nostalgic version of the world, I guess." She closed her eyes. "*Trees of green, red roses, too.*"

"The Louis Armstrong song," I said with a laugh. "'What a Wonderful World.'"

She opened her eyes with a grin. "*Friends shaking hands, saying how do you do.*"

"'*They're really saying,*'" I sang along, "'*I love you.*'"

We both cracked up, but then Viv grew serious. "To tell you the truth, I'm not sure I believe in a wonderful world. In my opinion, it can be pretty unwonderful…full of toxic, emotionally draining people. So, if you're wondering about this temple theme going on here, and my reasons for it…well, I wish I had peace of mind, but it's not like I can just plaster the walls of my mind with peace. So instead, I do what I know how to do. I make my home feel like a perfect, sacred place, a hiding space apart from the unwonderful world, that's all."

I rang the bell again and again, listening to its clear, crisp sound. What she would say if I told her I was a temple, a temple of the Holy Spirit? And she could be one, too. The atmosphere within me wasn't perfect, though.

The only perfection in me was the work of Jesus—the gift of Salvation—perfect and complete.

"I'll bet a hundred bucks," she said with a know-it-all tone, "you're the tropical beach theme type."

"Huh?"

"Your house. I'll bet you're going with palm tree wallpaper, dolphin shower curtains, seashell soaps at all the sinks."

I put the Tibetan prayer bell down. The dolphin shower curtain sounded cute, but palm tree wallpaper? No thanks. I wasn't going to tell her about the tropical toilet seat I had bought online. "You're the expert. Should I go all out with the tropical theme?"

"Organic modern, or tropical modern," she advised right away. "Keep it simple. But really, it boils down to whatever makes you happy."

"What about you, does this temple theme make you happy?"

"I'm not going to lie, I have no idea what makes me happy anymore." She went back to the wall and continued shading an area of the Golden Gate Bridge. "Just about done, two seconds."

"Are you drawing that from your head, or is there a picture you're using for reference?"

"All in my head, my wacky head. I know the bridge. I lived right near it…walking distance. But now, almost every doggone night, it shows up in this dream I keep having, the same recurrent dream."

"Tell me."

"If you really want to know." She pointed to one end of the bridge. "It starts here. It always starts here. I step onto the bridge and start walking."

"Nice."

"No." She shook her head. "It's not nice. I make it halfway across, and I wake up. I never make it further, and it frustrates me."

"A midlife crisis dream," I said, like it was a no-brainer. "I have them, too…only I'm eating a chocolate bar and wake up halfway through it. I never get to eat the whole thing. No big deal."

"What are you talking about, it's a huge deal! What if it never happens, what if I never get to walk all the way across the Golden Gate Bridge ever again?"

"Okay, so you've walked it before."

"Actually, no. And that's what bothers me. All those years I lived there, I only walked it halfway. It drives me crazy, all the things I could have done, but didn't. I could have flown a kite at Crissy Field, could have watched a sunrise at Bernal Heights Park, could have run for Congress. Seems like everyone is doing it…everyone is running for Congress. And now, I can't. And even though I traveled all over the place, I feel like I'm not going anywhere anymore. I'm not doing anything good."

"You can still run for Congress, Viv."

"Would you vote for me?"

"I thought we weren't going there."

"Meh, it doesn't matter. I'm too old."

"That's ridiculous," I said. "We're babies in Congress years. But what is it that you want to focus on…in your second half of life? I'm no dream interpreter, but I think that's what your dream is about."

"This is going to sound bad." Her eyes were intense. "Don't judge me."

"Why would I judge you?"

"I'm struggling."

"Viv," I said, slightly offended. "Why would I judge you for that? It's something we all have in common. I struggle, too."

"I don't know, don't get me started. It's just…everybody talks resiliency. And there I was going along, doing my thing…skies were blue, clouds were white. Problems came. I survived, stronger than ever. I was very resilient." She shook her head. "Then, one stupid thing I did and there's no bouncing back. I can recover from difficulties, but not mistakes…a certain mistake I made, and a stupid one."

"What'd you do?" I wasn't supposed to know about her drinking the lychee martinis, then crashing the golf cart.

She shook her head. "I don't want to get into it. But here I am now. All I do is sit around watching news. I should get out more. I miss the smiling faces, but are people even smiling anymore? I'm not seeing it. All I see is this monster fog rolling in and everything I looked forward to on my calendar has been canceled. I kid you not, I'm not counting down to anything, you know what I mean?"

Of course, I knew what she meant! Everyone in the world knew. Plans being squashed was yet another thing we shared in common, along with doing stupid things, falling down here or there. We entered the world fallen...in a fallen state. None of us were perfect. All of us were flawed.

"Viv, remember when my fog rolled in? You know what I'm talking about...right after we bought our backpacks and were counting down the months."

"The whole itinerary planned," she added. "I had every country mapped out for us...leaving two days after graduation."

"Yep, and the fog rolled in for me. I lost sight of all the plans I had for my life. But you know what? I did what I had to do."

"I didn't make it easy, did I?"

No, when she heard she was losing her backpacking companion...I was having a baby instead...she made me feel guilty.

"Did you like my postcards?"

"Yep. I know I never acknowledged them."

"Well, maybe unintentionally, I was rubbing it in your face."

"Oh, you were. But it's okay. Believe it or not, the fog cleared, and I was in the most wonderful world...babies crying, watching them grow." I blinked away tears.

"Are you okay?"

"It gets me every time, how fast it went by, how before I knew it, they were off chasing their dreams, with me running behind, trying to keep up."

Her face broke into a satisfied smile. "What are you waiting for?" She threw her hands up. "Pat yourself on the back!"

"Why?"

"Oh, for crying out loud, look what you've done with your life, my friend!"

"What, I loved my kids, that's all."

"No, you sacrificed."

"That's what love is. I would have given my life for them. I still would."

"I beg you, pat yourself on the back."

She wasn't going to let up until I did it. I reached my right hand over my left shoulder and patted myself on the back. "Just so you know, I don't deserve to be patting myself on the back like this. Loving them was easy."

"Stop being so hard on yourself. Everybody says parenting is hard, grueling."

"True, but loving them was easy." I let out a second-thought laugh. "Okay, raising them was really, really hard at times, so maybe I do deserve to be patting myself on the back."

It felt great reuniting with Viv. I didn't want to think about the impending foreclosure, and our time being cut short. "Back to you." I crossed my arms and stared at her sketch on the wall. "You make it halfway across, then wake up. What are your goals, and are you taking action steps toward them?"

"How about you?" She skipped her turn, sending it back to me. "What are you focusing on now?"

Obviously, the house. But also, my marriage, although I didn't want to bring that up, make her feel bad. I was writing to my heart's galore, but preferred keeping that private. And focusing on God, reading His Word and getting to know and love Him more. I could have mentioned one of those, at least, but sat down on the red velvet sofa instead. "It's your turn. You can't skip your turn."

She wheeled herself across the singing, creaking floor, then parked in the middle of the room. "I can't remember the last steps I've taken... meaningful steps toward anything."

"Okay, well, that doesn't sound like the Viv I know."

"I know, but midlife is a beast, a brutal beast. I'd love to take it by the horns, but I don't know how. It's eating me alive."

"Oh, please," I said of her wording choice. She was the only person more dramatic with words than me.

"You came over to watch a sunset." She wiped her nose with her arm. "I am not letting my drama get in the way."

I glanced out the wall of a window, at the sky—mostly blue with hints of pink. There was plenty of time. "What's bothering you the most?"

"I want to go someplace, but I can't. I can't go anywhere. I feel guilty for saying it, but I want to travel."

"No reason to feel guilty for that. Where do you want to go?"

"I'd be happy going to the movie theater, for crying out loud. But since you asked, if I could go anywhere, I'd go to where I left off last—" her voice struggled "—before everything in my life got all messed up."

"And where was that?"

"Between the ancient ruins of the Angkor Wat to the modern Wat Rong Khun. And after that, back to the Bay Area." She sniffled.

"What's wrong?"

"It's nothing like it used to be, and I miss it. I miss my old city by the Bay." She sobbed loud as a blowhorn. "I'm a hot mess, I know. But it's like eating a layer cake every year for your birthday, then all of a sudden, the scrumptious layers of your life fall out. The cake isn't the same." She reached down and pulled up the ends of her flowing maxi dress, using it to wipe her face. "Angkor Wat. I'm so in the mood to go to Angkor Wat."

It was the writer in me. I needed to foreshadow something good. Christ was good—the most powerful reality one could discover—and I wanted to foreshadow Him. She could go to Him. If her life was a cake, well, wouldn't she want to go to the master chef, the expert at picking up the collapsed, fallen-out pieces and reassembling them better than before, filling us with the fruits of Christ, and with layers of peace, joy, and hope!

"In all your travels," I said, beating around the bush, "did you ever find what you were looking for?"

"You mean a higher being? Nope, and let me tell you, I've got a bone to pick. I mean, wouldn't you think, as I was stumbling my way through South America, the ruins of Machu Picchu, that this higher being might have given me a few hints as to His whereabouts? You know—*Marco.* Polo. *Marco.* Polo—tell me if I was getting hotter or colder. But nope, never so much as a *polo.*"

Refusing to slip back into my cowardly ways, I opened my mouth, ready to pipe out the truth of God's whereabouts, and how thanks to Christ, we didn't have to be without His presence. But then Marita walked in carrying a glass bowl filled with the oddest things I had ever seen. They looked like superballs coated in spikes, or crimson-colored spiny sea urchins I had seen on the beach.

"What on earth?"

"Rambutan." Marita set the bowl on the coffee table in front of us.

"Ram..." I started to say, but was flabbergasted at the sight of them. "Rambut...what?"

Marita covered her mouth with her hands, to hold in a laugh. "Fruit. The most exotic fruit on the planet." With radiant eyes, she leaned close to my ear, to share juicy gossip. "Cousin to the lychee. Vivi eats them like gumballs. She cannot get enough."

I wasn't sure how I felt about any fruit related to the lychee, given what happened to Viv. "I'm more of a pineapple person." *Oh, and mango,* I thought but didn't say. "I like apples and oranges, lemons and limes." I was nervous they were going to push the fruit on me when I was content with life's simpler fruits. "Where do these come from?"

"Honduras." Viv licked her lips the way I did when key lime pie was put down in front of me. "Well, these ones came from Honduras. But I ate them back when I was in Southeast Asia. Marita gets them for me right here on Sanibel, at the Farmer's Market."

"Rambu...what?"

"Rambutan," they both said in unison.

"They look like porcupines...miniature porcupines, and inedible."

"I swear we're not tricking you. It's fruit." Viv leaned forward in her chair, and with fingernails painted the color of pearls—rhinestones on every other one—she pulled one of the so-called fruits from the bowl, then twisted it open and popped its rose-tinted ball of inner flesh into her mouth, dropping its skin on the table.

"When I threw my parties," she said, chewing, "I'd put a bowl of these out. It got everybody talking. Let me tell you, if you need a conversation starter, put a bowl of these out."

"We were talking just fine before they came out."

Viv rolled her eyes, like I was a plain Jane she wanted to transform. "We live on the same planet, Addie. How have you gone all of these years without trying a rambutan?"

Her good old notorious grin was returning to her face. She grabbed another one, then twisted it open and popped it into her mouth. Challenging me to leave comfort zones and try new things had always been a form of recreation to her.

"So," I refused to let the fruit distract what we were talking about, "what have you been up to? How do you spend your time these days?"

"Only because you asked, I feel like I'm on a lazy river ride that won't end. All I do is sit around thinking."

"Nothing wrong with thinking. Thinking is good, right?"

"Yeah, if my thoughts were nice, but they're not. I finally realized it's healthy to limit, even end, contact with toxic people. For too long, I figured I had to be there for them…they're family. I wished I had known sooner, it's okay to distance myself…for my own mental well-being. Still, I have all these memories…tons of them, and they show up out of nowhere. Sometimes, I sit around all day, bullied by memories. No need to make a hoopla out of it. I wish I could pick and choose what I remember and what I forget. If you know how to do that, let me know. Seriously, tell me if you know. Our minds are so complex."

What did I know about the mind? Not a whole lot. My Spirit had been made new by God long ago, but the rest of me—including my worrywart mind—didn't match up to that part of me made righteous before God through Christ. I was praying, though, reading His Word, and looking forward to the renewal of my mind. But I was also a work-in-progress for the duration of my life on Earth, and some projects were taking longer than others. Letting go, trusting God with my worries was definitely taking longer. I was about to mention it, but the colors of the sunset were taking over the sky, turning it irresistible.

"Grab a rambutan," Viv said with an indoctrinating gleam in her eyes, "and let's go see that sunset. Trust me, once you try one, your bones will cry out for more. They're loaded with calcium."

There she went so passionately pushing a fruit at me, when I could hardly find the words to tell her how, at the framework of my being, every part of me was already crying out for fruit…fruit of a different kind.

The enormous window of a wall opened automatically; there in the corner stood Marita, clicking away at a remote control. I got up, ready to take flight like a peregrine at top speed, but Viv's face turned hesitant.

"What?" I insisted. "What's wrong?"

"It's been a while, that's all. Husband number three and I, we loved our sunsets. I'm sure he still watches it every night, over the Pacific. But I don't want to get into all of that. He's a good guy, we'll leave it at that."

Marita's head bobbed with adamant validation, catching my attention. "It is true," she confirmed from across the room, where she was dusting the Tibetan prayer bell. "A true gentleman. Oh, how he loved her, and still does…loves his Vi. What a beautiful pair, and if you could have seen the parties they threw on that wrap-around deck overlooking the sea. Tell her, Vivi," Marita's voice rang out louder than the bell she was dusting. "Tell her how much he loved you, but you did not accept it. You rejected his love." She hesitated, and then in a mumble loud enough to be heard, "You do not believe that you are loveable."

By then the sky was one hundred percent pink, and the loveliest shades of it, to where even those who didn't like pink would have been calling it their favorite color. The pink from the sky was pouring in, flooding the great room.

"To tell you the truth," Viv's eyes had a desolate look to them as she held onto her words for a moment, "I blame Ron. I do."

"Your father passed away years ago, didn't he?"

"Yep, but I blame him, I do."

It wasn't hard to connect the dots. The mental games and abusive words she heard all throughout her formative years had damaged her ability to believe she was worthy of love. And even the husband who loved her—the good guy and retired heart surgeon—wasn't enough to mend her hurting heart. Viv needed more. And more was never in short supply when the more was from God, the Great Physician, the only one in the world specializing in spiritual heart transplants—putting brand-new hearts into people and doing so for free.

Viv reached over and grabbed another one of the fruits, then squeezed it like a stress ball. "I don't even care. I don't care about love. It's a hassle. But I'll admit," she glanced over her shoulder at Marita, "he did love me, and I loved him. I'm just no good at accepting or expressing love, crazy as that sounds."

It didn't sound crazy. I had trouble expressing God's love. Writing about it was one thing, but talking another. Marita, from behind Viv's back, was winking over at me, as if my moment had come to introduce my friend to God's greatest expression of love, Jesus, the only perfect lover, and the One I crowned King in my heart. The room was pink and softening the expression on Viv's face. What would her expression have been if she caught wind of how much God loved her!

He loved me, too. His love was in me. It was like I had a brand-new air-conditioning unit installed within me years ago. What it produced was pure and fresh, and I wanted a burst of it to enter the room, but first, the words had to make their way through my intricate systems, which, neglected for years, were rusty. I wished I had understood sooner the significance of renewing my mind...updating my ways of thinking according to God's Word. Then maybe the love of God running through me didn't have to go through rusty mental pipes, or get stalled in various twists and diverting kinks. I wanted the refreshing words that were making their way to the tip of my tongue to flow more smoothly, and not get stuck along the way.

Viv was savoring each bite of her rambutan like I did sea salt chocolate truffles. I privately asked God to help work on things with me, clean my filter for particles of insecurity, so the words trapped within might flow out more freely. I wasn't perfect, and would never be. Only God was perfect, His Words the only ones perfect.

"What are we waiting for?" I refused to look at Marita, still cleaning the bell. "If we sit here a second longer, we're only going to wish we had done it sooner."

"What?"

"Gone out onto that wrap-around deck of yours to watch the sunset! Let's go."

TWENTY-FOUR

Sitting in chaise lounges on the wrap-around deck, overlooking the sea, was like having special box seats for a private viewing of one of the most spectacular shows on Earth—the sun falling into the horizon. But Viv didn't seem to be appreciating it; perhaps it was the impending foreclosure, along with the accumulation of all her problems. There was a look of fear in her eyes, like a massive tidal wave was heading right at her.

I wasn't judging her for not appreciating the sunset. Problems did that. They accumulated and became all-encompassing, dulling even the brilliant moments. The look on her face reminded me of times in my own life, when problems were overwhelming. But the performance in the sky reminded me that no matter how tough things got on Earth, there was always something bigger and more beautiful to look at, if even for a moment each day.

I couldn't help but look back and forth at the sunset, and at Viv. The changing expressions on her face, from fear to apathy, told the tale of a person, who after captaining for so long her own high-seas adventure called life, felt whipped and forlorn, uncertain whether she had any strength left to brave another wave or enjoy the sunset ever again.

"Enough about me. I'm tired of talking about me," she insisted, when she felt my stare. "You, let's talk about you. Tell me the gist of what happened to you after we lost touch."

I rested my hands behind my head and went back to where the riptides of life took hold, sending Viv and me far off into opposite directions. Talking up a storm, I didn't stop even when Marita stepped out, bringing us iced tea.

"Osmanthus tea," she whispered, putting the glasses into our hands, then going back inside.

In between sips of osmanthus tea I told Viv all about the leading roles I played as mother, wife, nurse, and grown daughter to my mom, along with the greatest challenges each role presented. I shared with her my all-time favorite scenes, as well as my biggest tear-jerking moments.

"There you have it," I said around the time the giant beach ball of a sun dropped into the water. "There you have the gist of my life. And now, it's just me and Peter in that bird house next door, fixing things up."

She put her empty glass down and clapped. I joined her, assuming we were applauding the sun, which played its part beautifully.

"Glad you're clapping," she said. "You deserve it, you do."

"Huh? We're clapping for the sun."

"No, we're not. We're clapping for you."

I held my hands still. "For me?"

"Addie." She rolled her eyes, like I should have known. "As I sat here taking it all in...your crazy, marvelous saga of around-the-clock hours at the hospital to make ends meet, raising your kids, bickering with Peter, butting heads over parenting styles, fighting about finances, and how you went all those years without a date night, and were like strangers passing in the hallway, sleeping in different rooms, and how you resented him for not helping you clean or cook, and how he snores and you hum...well, I kept waiting for it."

"Waiting for what?"

"The part where you split up."

I let out a giant laugh because wow, I had gone overboard with the honest realities of my marriage, life, and raising four kids.

"To tell you the truth, I'm shocked to hear that after all of that, you're happier than ever, the two of you in that falling-apart shack next door."

"Well," I felt like Peter deserved a compliment, "he's a good man. My Peter is a good man."

"The difference between you and me is you didn't chase him out. I would have taken out my broomstick...scared him away. What you did is a skill of its own. I wish I had that skill...learned sooner how to keep the good ones and not kick them out just because we had a bad moment or two. Man, I wish I learned all of that sooner. Am I the only one, or do we all have things we wish we learned sooner? How about you?"

I stared out at the Gulf of Mexico, wishing I had loosened my grip sooner, surrendering to Christ, letting Him be Captain of my life. And trusted sooner the Word, like a nautical chart, steering me through the storms. In all my life roles, if only I had appreciated how precious the scenes with God were, I'd have written in more of them. Better late than never, though. All those things we wished we had done sooner, better late than never.

I was about to say some of that, but Marita came back out carrying that doggone bowl of rambutan. I wasn't going to give the fruit more attention than it deserved, nor talk under pressure, with her listening. "If I had a deck like this," I said instead, "I'd watch the sunset every night."

Viv let out a startling sob. "I'm sorry," she said right away. "I hate when I do this, when I cry and don't want to." But then she let out another sob, followed by a convulsive gasp.

"It's okay. I cry, too." I didn't want her feeling self-conscious with me, the one who dropped to my knees in the dirt, crying out loud with the osprey. "You saw me that day, didn't you? Bawling my eyes out in the yard."

"Yeah, but I didn't know it was you. My window, it's so high up." She wiped her nose with her arm. "I figured whoever you were, you were a hot mess because of your house."

"Maybe a little because of the house, but really, it was something else." I looked around for Marita, expecting her to poke her head out, flash me a thumbs up. But she was nowhere to be seen. "I was crying out to God… that's what I was doing in my yard that day."

Viv looked at me like I was strange.

I quickly swished around a bunch of words in my mouth, things I wanted to say without sounding strange. Even though I had never so much as mentioned Him, I believed in the Son of God, the risen Christ. But somewhere in my life, I stopped thinking of Him in the mornings, and praying to Him at night. He was still there, always there. But I stopped noticing. Finally, I opened my mouth, hoping my words would flow out nicely and she wouldn't think I was spitting at her. "Like you sobbed a minute ago about the sunset, I was sobbing that day in my yard…missing God's presence in my life, and how I used to acknowledge Him, but hadn't for so long, that's all. I could have cried out in my closet, but it's too filled with cockroaches and who knows what else…black widows lurking in the corner."

She didn't call me a goofball, didn't say a word as she stared out at the ever-present Gulf. It was glistening from the sun, even though we couldn't see the sun. It was there, though, just under the horizon. And God was there, too. Even though I had stopped paying Him attention, He was still there, always there, and never left.

Since Viv said nothing, I claimed the stage as mine. "I came here thinking this place would refresh me…make me feel young again because tropical islands do that." I let out a laugh. "I needed more than a tropical island, though. My aunt sent my mom's old Bible, and that's what did it. That's what had the child of God in me coming out…missing the God I loved as a child."

"We think we know people, but we don't." Viv sounded flabbergasted. "We know the obvious, surface stuff, and that's what we talk about. But we don't know what's really inside, deeper…even in our friends, who we thought we knew."

So true. If I had a new attic put into my house years earlier, would anyone have known? Probably not. I never invited anyone up into my attic. Jesus performed his labor of love in me—put in me a new Spirit, making me righteous before God. But how would anyone know if I kept the gift of salvation all boxed up for years, hidden away in the attic, serving no purpose other than being ready for Heaven one day?

"You think God heard you? You think He heard you crying?"

"I know He did. I know He heard me."

"How do you know?"

"I just do, He puts that knowing in me. I also read it in the Bible, He hears His children when they cry out."

Her mouth dropped open, displaying the giant gap between her two front teeth.

"What's wrong?" I asked.

"Tell me you're not one of them," she said with a grin.

"One of who?"

"I'll tell you what Ron used to say." She stole the stage with her gift of impersonation, gesturing her hands like smoking a cigarette. "He'd tell me, 'Stay away from them hippos, baby—herds of them eyeballing everything you do. They're everywhere, and they'll eat you alive with their enormous mouths. First, they devour the Bible, then they come after us. We're like dessert to them. Just the other night, one of them was chasing after me into the parking lot at the bar…beat me to the last parking spot.'"

"You mean hypocrites? He was talking about hypocrites?"

"Yeah, but six-year-old me thought there were hippos roaming wild in the neighborhood. And that he was sneaking out in the middle of the night—working as a hippo poacher. I'm not lying, I looked all over the house for ivory and teeth but couldn't find any."

I felt sad for my friend. The person who fed her lies still influenced her life.

"'Them Christians,'" Viv went on, her voice raspier than ever, "'them Christians are smoking crack, that's what they're doing. For crying out loud, the guy has been gone for over two thousand years. So, let's make a deal, baby. If you see Jesus Christ coming down from the sky, together with the Easter Bunny and Santa Claus, I kid you not, I'll buy you the Brooklyn Bridge. Heck, send Him my way. I'll buy Him a beer at Harry's. All He has to do is pay the tip. He can do that, right? The guy can pay the tip?'"

I wanted to mention He already paid…paid with His blood the price for our sins, but she swatted her hand in the air, as if swatting away the conversation. "Let's not go there," she said. "Seriously, my friend, like politics, let's not go there."

Privately scolding myself for having paddled around so long in my own insecurities, and for the conversation capsizing as it had, I sat up in the chaise lounge and looked around for Marita. I wanted to tell her to go find someone else. I was giving up, abandoning all efforts of offering hope and sharing God's love with Viv. But Marita was nowhere to be seen.

I was glad when Viv yawned. It was a slow, drawn-out, exaggerated yawn, accompanied by a series of loud gasps, and if I hadn't inspired her to become an interior designer, I would have encouraged her to become an actress. Her sleepy act would have won her an award.

"I used to be the life of the party. Look at me now, I'm a party pooper."

"You're not a party pooper. You're tired, that's all." I got up from the chaise lounge. "My time to go."

"No, I'm a party pooper. I really am."

I knew from being a mother how to detect when someone acted like they wanted me gone, but wished for me to stay. To lighten things up, I reached into the glass bowl and grabbed one of the funny-looking fruits, then tossed it at her like a superball.

Letting out a howl of laughter, she caught it, and whipped it back at me.

I caught it as well, and surprising even myself, I twisted its leathery skin open, and popped the rambutan into my mouth as Viv hooted and hollered. To my astonishment, it was like a chewy ball of cantaloupe but less sweet, and I vowed to never judge a fruit by its skin again.

"Okay, now I do have to get going."

"Sure, but don't go straight home. I beg you, leave from my deck, walk to the beach," she tilted her head toward the water, "and put your feet in, will you?"

I gave her a look. "Why?"

"You can, for crying out loud. No other reason than you can."

Maybe she wanted to live such a thing vicariously through me. "I could probably do that." I started down the steps, then stopped and looked back up at her. "On one condition, though."

"What?"

"Tomorrow you go for a…" I paused in search of a more fitting word than walk, "a stroll around the island with me."

"Tomorrow is no good."

"How about the next day? I'll come over and we'll go for a stroll the next day."

She shook her head. "Nope, physical therapy. I've canceled the last five. Marita won't let me cancel another."

I wanted to ask why she had canceled physical therapy, but didn't dare…didn't want to trigger more sobs. "Okay, the day after that then?"

"No can do. Mr. Lawyer is coming. Saturday is no good, either. Oh well, we tried. Now go put those feet of yours in the water!"

Her game of excuses was ridiculous, and her acting a disappointment to me. I wasn't buying it. "How about Thursday?"

She wheeled her chair to the edge of the deck. "I can't think what, but I've got something happening on Thursday." Her eyes were like a fibbing child's, and she looked away.

"Cancel it." I started along the winding wooden boardwalk through a field of sea oats. "I'll swing by late Thursday morning, be ready." I kept going without looking back. I didn't want to give her the chance to come up with more excuses.

TWENTY-FIVE

INTERIOR DESIGN TIDBITS

* * *

Welcome in that which brings life to your home.

* * *

Put one mismatched item in every room,
an item that doesn't fit in with your theme, color scheme, or patterns.

I was doing what she asked me to do, but it seemed like an insensitive thing—walking along the winding trail through the field of sea oats to the beach, while Viv, unable to walk, watched from afar. There had to be a profound and meaningful reason why she wanted me doing it.

Peter and my other friends at college never understood my friendship with the offbeat Viv. But they didn't know her like I did. We didn't just play dolls together. We learned our first cartwheels together, and lit our first match. I hid in the bushes with her when her drunken father ran through the streets at dusk screaming out her name. For a lot of kids, college was like an extension of their childhood, but for Viv it was her first time away from a dysfunctional home.

Granted, she had bad habits: wandering into my dorm room as if it were a thrift shop, rummaging through my closet for whatever she felt like wearing. Then again, when she decided she outgrew her dolls, she gave me all their clothes! In college she owned nothing of her own except her opinions, her views, and her passion for wanting world peace. She had so little—not even peace of mind—but wanted so much.

Nothing about her coordinated with the pattern of friends I hung out with who were proper, polite, and preppy. She unhinged me like none of them did, and got me talking, laughing, crying, and thinking about things I wouldn't have otherwise.

Halfway to the shore, I peeked over my shoulder and there she was, watching from that deck of hers. The deck was so lit up and what a shame, it took away from the stars. I gave a happy-go-lucky wave, while trying to ignore the uneasiness forming within me—the burden of living right next door to an all-consuming someone whose expectations of life and whose disappointments of it had always been and still were, it seemed, more numerous than the stars and bigger than the planets.

Whether it was serendipity, Divine Providence, or coincidence, Viv in my life was a complicated matter. It required filtering and separating her dramas from mine. I didn't mind us mixing together the contents of our minds for the sake of coming up with solutions, but I needed to be careful and not neglect my own dramas. They deserved attention, too.

My dramas, though, were nothing in comparison to hers. Her dramas had a way of knocking mine into perspective. A frog in my house, a wobbly toilet seat, and a husband sounding like a mating alligator when he snored were laughable, compared to what Viv was going through.

When I was almost at the shore, I heard a peculiar *honk*. It sounded like a goose, but there were no geese on Sanibel. I stopped walking and listened, then heard the *honk* again. It was coming from Viv's house, and I should have known, should have recognized the honking right away. It was the sound honking she had let out during our uncontrollable laughing episode the first day of dance class, and after that, we turned it into our own meaningful sound.

Some friends had ritualistic handshakes. We had her hilarious *honk*, followed by my quirky *quack*. Even though people looked at us, we did it all the time, and it became our custom. We thought we were hilarious, even if no one else did.

Honk! She did it again.

I had to answer back. If I didn't, she'd *honk* again. She was like that. She'd *honk* and *honk* and *honk* until I *quacked* back.

There was no one else around. I kicked my flip flops off, then stepped ankle deep into the warm water. *Quack!*

I waited for a return honk, but with much relief, it never came. She must have been satisfied. With my back to her, I stared out at the Gulf of Mexico. It was so immense in comparison to everything else, and I was in awe of its magnitude, how its tides carried shells all the way to the shore, washing up around my feet. But I was more in awe of the One who formed the sea, the One bigger and more powerful than it. I had no desire to swim out into the depths of the sea to where the seashells came from, but my desire was strong to draw nearer to Him. He desired that, too. He sent Truth all the way from Heaven to Earth, and His love washed up around us.

I didn't look, but was Viv still watching? What would she say if I told her I was appreciating the gravitational interaction, the pull between me and God that was causing my heart to bulge in His direction! I was dramatic, but if there was such a thing—a rise and fall to my appreciating God's presence—well, it was stronger than ever. I never wanted it to fall again, never wanted to be standing at the shore at high tide, unaware of the water rushing in.

Whether she was watching me or not, I went ahead and got down on my knees in the shallow water and prayed for Viv. I prayed she'd welcome the living, breathing, life-bringing Christ into her home, into her life.

Yay for the stars, her deck lights were out when I stood up again. If she had seen me on my knees, come Thursday, she might ask what I had been doing. Then, I could tell her I was going—not to a make-believe happy place—but straight into the arms of the One and Only real God. Going to a place of praise, praising the maker of me, the sea, the sand, and the shells. And going to the Author of my life, the One who penned me into being and knows how my story ends. That's what I'd say if she saw me on my knees in the water and happened to ask what I was doing. I was going to the reliable, practical, ever-present source of living eternal light…the One who loved me, and gave me strength.

I headed for home. If she didn't ask what I was doing on my knees in the water, would I tell her anyway? What were friends supposed to do— listen to each other's problems, or listen but also offer hope?

TWENTY-SIX

* * *

"The God who made the world and everything
in it is the Lord of Heaven and earth and does
not live in temples built by hands."
—Acts 17:24

*To the Lord of Heaven and Earth, to the One who does not live in temples
built by hands,*

*Soon, I'll be known as the island 'bench lady.' Here I sit on another bench—a
white wooden one parked beneath the canopy of a banyan tree on Periwinkle
Way. I'm not sure about the squatter's rights on Sanibel, but I could stay here
all day, sitting in Your presence.*

*You're the One who brainstormed me into being and knit me together in
my mother's womb. With utmost knowledge and proficiency, You elaborately
and intelligently designed me. You're my master architect, and once I accepted
the work of Jesus, You made me into a walking temple of the Holy Spirit.*

*I was reading from the Old Testament this morning how when the build-
ing of Solomon's temple in Jerusalem was finished, the people celebrated and
dedicated it to You. In the midst of their celebration, fire flashed down from
Heaven and Your presence (Your glory) filled the temple.*

*It will take the rest of my life here on Earth for me to be transformed into
all that You have in mind for me—more Christ-like characteristics—but that
same presence (Your glory) is already in me. Talk about reasons to celebrate!*

*You never left me. Even though in the year leading up to this trip I was
too busy and overwhelmed to give You a second of my day, You were here and
waiting for me to sit and talk with You, like I used to do. With every step I'm*

taking—crying out from my heart, reading from Your Word, repenting of my sins, sitting in Your presence, walking and talking with You—I feel close to You again, and refreshed. It makes me want to celebrate.

I'm no skilled musician, though, like King David. I've never touched a harp and can't read a note, let alone carry a tune. But the reality of Your presence and Your love has my heart writing a song of its own, my soul striking the tambourine, and my mind playing its own melodious harp and lyre. I'm so filled with joy and praise. My insides feel like Carnegie Hall. You, the conductor of joy, are at work in me, blasting sounds of re-joicing. My thoughts, emotions, and will are in concert together—nothing less than 'Carol of the Bells' ringing from within. At least, that's what I'm feeling when I sit here with You, God.

When Solomon prayed the dedication of the temple, even he knew the building was inadequate for You, who are present everywhere and cannot be confined to any human structure.

"But will God really dwell on earth with men?
The heavens, even the highest heavens, cannot contain you.
How much less this temple I have built?"
—2 Chronicles 6:18

And yet, You're willing to put Your Spirit here on Earth in an ordinary woman, a sinner like me. For that, I thank Jesus. He's the one who made me righteous in Your sight. And You're the One who sent Him. The plan was Yours…a plan of love. What else was it, but love? You loved the world so much. I feel so loved!

Love,

Finley (who is writing your verses on pieces of scratch paper and carrying them in her pocket, pulling them out and looking at them from time to time)

* * *

"But the Lord said to Samuel, 'Do not consider his ap-pearance or his height, for I have rejected him. The Lord

does not look at the things man looks at. Man looks at the outward appearance, but the Lord looks at the heart.'"
—1 Samuel 16:7

* * *

"But those who hope in the Lord will renew their strength;
they will fly up on wings like eagles;
they will run and not be tired;
they will walk and not be weary."
—Isaiah 40:31

TWENTY-SEVEN

As I waited for my morning coffee to brew, I copied the verses Mom had at the end of her letter onto scratch paper, and made it my goal to memorize them. I wanted God's Word to stay put permanently on the walls of my mind.

Coffee in hand, I went outside and sat down on the bottom porch step to write. But a low-hanging sea grape branch moving with the breeze kept brushing through my hair. I reached up and grabbed hold of the branch, pulling off one of its grapes. When I let go, the dew-drenched limb shook, giving me a refreshing shower.

I wrote about the refreshing twist, how I was God's project, His work-in-progress. The interior design tidbits were helping with the work I was doing on Hidden Potential. But the Bible—chock full of everything anyone in the messed-up world needed to know about God, humankind, and eternity packed into one place—was fast becoming my definitive resource for everything related to the interior design of me as a temple of the Holy Spirit. There was no tool more valuable and necessary than God's Word at work in my life. It was speaking Truth to my imagination, my reasoning, my intellect, my emotions, and my will.

Good thing Peter wasn't around, looking over my shoulder at what I was writing. He'd have told me it was over the top. But God's love for me and my love for Him *was* over the top. And I felt comfortable writing about it until an immature laughing gull flew overhead, interrupting my momentum.

"Ha…ha…ha…" went its raucous high-pitched *kee-agh* call, as if the laughing gull was laughing at me.

It was my imagination. Why would a bird have laughed at me? "Laugh at me all you want." I shook my finger at the bird. "I like what I'm writing, and some of my story is fiction, but I know well the difference between imagination and reality. Everything God...His Word, His love...is real."

The laughing gull flew off and I wrote again, refusing to let fear and insecurity devour the spiritual seeds rooting within. If I let that happen, if I continued to ignore God's Word like I had in the past, where would Truth find me next—a withering old lady about to be dropped into the soil, fighting off ravenous birds, kicking away rocks, and choking up excuses as to why I still wasn't ready to let Truth take root?

When I felt droplets of dew, I looked up at the sea grape tree. Several of its grapes in a single cluster were purplish and ready for picking, while others were hard and green. Not just the grapes, the sea grape leaves were of varying colors, too. Tough and hardy crimson leaves hung on sturdy petioles beside shiny ornamental bronze leaves, while soft and silky pinkish leaves were emerging right beside red-veined green leaves. Even the red-veined green leaves ranged in hue from light green to dark. The ruby and purple leaves that carpeted the bottom porch step where I sat were glorious.

The contrasting stages of maturity within a single sea grape tree was beautiful, and it got me thinking about the contrasting stages of spiritual maturity. People clustered together with others of the same faith—like grapes on a tree—but each person's spiritual ripening within that faith varied.

If in the spring of my life I told God, "Not now—come back in the summer," then when summer came, "Oops, God, I meant fall," and when fall arrived, "winter is around the corner, so how about You try me again then?" If I went on as I had in resisting Him, when would I ever have matured? Later rather than sooner, or not at all.

After a while, I got up from the porch step and went for a walk to the end of our road, where, under a towering Australian pine, stood a family. They were all in bathing suits and flip flops, as if they had left the beach and were wandering off the beaten track, which happened to be my road. The oldest-looking woman was pointing upward and the others were marveling, clapping their hands.

"What's up there? What are you all looking at?"

"An eagle," said a boy with binoculars to his eyes. "An American bald eagle...it flew from that tree."

My head held back, I saw the laughing gull that had been laughing at me and the osprey that lived outside my front door. Both flew right over us, but I didn't see an eagle.

"Are you sure it wasn't an osprey? Eagles and ospreys look a lot alike." I had been reading my wildlife books and learning the difference between all kinds of things—dolphin fins and shark fins, pink flamingoes and roseate spoonbills, water and cottonmouth snakes, good frogs and dangerous ones.

"Did it have a black chest?" I asked, staring upward with the group. "It has to have a black chest to be an eagle."

"Yup, I think so. I think it had a black chest, but I'm not sure. It's behind all those clouds right now."

They were large clouds, and eagles soared in circles. I didn't want to stand there all day, so I left the group and continued walking. But the experience got me thinking. Just like the wildlife books taught the differentiating characteristics of things in nature, the Bible revealed the distinct characteristics of certain things, too.

"Say what, child?" Ms. Viola had said one Sunday when I went up to the table where she sat during private question time. "You wonder if you're talking to the right God?" She picked up her Bible, lifted it high over her head, and held it there. "This is not a silly little storybook in my hands. It is the living, breathing Word of God and from it you will learn His characteristics and traits. Dear, sweet child, there is no reason for you to wonder if you're praying to the right God when in this book, He tells us who He is."

By then, her old and frail arms shook holding the heavy-as-a-brick Bible high overhead, and it caught the attention of the class. Crayons dropped, and the room went quiet.

"It's okay everybody," she said to the class, then stood up, "I was telling Miss Adele here, that when you are praying, there is no need to wonder if you're talking to some made-up, imaginary friend…not when you know what's in this book." She could have ended it right there, and I would have been satisfied with her answer. But Ms. Viola wasn't an ordinary teacher. She was extraordinary, so with the Bible still high over her head, and her frail arms shaking, she stepped up onto the tiny chair meant for children.

"Read, learn, study your Bible. It will teach you the characteristic traits of the One and Only true God, and teach you the difference between things, between God and His look-a-likes, good and evil, truth and lies, true prophets and false prophets, and right from wrong."

When the tiny chair she was standing on wobbled, the boy I had thought was a bully walked up and took the Bible from her hands, then helped her down.

"Believe me, children," she said in a whisper so low that everyone sat forward in their chairs to hear, "there will come a day when things are going to look confusingly more and more alike in the world, so you better know. You better know the difference between things!"

By then, I had already made it to the end of the road, turned around and was headed back, passing by Viv's house. It upset me...Ron, the self-proclaimed expert at identifying Christian phonies. He loved to call them out, and wasn't the only one. Declaring people authentic or fake had become a spectator sport. It was like bird watching, scrutinizing every chirp, observing every flap of their wings and flaunting of plumage, then calling it out the second they fell from the tree. "I thought she was a Christian. Guess not, guess I was wrong."

I pulled from my pocket the scratch paper with one of the two Bible verses I was memorizing—the one having to do with what God saw when He looked at me compared to what others saw when they looked at me. I liked what God saw. He saw my heart. I read the verse again and again as I walked, not wanting to forget there were always those matters that only God distinguished. None of us could have acquired the knowledge or skill to perfectly focus the telescope of mercy and grace into anyone's heart the way He did.

When a carload of people came down the narrow road, I stepped onto the grass to let them go by. They were *oohing* and *aahing* at Viv's beautiful rooftop sticking out from the trees. Good thing my house wasn't sticking out. They'd be gawking instead. Then again, no one had any idea of all the work underway inside.

It was similar with me. I was no model home, so to speak. I had so many flaws, and parts of me were a total mess. But a walking temple of the Holy Spirit, God was at work in me, whether others saw it or not.

My relationship with Christ had nothing to do with putting on a show of illusion and impossible perfection to impress others.

The nature books told me all kinds of things. Laughing gulls laughed, ospreys returned to their same nest year after year, roseate spoonbills probed for food in the water with their large, rounded bills. But when it came to people, who ever said Christians behaved perfectly? Only Jesus was perfect, and although I wanted to strive to be more like Him, acquiring Christ-like characteristics was a lifelong process that involved getting to know, love, and walk with Him daily.

The only perfect part of me was the part Jesus made righteous before God. I was horrible with numbers, but hopefully that meant I was at least one-third perfect. As for the other two parts of me…mind and flesh…they were far from perfect, and needed fine tuning in order to perform their daily tasks more harmoniously in sync with the Spirit of Christ within. But it wasn't easy. There were differences between flesh and spirit, and mine were on different pages, so to speak, and often, not even playing the same song.

But God saw Jesus' perfect and complete work of salvation and the Spirit of Christ within me and in all believers, and it differentiated us from non-believers. We accepted and took hold of God's Branch of Righteousness extended from Heaven to Earth, the one and only branch leading into God's presence. Even from then, however, believers still sinned. Sin we shared in common. But after falling from God's hand, instead of getting up by themselves and cleaning themselves off, true believers cried out to God. It was one of the behaviors to watch for in differentiating believers from non.

"You heard me cry out, when I was down on my knees in repentance for having fallen, fallen away from You. You heard my fallen chirps, saw my broken wings, and cheered me on in the Spirit as I limped my way back, and I thank You. Thank You for loving me so much!"

I said all of that out loud, even as the carload of people went by again and saw my lips moving. I had no earbuds in, nothing to make it look like I was talking on my phone or singing to music. But oh well, I continued walking and talking with the One who was known for picking people up when they were down, brushing the dirt off of them, and giving them a fresh start.

Laughing gulls liked to live around tidewater, roseate spoonbills in marsh-like areas, and osprey in almost any expanse of shallow, fish-filled water. I wanted to live in the palm of God's hand, and from there, learn to forage for food, sing, and fly…so should I fall, He would see and listen for my cries, then help me up again. I pulled the other verse from my pocket as another reminder. Believers knew in their hearts that when they were down and out and tired, if they hoped in the Lord, their strength would be renewed. And they would fly up on wings like eagles.

I arrived back and joined the group of tourists, still looking up, waiting, watching the sky for what we all hoped was a bald eagle. Sure enough, the clouds parted, and my own eyes saw it—the *Haliaeetus leucocephalus*—the majestic and regal symbol of our great nation soaring overhead. It was, after all, what the people believed it to be. The characteristics were there. I had read the books that told me what to watch for. Larger than an osprey, its chest and underside were dark, and it held its wings as it flew. When it landed in a nest high up on the tallest tree, we all clapped.

I clapped and clapped and was still clapping even when everyone else had stopped, but how could I not when there I was, not visiting, but living on a sanctuary island where the American bald eagle, once on the brink of extinction, was living and thriving. It reminded me that anything was possible, even when great things were at risk and entering extinction, there was always hope of a comeback, greater than ever. I pulled out my cell phone and took pictures, then texted them to Peter and the kids, it was so amazing.

But how much more amazing—the One who made nature, and thought up the entirety of space, time, matter, and energy, the master-mind behind the physical laws and the constants that govern them, put His Spirit not up in the highest, unreachable tree, nor in some elaborately adorned brick and mortar building, but took up residency in those who loved Him, like me.

I left the group and headed for home. What else was it but love? Whoever believed in Him would not perish but live eternally with Him. And He put His Spirit in those who believed, making them walking, talking temples, sanctuaries of the Holy Spirit. Such walking, talking sanctuaries of the Holy Spirit were out there all over the world, their numbers ever-increasing.

More than once, Mom had tried telling me how amazing it all was, how not only was God present with us, but His presence brought all kinds of things…hope, strength, peace, wisdom, and so much more than what we could have imagined for ourselves. Mom had been right all along. God's love was amazing.

TWENTY-EIGHT

INTERIOR DESIGN TIDBIT

* * *

Replace old, space-robbing kitchen appliances,
and enjoy the amazing features only new appliances offer.

My stomach growling, I stood in the kitchen with my hands on my hips, glaring at the nasty old oven that came with the place. The thing was filthy, and the reason I had been eating fruits, nuts, and salads that didn't require cooking. Even the osprey was eating better than me—I saw it through the kitchen window, sitting on a post, picking apart a fish—although I liked my fish broiled, baked, fried, or roasted. I wanted to haul the heavy-as-an elephant oven down the steps and out to the drive, but a new oven wasn't in our budget.

When my stomach growled loud as a launching space shuttle, I sat down with my laptop on the kitchen floor, and took off on a mission all over the world, landing on a website featuring a contemporary stainless steel double electric wall oven with an eco-friendly, two-hour self-clean cycle.

I called Peter, who was still in Michigan but coming home in a day. "Glad everyone is having you for dinner, good for you. How are those good old Michigan pot roasts and meatloaf tasting? I'm still eating pretty much locusts and wild honey here."

"Nope," he said automatically, "no new oven, if that's what you're getting at."

"Why not?"

"Why not…are you kidding me? It would be financially reckless, that's why. Unless I win this account, or you're planning to go back to work, no way…not right now. Don't forget, we need a washer and dryer, too. We have to pick and choose, right? That means putting things on hold."

Peter was right, and I felt bad for having pushed it. He was the one bringing home the bacon. "What about a small microwave, then?"

"I was thinking a grill."

"A grill? What about coyotes, bobcats, and palm rats smelling your steak? What a fun backyard barbecue that would be."

I spent the rest of the evening searching online for recipes that didn't require cooking. Ceviche looked good. All I had to do was marinate shrimp in the juice of lemons, letting the citrus do the cooking for us. But just like with the lemon bars, I stubbornly wanted to use lemons from our own trees, so I put that recipe on hold for the day when there was fruit in my yard.

In the meantime, I could have tossed shrimp into a pan, put it out onto our drive, and let Chef Sun sizzle it up, sauté us an appy. People did that with eggs. I'd even add a few tablespoons of olive oil, finely chopped garlic, fresh flat-leaf parsley, salt, pepper, a drizzle of lime juice, a splash of fine sherry, and put the pan on top of the minivan, so it would be closer to the heat. Or Peter and I could cook kabobs over an open fire in the yard.

Enough procrastinating with crazy ideas. I turned the old filthy oven on to 150 degrees, then poured half a cup of ammonia into a dishpan, setting it on the top shelf of the oven, then putting a boiling pan of water on the bottom shelf.

"Ha-ha-ha," I said to the oven, as if it were a horrible beast. "Like it or not, come morning, your detestable insides will be clean. Night-night, you filthy, nasty, wretched oven."

TWENTY-NINE

* * *

"What agreement is there between the temple of God and
idols? For we are the temple of the living God. As God
has said: "I will live with them and walk among them,
and I will be their God, and they will be my people."
—2 Corinthians 6:16

To the One who lives with us and walks among us, to You, my God, hi.

*I'm back on the bench outside the general store. They have great coffee, al-
though I finished mine a while ago, and I'm still here. I don't want to go. I
want to sit with You, although I should get up and move to another bench—or
they might start charging me bench rent.*

*So, even though they had celebrated and dedicated Solomon's magnificent
temple to You—with good intentions of bringing You glory—things got complicated. There was a repetitive cycle of good kings in reign, then bad kings in reign,
good kings, then bad, and along with that the people got caught up in bringing
You glory for a while, then not bringing You glory, bringing You glory, then
not—over and over again. The bad kings kept undoing what the good kings had
done, and the good kings kept undoing what the bad kings had done.*

*When the bad kings were in reign, idols crept into the temple and the people
turned away from You. When the good kings came, they chased the idols out and
the people returned to You. It was during a good king's reign that the temple was
restored back to Your original design—that place on Earth in Old Testament
times (before Jesus came to Earth) where You were especially present to the people.*

*Because You cared about the people, when yet another bad king began to reign,
You sent Your prophet Jeremiah. A true prophet, Jeremiah urged Your people to*

humbly return to You and repent. But the words of a true prophet didn't sound appealing to people who preferred the tantalizing lies of a false prophet.

Yet another bad king came to power in the temple and even after doing evil in Your eyes, this bad king refused to humble himself before You. His heart was hardened, and he went on influencing the people to follow detestable practices that defiled the temple.

Then came another good king and upon hearing Your Word, the good king Josiah launched tremendous efforts to rid the temple of idols. It involved hauling and pushing out, tearing down, cutting into pieces, smashing, burning, and crushing the idols. But even after all of that, another bad king came into power and with him, the cycle continued. The temple—once filled with Your presence—was eventually ransacked, corrupted, and destroyed by the Babylonians.

You know I've gone days, weeks, months belting out praises and celebrating Jesus' work of salvation in me, but also entire stretches of time without so much as thinking of You. A distraction in my life takes over and before I know it, I'm no longer living in a glory-to-You sort of way.

I'm a temple of the Holy Spirit, but still stand vulnerable to idols creeping in. It's happened before and can happen again. Help me, Lord, to recognize the idols in my life, all those sneaky rascals that disguise themselves in fancy packaging, masquerading in costumes, deceiving and playing tricks on my mind. They appear harmless at first, but before I know it, they consume my time and energy, keeping me from what matters.

I've tried talking to the kids about idols. If you let them into your life, let them run wild, they'll try taking ownership of you. Like slumlords, they'll keep you in rundown places, leaving you with no time or energy to work on fixing up the broken areas of your life. The kids think I'm overexaggerating (I used to think the same of my own mother, who happened to be melodramatic with her words, too). But how can I not be when there are so many things in this world that have gotten in the way of, and even tried to destroy my relationship with You?

When I don't recognize them for what they are, when I allow idols into my life, they trick me into thinking Your love for me has faded, and the work You did in me was only a feel-good façade. They interfere with my walking and talking with You, and sitting in Your presence, and my faith begins to crumble and I forget how much I love You. But then I read Your Word and it reminds me of the Truth: that Your love for me is unfading. And the labor of love Jesus did for me was perfect and everlasting. A temple of the Holy Spirit, resurrection lives in me!

I wish I could go on and on, writing You my thoughts, but it's time for me to get up from the bench and go to the beach, or the kids will be waiting. Just know I need You! As long as I live in this temporary world, I stand vulnerable to ransacking idols and need you as my good king, the one and only good king reigning within. My landlord, too, please be the landlord of my life. And if those sneaky idols try creeping in, help me recognize them for what they are and kick them all out!

You specialize in that. You took on my sins, and made me righteous. It wasn't just a beautification project. The work You did in me was a matter of life and death, and I thank You, my Lord.

Love you. Bye-bye.
Finley (who wishes she could wear a t-shirt that says, Work in Progress, *or* Masterpiece in the Making, *or* Restoration Underway *because although there are things that I'm continuously working on with You, at least the work is underway)*

P.S. I keep wondering if my book club sisters would want to join me in reading the Bible in a year. Or one book from the Bible. Granted, at the start of our group so long ago, we vowed to never talk religion or politics, but still. We've read and discussed everything from murder mysteries to literary masterpieces, to romance novels. We even read The Velveteen Rabbit *once, and the discussion that followed had us all crying like babies. Why can't we talk about You, God? I'll ask them when I get home. We could read the book of John or something.*

THIRTY

Blame it on having read Mom's letter to God right before bed, I woke the next morning not to an alarm clock, but an urgency within. I was more than ready to ask God's help with the evacuation of idols in my life.

At the same time, I had to deal with the oven, and when I opened its door and poked my head inside, I gagged. So much for ammonia—the heat- and acid-resistant porcelain enamel walls were still coated in stubborn, built-up grime. It grossed me out…cleaning out other peoples' gunk. My own gunk was one thing, but someone else's gunk another.

As I slid my hands into a pretty pair of purple latex gloves, I wished Mom was with me so we could have enjoyed our own discussion. She and her book clubbies never ended up reading the book of John or anything from the Bible. They read more romance novels, though. I used to hide in the hallway, spying on their juicy discussions while covering my mouth, trying not to laugh. All kidding aside, Mom loved good, in-depth talks, and if she was with me, I'd have told her what my idols were.

"They're whatever I'm doing when I hang an *out to lunch* sign in God's face," I mumbled as I stuck my face into the scummy oven. "At least, I think that's what they are."

Although different for everyone, for me idols were the nonessentials that barged into my life and took over, occupying every free moment alone that I had, stealing my attention and pulling me away from sitting on a bench in God's presence, or walking and talking with Him. Looking back on my entire adult life, whenever I found myself on a bench the first thing I did was pull out my cell phone and read local, national, and if time allowed, world news. And if ever I went for a walk, I called a friend and yacked the whole way. Reading news and yacking with friends was good.

But I chose it over reading God's Word, sitting in His presence, or walking and talking with Him instead.

I needed to continue reading about and learning the difference between idols and sin. I wasn't sure what it was, but a certain multilayered emotion of mine (a mixture of disappointment, disgust, anger, and fear, otherwise known as resentment) also had a way of taking over. It hardened my heart, hijacked my prayers, and encroached upon that special place within me, that inner sanctuary, the *sanctum sanctorum* where God and I met up.

When outside on the bottom porch step, with the branch from the sea grape tree brushing through my hair, my thoughts drifted joyfully toward God. But with my face in the dark, scummy oven cavity, the icky, built-up bitter thoughts surfaced, interfering with my peace of mind.

After all our years of working so hard, why could Peter and I not afford a new refrigerator, or even a washer and dryer, let alone an oven? Why was every purchase a huge ordeal involving debate, bickering, penny pinching, and guilt? Thanks to Mom we were living on Sanibel, but still, where had all our hard-earned money gone, and after all those years of working overtime, why hadn't we leftover play money?

"We should have bought a starter home when we first got married, shouldn't have rented that apartment those first five years, like we did."

"How could we have bought a house when all our money was going to student loans, childcare, cars that kept breaking down?"

"We should have deferred our student loans, like I wanted to. Bought a house right away. And when we did buy a house, we shouldn't have stayed in one place. We should have bought and sold every few years, growing with the market. We could have made our way into a mansion."

"You didn't want to move, remember? You loved the willow tree, wanted the kids to grow up in one house, grow up with that willow tree."

"Well, the neighborhoods you wanted us moving to didn't even have trees."

The more I scoured the cruddy oven, the more resentment surrounding financial decisions Peter and I had made in our marriage surfaced.

"Remember way back when I told you about that brand-new online book company? I loved books and had a gut feeling it was going to be huge. All I wanted was to invest ten thousand dollars the week it went public, remember?"

"Honey, we didn't even have ten dollars back then."

Still, we should have invested, should have done a lot of things. I was putting a lot of muscle into scouring the oven. We should have gone on a honeymoon, too, but no. Hyper-responsible Peter said we had to first pay off student debt, be one hundred percent debt-free, so we pushed our honeymoon off until a futuristic debt-free day that never came.

I got all worked up, angry and resentful whenever I cleaned, not to mention I was always cleaning. I was the only one who cleaned. Peter never cleaned an oven before, nor a shower, nor toilet.

But like the good king Josiah (Mom mentioned him in her letter), shocked and upset over the idols in the temple and wanting them gone, for the first time I was shocked and upset over the resentment in me. It was like a built-up grime...my insides coated. I wanted it gone.

After pulling out what looked like a scorched cockroach and dropping it in the trash, I went to the sink, gasping for air and splashing water on my face. As I stared out the window above the sink, I wished I was on the beach, walking and talking with God instead. He wasn't with me only in the pretty places, though. God was with me in the gunky places, too.

And nowhere in the God-written manual did it say that back when I was made new, I was also made sin or idol resistant. Nor was I designed with a self-cleaning feature. Christ was it. He was the One God gave to remove the icky grime built up within me. Christ was a feature like no other, the greatest feature of God's love.

I put my face back into the detestable oven.

"Did you go to Him today?" Mom would ask Luke and me as she kissed us good-night. "Did you bring Jesus your daily sins?"

Oh, come on. It wasn't like I hurt anyone, stole, cheated on my tests or did anything horrific. Why bother Jesus with my petty stuff; how so and so talked behind my back, so I said stuff about her, too?

"Bring everything to Him, your daily troubles, struggles, hurts, and pains," Mom would say. "If you don't, trust me, it accumulates like plaque on your teeth, only we're talking a hardening of your heart. So please, brush your teeth, floss, and bring Jesus your daily gunk!"

Poor Mom, she tried, but Luke and I gave her a hard time. And soon we did more than roll our eyes. We talked back, until she threw in the rag, reserving all such topics for church on Sunday. But even then, we kicked and dragged our heels, and eventually she settled for taking us every other Sunday, if even that.

But what she once taught me was soaking in, and making sense. If I hadn't cleaned my oven on a regular basis, then what would have happened to the overflowing corn soufflé from ten Thanksgivings past, or the spilled blueberry muffin batter that set off the fire alarm, or the burnt cheese from all the casseroles I filled too high? It would still have been in there, and even though I never spilled anything horrific, a spill was a spill, and even the slightest dripping not taken care of would turn into a built-up stubborn residue of its own over time.

With that in mind, I prayed and prayed, telling God I wished I had listened sooner, and followed Jesus' simple instructions, had gone to Him regularly—*forgive me of my daily sins*—and savored all along the dough rising as Christianity's recipe claimed. Instead, I let all kinds of stuff—nonchalance and apathy, pride, procrastination, busyness, idols, and sin—get in the way and take over. Instead of taking them to Jesus, I let even my drippings of resentment, small at first, bake alongside God's goodness, robbing it of its precious rising space within me.

No wonder I pouted the night the Bible arrived in the mail! I was holding the cookbook in my hands yet hadn't appreciated the aroma of God's presence rising forth in my life.

I came out of the oven, dipped the rag into a bucket of cleaner, then went back in. I no longer minded the oven work. The Custodian of My Soul was with me, reminding me how loved I was, that He was willing to do my inner janitorial work for me. I simply had to bring everything to Him…not just the big spills but the drippings, too.

Whereas most ovens—obviously not the one I was scouring—had self-cleaning features, people did not. The oven I had found online boasted a cleaning feature where all I'd have to do was touch a button, then stand back as it heated to 900 degrees, mechanically interlocking its doors during the high-temperature cycle, keeping me out.

"I know that's not how You designed me," I said to my Maker. "You don't want to keep me out of it. Nor did you design me with a self-cleaning feature. Thank You," I whispered. "I love Your method, and how You designed me with a special ability—the ability to repent."

Down on my knees, I dipped the rag back into the bucket of solution, grateful for God putting in me another much-needed feature—receptivity to the Holy Spirit, and to His Word. All of it was working together, and the receptivity igniting in me a desire for change.

"Only You, Jesus," I squeezed the excess solution from the rag, "only You can remove my built-up interior scum. But when I repent, I can keep from spilling forth the same old messes again and again. Help me to repent!"

My insides felt lit up and warm with love for my house guest within. I didn't know how God put up for so long with my unwillingness to even think about such things. It had driven me bonkers back when Peter and I moved into our willow tree home and he procrastinated a whole year before getting around to knocking out an unwanted wall. Yet God knocked down the barrier between Him and me, and I hardly showed appreciation.

I was glad no one was around to find me with my knees stuck to the kitchen floor, and torrential tears coming from my eyes. The supernatural, voice-activated cleaning feature, whereby God heard the cry of my repentant heart and responded, had been triggered within me and no one needed to see it. His method of working was so beautiful and quiet that soon I was savoring, appreciating like never before the bread of life rising within.

A couple of hours later, I headed for Viv's house, never wanting to forget that cleaning an oven wasn't an every-other-year sort of a thing. Once I baked stuffed bell peppers, or a dish of garlic, tomatoes, and marinated eggplant, it was going to need to cleaning again. And once I walked anywhere in the world, lived another day, I was going to need a cleaning, too.

Forgive me my daily sin, Jesus.

I headed through the line of trees and into Viv's yard with a bounce to my step. Perhaps it had to do with God's love for me, and how He didn't want me stuck in a stagnant state of resentment, but moving out of it, into new things. I loved Him, too, and didn't want to be just a dwelling place for the Holy Spirit. I wanted to be a lovely dwelling place for my house guest within. And bring glory to God.

I went around the side of her house, where I heard talking. "Do you know how much God loves you?" I practiced beneath my breath, just in case.

THIRTY-ONE

INTERIOR DESIGN TIDBITS

* * *

While caring for your ailing home, don't neglect yourself.
Step away from it all and go outside to refresh.

* * *

Enjoy one step at a time.

Viv was out around back, sitting in her chair when I arrived, and Marita was working on her hair.

"Hello, precious," Marita said the moment she saw me. "I am making Vivi's hair into a French twist…almost done."

Viv had on enormous sunglasses, covering half her face. She was all dressed up in cream-colored leggings, a long-sleeved poncho, and ballerina flats, which made my usual ponytail, workout leggings, white t-shirt, and flip flops seem underdressed in comparison.

"Ready for our stroll?"

"Yup," she replied, not moving her lips.

"She can't talk when I do her hair. She moves her head too much. But yes, she is ready…more ready than you know." Marita gave me an exaggerated look, telling me there was drama behind Viv being more ready than I knew.

Since the sun was only going to turn hotter, I acted oblivious to the expression on her face. I didn't want her calling me to the side, talking behind Viv's back, wasting what was left of the fleeting morning sun.

Marita pulled a yellow silk scarf from her pocket, wrapped it elaborately over Viv's hair, tying it on the side. "Done," she declared.

I took hold of Viv's chair. "Hold on tight, my friend!" Turning it around, I pulled it up and onto the same boardwalk I had taken on my walk to the beach a few nights earlier.

"Whoa, hold the reins," Viv said. "We're not going to the beach, are we?"

"To the shore and back, yes."

Viv shook her head. "I was thinking the road...we'd stroll up and down the road. This chair isn't made for sand. You'll feel like you're pulling an elephant."

She had no idea all the people in chairs and on gurneys I had pushed and pulled up and down the halls of the hospital. If only I could have brought them to the seashore instead. "Don't think twice, Viv. I can do it. I want to do it."

"Meh." She shook her head again. "I don't think so."

"Your friend says that she can do it," Marita interjected, "let her do it. Sit back, relax, and enjoy the ride. Go to the shore and come back. It'll be good for you."

When Viv put her hands up in surrender, I pushed her chair along the bumpy boardwalk, making it a short distance before Marita was calling after us.

"Girls, girls, come back!" She waved a spray bottle mister in her hand.

Although the late morning sun wasn't hot enough to toast our noses and cheeks, it was quickly preheating, and set to be an eighty-seven-degree day, hot enough for frying. With that in mind, I left Viv where she was and ran back.

"You have no idea," Marita disclosed to me the second I returned, "no idea how long it has been since that girl has been to the beach."

"Well, she's going today," I said, encouraging no conversation behind Viv's back.

"I shouldn't be telling you this, but the second she opens her eyes in the morning, she is already looking forward to her first cat nap. She told me so the other day."

"Nothing wrong with cat naps."

"They're the highlight of her day...every hour on the hour...one after the next, cat naps all day long."

I felt after that I had the right to ask the one thing I wanted to know. "Will she ever walk again?"

"If she wants to walk, yes, she can walk." She glanced over at Viv, then back at me. "Don't say a word, but I will tell you quickly what I think is going on." She took a step closer to my face. "She thinks because she is not good enough that she does not deserve to walk."

"What on earth?"

"The golf cart incident...she can't move past it and is canceling everything good in her life. I don't know what happened to her as a child, but it was bad, and it plays a part."

It wasn't for me to share, but Marita was right. Viv had tried to be a good girl, but even when she broke a glass out on the front porch steps, her father canceled her birthday party, and when he caught her mumbling the slightest thing about him under her breath, he canceled her going on the youth camping trip. So after the golf cart incident, perhaps she was doing what she knew best...one thing after the next, canceling everything good in her life.

"She lives stuck in a wishful place," Marita's words were coming out faster than I could keep up. What kind of coffee did she drink? "She wishes she could do things, go places, laugh, and love. But if you ask me, her wishing keeps her from doing, and from going to the real places all around her...the places she is meant to go."

"Like where, where is she meant to go to?"

"Aye, aye, aye, to the seashore, and to sunsets, to the Farmer's Market, and the theater...and to God, the giver of fresh starts! But all she does is shush me up. And now, if you want to know what I think...I think she believes a lie...that passively observing life from a distance is good enough... and keeping a distance from God, too."

"Um, hello," Viv called from the boardwalk. "It's now ten degrees hotter, just saying. How about you reconsider hauling me to the beach?"

I had all the more reasons to haul her to the beach. Everything about life, including our love for God and His love for us, was meant to be experienced up close and personal, as active participants and not idle spectators seated far away.

But Viv was right. Florida's sun had finished preheating and was already broiling. I didn't expect it to happen so fast and almost needed oven mitts on as I took hold of her chair, struggling to push it over a broken plank of wood. For Viv's sake, though, I refused to let anything stop me.

And for added oomph, I recalled a quote from Kahlil Gibran, another old favorite writer of mine whose works I read in college. "'For to be idle is to become a stranger unto the seasons, and to step out of life's procession, that marches in majesty and proud submission towards the infinite.'"

I couldn't stand to see Viv a stranger unto the seasons or sitting along the sidelines of life's procession. *March, march, march—proceed*, I chanted beneath my breath, determined not only to bring Viv closer to the seashore, but to Jesus, and to God, whose love for her was more infinite, endless, and immeasurable than the sea!

"Hold on tight," I said when I made it to the end of the boardwalk. I spun her chair around, pulling it backward through the trail of sand lined with massive sea oats. It felt indeed like I was hauling an elephant, but I had to keep going, had to help my friend feel a part of life's procession again.

To help me along, I pretended we were in a parade and I was pulling a precious float. The sea oats were like bystanders, cheering us on.

"You're making me nervous, Addie. You sound like you're about to pass out. I told you this was a bad idea."

I could hardly talk. "Spray...bottle...please."

Viv held the bottle up and misted my face. "Let me hear you say a coherent sentence or two so I know you're okay, and not regretting this."

"My flabby arms need this. It's good for them."

I wanted to say more...tell her it wasn't just a good workout for my arms but for my mind, too. I had read that physically active people had a lowered risk of developing Alzheimer's, and if they already had the disease, then exercise maybe altered its progression by slowing down mental decline.

By then, though, we were making it through the scruffy, wide-open beach plant section, which proved even more challenging for the no-terrain wheelchair, and my unfit body hauling it along. Still, it was nothing in comparison to my former workouts lifting Mom from the tub, wrapping her body in a towel, and carrying her to bed.

When the sand got deeper, and the pulling impossible, Viv twisted in her chair, to see where we were at. I looked over my shoulder, too, and felt like giving up. The water line looked far, blame it on the tide being out.

For self-motivating purposes, I focused on the two clouds in the sky. One was shaped like Mickey Mouse, and I walked with the Mickey

Mouse-shaped cloud until it changed before my eyes into what looked like a princess with a tiara. Not wanting the princess cloud to beat us to shore, I picked up pace, watching it change into what looked like a castle. Wanting to get Viv to that castle in the sky, I sped up even more.

Watching clouds change was fun but watching people I loved—Mom and Viv—change from who they once were into unrecognizable forms wasn't fun. The Viv back in college hadn't just a wanderlust, but a passion for getting herself and others involved in causes that made the world a better place. I didn't like seeing her detached and disconnected like a solitary cloud floating through the sky.

She didn't feel worthy of marching joyfully along, but what did that even mean? Only perfectly good people who never screwed up were allowed to move forward in the world? No one was perfect but Jesus, and He didn't come to cancel or condemn, but to forgive. Talk about love! If God only loved the perfect people, He would have loved no one but Jesus, who shared His same divine nature. Instead, He loved the world so much. He wanted to adopt us as His children.

"I'm an idiot," Viv said. "How could I have forgotten?"

"Water…you mean water?"

"No, how much I loved the beach. I used to be a beach person…loved everything about it."

Even though we were still far from the shore, I didn't want to pass out. I turned her chair around so she was facing the water, then dropped onto the sand behind her so she wouldn't see the exhaustion on my face.

"What happened to me?" She sniffled, then cleared her voice sternly to chase away more sniffles. "How am I not a beach person anymore?"

I put my hands down like a terrestrial creature, and crawled on all fours around to the side of her chair, then reached up and grabbed the spray mister, untwisting its cap and downing the contents.

"A morning person, too. I kid you not, I loved mornings…my favorite time of the day. Now, it's good for me if I'm up by noon." She slid her giant glasses down on her nose and gazed over them at the distant shore. "My third husband…the good guy…he was a morning person, too. We loved them together."

I took my pulse, then moved into a more comfortable position in the sand. "Your love for the beach and for mornings," I refrained from saying her third husband, "is still in you. Things just got in the way. At least you're remembering and realizing." I ran my fingers through the sand. "The good thing is, beaches are everywhere and mornings keep coming. Every twenty-four hours you have a new morning to love."

"We can agree to disagree, and call it a day."

"What do you mean?" I didn't think I had said anything that anyone would have disagreed with.

"I have no love left in me."

"No love left in you? Oh, come on, Viv. Love isn't something we run out of."

"Speak for yourself. Mine ran out. Trust me, none left."

"Sounds like you're talking about crude oil," I said with a laugh, then stared out at the Gulf of Mexico. Like crude oil stored in barrels in underground caverns, Viv was keeping her love hidden away…for emergency purposes, or slow-releasing here or there. But she didn't have to. "Seriously, Viv, love doesn't run out. It's a replenishable thing with infinite supply. And God…the source of it…loves to replenish."

She gave me her typical *thanks for being my friend* smile, but shook her head, like I was talking nonsense. "When did you become a guru, Addie?"

"Oh, stop, I'm no guru." I put my mouth on safety lock, not wanting to overdo it. But what I did know about love? When I had one baby, I wondered how could I ever love two, but when I had Mallory more love came. Then Charlie and Henry arrived, and my love wasn't spread thin or in limited reserve, but multiplied exponentially. There wasn't space enough in me, let alone barrels in the world, to store and reserve the immeasurable and uncontainable love I had for my kids alone.

And God, the source of love, deserved credit. If only I could have presented my thoughts to someone. I didn't know why I craved so badly to talk about God…talk about Him to Viv, or to anyone. If I was still in school and the assignment was to present on a three-fold poster board any topic of interest, I'd have picked God. Without having to feel self-conscious, I'd be a student doing her assignment, presenting the three-fold aspect of God, describing His continuous love, how in a roundabout way, like water, it had always been present, in different phases...precipitating, evaporating, and condensing.

Love was sent from Heaven to Earth, then resurrected back up to Heaven, and came pouring down again. God's love never ceased to exist. It wasn't always visible in the form that maybe I expected to see it in, but it was there in the infiltration of hearts, and around the surface of the Earth, and in the runoff, too.

Rightfully so, I would have gotten a poor grade on such a project—in reality, resurrection was nothing like evaporation. Evaporation—the process that changed liquid into vapor—was invisible, whereas the resurrection was not. People saw it clearly. After Jesus' body was gone from the tomb, they saw Him alive in the resurrected Christ form. Once He went back up to Heaven, He wasn't a cloud floating through the sky but was seated at the right hand of His Father.

"Is my nose red?" Viv asked.

"No, not at all."

"You swear?"

"It's not red. I'll tell you if it gets red."

"Good, I don't need the sun aging me even more."

"Oh, please, you look like you're thirty."

"Nice of you. But I feel like I'm ninety."

"Why?" I gave her an incredulous look. "Why do you feel ninety?"

"I don't know, I make a big deal of stuff I never did before."

"You've always made a big deal of everything," I said with a laugh. "And that's a compliment. Better to be passionate about something, than passionate about nothing."

She sniffled. "Yeah, I never thought I'd get old. It was happening to everybody else. I thought it would skip over me. And now, it's this big mental hoopla in my mind. When did it happen?"

"First of all, you're not that old."

"What are you talking about? I left the spring of my life a long time ago. It's not even summer for me. When did fall arrive? I won't lie, fall isn't colorful for me. I feel like it's going to be short, which means winter is just around the corner. Hey, don't look at me like that. It's coming for you, too. There's no stopping it. Ready or not, it's coming for us both, my friend."

"You think I don't know that?" I pointed to my forehead. "There were four lines this morning. Don't tell me if there's a fifth. I don't want to know."

Whether she meant to or not, her words were getting me all worked up. How could they not when I, too, had taken one too many mornings of my life for granted? Spring and summer rushed by too fast, and no matter how old or young my face looked, there was no going back to my younger self, or my favorite season on Earth—when my kids were little and on my days off, we stayed inside in our pajamas and made a mess, and played all day.

When Viv slouched forward in her chair, like a wilting morning glory—its short-lived splendor over forever—I wanted to do more than point out age lines on my forehead. I wanted to point out the only thing I knew of that put aging on Earth into perspective—eternity.

But I didn't want to sound like Peter, always responding in a quick-fix, solution-oriented manner. He wanted to move my problems to his "done" pile, and I wanted long, drawn-out wrestling matches with my inner thoughts, and thinking-out-loud sessions with people who did nothing but listen and cheer me on as I reached my own victorious conclusions.

But when Viv let out one of her notorious sobs, I had no choice but to steer our heart-to-heart down a more optimistic road. Otherwise, I risked becoming misery's best friend.

"You're in a rut, that's all," I said.

"Yep, another one. You know how many ruts I've been in lately? I won't lie, I think that's what life is all about…falling into ruts and getting ourselves out. I'm fine with that. It is what it is. But some ruts are harder to get out of, that's all."

The rut thing we shared in common. All through the years, more days than not felt like rut-filled obstacle courses challenging me to the core. "Let's just pat ourselves on the back." I got up from the sand, which had become too hot to sit in.

"Yeah, then call it a day." Viv reached over her shoulder and patted herself on the back, as I was also doing. "Here's to all the ruts we've fallen into…and the ones we're still trying to get ourselves out of."

I eyed the distant turquoise water. "It looks so refreshing, what do you think, shall we proceed?"

"Is my nose red?" She pushed her face forward for me to inspect.

The moment I put my hand over my eyes like a visor and looked at her nose, a fire alarm went off within me. It was redder than red velvet cake. The look on my face had Viv pulling the scarf off her hair and wrapping it around her face, covering her nose and mouth.

"It might not be from the sun," I said, trying to calm things down. "You were sniffling and sobbing."

"Oh, for crying out loud. I sniffled twice, and sobbed once. Not enough to turn my nose red. We have to go!"

I took hold of her chair, not bothering to ask if my nose was red, too, or whether the fourth and minor line on my forehead had turned major. If my forehead was sheet music for a symphony, it was getting more intense.

"I know what you're thinking. You're thinking I'm a *bah humbug*," Viv said as I tugged her chair back from where we came.

"Nope, wasn't thinking that at all. Our rut conversation…I was thinking about that."

"Then I'll admit. I do think there's more to life than falling into ruts and getting ourselves out. The younger me keeps reminding me…feeling grateful in our ruts, that's what it's about. I don't know why I forgot about it, but gratitude had a way of always pushing me out of my ruts. Why do you think I used to do that gratitude activity…remember that?"

Of course I remembered. She used to write out things she was grateful for and pin them to her shirt, walk around campus like that. "Do you still do that?"

She answered with a sob, and I wasn't sure if that meant, yes, she did still do it, or no, she didn't, but wished she still did.

"I'm grateful I can show emotion," she said. "When I was little, I couldn't. If I showed anger, Ron showed more. If I expressed happiness, he ruined it…popped my balloons. I didn't grow up watching Mr. Rogers, like you. I didn't know that expressing my feelings was okay."

I wanted to respond with a compassionate sniffle, or better yet a sob, but as I was about to give her one or the other, Viv changed the topic.

"Enough about me. I mean it. Let's talk about fun stuff…and you. Remember you went through that Hemingway phase…obsessed with going to Spain, falling in love with a matador? And if that didn't happen, then a French chef in Paris?"

"A poorly laid-out plan," I said with a laugh, "being that I dropped out of Spanish and wasn't even taking French. But you know what?"

"What?"

"Reading *A Moveable Feast* was enough, enough to inspire me. No wonder my old book collection went missing. My mom sold it at her garage sale for my own good."

"So, what are you reading now, Addie, what's your book of the month? Better not be *Old Man and the Sea*. I don't want to hear about you on the news tonight—woman in boat, last seen drifting toward Cuba in pursuit of a fish."

Maybe it was the heat; I couldn't remember whether I had mentioned I was reading the Bible. "Talk about a feast like no other," I said with a pant. "The Bible...it's a feast for my soul."

When Viv said nothing in reply, I stopped walking long enough to swing my head around the side of her chair and read the reaction on her face. Sure enough, it was the same look my boys gave whenever they smelled broccoli in the house. The look on Viv's face had me shaking my head in frustration at Marita for having appointed me with the seemingly impossible feat of sharing God's love with Viv in the first place.

I wasn't a pushy person, or the type to force-feed anyone anything. Even when Charlie went through his phase of refusing to eat food that wasn't white, I never shoved greens down his throat. If greens made him gag, how would me talking about how much I loved greens make them more appealing? For that reason, I decided not to dish out the scrumptious things I was reading from the Bible, unless Viv asked.

"Hey," she said then, "I know you're out of breath, but what's one thing your grateful for?" She snapped her fingers in the air. "First thing that comes to mind...blurt it out!"

"God is with me in the ruts."

"Um, okay, and if you were me," she said, making it a game. "One thing you'd be grateful for if you were me."

It wasn't my place to point out what another person ought to have been grateful for. But when I glanced over my shoulder to see how far we had yet to go, I spotted Marita, who loved Viv like a daughter and went to extremes fussing over the details in her life. "Marita…be grateful for Marita." I squinted my eyes to better see her alongside Viv's house, caught up in the branches of a sea grape tree. "What in the world is she doing?"

"Collecting sea grapes. Eight cups of the pinkish, purplish grapes so she can make sea grape jelly."

"Why not buy it? They sell jars of it over at the general store. I saw it there."

"Nah, she likes making it herself. Once she has enough grapes, the rest is easy—four cups of water, five cups of sugar, one box of thickener, and a teaspoon of butter. I've helped her make it. She boils and drains the berries, uses a colander and a cheesecloth, then has me mash it all together. It's so good, I kid you not, it's my splurge. I eat it on crackers with—" Viv sniffled three times, and after that, let out what sounded like a combination of a sniffle and a sob, "crackers with cream cheese."

"What's wrong?"

"I'm letting her go tomorrow."

Whoa, it felt like I was pulling a broken buggy through the sand—the plight ahead more daunting than ever. Without Marita, who would run Viv's errands and fuss over every detail of her life? Who would wake her from cat naps, put her hair into French twists, and wipe the mascara under her eyes? Who would buy her rambutan, and make her sea grape jelly? My head was a dizzying mess. Her lawyer and I could take turns every other day, or go one week on and one week off, which would give us a break in-between.

Then again, there was the impending foreclosure, which for Viv's sake, was hopefully weeks away yet. But for me, it meant I wouldn't have to be consumed on a long-term basis with handling the complexities of her life. Still, I'd have to set boundaries…two cat naps a day, apples and oranges instead of rambutan, and ponytails instead of French twists. Oh, and store-bought jars of sea grape jelly.

"Addie, you sound like you're gasping for dear life. We're almost back. Did you hear what I said, I'm letting Marita go tomorrow. I have no choice."

Yes, I heard, but as I struggled to pull Viv's carriage along the tracks we had made earlier in the sand, it was all too much for me. I needed a catnap of my own, to give my brain a rest from going there, imagining spending my days making sea grape jelly for Viv, when all through the years I hardly had time to make homemade suppers for my own family.

"For the record," Viv said when I heaved her chair up and onto the boardwalk, and from the corner of my eye, spotted Marita waving from under the sea grape tree. "I'm going to miss her. She is what I'd picture a loving mom to be. But you know what? My own mom up and left me… left me with Ron. He lacked self-awareness, as most toxic people do…and never changed. Was I loved as a baby? I'll never know. I don't remember. But enough about me. We're back and you need water."

THIRTY-TWO

When Peter returned from Michigan, we were more determined than ever to take noticeable steps forward with the renovations of Hidden Potential, and to also have fun. I cranked up Latin and Mediterranean guitar music loud as it would go, and over the next several days, we went about knocking out a short wall in the great room and removing the eight-and-a-half-foot drop ceiling that exposed the beams and rafters, all the while doing the rumba here or there, and a bit of flamenco.

"You think it's too loud?" Peter said of the music.

"Who cares if it is? If you're worried about the birds, they love it."

If Viv opened her windows, or if tourists on rented Surrey bikes peddled down our road, they probably assumed the music mixed with laughter was coming from tropical creatures. But it was Peter and me, pretending to be in the spring of our lives, drumming in sync, tapping our beaks like a couple of red-bellied woodpeckers, courtship-dancing in our secluded birdhouse up in the trees.

Peter turned the music down a tad, then took me in his arms and spun me around. "We should have bought a place in South Beach," he said, looking hipper and happier than he had in years. "We're young enough for South Beach, aren't we?"

I let out a laugh. "Of course we are, but you know what?'

"What?"

"I'm glad to be on Sanibel. It's just right for us, and look at us, we're doing it. We're reclaiming Hidden Potential, and reclaiming us." Even my sore spot of having never had a honeymoon was already starting to heal, and it sure felt good.

When not working on the house, we walked the beach, drank coffee on the front porch, or found ourselves on lengthy phone calls with one of the four kids. Peter also spent countless hours on his laptop, and I reading the Bible, and also writing. I was writing more than ever, filling a binder with all kinds of things, and how could I not when everything on the island from the water to the shells to the trees were like muses!

Even the foliage-topped ornamental stalks of *Cyperus Papyrus*, every time I walked through the scruffy beach plant area, made me want to write. I wanted to pick a piece of the grass, dip it into the inky blue Gulf of Mexico, and scribble my heart out onto sea grape leaves. The pen shells, too…the mere sight of them, their fine tips pointing out from the sand, made the inkwell of my heart bubble within.

Peter and I kept our momentum on the house going. It pained us to do so, but we removed the distressed pine wood flooring in the kitchen. Devoured as it was by termites, we were left with no choice.

"I'm about to start the movie," Peter said, sitting on the torn apart floor, ready to press play on his laptop.

Stepping over him, I rushed around the kitchen finishing up our cocoa-cayenne popcorn. It was Marita's recipe, which I had found in my mailbox along with a jar of sea grape jelly and more of Viv's interior design tidbits. I wasn't sure if Viv had gone through with her plan of letting Marita go. I was avoiding going next door, wanting instead to spend time with Peter and not get carried away in tidal wave drama.

After sifting together three tablespoons of confectioners' sugar, one tablespoon of cocoa, 1/8 teaspoon of allspice, and a dash of cayenne pepper (enough to give it a kick), I tossed it into a bowl of warm, air-popped popcorn with olive oil. I then sat down on the floor next to Peter and we played a one-hour video on how to lay Cuban-style mosaic floor tiles in hopes of turning our small kitchen into a soulful, old-world environment.

"Remember psychology class freshman year?" I asked Peter the next morning, while down on my knees, spreading wet cement across a small area of kitchen floor.

"Um, no…I never took psychology."

"Yes, you did, you nut…you lychee nut. You were in my class. You sat behind me."

He placed a sheet of precut tiles over the wet cement. "So, what about it?"

"Well, I was thinking how we learned about the basics of love. Do you remember that?"

"If I don't remember the class, how would I remember that?"

"We learned what can happen to babies without love. Some don't grow or develop properly and can even die." I used my hand like a compress, smoothing it across the sheet of tiles that Peter was putting down. "What do you think? Babies who make it to adulthood having never had love… are they able to accept love later in life…can they ever love themselves?"

Peter raised his eyebrow. "Let me guess, this has to do with that certain somebody, our neighbor?"

He wasn't crazy about Vivienne living next door, and hadn't even gone over to say hello yet. I hesitated to answer as I crawled across the floor, putting down more cement. Whenever I rambled with concern about the all-consuming complexities of her life, he quick-fixed it by telling me it wasn't my problem, then returned the conversation right back to us or the work we were doing on the house. I didn't blame him. In all our years of marriage, we had never focused on just the two of us.

"I promise I don't want to talk about her," I crawled further across the floor, "but I wonder, do you think she'd open up for true love if it showed up knocking on her door?"

Peter put down another sheet of tiles. "If she's smart, no. She'd double bolt her door. Three husbands are enough. But again, her problems aren't your problems, and I don't want them to become mine, either."

I didn't want to overdo things by telling him I was talking about God's love, and the One who showed up knocking on the door of our hearts. Would Viv have opened herself to Jesus?

When all the sheets of tiles were placed, Peter hopped into the shower, and I went out onto the front porch to write. But as soon as I started, I was interrupted by a commotion down on the driveway. I pushed my nose to the screen and saw a disheveled Marita, her bun a mess, running toward our house, wiping her eyes with her fists.

I rushed outside, meeting her halfway down my porch steps, as she had already rushed halfway up. "I'm sorry," I said right away, assuming she was all worked up from having been let go.

"No, no, no. It is not about me. Vivi...she needs your help!"

"Tell me," I insisted.

"After she let me go, she asked me to do one last thing, and what was I to say, no? I dragged her in her chair out onto the beach, like you did that day, only farther. She made me pull her all the way to the shore. And she is still there!"

"Oh," I said, trying to understand the emergency. "So she's on the beach...and it's almost sunset." It sounded nice.

"I just know she is going to do something crazy."

"Yeah, that sounds like Viv."

"I tried to stay with her but she swatted me away. Who knows what she is planning to do there all by herself, no way to get home!" Marita closed her eyes and grimaced, as if whatever her imagination was picturing—mine imagined Viv watching the sunset—was too much to handle.

In case it was an emergency, though, I didn't want to be blamed for not responding. With Marita at my heels, I hurried down the driveway, glad that Peter was in the shower and I didn't have to explain.

"At least we don't have to worry about her nose burning," I said as we went.

"I am done praying for her nose."

"You prayed for her nose?"

"Who do you think went out and bought an aloe vera plant for it the other day? Of course, I prayed for her nose, and I would pray for your nose, too, if you needed me to. And speaking of noses, you probably think I am nosy, but I'm not. I like to know what is going on in people's lives, so I can pray for them. It's what I do. I do not say 'amen,' there's no end to my prayers. Everything I know about her and you and other people I bring to God in prayer. It's what I believe God wants me doing, and I can't help it. He has given me this desire to pray…this way of serving Him, and helping others."

I was out of breath from walking so fast and feared she'd pass out from talking so fast. For her sake and mine I stopped abruptly, causing her to bump into me like a fender bender.

"I am sorry," she said.

"No, I'm sorry. I shouldn't have stopped like that. I needed to catch my breath. Do you think Viv will ever feel God in her life?"

"When it comes to God, we do not rely on feelings. His Word in our hearts and our minds is more than a feeling. She needs to hear the Word of God, and let it do its special thing in her heart."

Probably, she was going to tell me it was all up to me to share God's Word with Viv. I walked.

"All you can do is tell her—" she tried to keep up with me "—tell her how much God loves her. And pray…pray that she turns her face toward the light."

Sure enough, there she went with her relentless pressuring. Bothered, I kept walking, and when I reached the arching entryway, I went into the tunnel of trees, slowing my pace only when I tripped on a root.

"How'd you know I was a believer in the first place?" I asked.

"Easy, child," she said at my heels. "Your cross necklace."

"Oh." I didn't expect that, and let my fingers fumble their way around my neck until they felt it—the small silver cross I had worn for years. But just because a person wore a cross necklace didn't mean they were John the Baptist-compelled to make their hearts ready for Jesus. Did she know how awkward it was for me, how anytime I tried, my words came out like detached, self-propelled freight cars all bumping into one another and not going anywhere?

As we neared the end of the tunnel of trees, I caught sight of the sand, water, and Viv in her chair, way down by the shore. I was about take off in a jog when Marita took hold of my arm.

"I will say good-bye now, precious."

I tilted my head toward Viv. "Aren't we going to get her?"

"Not me, no." She looked up at the bits of daylight still twinkling through the branches, and smiled. Heaven knew what she was smiling about, a private joke between her and God. "I must go now. You won't be seeing me around."

"I'm sorry she let you go."

"No, it's okay. I was ready. Just know I will pray. I will not pressure you. I will pray." She turned like she was about to leave, but as usual had one more thing to add. "A little bird told me that you write?"

I nodded hesitantly, even though I had been writing morning, noon, and night, in every in-between moment when not spending time with Peter, or working on the house.

"Keep writing, precious," she said, despite my hesitant nod. "Write about God!"

"What if I'm writing a romance?" I said, bothered because there she went again.

"The love of God is the romance the world needs to read. You know that phrase, dance like no one is watching?"

"Yes."

She looked me straight in the eyes. "Write like no one is watching. Write to the glory of God, like no one is watching, no one is reading what you write, okay?"

I didn't reply.

"Aye, aye, aye, what do I know?" She shook her head. "I am just a person who loves to pray. And now, I will be praying for you. I cannot help it. Like I said, it is what I do."

As I stood there watching her go back down the long chamberlike trail leading to our road, I squinted my eyes, trying to see the beauty in what she said, and with the slightest tilt of my head, her words became like shimmering specs of reflected light, ever so slightly shifting ideas within me, bringing new things into focus.

I had already been writing about God, although not a romance. More of a nature book, how when I first arrived on the island, His presence in my life was seemingly endangered, and my love for Him on the brink of extinction. But those were just feelings. God wasn't disappearing. His presence wasn't running out. I had neglected to care for my relationship with God. But since then, I had been filling my mind with Truth…relying on it rather than my own feelings… and sure enough, my love for Him was flourishing, greater than ever.

When I could no longer see Marita, the things she had said were still with me, and I was grateful. I turned and headed through the scruffy beach plant area, toward the shore, praying as I went, thanking God for the dune daisies stretching across the sand on their vines, how in the mornings I had seen them on their neck-like stems turning their bright-eyed faces toward the sun. I prayed that Viv would catch word of God's love for her, then turn her face toward His warm, loving light.

When I got to Viv, the sun was dressed in hot pink and performing its slow descent with the matching clouds waltzing around it. My insides applauded the Creator of the longest-running show that never, in the history of the world, missed a night of performing.

"I knew it. I knew she'd run and get you," Viv said, without looking at me. "I swear I didn't want her to. Everybody is trying to save me, and it's driving me bonkers."

I sat down in the sand next to her chair. "Who all is trying to save you?"

"I'm sure Marita told you. Mortgage brokers, Chapter 13 attorneys, so-called mortgage negotiators…I could go on and on…private financiers, my own mortgage holder, for crying out loud. Stop me, or I'll keep going."

"Okay, stop."

"Thanks. I kid you not I've been inundated with junk mail all because my name and my address have become public information offered throughout the court system. Would you believe it's published in journals? No wonder crooks and con artists are finding me, sending me stuff. I'm not lying, this one guy offered to take title of my house, then invited me to pay him rent."

I opened my mouth, then closed it, unsure what to say.

"I wish she didn't run to get you. I know how crazy busy you are, wrestling with a floor, or knocking out a wall."

"Nope, just writing."

She turned her face from the sunset and looked at me. "Where?"

"What do you mean, where?"

"Where do you write?"

The question threw me. I would have expected her to ask what I was writing, not where I was writing. "Anywhere," I said. "From the kitchen floor, to the front porch steps, to the hammock, and the beach, wherever I happen to be…no particular spot. Why?"

"Well, I did something cool for a writer client of mine, turned the most ordinary corner into a cozy writing nook. It's a cinch to do. All I did was take a small antique farm table, bathed it in white, paired it with the coolest floor lamp, which I topped with a soft striped silk lampshade. The ambience I created in that corner for my friend to write in was so inspiring, she went on to write a bestseller." She lifted one eyebrow. "I should be getting royalties, don't you think?"

"Are you still friends?"

"No, but that's beside the point. What are you writing?"

"Oh, um, let's see." I ran my fingers through the white, silky sand. "I'm filling this great big three-ringed binder with all kinds of stuff, clearing this head of mine, and also my heart. It's a bunch of scribbles, I think, but meaningful scribbles. At least they're meaningful to me."

"Well, whatever it is, if it ends up being a novel—"

"Oh, it will."

"Good, make me into one of your characters, will you? Childhood friend you lost touch with and always wished you hadn't. I'd be a good character in a book…just make me happier than I am. I'd love to read a happier version of me. Who knows, it might just make me happy reading about a happy me."

A girl chasing sanderlings up and down the shore captivated our attention. Viv looked ready to cry.

"What's wrong, Viv?"

"Pathetic you have to ask. It's one thing after the next with me, isn't it?"

"Well, what's wrong now?"

She stared ahead at the sunset, and I should have, too, but the expression on her face was a show of its own. "It doesn't matter where I am or what I'm doing, Addie. I mean here I am, watching a sunset, and a painful memory featuring me pops into my brain. I'm not exaggerating. It happens all the time, and totally takes over. It's emotionally taxing, and drains my energy." Her eyes were burning, and her teeth clenched. "A minute ago, it was *Little Girl Me* making dinner for Ron, but when Ron comes home, he's not hungry. He's drunk and mad, so *Little Girl Me* runs under the kitchen table to hide."

"That happened to you? I'm sorry."

"Yeah, and when I crawled out from under the table, Ron picked up a kitchen chair, swung it, and knocked my front teeth loose. He swore he didn't mean to hit me…just meant to swing the chair, for crying out loud."

The girl was still chasing sanderlings up and down the shore, but Viv's eyes were closed, and I felt sorry that she was missing the beautiful scene in front of us, watching instead the vintage film playing in her mind. It seemed like most of her memories featured the walloping hurts and pains of her life, with all of them starring her—a self-perceived worthless, un-lovable, no-good person.

Glancing back and forth at the sunset and at Viv, I wanted to do something, wanted to help. I privately pleaded with God. It wasn't fair! Couldn't He open her heart to the Light of Christ…let Jesus do His re-storative, renovating work in her, shutting down the old movie theater operated by Ron in her mind, and transforming her interior into a new atmosphere, into a temple of the Holy Spirit, filled with peace?

If God created and produced the scene in front of us—a pink beach ball of a sun falling from the sky, birds diving beak-first into the water, dolphins circling, and a mother running after that happy girl chasing sanderlings up and down the shore—then surely, He was capable of pro-ducing in Viv new and spectacular scenes of joy starring her and Him. At least, that's what I wished for my friend, wished so badly she would hear of God's love for her, and the promises He had for her, and turn to Him.

"Before you showed up," Viv said, "I was sitting here trying hard to listen to the waves, see if they had good stuff to tell me. But I couldn't hear the waves. You know why?"

"Um, there's hardly waves here?"

"No. All I hear is the sound of guilt. He was my blood, and I was the only one he had left…and I cut him out of my life."

"You had to, Viv…for your own well-being. And you put up with it long enough…kept him in your life out of guilt and obligation. It took courage doing what you did…distancing yourself from such a toxic person."

"Why was he so mean? How could he do that to me?"

"Stop trying to find an answer to that," I said. "You're a good person. You did nothing to cause it, and you're nothing like him. Stop listening to past lies. You want your scars to heal? Listen to what is true! When it comes to love…listen to God."

I stopped and listened for a moment to the subtle waves, which were beautiful-sounding but not telling me anything. I'd rather listen to the One who caused the waves, who made the sea, and was more powerful, letting His Truth reach my soul like a battle hymn, telling me, *You can, you can, you can…with Christ alone, you can!*

"You want to know why I came down here?" Viv asked.

"Yeah, why?"

She looked at me with plotting eyes. "I'm ready. No, I'm more than ready."

"Ready for what?"

"Ready to take a step, that's what!"

My mind went there right away, assuming she meant a step toward God, and that I was about to experience one of those prayer-answering moments in which Viv, like a dune daisy, but with ears to hear and eyes to see, was ready to tilt her neck and turn her face toward God…to at least hear of the love He had for her.

But then, she bent forward at her waist, reached down, and pulled her ballerina flats off, letting them drop into the sand. "I'm ready to stand up and use these feet of mine, take my first step, right here, right now."

It wasn't the step I anticipated. A part of me wanted to coordinate a celebration—light the fireworks, start the band, my friend is taking a step—but another part of me wanted to call her physical therapist and get their approval. As her accomplice, the spotter by her side, I wanted to know was it the step we had all been waiting for, or a grandiose stunt happening too soon?

"Are you sure?" I got up from the sand and brushed my legs off.

"Yup, you inspired me."

"How'd I inspire you?"

"That night you left my deck and walked into the water."

"Well, it was you who asked me to do that."

"Yeah, but I didn't like it."

"What do you mean…you said I inspired you?"

"I don't want to live vicariously through you or through anyone. It's my life, and I want to live it. But you know what? It's going to be me stepping into the water right now."

I looked down at the sand. It was damp and densely tiled with miniature pastel-colored coquina shells, but we were still several steps from the water. "You mean a few steps?"

After a quick shrug of her shoulders, like she didn't care how many steps to the water we were, she wasted no time and inched her buttocks to the edge of the chair, pointing her right leg, then flexing her left. She left me no choice but to stop questioning and take my position as trusted spotter.

"It's not dance class," I said after she pointed her left foot, then flexed her right. "Don't do anything crazy!"

"Just don't laugh if my face hits the sand."

I took hold of her and bent at my knees. But when the moment arrived, she fell out of readiness mode and a miserable expression overtook her face. "Uh oh, what's wrong?"

"Oh, man." She shook her head, her moment of triumph put on hold. "Why does this happen to me?"

"I don't know, what?" I relaxed my stance.

"His belittling, condescending tone. I can't get it out of my head. 'Who do you think you are young lady? You're certainly not the birthday girl. Take your hat off, pop the balloons, tell your friends to go home!'" She pressed her lips together. "It's like a dark cloud that shows up, ruining all my beautiful moments…holidays and sunsets and days at the beach. Addie, I'm not exaggerating. You have no idea!"

And she was right, I had no idea what she went through and what it was like to have never been the birthday girl, or Daddy's princess. If my parents were still alive, I'd have thrown my arms around them for loving me, making me believe I was like a precious, priceless pearl.

I didn't know what to do, and when I happened to glance over at the distant line of trees, I spotted Marita, standing at the arch, the entrance to the tunnel. She blew me a kiss, then put her hands together to form a church and steeple, as if to tell me she was praying.

Knowing she was right there praying gave me the boost I needed. I snapped my fingers in the air, the way our dance teacher used to do.

"Alright, Vivienne Watts, let's get this show rolling. You can do it...you can, you can, you can! Just don't try anything fancy—no *right, left, demi-plié, straight left onto left demi-pointe*—one simple step, you hear?"

Giving her no time for rebuttals, I bent at my knees and once again took hold of her arms, unsure what I was getting myself into. Was I going to end up assisting or grabbing onto her for dear life? Regardless, I was more than experienced, and ready for either.

Viv set her feet flat in the sand, then took hold of my arms, squeezing them tight. My heart pounded as she let me pull her all the way up into standing position. Once she was steady, I moved to one side, keeping one arm around her back, and the other like a bar under her arms. Marita was praying, I was praying, and God was there with us.

As quickly as the sun dipped below the horizon, it happened...Viv took a step. To be sure I didn't imagine it, I glanced back at the sand, and sure enough, her footprint was there.

"More, I want to take more!"

So—one, two, three, four—we were marching toward the sea, and I was praying beneath my breath, slightly out loud as we went. *With Christ alone we can...we can, we can, we can!*

Viv gave me a look like I was strange and overly dramatic, but oh well, so was she. I ignored the look and proceeded straight ahead, wishing I could look back to see if Marita was still there, praying near the triumphant arch. And maybe there was a glass floor to Heaven and Mom and old Ms. Viola were watching us, too, cheering us on.

"No *waaaaaaaay*," Viv screeched like a seagull when after several slow steps, her toes reached the foamy water. "I forgot how warm the Gulf gets."

I laughed with her just a little, but didn't want to get carried away. I steadied her down into a sitting position on the sand, close enough for the white foam to still touch the tips of her toes. There in our new section I stood for a moment, breathing in the wonderful salt air and glancing over my shoulder at the line of distant trees. Marita was gone, but her prayers were still with us.

"Hey, I'm curious," Viv said after we sat quietly for a moment, "what were you doing kneeling in the water that night? No big deal, just wondering."

It was no big deal to her, but her question reached my soul like a wonderful writing prompt. If only I were alone in a writer's corner with a laptop, I would have answered at ease. I glanced up at the splotchy sky, which looked like a piece of pink stationary, but it wasn't for me to write on.

"If you really want to know," I sat down next to her, "I was praying, telling God how sorry I was for choosing to sit in the back row most of my life—far from Him—when all along, He had a nice seat for me up front." I stopped to breathe, but was on a rattling roll, and all the writing I had been doing was helping with the rattling. "And I was thanking Him for His presence, how I don't have to travel to some faraway, extravagant place to meet up with Him, or play hide-and-seek or wonder His whereabouts."

"Why not?"

I looked at Viv and smiled. "He tells us in His Word exactly where He puts His presence."

Viv tilted her neck, and turned her face slightly. "Where...where is God's presence in the world today?"

"Well, it's not in the stars, the moon, or the sea." But when she asked again, I had to say more. "It's with me when I pray...and when I praise Him...the Holy Spirit is in me...in anyone who—"

"Let me guess, anyone who believes in Jesus as their Lord and Savior," she said, like she had heard it one too many times before and thought it unfair to those who didn't believe. "You believe all that?"

I nodded. "I believe the book I'm reading is more than a book. It's the living, breathing, Word of God. He breathes new life into those who believe, and they become temples of the Holy Spirit. Talk about restoration projects. Jesus restores us back to God!"

Viv shook her head, then stared at me with one eyebrow raised. "Okay, so you're into all of this." She let out a laugh. "Don't feel self-conscious, you know I admire passion. I admire passionate people more than I do the boring, bland ones who don't care about anything. Might as well go for the gusto, right? And good for you, my friend, but mark my word...no Spirit of God would ever want to spend so much as a single night in me. How do I say it? Meh, I just will. There's five-star resorts and motels—and then there's me. I'm more like the roadside no-tell hotel. And believe me, I'd be way more than a restoration project for God. We're talking demolition, then ground-level construction." She picked up a broken calico shell and held it in her hand. "If we're talking seashells, I'm like a cracked oyster… that not even a mollusk would take up residency in."

"Oh, please," I said, "it doesn't matter if you're a luxury resort, or a cracked shell, so to speak. The God of passion wants to restore all people…restore them to Him. It's why He sent His one and only Son into the hot mess of a world, to take on our sin…talk about passion, the passion of Christ. He loves you, and everyone, and if only we believe, He spares us demolition…I mean, damnation. I'm no good at talking about this…I never have before…but it's Jesus. He makes us move-in ready for the Spirit of God. He'll make you a walking temple of the Holy Spirit too. You won't be disappointed. The Father, Son, and Spirit are restoration specialists like no other."

Viv tossed the shell into the water. As she picked up several more, hurling each one out into the sea, I sat there for a second critiquing my goofy way of wording things.

"You know me, Addie. I've always been the free-roaming type, and I like that about myself, so why would I want to confine myself to *one* pasture when I like tasting from *all* the pastures? Do you get what I'm saying?"

"I get what you're saying." I was glad for the conversation, glad we could talk that way, and weren't like two monstrous heads bickering and belittling each other for believing differently. "You think it's rude and unfair to everyone else that Christians believe Jesus is the way to God—the only way to salvation."

"Yeah," she nodded. "I'd never march into a client's home, knowing their style was eclectic, and tell them to get rid of all the patterns and colors and only keep this *one* pillow, because this *one* pillow is the *only* right pattern and color. I'd never do that, and I don't get why anyone would. My point is, you like the Garden of Eden as your fabricated design, and if so, good for you. But it's not my thing, and never has been my thing."

By then, a pathetic hermit crab caught our attention, and how could it not? It was flipped onto its back and trying so hard, but struggling, to right itself in the sand.

"The poor thing, help it," Viv urged, sitting too far herself to reach it.

"Nah, let's watch it a moment."

"Watch it a moment, why? Do you not like crabs?"

"I love crabs," I said, having lived with them for years in my own house, thanks to Charlie and Henry's crab fetishes.

"Well, if you love crabs, then help the poor thing, for crying out loud!"

The disoriented creature struggled to right itself in the sand, and my mind went there again—to God. I kind of feared what was happening to me, how even a hermit crab trying to right itself in the sand was pointing my thoughts toward God.

"I'll slink my way across this sand…help it myself, if you don't help the poor thing right now," Viv said, annoyed at me for sitting there, watching it. "Obviously, it can't do it by itself, Addie. It can't right itself."

Nope, and neither could we.

We can't, we can't, we can't…without Christ, we can't! Anything is possible with Christ, but without Him, we can't. We cannot right ourselves before God!

Viv gave me an impatient sigh, but I had already come up with a plan, a good plan in which I didn't have to get up from where I was sitting, or risk having the crab clamp down on me.

"Aha, I see what you're doing," she said when I picked up a branch. "But here, I think you should use this instead," she tried handing me a pen shell, "in case that branch isn't strong enough."

And people tried telling God what they thought He should have used instead. But God didn't need a plan B, C, or D, when His one and only plan was perfect and sufficient. "Nope, I'm using what I'm using. The branch is perfect. It's all that's needed."

And the Branch of Righteousness, the perfect, sinless Jesus, seated at the right side of His father in Heaven, was all that was needed for God to reach down into the world that was turned upside down with sin and to right us before God.

"No, wait," Viv reached for a piece of driftwood, as if she still didn't think the branch I had chosen was sufficient, "I'd use this if I were you."

I stretched my arm out, and using the branch that I chose, gently flipped the crab over, righting it in the sand.

"Loving of you," she said.

"Loving indeed," I smiled. What else was it but love?

Later that night, I went out onto my front porch step to write about something. I was loved by God, but He didn't force me to love Him back. He didn't force me to accept His saving hand. He gave me free will. I didn't want to squirm around like a disoriented crab on its back, trying to right itself, and was glad for the choice I made. I liked crawling to where He had called me.

When Peter came out onto the porch and asked what I was writing about, I didn't feel like telling him. "Just stuff."

"Stuff for that bestseller of yours?"

"Writing about a crab I saw on the beach earlier."

"Um, you mean a children's story? You're writing a children's story?"

A child of God story, I thought but didn't say. I shrugged my shoulders. Whatever I was writing, I was writing like no one was watching… writing to the glory of God, and it felt nice.

THIRTY-THREE

Create a cozy outdoor niche under the stars.
Pick out a spot in your yard, then put down a sofa, chaise
lounge, low table, and swivel chairs. Be sure to go with
furniture that's crafted to withstand weather and time.

Peter and I spent the next several days, sunrise to sunset, working on the house. When he had conference calls and reports for work, I either snuck to the beach and walked, or I wrote.

"What on earth?" I shouted with surprise when I returned after sunset and found him under the lit-up house pulling one of my wish-list items—an onyx-colored outdoor furniture set—from a giant delivery box. "*Woo hoo, woo hoo, woo hoo!*"

"Yep," Peter said with a giant grin. "I won over a new account, and wanted to surprise you with something on your wish list."

"*Woo hoo!*" I did a dance. Peter and I had a new spot to sit out under the stars, and for me to drink coffee in the morning and write.

"We can get the washer and dryer and other things, too." He looked at my dancing feet coated in sand. "You should add an outdoor shower to that wish list of yours, instead of the tummy tuck."

I stopped dancing. "Wait a minute, Peter, did you find my written-out wish list?" I had told him about the outdoor furniture, but not the other things on my list.

He didn't need to answer. As he reached into a giant box, pulling out a swivel chair, his expression gave him away.

"Were you snooping through my binder? How much of my writing did you read?"

"Simmer down, Adele. You left it open. I didn't think it was a big deal. Sorry, I won't read it again." He opened another box, flipped it onto its side, then pulled out a coffee table. "But a tummy tuck? Tell me you're not serious about that!"

I said nothing as Peter took one end, I the other, and we carried the table across the yard to where we had repaired the crumbling stonework of a terrace. I didn't expect him to understand why a tummy tuck had for a fleeting moment entered my mind and made its way onto my wish list.

His tummy never housed a seven-, eight-, and two six-pound, kicking and pushing babies like mine did. During the nine months that each of them dwelled in the less than twelve-square-inches of living quarters within me, they needed more room to grow, and stretched and expanded the space they were in.

We positioned the table, then went back to the boxes and pulled out a chaise lounge. "Let me guess, it was Viv's idea?"

"Nope, not at all. This cozy niche under the stars was her idea and a good one. Why would you think me wanting a tummy tuck was Viv's idea?"

"Ah, let me see…way back when you colored those strands of your hair green and gave away one month's tuition to the local food pantry, then waited tables to make up for it…well, those were her ideas. The two of you fasting for that month…her idea…I could go on and on."

"Her intentions were good. What's wrong with wanting to experience a profound internal awareness of the issue of world hunger? I'm not ashamed that I let her influence me with that, even though I cheated our fast when she wasn't around, when you brought me those boxes of ramen noodles."

"Okay," Peter grinned, "so you see why I asked if it was her idea."

I shrugged off his snooping into my writing. I wanted to enjoy the new furniture moment. And I wasn't that upset. "Just know Viv isn't some influencer in my life. It was a hundred percent my idea, and to be honest, I wouldn't get a tummy tuck. I'm too scared." I picked up my end of the chaise lounge, Peter picked up his, and we headed for the stone terrace. "What about you, don't you ever wish for things…even if they seem outlandish?"

"Sure, I do. I wish I could see in the dark like an owl, wish I could win over more accounts, so we could buy all the things on your wish list, all the things this place needs. I wish it didn't need so much...wish we could buy a boat instead. You did a great job with the oven, but I wish the whole kitchen was done, and it wasn't such a painstaking, costly gut-job itself."

"I wish that, too," I said, and by then we had put the chaise lounge down and were back by the boxes, opening more.

"For the record," Peter pulled out a white and turquoise striped cushion, "I like your stomach the way it is. We can move on, but I wanted to say those stretch marks of yours, they're like hieroglyphics."

"Hieroglyphics?"

"Yeah, they tell part of our history, that's all, and I like our history."

Right then and there, I wished for another quarter of a century with him by my side, and I should have told him that, but some wishes were awkward to say out loud.

Once all the furniture and cushions were placed, Peter went over to break down the boxes, and I dropped down onto a swivel chair. In light of him snooping through my binder and reading what I wrote, was it even possible, what Marita had told me to do—write like no one was watching, write to the glory of God, like no one was watching?

I stopped swiveling and looked up at a group of stars. When I was younger I did more than look up at a group of stars. I danced along the imaginary lines of the constellations. Mom and Luke saw me through me the window, stargazing in the yard, and later in the house, studying for my astronomy test. They didn't see into my imagination to know that I was doing more than gazing at the stars and memorizing a study guide.

I was getting to know and personalizing the far away and distant, encountering it for myself...tip-toeing from the curve of the Big Dipper, and with pointed toes, star-hopping through outer space, landing on Arcturus. After stumbling out of place from its brightness and rebalancing myself, I danced around it, while singing beneath my breath over and over again the scientific facts I had learned in class.

It was my way of learning the facts in a more active and meaningful way, and the reason for my A's. I did the same with geography while learning states, countries, and continents.

I got up from the swivel chair and since Peter was still collapsing boxes, I settled down on the chaise lounge, closing my eyes. Writing was an unusual activity, different from dancing and less carefree. A person dancing alone in their house left no evidence of their dance behind, but a writer left line after line of words. And just as the imaginary lines around the stars formed animals, mythical persons, creatures, and gods, writers formed patterns, too.

What if one day, someone was on their back in the grass—not gazing up at the massive spheres of gas in the sky, but following along the lines of something I wrote? Where would the lines take them? Maybe somewhere good, and for that reason there was a responsibility attached to writing.

"One more thing." Peter came over to where I was. "I'm not going to read your writing unless you want me to. But the crab you wrote about, the one that was turned upside down in the sand—"

I kept my eyes closed.

"It didn't need to be flipped over."

I opened them. "What?"

"Yeah, it was entering the molting process. You know, outgrowing its shell, getting ready to leave...move into a bigger shell in order to grow."

"Seriously, Peter, how much of my binder did you read?"

"Not much. The wish list and the crab. You mentioned you were writing about a crab, and I was curious to see where you were going with it. I didn't realize you were relating it to the hand of God coming down to Earth to right us upside-down people."

I folded my arms and re-closed my eyes. Great, not only had I interfered with the growth of a crab, but Peter didn't like what he had read, my overly dramatic, hyper-spiritualization of things. And maybe he was right, I was overdoing it.

"I'm calling it a night," he said, like it was no big deal about the crab and my writing. "I'm heading upstairs. You coming?"

I got up from the chaise lounge, but felt such a headrush, I dropped back down. "I'll be up soon." I needed a moment alone. Like the crab, I had been going through a molting process, too...outgrowing desires, leaving them behind, and setting my heart on new and bigger things.

And what if Peter didn't like such growth in me? I no longer wanted to crank out a shallow romance. I wanted to write to the glory of God, so if someone reading what I wrote happened to be in a place of darkness, they'd catch glimpse of God's bright love. But I didn't want Peter thinking I had gone overboard.

"To tell you the truth, Adele," Peter said from the porch, "I liked what I read…wanted to read more. Your writing turned sloppy, though. You might want to only use your laptop from now on. At one point, it wasn't even readable. Why'd you write so sloppy all of a sudden?"

I sighed with relief that he wanted to read more. It meant he wasn't disappointed or concerned that I was writing too much about God. But I didn't tell him why my writing got sloppy. When I tried writing about the villainous disease that stepped on Mom's toes, for the first few minutes my pen waltzed formally across the paper. But as soon as I felt a pattern forming, and my words and thoughts advancing together—*step, step, close*—things fell apart.

If only Peter knew what that sloppiness was…my words trying to hold my thoughts up and my thoughts stepping on my words or knocking into them. The sloppiness was okay. Some dances, like some writing, only God needed to see. He knew I was struggling, couldn't get over and around certain aspects of the imperfect world, and He didn't mind me working on things alone with Him.

If furniture makers crafted furniture to withstand weather and time, I wished so badly God would have crafted Mom's mind to withstand the duration of her life on Earth. Where was He when they found her alone in the middle of the night, sitting on that bench? It didn't seem right when a person's insides wore out before their outsides, nor even when their outsides wore out before their insides.

But the more I prayed in honesty to God, the more my insides told me it wasn't God's fault. He didn't design us to deteriorate and die, but to live. Anything short of living was the consequence of what unfolded in the Eden. And even then, He went about providing us a way around such consequences so we could go on living eternally with Him.

"Christ's workmanship in me," I muttered out loud, "that's what withstands weather and time and lasts into eternity. Nothing I obtain lasts longer than righteousness. No storm, disease, wear and tear, or sandy feet will ever destroy what Christ has done in me." On that truth alone, I could have sat resting all night, although the chaise lounge was pretty comfortable, too.

When I got up from the chaise lounge and headed in the moonlight up the front porch steps, did I blame the builder for the current condition our house was in? No, he'd built it well. I didn't want to blame God for what happened to Mom's mind. Everything God made was good. If Hidden Potential burned down, I couldn't have blamed the builder. I'd have blamed the person playing with fire in my yard the day before.

THIRTY-FOUR

The kitchen proved itself to be the motherlode of all gut-jobs. The few things we kept in place were the oven I scoured, the nostalgic deep-basin farm sink, and the original wooden cabinets. We did rip off the cabinet doors, though, something we never could have done back when we had millions of mismatched cups to hide. After patching and filling the screw holes where the doors had been, Peter painted the original wood-work bright white, and I painted the interior shelving taupe. Wow, how it made our white vintage dinnerware pop!

With coffee in hand, I hurried around the house early in the morning, peeking out the windows to see if the painters were there. They had been prepping Hidden Potential for days, power washing, cleaning its trim, scraping, sanding, replacing rotten wood, and the day had come.

I unwrapped a bowl filled with Kalamata and Spanish olives I had bought at the Sanibel Farmer's Market and marinated overnight in minced garlic, dried chili flakes, lemon, orange zest, vinegar, sugar, salt, and pep-per. It was going to be for Viv and me, for when we sat in the yard watch-ing the house get painted.

Every several days or so, she and I had been taking morning strolls up and down our road. I bought her fruit on Sundays, but other than that, I wasn't spending much time with her. Mostly, I was focusing on Peter, the house, reading the Bible, walking and talking with God, and writing. Peter had reunited with Viv, but the reunion was short and nothing worth writing about—very undramatic.

"Can't believe today's the day!" I went into the bedroom to pull my hair back into a sloppy ponytail. "I'm so giddy I can't take it!"

"Giddy," Peter grinned. "I don't think I've ever heard a single person use that word. What does it even mean?"

"Excitement to the point of disorientation."

"Um," he wiped a smudge of taupe-colored paint off my nose, "are you giddy that Viv's coming over, or giddy that the house is getting painted?"

"Both. Viv doesn't know she's coming over. She thinks we're going for our usual stroll." I hurried into my closet to change into my black mid-length workout leggings and white t-shirt, "The other day, she told me that watching a house get painted is like watching a show on Broadway, and she cries."

"Why does that not surprise me?"

I let out a laugh, then slipped my flip flops on and headed out the door. Viv was in her chair waiting for me at the end of her ramp. She never wore the same outfit twice, but had on the exact orange leggings and semi-fitted floral shirt that she wore the last few times I saw her. For me, wearing the same thing was no big deal, but for her, I suspected it meant she was struggling without Marita. I was glad her physical therapist was showing up four days a week, and I wasn't the only one in her life.

"We're going somewhere special today," I announced. "You'll see where in a minute."

"Oh, for crying out loud," she flung her uncombed hair out of her face, "you know I don't like surprises!"

"I'll give you a hint. Listen."

Even with all the commotion coming from my yard—truck doors opening and closing, and muffled conversation—she had no idea. I didn't want us missing the opening act—Hidden Potential getting its first stroke of paint—so I took hold of her chair and quickly as I could, headed around the side of her house.

Once we reached the bumpy banyan trees at the edge of her property, I said, "My yard. We're going to my yard."

"Your yard!" Her voice was reactive, as if we were leaving the castle grounds, heading into the spooky forest. I didn't blame her. Other than repairing the stone terrace and putting the furniture set out, Peter and I hadn't yet gotten around to yardwork.

She gripped the armrests of her chair, and after making it through the line of fruitless trees, then plowing through the field of pointy, blade-like grass reaching her seat, we came up and around the side of the house to where the painters were starting. Viv clapped her hands at the sight: tarps spread out, cans of paint opened, painters in their costumes climbing tall ladders, dipping brushes in and swirling them about.

I parked her chair on the stone terrace, right beneath the awning of the fifty-foot apple blossom cassia tree. Already, it had become a special spot for me and when I sat there writing, its dark chocolate-colored seed pods and sweet fragrance attracted oodles of yellow sulphur butterflies.

"I don't know what to say." Viv's eyes fluttered about. "I'm proud of you. I'll start with that. Right here in the midst of total yard chaos, you've created this cozy outdoor niche!"

"Well, it was your idea."

Her eyes had already moved on and, like a hawk, were watching a painter high up on a ladder as he spread the first stroke of color. "Is that primer or paint?"

"Both. It's primer and paint mixed together."

"Why'd you do that?" Her voice turned critical. "Why'd you mix the primer and the paint together?"

"Reduce the number of coats…get it done sooner. Why, would you not have done that if you were me?"

"Well, you wouldn't combine all four movements of a symphony, then play them at once, to save time, would you? When you cook, you put the garlic in by itself a few minutes, right? You don't put the garlic, onion, celery and carrots all in at once, to save time."

"Um."

"Don't get me started, never mind. But white," she made a face, "why white?"

"Brilliant white. I went with a brilliant white, not dull. And besides," I pointed out the orange and yellow scarlet milkweed growing alongside the shed, and the dark rosy-pink flowers of the apple blossom cassia near the bottom porch steps, and the glowing yellow flowers of the Oncidium orchid, "I figured those were color enough."

She gave me a megawatt smile. "Pat yourself on the back, you know why?"

"Why?"

"You gave thought to it, that's why. It drives me bananas when people paint their houses white for no other reason than they were scared to pick anything else. But you picked it for a reason." She clapped her hands. "I love it—I love the brilliant white, but what about the inside? Tell me the inside isn't going to be all white."

I dropped down into the swivel chair. "I have no idea. But when the time comes, Peter and I will get you up those porch steps, so you can go inside and help us figure it all out."

Speaking of Peter, he was standing under a tree with our bowl of olives. "Hey," I called out to him. "I see you over there. I see what you're doing."

He walked over, giving us both an acknowledging nod, then surrendered the bowl on the table in front of us.

"You think you can build a ramp?" I asked.

"Not for me, I hope," Viv interjected before he could answer. "Don't you dare build a ramp for me! I'm not even going to be here that much longer. And besides, you watch and see, I'll be out of this chair in no time, marching right up those steps of yours, to say good-bye. I kid you not!"

Peter looked relieved. "I would have built a ramp for you, if a ramp was needed," he said in a super-sweet voice. "If I fixed the porch steps, I'm sure I could have figured out how to build a ramp."

Viv looked at me, then back at Peter with a look of awe on her face. "You know what, Peter?"

"What?"

"You're a good guy. I'm not kidding, you are!"

I had to roll my eyes. It wasn't that I disagreed, but it was like she was talking about some rare creature of which there were a few remaining in existence.

"Being a good guy is easy. I love my family, love my wife. They deserve my best and nothing less. But thank you. I'll let you ladies talk now. One of the painters is calling me over."

"Unless it's a show," Viv said the second he left, "looks like you two are still in love. Are you?"

She had shared her struggles. I didn't want to reply with a sickly sweet, artificial answer making her think everything was perfect when nothing was perfect. Our marriage had never been perfect, and if she knew how all through the years I had mumbled beneath my breath in annoyance at him and he at me for this or that.

"The two of you together still, not loathing each other," she popped an olive in her mouth, and in a raspy whisper added, "what's your secret?"

I had no idea what our secret was. I looked over at a pair of doves resting on the bottom front porch step. Doves mated for life. What was their secret?

"You're not seeing us in our old setting. In our old setting, we were overly scheduled and running around like fools, trying to keep up. We were hardly home at the same time, and when we were, we spun like tops, bumping into each other without stopping. I don't know how we did it. It's all a big blur now."

"Well, you're still together. And, unless you're both a couple of actors, looks like you like each other. There's got to be a secret behind that at least."

I glanced back over at the pair of doves. They hadn't budged and good for them, sitting so peacefully on the step beneath the flowers of the apple blossom cassia. Probably, they had already built several nests together, raised multiple broods, and consumed their morning seeds. That was their secret—do what you have to do, don't complicate things, and enjoy your moments of rest together.

Viv was waiting for me to answer, but if only I could have written out my answer instead. Writing about love was easier than talking about it. In writing, I could have so easily answered along the lines of: Peter and I seeded a crop together…our family. And we were both fully committed to maturing it to harvest, which required decades of hard work. We were like two farmers who shared land together. We loved our land and what we had planted more than we loved ourselves as a couple. Since we both had different weaknesses and strengths, plowing through together worked better than going alone, and so we worked sunrise to sunset, putting together whatever we had to offer for the sake of the crop, operating like a single machine combining several jobs into one.

I let out a laugh.

"What's so funny?"

"I can't tell you our secret…I don't know how to make it sound normal. It was a labor of love, grueling at times, especially during our drought seasons…but we survived, we made it through. Peter is a good guy, which helped a lot. Be careful who you seed a crop with."

"Anything else?"

"Yeah, for every annoying flaw in him, I had to recognize an equally annoying flaw in myself. It was humbling, but I had to do that."

Viv popped an olive in her mouth. "I guess falling head over heels in love and staying in love for the long-haul isn't necessarily romantic."

"Oh, actually," I lowered my voice to a whisper, "I'm not sure I ever fell in love."

Her expression changed, as if I had released horrible, shocking, breaking news, and poor Peter!

I got up from the swivel chair, making myself more comfortable on the chaise lounge instead. "Here's what I mean. Falling is a temporary act. Whatever we fall into...ruts, moods, water, love, whatever...we don't stay there." I pointed toward the house. "If that guy falls from the ladder and lands in a bucket of paint, he's not going to stay in the bucket of paint. He's going to get out of it."

"Well, I hope so!"

"Yeah, so, when I said that, what I meant was that my love for Peter was more than a single moment of falling."

"What was it then?"

"Hmmm, I'd have to think about it." I ate an olive, kicked off my flip flops, then stretched my legs across the chaise lounge.

It had been like a dance, a first dance. I wanted to dance with him, he wanted to dance with me, and neither of us knew what we were doing. We stepped on each other's toes, but didn't care at first. I got caught up dancing with him, like nothing else mattered. But then the stepping on each other's toes started to bother me. I can't tell you how many times I went to my corner and he to his. We both learned bad moves of our own...tried them out on each other.

And before we knew it the dance floor was filled with kids. We couldn't even hear each other. Forget whispering. We were shouting. Peter kept telling me to enjoy it, that it would be just the two of us one day, dancing on the quiet dance floor again. Whenever our old favorite song came on, the one we first danced to, Peter looked around the crowded room and so did I, and for a quick second our eyes locked.

"Peter and I," I told Viv as we stared up at the house getting painted, "it's been like a first dance that never ended. We'll go on and on until the music dies."

Her expression softened. "You should be a greeting card writer!"

"You're not the first one to tell me that."

I rested my hands behind my head and pointed my toes, feeling optimistic for Peter and me. We had made it and were on that quiet dance floor again, learning new steps. I looked over at the doves, digesting their seeds. We were digesting the last couple of decades of our life together, resting in the present, and appreciating the overall significance of what we went through, the good songs and the bad.

"I tried." Viv spat an olive pit out, then licked her lips. "I tried forcing husband number one to love me. I told him I'd jump off the Golden Gate Bridge if he left me. I regret that. It's one of the reasons I want to walk the bridge all the way across…healing in more ways than one. He was a kid, and so was I. We put each other through a nightmare."

She put a few olives in her mouth. "I did everything I could to keep husband number two. Tried so hard to change myself—anything to make him love me." She swallowed hard. "I should have been an expert by the time my third came along…but nope." She wiped the corners of her eyes with her pinkies. "I wasn't raised to believe in good things, so I grew suspicious, not trusting that his love for me was real. That's the reason I ended it, as crazy as it sounds."

"Did he want to end it, too?"

"Nope," she said right away. "He wanted to make it work, but I said all kinds of nasty things to him. And even when he was nothing but nice, I kicked him out." She let out a sob. "I told you watching a house get painted always makes me cry. Dull and worn out, imperfections everywhere. Then, *ta dah*, all is new. Witnessing beautiful transformations…it's always an emotional experience for me, I can't help it."

Just then one of the painters lit a cigarette, then sat down on the bottom porch step, unintentionally scaring the doves off. He gave us a nod.

"He must think I'm a nut case, sitting here blowing my nose, sobbing." Viv wiped her face with a napkin. "Enough, I mean it. Enough about me. Don't let me go there anymore…to me! Your sweet little house…Hidden

Potential…is on its way to reaching its potential. I don't even want to think about my potential…the potential me and my third had together."

I didn't want her feeling like she was the only one with problems. I didn't share as many of mine with her because I was writing about things, and writing was like therapy—a cathartic experience. "The other night," I said, "I was sitting right here in my cozy outdoor niche, under the stars….and I let myself cry."

"Aw."

"Yeah, thinking about my mom." I stood up and walked a few steps over to a decaying, hollowed-out tree occupied by a honeybee colony. I didn't feel like telling her what I sometimes struggled with—

How could our loving God have left my mom out to dry on a bench in the middle of the night? Where was He when she wandered blocks from our house only to sit all alone in the dark? It was a question that stung me over and over, leaving me with lingering twinges of pain.

Viv and the painter had become engaged in small talk. I did my own thing, pulling from my pocket another Bible verse Mom had scribbled onto scratch paper. I had been putting verses into my pocket daily, then waiting for the right moment to pull them out and read them.

> "And if the Spirit of him who raised Jesus from the dead is living in you, he who raised Christ from the dead will also give life to your mortal bodies through his Spirit, who lives in you."
> —Romans 8:11

I read it again and again as I circled the decaying tree, until an ever-so-subtle thought buzzed through my mind. The Spirit of Him who raised Jesus from the dead had been living in Mom. He didn't move out when she was physically deteriorating. His Spirit dwelt in her and was at work in her right up until the end, including that night when she sat on that bench not knowing who or where she was.

She had more than a beautiful memory in her mind. She had a house guest who never left her. She wasn't alone. Up until the very end, Mom wasn't alone. She had the company of Christ in her.

Viv and the painter thought I was looking into the decaying tree, at the hive filled with bees and honey. But really, I was looking into God's

Word and finding peace knowing that Mom was filled with more, with the stored-up Word of God in her and the Spirit of Christ.

"Still," I prayed beneath my breath, "the image I have in my mind— Mom sitting alone at three in the morning on *a bench, a bench, a bench*— it's always with me. And it makes me sad."

By then, Viv had wheeled herself away from the stone terrace area and was over by the porch steps, laughing with the painter. He was on cigarette number two and still sitting on that bottom step, where the doves had sat and where I loved sitting, too. I sat there when I wrote and when I prayed, and it was like a wooden bench of its own.

A bench, a bench, a bench.

My mind wouldn't get off the chant, until it struck me.

"Oh my Lord!" I shouted, startling the painters on their ladders, the birds in the branches, and even Viv and the guy she was chit-chatting with. I went over and sat right down next to him on the bottom step.

He stomped out his cigarette, but us sitting on the step together was awkward. It was like one of those *who's on first?* moments. He looked at Viv. Viv looked at me. I looked at him. When he looked at Viv again, it was her turn to look back at me, and so she did. "What's going on here, Addie?"

"You want to know? I'll tell you. That horrible disease, like locusts eating away at my mother's mind…well, it had her wandering out the front door in the middle of the night. Police found her sitting on a bench."

Viv cracked her knuckles, as if she wanted to fight the horrid disease. The painter cursed with compassion, then apologized for having cursed.

"But guess what?"

"What?" they said in unison.

"Mom knew where she was going. A part of her, deep inside, knew where she was going."

"Where?"

I shook my head, still freshly appreciating the profoundness of it, but also wanting to prolong the wonderful suspense. "She was meeting up with God on a bench!"

Viv looked at me pathetically. Scratching his head, the painter got up and walked a few feet away, then lit a third cigarette. "You mean to say that God was on a bench?" A halo of smoke floated above his head.

"Before my mom got sick, she loved to sit on benches, praying and writing letters to God. It was her thing. I've been reading the letters she wrote to Him while on those benches—benches right here on Sanibel, all over this island."

The painter looked at Viv, and she looked at me. It was still my turn. They wanted it to be my turn. "Guys, my mom wasn't alone the night police found her. God was still with her. See that deteriorating tree over there? It's got a beehive in it. My mom, she had the Spirit of Christ in her, and no disease destroys that! Even as parts of her deteriorated, He was still with her, in her *sanctum sanctorum*—"

"Her what?"

"Inner sanctuary, where the two of them met up."

"Um," the painter probably felt like he had to say something, but didn't know what. "That's all pretty cool. So, do you want us to paint the porch steps, too...and what color?"

I looked at Viv and shrugged my shoulders. I had no idea what color to paint the porch steps.

"Paint them white," she ordered, confident as a high-ranking commander. "It's a no-brainer, paint the porch steps white!"

Hmmm...I took a few steps back, trying to picture it—a white house with white steps. "Are you sure that won't look kind of boring?"

"Hold your horses, friend. I'm not done. And trust me, I know what I'm doing." Her tone was passionate. "After this wonderful man here paints the steps white, you, my friend, are going to paint by hand a wide swath of turquoise to mimic a runner. You need to add whimsy to your dollhouse by the sea."

"Love it. I never would have thought of that myself."

Viv cleared her throat, commanding further attention. "I have another idea." She straightened her spine, sitting upright in her chair. "On that bottom porch step, I want you to paint the words, 'In loving memory of Mom, I sit here not alone, but with God.'"

I didn't say anything, but understood then why my friend was so good at what she did. All I could do was nod. I didn't want to sob.

With that, the painter tossed his cigarette and looked at me. "Alright then, we'll paint the steps white and you can do the rest."

THIRTY-FIVE

* * *

"For every house has a builder, but God
is the one who made everything.
Moses was certainly faithful in God's house, but only as a
servant. His work was an illustration of the truths God would
reveal later. But Christ, the faithful Son, was in charge of the
entire household. And we are God's household, if we keep our
courage and remain confident in our hope in Christ. That is
why the Holy Spirit says, 'Today you must listen to my voice,
Don't harden your hearts against Him as Israel did when
they rebelled, when they tested God in the wilderness.'"
—Hebrews 3:4–8

To the One who made everything,

*Here I am again, meeting up with You on another bench—this one tucked
within a mangrove forest over at the wildlife refuge. I found the secluded spot
after walking on the Indigo Trail, over the tropical hammock. I could sit here
all day, breathing in the smell of the salt marsh, resting in Your presence.*

*All over this island are trees with heart-shaped leaves, and I can't stop no-
ticing them. This morning, I pulled one off a branch and stuck it in my pocket.
A minute ago, I pulled it out and already it's dried up and crumbled. The
vibrant, heart-shaped leaves are reminders that my heart must stay attached to
You via Your Word. How can my heart beat according to Your will if it's not
attached to Your Word? Whatever I do unattached will dry up and crumple.
Your Word, it lasts forever. You've pressed and preserved Truth within the pages*

of the Bible, but it's as living as when You first spoke it. You are Your Word and Your Word is within me, and for that, I thank You.

Last night I made my way through the entire book of Haggai. I'm not bragging, it was only a couple of pages long. But I was excited to read about Your people in 538 B.C. returning to Jerusalem to rebuild Solomon's temple that was destroyed by the Babylonians. The people must have been a wreck. The temple was their connection to and the focal point of their relationship with You.

I love living in New Testament times. Christ is now our connection point, our focal point. It's one of the things I love about Christianity. It's about a person, not a place, and about going to Christ, not a building. Church is important, to stay connected to others in the household, and to learn and worship collectively. But my relationship with You is personal.

So, back to the little book of Haggai in which the people were all ready to start working on the rebuild and restoration of the temple. Even though they knew there was nothing more important than restoring the temple and their relationship with You, as passionate as they were, they got diverted.

They lost their purpose and forgot their priorities. Duh! How could they be so dumb? One moment they were passionate about rebuilding a place for Your presence, and the next moment they got all distracted to the point they let their work on the temple flounder for over fifteen years.

But then it struck me. I've done similar. You know the times in my life when I was passionate for You, but then different priorities took over. I stopped praying, Bible studying, and meeting up with others in Your household. Halting everything related to me as a walking temple of the Holy Spirit, I put my relationship with You on hold.

It's easy to put things on hold. There's always those things in life pulling my attention away from where it should be. If there are two birthday gifts with my name on them, there always seems to be three problems. As much as I want to unwrap and enjoy the blessings You have for me and to live in a state of authentic gratitude, problems and their associated stress pile up in front of me, hindering me from seeing and appreciating the blessings and gifts You have for me.

It's like the walls of my mind are painted in two contrasting colors—humility and self-pity. Self-pity is a more dominating color and tends to pull my attention away from humility. When self-pity dominates, it produces an atmosphere of entitlement—I expect pity for my circumstances. I'd rather the walls within me were painted in humility. Then, I'd realize I can't solve this situation without You, God. Help me, I'd cry desperately—then find myself filled with an atmosphere of gratitude instead.

How simple if I could go to the store and buy cans of humility, then pour them over my thoughts. But stores don't sell cans of humility. Still, that doesn't mean I'm stuck with an inner atmosphere I don't like. Attitudes aren't permanent features that we're stuck with. If I want humility, I know where to get it. It comes from knowing You, my Creator, and the more I know You the more I love You, and want to spend time with You. I know that You love me, and that every good thing—salvation, for starters—is a gift from You.

So, back to the people I was reading about last night. They got sidetracked for their own reasons. They were pouring their energy into rebuilding their own homes rather than restoring the temple. Then through Your prophet, Haggai, You asked them a specific question. "Is it time for you yourselves to live in your paneled houses, while this house remains a ruin?"

I personalize that question. How can I read such a thing without personalizing it? The Bible is the most personal book I've ever read, and even now, I keep holding my pen still just to sit here and think things through. The people picked back up again, working on the temple. And I'm glad I've picked back up again, too, working on my relationship with You.

You promised the Old Testament people that You would fill their house— that new temple they were building—with glory. And You would also grant peace. Well, sure enough, You fulfilled that five hundred years later when Jesus Himself entered the rebuilt temple, filling it with His presence. Structurally and decoratively the second temple wasn't as spectacular as the first—and the people had been reminiscing over the great glory of the former—although once Jesus stepped foot inside, there was far greater glory than the former house, indeed!

Here we all are, so loved by You that You sent Jesus—the only name under Heaven given among men, whereby we must be saved. And now, Your glory is walking around all over this world in those who believe.

The day is coming when I'll look back and miss my stint on Sanibel, sitting on the benches surrounded by tropical flora, while appreciating overwhelming peace from the presence of the Holy Spirit within. It'll hit me in the dead of winter, when a bitter, cold, wintry mix of rain and snow is descending upon Michigan. I'll grieve the vibrant, heart-shaped leaves, but remember to stay attached to You, no matter the season I'm in.

Soon I'll be sitting in traffic, not on a bench in a wildlife refuge. Things are going to get busy again, but when that happens, I pray I don't hang an out to lunch, be back soon *sign on the door of my heart. Wherever I am, may benches remind me to stop and sit for a moment...sit with You in Your holy presence.*

Love,
Finley

P.S. Help me lay aside that which gets in the way of me seeing Christ, me moving closer to Christ. No matter where I am on the boardwalk of life, like Florida's year-round blooming wildflowers, may I always keep my eyes and ears open...open to You no matter what.

THIRTY-SIX

After the painters doused the porch steps in white, I took Viv's advice and hand-painted the turquoise swath. Then, in a small font, I wrote in memory of Mom—*I sit here not alone, but with God.* Beneath the outstretched arms of the sea grape tree and the flowering apple blossom cassia, I spent many mornings on the bottom step, and felt like an undisturbed barn owl nesting in a secret, hollowed-out tree.

Peter and I continued working on our lovely dwelling place by the sea. We replaced her windows and added weather-resistant, white-stained cedar shingles. Despite our measly budget, we hired Daniel, a young landscaper, who on his first trip out to the house confirmed our worst suspicions. Reviving the neglected grounds around the place was going to be more daunting than we imagined.

"We can work out here together," he said as we followed him on his trek through our tropical rainforest of a yard. "It'll cost less if you're willing to do some of it yourselves."

I looked at Peter. The sun was poking through the branches of the gumbo-limbo tree casting a monstrous shadow on his face. "I can mow a lawn, no big deal. I've always mowed the lawn. But this isn't a lawn. I wouldn't know what to do if I—"

"If you what?"

"Came across a s…s…snake."

No wonder he was wearing the knee-high, yellow rubber boots that came with the house, the ones I wore the day I ventured out to look for fruit in the trees. Peter was afraid of snakes.

"Don't worry. They want nothing to do with you, either." Daniel moved along, pointing out endless clusters of glossy-leaved shrubs with bright red, ornamental berries. "Brazilian peppertree shrubs. It all has to go."

"Why? They're so pretty."

I didn't like his answer, that Brazilian peppertree shrubs were a damaging species, growing out of control—up to fifteen feet high—and forming closed canopies of their own, serving no purpose to Sanibel's wildlife whatsoever.

"It seems like everything has to go. Tell me my fruit trees can stay!"

"Sure, but you've got all this deep-rooted bad stuff growing out of control, blocking them from the sun. We have to get rid of the bad stuff so the good stuff can grow."

The ornery shadow returned to Peter's face. "This sounds like a lot of work. It's going to take over our lives…way more than yardwork here."

"Garden restoration," I said, like nothing else mattered. "And we can do it. We have to do it." Peter and I functioned best as opposites. When he turned into the pessimist, I had to be the optimist. "Think of it as one big month of playing in the yard. We'll make it fun. I don't know how, but we will."

We picked a start date that worked for Daniel, and in the days leading up to it, we tried not to think about how daunting it was going to be. "No talking about the yard," I said as we sat trying to relax on the candle-lit front porch, long after dark. "And no talking about finances or work, either."

"What about the kids? Can we talk about them?"

Each of them had been encountering turbulent situations of their own, and usually the moment Peter and I lit the candle, then settled down on the front porch, one-by-one they'd call or text. I was grateful for the help of a landscaper to guide us with our yard, but if only there was some-one—an air traffic controller, perhaps—to help guide our kids on a safe and expeditious journey through the rough patches of early adulthood.

Peter and I were squeezed together on the wicker loveseat that came with the place. He took a call from one child, as I hung up with another, and was then on the phone with the third, while the fourth was texting us both. It reminded me of when they were little. One got upset and whined, then the second chimed in, and since whining was contagious, the third joined in, until all four were whining, wailing, and tugging on the hem of my skirt.

"I used to feel like a superhero," I told Peter in between calls.

"Um, what do you mean?"

"A hug, a bowl of ice cream, a talk here or there, and I had the power to make things better…Wonder-Mama."

"Well, you know everyone warned us it was coming…bigger kids, bigger problems."

So true, and I felt powerless, like my hands were tied behind my back as they nose-dived and tried to turn situations around, without success.

"Did we not prepare them?" I stared into the flickering candlelight. "I know I could have done more…when it was still my job to work on them, when they were living under our roof."

"I don't know. We did our best."

"I want to think that, too, but it all went by so fast and all of a sudden, they were off…like planes on a runway, one after the next. I feel like all we can do now is stand here, watching, waving." I laid my head on his shoulder. Could I have done a better job of inspecting them before they took off, working on their systems, taking that extra time to make sure those critical parts—morals, values, attitudes toward life and selves—were in check and secure?

But too late, or so it seemed, they were off on the flights of their lives, and we couldn't go with them. The journey was theirs, not ours, and all we could do was listen to their voices when they called, and from a distance, guide them wherever possible.

My mind, running smoothly for weeks, was rattling and shaking again, getting all worked up over Lucy not breaking up that pattern of hers. She and her no-good boyfriend were still on-again, off-again every other weekend, and it was making Peter and me feel a sort of emotional motion sickness. Whenever she announced on speaker phone their relationship had ended, we performed a quiet high-five routine. And when we heard they had gotten back together again, we wrinkled our faces like bulldogs.

Her broken voice always sent my mood crashing, but it devastated me more when she kept taking him back into her life. I closed my eyes, wishing she would have listened to my advice…kicked him out of her cockpit, enjoyed a solo flight for a while.

"You're going to like this," Peter said, once his texting with the boys, and my phone calls with the girls for the third night in a row were settling down. "Mrs. P delivered a bag of groceries to Charlie and Henry."

"No!"

"Yep, left it on their doorstep, rang the doorbell, and ran…well, not fast. They saw her."

"I'm speechless."

"I know, right? Charlie said he'll text you the details tomorrow…there were homemade brownies in the bag."

Goosebumps covered my arms and my eyes welled with tears. The willow tree. The night of our party, she had seen them under the willow tree, chowing down on brownies. Despite the unrest happening—chaotic situations my own kids were going through, and things on the news—it was still a wonderful world at times, and people—most of them—had soft and loving, gooey parts to their hearts.

Still, I was huffing and puffing, overtaken by worries for Lucy our first day into garden restoration. Had I not taught our daughter to watch out for people tangling around her like needy vines, and to protect and appreciate her precious space?

Peter was huffing and puffing, too, and I assumed he was all worked up over the same thing I was. "It's tough, isn't it?" I asked, my bottom lip protruding.

"What are you talking about? Tough isn't the right word. Pull out your thesaurus and pick out a better one. I've never heard you underexaggerate anything like you just did. This is tougher than tough…excruciating is more like it. I didn't sign up for this…hacking away at miles of vines… rounding up air potatoes. So yeah, how'd I get drafted into this? And I repeat, I don't mind yardwork. You know that. I'm good at mowing the lawn. But this—"

"Oh, come on, Peter, you've got to be kidding me." Granted, he was dealing with his fear of snakes, and for that, I felt sympathetic. But at least he had bought a pair of brown boots, and wasn't wearing the bright yellow rubber ones. "Listen to me, the sooner we clear all of this out, the sooner there'll be fruit in our trees, and you get to eat your lemon bars. You still want those lemon bars, don't you?"

When he didn't answer, and his face looked irritable as ever, I called over to Daniel. "Hey, Daniel, you were telling us that air potatoes are part of the yam family. Well, I was thinking I could save on groceries, make Peter homegrown mashed air potatoes tonight, and tomorrow a baked air potato, and the next day air potato fries."

"I don't recommend that," Daniel said. "If you were in Asia or Africa, fine. They're food crop there. But here in Florida, the strains aren't edible. Potentially poisonous, not to mention bitter."

"In other words," Peter looked at me sternly, in case I didn't understand, "don't make me air potatoes!"

"I was kidding. I would never."

Despite our grueling day in the yard, Peter and I met up that night as usual on the front porch. I got there first and lit the candle, and when he came out, with a groan from sore muscles, he dropped down next to me on the loveseat.

"You know what Viv would say?" I rested my head on his shoulder. "She would tell us to pat ourselves on the back. If ever there's a time, it's now."

"Why?"

"It's happening, that's why. As grueling as it is, it's all coming together and we're doing it."

"Doing what?"

"Returning this place to its original splendor, that's what." My grandiosity was coming out. "Then again, no, I take that back. We're not returning anything to its original splendor. We're bringing it to an even greater splendor, that's what we're doing!"

"Well," he groaned as he lifted his feet onto the shabby wicker table, "you sure have a way of seeing things, and good for you."

"You know what else?"

"What?"

"It's time we rename the place."

"What's wrong with Hidden Potential?"

"Nothing, but Hidden Potential is surpassing her potential, so we have to rename her."

"Sure, how about Hidden Costs instead?"

There I was, about to pat his back for him, even rub his back, but after he said that I wanted to pinch him instead. "Remember the porch rules, Peter…no talking money or debt."

"Okay, fine. What do you have in mind…any ideas for a name?"

I had been thinking about it for days, and yes, already had a name in mind, inspired by the words of King David in that scripture verse I had read on the kitchen floor. From that first night when the Bible arrived and I opened it, the verse had inspired in me a desire for spiritual restoration and the relaunching of my long-since put-aside pursuit to know and love the Lord, my God, with all my heart, soul, and strength.

"How lovely is your dwelling place, O Lord Almighty!
My soul yearns, even faints, for the courts of the Lord; my
heart and my flesh cry out for the living God."
—Psalm 84:1-2

"Lovely Dwelling," I told Peter, although I didn't mention the deeper meaning behind it: that I had been wanting like never before to appreciate the Holy Spirit dwelling in me. "Let's call this our Lovely Dwelling Place by the Sea."

He was quiet for a moment and then, "Pat yourself on the back. You know why?"

"No, why?"

"I like it. I like that name."

Early the next morning, so early the sky was still orange from the waking sun, I wanted to make rounding up air potatoes fun. I grabbed a couple of old wicker baskets left with the house and after handing one to Peter, we went down the porch steps like a couple of kids on an egg hunt—me more excited than him.

"On your mark, get set, go!" I announced at the bottom porch step, then took off in a sprint, hoping Peter would find fun in it, too. A short while later, as he stood in a patch of grass, I moseyed on by, showing off the contents of my basket. "*Ha,* I've got more than you do."

He raised a *who cares* eyebrow, but soon his competitive side kicked in and he took off quick as a lizard darting through the field of weeds. Daniel was already at work high on a ladder, but it was easy to miss him all dressed up in branch-colored camo.

Once my basket was half full, I set it down in the sandy soil and picked up a potato. I put the potato in my throwing hand, and held it like a baseball at chest height, near the middle of my body. Then I put my feet and shoulders in line with Peter, who was far across the yard, and stretched my arm all the way back, into the strongest throwing position.

"Hey, Peter, catch!"

He looked unsure whether I was going to do it, but dropped his basket in case. Then, with wonderful force, I pitched the potato toward him hard as I could and ran toward first base—the rubber tree that Daniel was in.

Peter missed, and the game was off to a good start. But as I approached the base of the tree, my foot tripped on a root and my ankle twisted. I hopped, skipped, and then skidded down into the dirt.

"Ouch!" Daniel commented from the tree.

"Uh oh." Peter ran over. "Are you okay?"

I flexed my foot and was fine, just disappointed at myself for thinking I could make the yardwork fun. My face, optimistic all morning, turned down and out.

"*Just what makes that little old ant think,*" he sang from the old classic song we used to sing to the kids, "*he can move the rubber tree plant?*"

I loved that he was taking his turn as the optimist. I took his hand when he offered it and sang along, "*Anyone knows an ant can't move a rubber tree plant.*"

We were an act, not only singing, but groaning from sore muscles and laughing as he struggled to get me up and off the ground. "*He's got hiiigh hopes,*" we belted out in awful unison, which I found funnier than it was, "*he's got hiiigh hopes.*"

"We're not always this strange," Peter told Daniel when he came down from his ladder for a drink of water. "At least, I don't think."

"Ah, don't worry about me. I wasn't thinking you were strange. But I have to admit, in all my years of landscaping, I've never seen anyone have that much fun rounding up air potatoes."

"In all your years, Daniel?" Peter grinned. "You're no older than my daughters. How long have you been doing this?"

He chugged his water, then wiped his face. "Well, let's see, sir...I learned to tie fallen fronds into piles with twine before learning to tie my own shoes, climbed my first *Hevea brasiliensis*, like this one here—" he tilted his head toward the rubber tree "—when I was seven, took a machete to the top and released the dead branches."

"Wow," Peter mused, "so that's why our yard isn't too atrocious for you."

"No atrocity here, no. But even if it was, if a person my age doesn't have it in them to take on the atrocities of the world, then I fear for the generations to come." Poised like a high-ranking commander, Ivy League graduate, or valedictorian from the University of Landscaping, he looked Peter in the eyes. "There's a battle going on in your yard, sir, but I've fought a lot of battles, and I'm more than experienced. We're going to win this, you'll see."

"I like your confidence."

"Call it what you like, sir." Daniel wiped his face. "All I know is I grew up working side-by-side with my folks, who taught me everything I need to know about landscaping and life."

Oh my. How could I have gotten Lucy there...a red-eye flight, perhaps? I winked at Peter, hoping he'd read my eyelid sequences like Morse code, then go out on a limb and ask Daniel whether he was single or not. But even after all our years together, Peter flunked when it came to reading my eyelids.

"What's wrong, another bug in your eye?"

I swatted him away, like *he* was a bug. "So, Daniel, when it comes to garden restoration, my friend next door says gentle intervention is the way to go. Do you agree?"

"Not at all, declare war! The vines in your yard are growing up to eight inches a day. They'll take over if you let them, it's the nature of the beast."

"Then back to work we go," Peter said.

"Back to work indeed," Daniel agreed. "I have a tendency to talk too much, which I got from my dad. We talked all the time when we worked."

"Oh," I said, detecting grief in his tone.

"Yeah, first job I'm doing without him. My mother used to work with us, but she passed years ago."

"So sorry," Peter and I said in unison. "We're so sorry!"

Daniel looked down at the ground, then back up at us. "My dad was a great guy. I wouldn't mind being like him—not many guys can say that of their dads, but I can." Daniel picked up a machete, and with a heavy blow, started chopping away a tree right beside us.

"Oh, wait," I had to stop him. "What are you doing to that poor tree?"

He held his machete still. "It's a strangler fig, doing what strangler figs are notorious for—wrapping itself around this innocent palm, blocking it from the sun, and slowly but surely, strangling it to death."

"Oh."

"If the palm was thriving," he patted its trunk, "I wouldn't intervene. I'd let the two trees be. But as you can see, this here palm is suffering... dying *because* of the fig."

Peter and I studied the two trees involved in the dispute and tried deciphering the bully from the victim. The arm-like branches of the strangler fig were wrapped tightly around the slender, slouching trunk of the puny palm, and the two didn't look to be hugging.

"My mom was the fig expert," Daniel said. "We'd hack away at figs. She'd tell me to think of the strangler figs, so to speak, in my own life—you know, things that creep in, block us from the light, and over time strangle the life out of us. She was referring to other things, but since we were out landscaping, she used landscaping language to teach me stuff." He smiled and shook his head. "She was one of those people whose thoughts were always on the good Lord above. Everything from a bug to a palm tree had her thinking of Him. And she talked so naturally about Him, like talking about a friend."

"My mom was sort of like that, too. So, what did she say to do... about the strangler-fig-like things in your life?" I hadn't mentioned to Peter what Mom had written in her letter, the one I read right before I cleaned out the oven and asked Jesus to help rid me of the idols in my life.

"Well," Daniel said with a laugh, "just as a landscaper honors the grandeur of the native plants in one's yard, she'd tell me that God knows what belongs in my life and what doesn't. Work intimately alongside Him and trust. Trust that He knows what needs to be removed and why. Removing the bad stuff reveals beauty hidden within, and produces fruit in one's life…that's what she used to say."

Peter raised a brow at me, as if wishing, too, that our daughter was there. "So Daniel, do you have other family, friends, a girlfriend here on the island?"

"Yep to all of that, except for the girlfriend…not at the moment anyway," he grinned. "I'm doing my thing right now, soaring."

"Soaring?"

"Alone like an eagle."

"Something your mother taught you?"

He shook his head with a laugh. "Nah, something I know about myself and gaining strength…gotta soar alone from time to time."

Peter looked amused, like he could have stood there all day listening to what the grown kid was saying about landscaping and life. We were both disappointed when he turned and climbed back up his ladder, disappearing into the tree.

I reached down and picked up an air potato, then waited for Peter to notice.

"Uh oh." He opened his hands the moment he saw.

"Uh oh is right…hot potato!" I tossed it to him, and he caught it, then sent it right back. "Hot potato, hot potato." Back and forth we tossed the spud, holding in our laughs like a couple of kids who should have been working but were procrastinating and goofing off instead.

Soon, we got back to work, filling our baskets to the brim several times over, then dumping the potatoes into giant garbage bags that Daniel said we could bring to the Farmer's Market. Environmentalists would dispose of them.

The rest of the day, I couldn't get that song from our game out of my mind. *Hot potato, hot potato,* I hummed, and even when Lucy called, "*Potato, potato, potato,*" I answered.

"Mom, are you okay?"

"Hi, my little sweet potato." I put her on speaker phone, not minding if Daniel up in the tree happened to overhear me talking to my sweet, sweet, sweet potato of an oldest daughter.

"You sound out of breath, Mom. What are you doing?"

"Dad and I are out playing in the yard. What's up with you, my daughter?"

"Dirk and I are back together."

I took her off speaker.

"Are you there, Mom?"

Yes, I was there, but what did she want me to do, throw confetti and shout hooray? I looked around the yard for Peter and when I spotted him tying shut a giant garbage bag stuffed with air potatoes, I hurried over, wrinkling my face like a bulldog. He knew what it meant and did the same back at me.

"Mom, I don't want you freaking out."

I preferred the word "worrying," but didn't have the chance to tell her that.

"I'm helping Dirk with those things…his moods, his temper. I want to help him. I believe in him."

Who did she think Dirk was, Mr. Potato Head, a toy she could change—pull off the angry-looking parts and snap on kind-looking ones instead? I was the angry one; my daughter thought she had to be the one to change another mother's son! Peter marched along with me over to the porch steps, where we both sat down.

As Lucy went on and on about the high hopes she had for Dirk, I handed the phone to Peter, then put my head in my hands. Why couldn't I have talked naturally about certain things? Let my kids know that the Landscaper of their souls loved them and cared. God cared about the intricate details of their lives, including the grounds around them and the people and things they surrounded themselves with. And He'd work alongside them, helping to pull whatever it was that was wrapping around their hearts, souls, and minds, strangling their joy, hindering their view of Him. But if I tried—after having never talked like that before—my words would have hit them like surprise balls coming out of left field.

If I was a roly-poly, I'd have tightened myself into a protective ball, then dropped off the porch step into the dirt. But I wasn't a roly-poly, and there was more I could do than roll up into a protective ball. I could pray to God, which I did, letting Him know how vulnerable I felt as a mother. One moment I was having fun with my husband, and the next wanting to burrow beneath a rock, terrified of all the joy-predators out there in the world. I also told God how sorry I was for not including Him more as we raised our family.

I came out of my protective ball with God when Peter put Lucy back on speaker phone. "The reason I called in the first place," Lucy's words came out like a drum roll, "is that we're looking at rings."

Holy moly, roly-poly. "Run for dear life!" I wanted to tell her. "Run from his temper, run from his laziness, run, run, run or he will be the thorn in your side until death do you part!" But we had already told her that so many times, and she didn't listen.

Peter's eyes looked ready to pop out. I had to do something. "I have an idea, Lucy." It was all I could think of, but a good one. "Why don't you two lovebirds come to Florida...a long weekend away, stay with us." I gave Peter the *trust me* wink, and his brows lifted. "You won't believe the sunsets here."

"Okay, but just so you know, we both want to get married in Hawaii."

"Why in the world, when your parents live on Sanibel?"

"Hawaii is Hawaii...the plumeria flowers alone...I love them."

I jumped up from the porch step and, taking her with me on the phone, went over to the most unusual-looking tree in our yard, the one with leafless, naked branches. I took a quick selfie holding a branch, then texted it to her.

"What an ugly tree, Mom. Did you mean to send that?"

"It's a plumeria tree. Right here in our yard, we have a plumeria tree!"

"It has no leaves. It looks dead."

"Nope, alive. Our landscaper, a wonderful guy, your age, told me it gets its leaves every May, along with its flowers... pink or yellow, we're not sure which."

"Wow, I guess if we have our wedding there instead...as long as we get married in May...we could pick the flowers ourselves, make the bouquets."

At that point, I didn't reply. I wasn't encouraging a wedding. I wanted them to come visit, so we could talk with them in person.

"Let me run everything by Dirk. I can talk him into it, as long as he can have his pig roast with pineapple kabobs at the reception."

We ended our call after that and I went over to Peter, who all that time had been sitting on the steps, running his hands through his hair, and hopefully not pulling it out. "I don't want to talk right now," I told him. "I'm speechless. Let's meet out on the porch tonight, and talk then, okay?"

After all of that, we were no longer carefree kids running through the yard, laughing and playing *hot potato, hot potato*. We were in rotten moods as we went around picking up the doggone spuds.

"Hey," Peter snapped when the two of us tried snatching a giant spud at the same time "that one was mine!"

"Was not." I batted him away. "Finders keepers; losers weepers!"

THIRTY-SEVEN

* * *

Garden restoration is about making choices, one after the next, and letting go of that which doesn't belong, that which hinders beauty.

* * *

If you don't get at the roots, it all comes back with a vengeance.

Despite my intimate roly-poly moment with God on the bottom porch step, over the next couple of weeks, my worries grew as quickly as the vines in my yard. For the vines in the yard—the ones wrapping around the fruit trees—I used a pruning saw, and for the deep-rooted ones, a pitchfork and sometimes a small hatchet. I kept an eye out for new shoots, digging them up the moment they popped. But for the worries in my mind, I was hardly trying to stop them.

Peter made several trips to the Farmer's Market, handing our bags of unwanted air potatoes over to the environmentalists. I could have rounded up my worries, handed them over to God, but chose to hold onto them instead. In my mind I equated worrying with loving. Loving mothers worried, right? If we couldn't fix our kids' troubles, instead of doing nothing, we worried. It wasn't productive, but made me feel like I was doing something—carrying the weight of Lucy, Mallory, Charlie, and Henry's burdens on my mind.

Living afar had become harder than I imagined. I didn't tell Peter how I wished that I had waited until they were in their thirties before moving away. But, exhausted after making it through their teenage and college phase, I hadn't thought things through. Their emerging-into-adulthood phase was also emotionally all-encompassing. Was there going to be a break before their getting-married phase, and another break before their having-babies phase? I needed to build up zest for the grandma thing.

I caught word from Henry that Charlie had picked back up again and was playing his favorite video game morning, noon, and night, reaching all-time high-ranking levels, while compromising his job. Sure enough, his fingers were tapping the keyboard even as we talked on the phone. And Lucy wouldn't stop texting me pictures of her finger with rings on it, wanting to know every other hour which one I liked. As for the other two, well, they had worrisome things going on as well, situations they were dealing with.

Watching kids cross the mile marker into adulthood with penalties and poor spirits was all-encompassing for any mother. I didn't want to be that screaming parent on the sidelines, coaching their every move. I just wanted to cheer them on with words of encouragement and be able to hand them whatever essentials they still needed from me.

Of these four, which do you like best? Lucy texted.

I stopped pulling out a patch of poison ivy at the base of the lemon tree, and walked beneath a shadier tree to better see. She and Dirk should have been picking out a ring together. But Lucy was my indecisive one, and for that, I blamed myself.

"Give her mint chocolate chip," I ended up saying every time we went for ice cream and she'd stand twenty minutes, nose to the glass, unable to pick a flavor.

"No, wait, what's in this one, Mommy?" she'd say, as if picking ice cream was a life-or-death decision.

"Chocolate covered peanuts and fudge."

"Coconut in it, too?"

"Nope, peanuts and fudge, that's all."

Even as her sister and brothers were already halfway done eating theirs, she was still trying to decide. If I let her, she'd have asked to sample all fifty flavors in the shop, oblivious to the line forming out the door.

"Just get what I'm getting, chocolate turtles," I'd say, looking up at the giant descriptions written on the chalk board behind the counter. "Chocolate ice cream with chocolate covered pecans and caramel."

"But Mommy, what if I don't like it? What's in this one…this pretty blue one?"

"I don't know. Why not just try it?"

"No, I want to know about this orange one first, Mommy. What's in this orange one?"

"I don't know, but I'm going to order for you now." By then, by her sixth or seventh inquiry, my patience had melted. "She'll have mint chocolate chip, please."

Go with the second ring, I texted, then returned to the base of the lemon tree, pushing and pulling the saw across the vines, wishing I had done a better job at teaching my daughter the process of elimination. If I had, she would have eliminated her current boyfriend long ago.

When I heard singing coming from Viv's drive, I dropped my saw and ran over. She had been singing the last couple of days, on her way to the mailbox. It didn't matter the song, her raspy, sultry voice made them all sound alike. But there was something different—a refreshing snappiness to her voice—that had me curious.

"Look at you!" After wearing the same clothes several times in a row, she had on a yellow maxi dress with a colorful scarf, and her hair was in a French twist. "What special event of the decade are you going to?"

"No event, a dinner party at my place is all." She wheeled her chair to the mailbox, then took a couple of extra steps of her own to reach it. "Yay, no junk mail, no foreclosure notices." She sifted through the mail. "I'll take it."

"A dinner party," I said.

"Yeah, and I have to scoot. I haven't even ordered the sushi yet."

"Sushi. For how many?"

"Two."

I gave her a look.

"Take that look off your face. I swear, I'll fill you in later, but for now, I'm not lying. I have to scoot."

"Too bad. Lucy sent more ring pictures."

"Oh, for crying out loud." She took my cell phone and within seconds, her expression went from poker face, to *no way*, to *aha!* "It's a no-brainer. This one, tell her to go with this one."

I squinted to see. It was different than the one I had texted her to go with. "Why that one?"

"Bling, that's why…the biggest bling. That way, she can sell it later if she needs to, and walk away with cash."

I shook my head. "She's the one paying for it…took out a credit card to buy her own ring."

Viv looked ready to pass out. "Did you not teach her to pick out partners with money? Trust me, I've married with and without, and things are a heck of a lot easier with."

If only Viv knew, I had been beating myself for days—not over that—but over all the other things I wished I had taught my kids. "I don't care if the guy has a million dollars or one dollar, Viv. I don't like him. But it doesn't matter. Lucy's in love and there's no talking her out of it."

"Well, sure." She shrugged her shoulders. "Sometimes we crave love so much that we pick the wrong person. Our cravings get the best of us. Then love becomes an icky thing. And it's so unfair. One person loves more than the other and they give and give and get nothing in return. But don't get me started." She turned and went down her driveway. "You know I have a sour taste in my mouth when it comes to love. I'm working on that, though, working hard. But you…you can flip out all you want about who your daughter loves, but it's her life."

Back in my yard, I waved at Peter and Daniel, who were loading equipment onto the truck, and since we were done for the day, I plopped down onto the hammock. "What is love?" I asked God. "And what's in it? The thing I don't like about love is worrying. Is it an ingredient in love, or something I've added?"

I closed my eyes and remembered a description of love I had memorized weeks earlier, the words of the Apostle Paul in 1 Corinthians 13:4–8. It was as detailed as the ice cream descriptions had been on the giant board behind the counter.

"Mommy, what's love? What's in it, and what's not?" If only Lucy was still of that age, and still asking.

Love is kind, love is patient. It doesn't envy, or boast. It's not proud. It is not rude, it is not self-seeking, it is not easily angered. It keeps no record of wrong. Love doesn't delight in evil, but rejoices with the truth. It always protects, always trusts, always hopes.

Worrying wasn't an ingredient God included in His description of love. If pecans were removed from chocolate turtles ice cream, it wouldn't be chocolate turtles ice cream anymore. But if I took my worries out of love, it would still be love.

"Hey, what do you think?" I asked Peter when he came over and joined me on the hammock. "You think worrying is part of loving?"

"Nope," he said right away. "I see what it does to you...serves no productive purpose. I think you can get rid of it and enjoy love more."

"What if it's a part of me...who I am as a mother...a mother who worries."

"Well, it doesn't enhance motherhood in any way. Let it go and I guarantee you'll still be a loving mother...a loving mother who doesn't obsess." He got up, kissed me on the forehead, and went up into the house to shower, then work on his reports.

I re-closed my eyes. The out-of-control worrying that entangled my joy didn't belong in me, and was every bit as invasive as the non-native vines in our yard. Still, why were worries so hard to get rid of? Doing so required time and prayer, working alongside the Landscaper of my soul until the root of worry lost its energy.

No sooner had I fallen into a pleasant catnap when a delivery truck rolled down our drive. What startled me more was Peter, who burst forth from the house like an excited dog, rushing three-quarters of the way down the porch steps, then jumping the rest of the way.

"What on earth, Peter?" I put my feet to the ground.

"It's here, something I bought for us...money left over from my last bonus...a surprise!"

Instantly, my mind took me to wonderful places—Peter and I sitting in a jacuzzi—not that we needed one in Florida, but the jets would have been nice on his back, and we could have filled it with cold water instead of hot. I rushed over and stood beside him as the delivery people opened the back of the truck and pulled out an enormous, flat box.

There went that fantasy. "It's not a hot tub, is it?"

"Nope." Peter squeezed my hand. "Better."

"Okay, then a gigantic seashell mirror for the bathroom…a great heron painting for our wall." I wanted to collect framed pictures of Sanibel birds and put them in every room.

"Way better than any of that!"

I squeezed his hand. "I can't think…give me a hint."

His expression turned boyish. "All those bags of potato chips I bought."

I had assumed his recent potato chip spree was a craving from all the air potatoes we had been gathering from the yard. I looked at him, like I needed another hint.

"What do I like to do when eating potato chips?"

I let go of his hand. My body stiffened and my ears went flat. If I were a cat, I would have hunched my back, puffed up my hair and tail to make me bigger and scarier. "No, Peter, tell me it's not a…not a…" I hissed, and couldn't say it, the two-letter word, TV.

He knew better. He knew it was the last thing I wanted when all through the years nonstop sports and endless news was the constant background noise in our house. Even during conversations, our eyes were on it, and not each other. Why would I want a TV?

Already, there was a familiar gleam in Peter's eyes, like when his old work days were done and he was ready to hunker down on the sofa the rest of the evening with his bag of chips. The only thing lessening that gleam in his eyes was the smokiness in mine. I was heating up on the inside.

"Don't be a nervous Nellie," he insisted, not even looking at me. "This baby here isn't what you think. It's far more advanced than our old TV." His eyes were tuned into the scene in front of us, of the delivery crew pulling his giant baby from the truck. "I shouldn't call it a TV. It's an insult to call it a TV. It's a flat-screened, wireless, surround-sound, home theater system!"

He had the audacity to look at me then, as if I were a contestant on the *Price is Right* and should have been jumping, screaming, throwing my arms around him. When I did none of that, he escorted the team up the stairs and into the house with me trailing behind.

I wasn't going to admit it, but the object getting unloaded in our great room looked like state-of-the-art technology from another world, from a technically advanced planet far, far away from where we had been living all our lives. I was impressed.

But quiet as a finch, I perched myself on a stool as they all talked and joked and set everything up. Soon, their voices were drowned out by blaring political news that filled every room of Lovely Dwelling. The talking heads were going at it, like a pandemonium of noisy, fighting parakeets, and Peter was already a part of the wild uproar. The channel switched to sports, then back to news, then to sports, then news again.

"Thoughts, honey?" Peter shouted from across the room.

Yes, poor Viv and the quiet one-guest dinner party she was trying to have. As the technicians performed volume checks, I went around closing all the windows.

"Like it?" Peter asked in his broken, TV short talk, which used to drive me crazy. Whenever the TV was on his sentences became fragments, and what should have taken ten words to say, he edited down to three or less.

I walked over to where he was and put my hands on my hips and my lips to his ear. "We could have flown our kids out to see us for the price of this…Dirk and Lucy, who are struggling to afford tickets."

"Then tell them to buy a fake diamond, like we did. I'm not spending a dime on that guy…one-way rocket to Uranus, maybe…let him get a job and buy his own ticket."

Peter got an entire stadium of surround-sound cheers for those comments, and it sounded like it was coming from my bedroom since the wires even went into there. It was a touchdown on TV occurring at the same time. When the hoopla calmed down, I stood there with a pout forming on my face and didn't know how to remove it. Peter rubbed the back of my neck, but it didn't soothe me.

The rest of the evening I muted myself. I said not a word, although Peter didn't seem to notice. He tore open his bag of chips, and since we hadn't even bought furniture yet—except for the outdoor terrace set—he plopped himself down on the dirty sofa that came with the place.

I spent the next several nights fleeing from the bathroom to the kitchen to my bedroom in search of a quiet corner to perch. But the walls of Lovely Dwelling were thin as tortilla chips, and I was thin-skinned, too. It didn't matter we were off on a sanctuary island in the Gulf of Mexico, or tucked within the branches of a banyan tree; news reports from around the world, along with things happening in our own country, went blaring through the house. Although I didn't want to bury my head in the sand and be ignorant to what was going on, hearing it rattled my heart, soul, and mind. I didn't want to get all hysterical. I wanted to help, but didn't know how.

Band after band of breaking news consumed us both, and soon Peter and I were spending our nights in heated debate. We weren't the only ones. Everyone we knew was on one side or the other, bickering over what America was. If some of its ingredients were taken out, and others were added, then America wasn't going to be America. It was going to turn into a new flavor altogether. Some wanted the new flavor, and others wanted what they loved as a kid. They didn't want the original recipe altered.

The world was getting scarier by the day, and it triggered the protective mother bird in me. If only I had a giant nest in which to shelter my family, hide them under my wings. Ignorance was bliss but unacceptable, and knowledge was irreversible. The more news I watched, the more I wanted to know, and the more I knew, the more I grieved. I wanted my kids to inherit a wonderful world.

"Remember when I researched every school in the district," I said to Peter one night, "making sure to send them to the safest, the best?"

"Yep," he answered, his eyes on the screen.

"Well, I can't do that with the world. There isn't world choice. There's one world in which we all have to live. And it upsets me. Our kids are in attendance in a scary, messed up world."

When Peter didn't reply, I escaped to the porch to hear my own thoughts. I wished I had taught my kids where they might go for comforting refuge…how to dwell in the shelter, rest in the shadow of the Almighty. But I was hardly going to God myself lately, and even if I was, talking about it to my family, when I hardly talked about it before, would have been over-the-top strange.

Like a cuckoo-bird, every hour on the hour Peter poked his head out onto the front porch. "Want me to join you, or are you okay with your alone time?"

"I don't care."

"Of course you care. Want me to join you or not?"

"Sure, but to warn you. I'm upset with myself."

"Why?"

"What am I doing to help?"

"What do you mean?"

"You and me reacting to the news, debating all day long, talking like a couple of know-it-alls…it's good conversation and great venting, but that's all. It's not helping matters. It's not changing anything. And my worries—"

"Weren't you winning that war?"

"I'm getting re-attacked with a vengeance, and you know why?"

"Why?"

"I don't like living this far from our kids," I blurted out. "I'm missing them more than you know. What was I thinking?"

"You weren't. I don't mean to sound harsh, but you weren't thinking. You had an extra strong cup of coffee that day, or—" he stopped, and with one foot on the porch and one foot still in the house all that time, he swiveled his head like an owl, to hear what was happening on TV before swiveling it back to me.

I had no idea how he found the flexibility to do that without pinching a nerve. "Unless you put both feet out on the porch, I don't want to talk."

He stepped his other foot out onto the porch and sat down next to me on the loveseat like he used to do. I didn't bother to light the candle, though.

"That TV gets in the way of me hearing the ospreys. I had to come outside, stand on the top porch step and stare at their nest, to make sure they were still there."

"Were they?"

"Yep, two heads popped up. I miss when it used to be quieter around here."

"I get what you're saying, I do. But even before the TV, all we were doing was talking about the kids. And I hate to say this, but the kids will have problems in their thirties, and their forties, too, and when they're our age, they're still going to be having problems. You know why? Because problems are part of life. You get rid of one, another pops up. That's the way it is."

"True," was all I said.

"Look, at the end of the day, honey, too much of anything isn't good, I agree with you on that. I bought the TV...figured it would give you a break from too much quietude and thinking. I'll make a deal." He looked me in the eyes. "We can go back to reading news on our phones, and we'll watch fun stuff...you name it, I'll watch it."

He went inside and I stayed put, looking up at the sky until oh no, a star fell! And what if it happened to be my favorite star, playing its part in the...the what constellation? Oh my, like I often forgot the names of movies, I forgot the name of the most well-known constellation. Its name wasn't even on the tip of my tongue and perhaps it was happening—one by one my words falling off the tip of my tongue, like tiny bits of dust and debris falling into the Earth's atmosphere and burning up.

I had heard on the news that people who did four or more crossword puzzles per week weren't as likely to develop Alzheimer's as people who worked one. I went inside, up to my room, and closed the door. I had ordered online a bunch of intellectually stimulating crossword puzzles that required several mental activities all at once—word, geometric skills, even logic. I opened the drawer of the distressed vanity that came with the place and pulled them out.

I tried to concentrate, but couldn't. "After our porch talk," I poked my head out at Peter, "wouldn't you have turned that blasted news down?"

"I'll turn the channel if you join me."

"No, I'm doing crossword puzzles."

After that, I became like a ticked-off cuckoo bird, poking my angry head out every hour on the hour, until eventually I put the crossword puzzle book away and went to bed. "Turn that blasted news down," I shouted from bed. "I beg you, please!"

"It is down," he yelled from the other room. "You're a light sleeper."

"Oh, shush, I am *not*."

The bedroom door opened and a flying pillow came in for a landing right on my head. The pillow must have hit me in the right spot. I remembered: "Big Dipper!"

"Who, me?" Peter said from the doorway. "Are you calling *me* the Big Dipper?"

As mad as I was, his being offended thinking I called him the Big Dipper triggered the funny button in me. "No, I wasn't calling you that. I have a different name for you."

"What is it?"

The word was ready to jump, but still, I didn't want to laugh. "A...a..."

"What? I'm a what?"

"Couch potato!" I shouted at the top of my lungs.

As hilarious as I was, my choice of words made no splash. Peter left the room, closed the door, and I lay back down in the old iron twin beds we had pushed together with an awkward crack in the middle. I formed a pillow fort around my head, using the one he threw at me as the roof.

No sooner had I fallen asleep when Peter woke me with the noise of his bathroom duties—closing the door, brushing his teeth, cabinets slamming.

Like a Greek mythological monster woken from sleep, I stormed out of the bedroom, ranting and raving. "I can't take it!" I went into our spare room and sat down on the floor in the corner, frustrated with the uncomfortable crack in our bed, the cracking divide in our country, and what seemed like a crack in my faith. I was hardly praying, and instead letting the worries eat away at me from the inside.

And there it was—the Bible along with Mom's folder of letters to God poking out at me from a bunch of clutter. I forgot how it even ended up in the pile-up room, but brushed the dust off the Bible, then opened the folder and pulled out another one of her letters to God.

THIRTY-EIGHT

* * *

"A new commandment I give you: Love one another.
As I have loved you, so you must love one another."
—John 13:34

* * *

"I will give them a heart to know me, that I am the
Lord. They will be my people, and I will be their God,
for they will return to me with all their heart."
—Jeremiah 24:7

To the One I've returned to with all my heart,

I look up at the sky and can't help but think of You. Not only did you create the stars, but You also count them, and call them by name. And not one of them is missing, thanks to the greatness of Your might, the strength of Your power. You know what's going on in the sky, and on Earth, and You know the details of everything.

I love sitting with You in the mornings, but tonight I'm nocturnal as a raccoon. What's to blame—the café Cubano I drank at four? Long after the kids went to bed, my thoughts were moving ahead of me, fast as a high-speed ferry en route to somewhere exciting. I followed my venturesome thoughts and should have known they were leading me to the beach.

Here I am, not on a bench, but sitting right smack in the sand, grateful for the light of the moon so I can write You this letter. And grateful that no one but the mother loggerhead sea turtles are out here to see me on the beach in my pajamas in the middle of the night. You see me, though, and for that I'm glad. Even on a barrier island in the Gulf of Mexico, there's no such thing as being off the grid from You.

"Where can I go from your Spirit? Where can I flee from your presence? If I go up to the heavens, you are there; if I make my bed in the depths, you are there. If I rise on the wings of the dawn, if I settle on the far side of the sea, even there your hand will guide me, your right hand will hold me fast."

—*Psalm 139: 7–10*

Before I came out here, I was reading in the book of Jeremiah the analogy of You being the potter and we the clay. When I feel your finger at work, poking and prodding sections of my heart—it feels uncomfortable, but in the end everything You do restores glory.

You didn't create us to be thoughtless lumps of clay, though. You've given us minds of our own and choices. But if I choose to give You only a piece of me to work with and hold back the rest, it's like putting just one foot up on the pottery wheel, or saying, "Here, God, You can have a crescent of my heart—a beautiful sliver of my whole to work with, but no more."

I look up at the full and glowing circle in the sky, and it reminds me that You want more. You want more than a quarter, more than a half, or a gibbous. You want my entirety handed over—all of Finley Child, full as the moon—and I want that, too. I want to give You more than just a bit of me. You've offered me nothing but fullness.

"For in Christ all the fullness of the Deity lives in bodily form, and you have been given fullness in Christ, who is the head over every power and authority."

—*Colossians 2:9*

When I accepted Christ, and the Holy Spirit made His home in me, I was given everything I need. Through Christ You offer me Your wholeness. Through Him I learn who You are, and experience Your love fully. And Your grace, it overwhelms me. Why would I choose to hold things back and give You only a sliver of me in return?

Even as I write You this prayer, I hear wave after wave lapping the shore, and verse after verse of truth coming to mind.

"From the fullness of his grace we have all received one blessing after another."

—John 1:16.

There may be a far side to the moon, but there's no far side to my heart. You see all of it, even the dark splotches and lava-like basins left by the damaging asteroid impacts of life. And still, You invite me to live fully, not partially, in the palm of Your hand.

My desire to fully surrender waxes and wanes, and it's hard to give up control, hard to hand over my problems and worries. But lately, it's greater than ever, this uncontainable desire to accept Your wholeness and walk in Your will for my life. It's why when I first stepped out onto the beach tonight, I picked up a pen shell and drew a big heart in the sand. I stepped one foot in, then the other, and that's where I've been sitting—in this big heart I drew in the sand.

If other insomniac beachcombers happen on by, they'll see just a woman sitting in the sand. But I'm more than just a woman sitting in the sand. I'm a woman sitting in the palm of God's hand. And because I've got choices, so many choices, I'm choosing to hand over more of myself to You, Lord, so You can do Your thing in me, sculpting that which needs sculping, and smoothening out whatever cracks need smoothening out. You know what needs to be done.

To You, my heart is like a translucent precious stone and my flesh sea glass. As if looking into a glass bottle, You see all the contents of my being. If there's sin, please make me aware, and together we can sift through things and rid me of what isn't needed.

I thank You. You are Your Word and Your Word is within me—a message in a bottle.

Love, Finley
(Or, according to Your Word, You know me also as Your "beloved child, daughter, crowned with glory and honor, a new creation, loved, precious, living stone, temple of the Holy Spirit." Of all those names, "Loved" is one of my favorites. What a nickname to have, "Loved by God!")

P.S. I'm still wide awake. Blame it on me drinking that second café Cubano, but also, You've given me a mind and it wants to think. I love how up in the sky You placed the sun, moon, and stars. And in me, a heart, soul, and mind. The three govern my body like a checks-and-balance system. If my mind lacks the knowledge of Truth, it will go along with whatever my heart says. But if my mind is packed with Your Truth, and my soul filled with Your light, then together my mind and soul will stop my heart from beating down the wrong path into darkness.

THIRTY-NINE

The next morning, still in my pajamas, I sat drinking coffee on the bottom porch step. If there was one special picture I'd forever keep framed and hanging in my mind—a picture of Mom I was never going to take down—it was of her on Sanibel Island sitting in that heart she drew in the sand. And to think she wasn't just sitting in the sand. She was in the palm of God's highly skilled hand. Mom was up on the potter's wheel like a piece of art, a masterpiece in the making, working with and putting her trust in Him, the One who breathed beauty into the world and everlasting light into her.

I wanted to be there too, in the palm of God's hand. "Continue to work in me," I muttered beneath my breath, "Please, bring about Your ideas, projects You want done in me, a beautiful dwelling for the Holy Spirit."

Viv was right about restoration; there were choices that needed to be made one after the next. Just as fruit trees should be spaced at least twenty-five feet apart, I wanted to space my busy moments, leave space between for quietude and prayer. Accepting and receiving wave after wave of God's love, for me, was also a choice—as was looking forward to fruit in my life with great expectation.

When I finished my coffee, I got up from the porch step and walked over to a nearby patch of dirt where I had planted a native blue porterweed (*Stachytarpheta jamaicensis*) in full sun. It was the larval plant for the tropical buckeye butterfly, which I wanted to attract. Sure enough, they were fluttering all around, and when I stretched my arms out, a few landed on my hands.

I didn't ever want God to think, *where was Adele? I gave her my flawless and purified Word, to be her host plant and to feed her soul. I even gave her a mother who was a believer, but where was she? She fluttered near me for a season, then soon her worries and the cares of the world took her elsewhere.*

But the tumultuous world alarmed me, and gave me reason to be terrified. I wanted the simple-sounding words of Jesus—*love one another*—to hit the doom and gloom area of my brain like falling two-by-fours...remind me that love was God's answer to the world. Even the issues worth debating, worth the continuous dialogue and holding one's ground, needed to be done out of love for one another. I needed to pray for those I disagreed with, those with differing views. Pray, too, for the hand of God to stay open. There was no better place to go for breaks to be repaired, cracks to be smoothed out, than the palm of His loving, working hand.

I didn't eat chips, but spent that evening and the next several as Mrs. Couch Potato, sitting beside Mr. Couch Potato watching what Peter let me pick out—home makeover shows on TV. As Peter and I talked about ideas we wanted to implement in Lovely Dwelling, I couldn't help but anticipate the ideas God wanted to implement in me. On the shows, however, the homeowners went away and when they returned the house was done for them. That wasn't how God was working in me. I was present and making choices, working intimately with Him.

The homes on TV experienced transformation in a weekend, but the detailed work underway in me—not all, but some of it—was going to take a lifetime. As impatient as I was in wanting everything done, I looked forward to experiencing God's presence, His grace, and His mercy throughout the ongoing episodes of my life. Whatever I lacked, Jesus was God's full supply. I needed to stay tuned to Jesus.

I once heard, though, what I thought was a cardinal and it turned out to be a mockingbird instead. I didn't ever want to be mistaken when it came to God's voice—thinking I heard God when it wasn't God. For that reason, I chose to stay tuned within the boundaries of His Word and started back up again, reading from the Bible a few minutes each morning.

I was sitting on the bottom porch step with it opened in my lap, reading Jesus' words from the book of Matthew, how those who hear His words and do them are wise builders. They have built their homes on rock-solid foundations. The winds howl, the rains come, but the house stands firm. Those who hear His words but fail to live by them are foolish builders.

When I heard the *kukukkukkuk* of a pileated woodpecker, drilling into one of the wooden pilings that held up our house, I jumped up and hurried over, shocked to discover tiny holes up and down the beam. "Shoo. Shoo, shoo, shoo or my house will fall down!"

I put my hands on my hips and stood there thinking about certain ever-persistent behaviors pecking away at me, distracting me from my quiet moments alone with God.

"Shoo!" I shouted when, sure enough, the compulsive woodsmith returned. "Shoo, shoo, shoo!"

"I hope you're not shooing me away." Peter must have tiptoed down the steps. "Everything okay this morning?"

"Yeah, I don't want Lovely Dwelling to fall down."

"Well, that's enough to cause a headache. Let's not think those kinds of things. Guess what? We're taking a break from Lovely Dwelling and having fun today instead!"

"Doing what?"

"Something I've been wanting to do for a while. Hurry upstairs, put on shorts and a t-shirt, nothing fancy. Bring a hat and sunscreen, we're going out on the water today…that's all I'm going to say. The rest is a surprise."

My imagination kicked in, and the images my mind produced were so wonderful I couldn't even say the word, *boat*. I kissed him on the cheek then ran upstairs, picturing myself on a dolphin-watching cruise, or off to a nearby remote island I had heard about, where boaters stopped for lunch, or yet another remote island to search for rare shells. Even as I splashed my face with water, I imagined Peter dropping the anchor and me doing a cannonball off the side of a yacht.

A half hour later, there I was—no yacht, or even a pontoon—but seated low to the water in the cockpit of a single-person kayak. It was a water vessel nonetheless, and I was more than ready to make my way across Tarpon Bay, nestled within the J.N. "Ding" Darling National Wildlife Refuge.

There were ten of us in the group, and as we left the sandy shore, my thrill kicked in for doing something I had never done before. I had canoed with the kids, but it was more like tipping over a million times into a cold Michigan river. I didn't want to tip like that in the kayak, not into wildlife refuge water.

"What if I see a gator?" I asked in a laid-back voice, not wanting to sound like it was a big, worrisome deal to me, even though it was. "Do I push it away with my paddle, or kayak right over it…the gator?"

Two or three random voices in kayaks around me assured me there were no gators where we were going, and the only crocodile on Sanibel preferred hanging out at a swamp near the country club. I didn't know if they were serious or having fun with me.

Like test-driving a new car, I shifted my buttocks in the seat, gripped the paddles, and practiced going forward, then in reverse, then to the left, and the right until I felt comfortable with the basics. When I glanced over my shoulders, Peter's face had a boyish and adventurous look to it. It made me want to be an adventurous, carefree, outdoorsy girl.

To my delight, the crystal-clear water was barely deeper than a bath, and filled with tiny crabs, jumping mullets, and adorable creatures resembling toddler bath toys. Right in front of my kayak, a bird below the surface of the water popped its long neck up as I approached.

"Oops, sorry," I whispered, trying to stop my kayak, but without success, steering around it instead. "Don't mean to interrupt you as you look for your breakfast."

The inky black anhinga with clusters of silver on its feathers attempted to fly away but its wings were wet. It vigorously flapped them dry while running on water.

As our group moved across the bay, I felt like an honored guest in an enchanting kingdom, a province of nature bordered by mangroves, and I was overtaken by its charming inhabitants, especially the chorus of birds.

"How's it going?" Peter let his kayak tap into mine. "Are you enjoying?"

"I sure am!" But that was an understatement for what the pristine setting was doing to my insides. I wanted to stand up in the kayak, spread my arms like the wings of the anhinga, fan them open in a semicircular shape, and give praise to the Creator of it all. And to think the Creator of it all was the One reigning in me, the Ruler of my heart and kingdom within.

"Hmm, I hit a rock," Peter said when his kayak bumped lightly into a grayish thing, twelve feet long. "That, or a floating blimp."

Our guide did a U-turn in our direction. "It's a majestic manatee, although with algae growing on their skin, they look like rocks." Her tone was of a passionate museum curator. "But it's a gentle, slow-moving, giant herbivore, eating its grass for breakfast."

The mammoth mammal rolled slowly, then looked up at Peter with small, inquisitive eyes. "I think it wants to be my friend," he said, drawing laughs from the kayakers circled around us.

"Since you're all here," our guide's voice rose with passion, "let me tell you about the back-bay ecosystem. It's an animal sanctuary…for the most part, a place of undisturbed refuge."

Undisturbed refuge, undisturbed refuge.

Didn't most creatures on Earth long for places of undisturbed refuge? I liked those words and wished I had paper and pen.

"So," the naturalist went on, "the mangrove estuary, it's where fresh water from the river meets up with salt water from the sea."

Estuary, where fresh water from the river meets up with salt water from the sea.

I liked those words, too, and they drifted through my mind, attaching to other words as they went.

Estuary,
where fresh water from the river
meets up with salt water from the sea.
Inspiration,
where something on the mind of God,
flows into our minds.
How beautiful a moment,
an estuary moment
when the contents of Eternity
meet up with the contents of our minds.
Every bit as lovely as when
Fresh water from the river meets up with
salt water from the sea,
estuary moments!

"What you're seeing is an animal sanctuary, a safe haven," the guide was saying. "And all these mangroves, they're protected as well. If you take the mangroves away, the ecosystem falls apart."

If you take away the mangroves,
the ecosystem falls apart.
If you take away God,
systems fall apart.

Soon she announced it was time to line our kayaks up and enter single file into the mangrove forest along the Commodore Creek water trail. Peter had made his way up front, and I was about to fall last in line. I sat upright in my seat, touched the paddles to the water, and picked up speed much the way I had leaving work in my minivan, speeding my way to the ball field each night, picking the twins up after practice. I was always speeding back then, always rushing, yet still, the last to arrive, the last parent in the pick-up line. The thought of those days behind me—when my kids were little—made me sad.

In a line, our group entered the winding, maze-like tunnel of mangroves. The sun found its way through and made everything glisten, except for my memories. I wanted my memories to glisten, but my mind was thick with regrets. I wanted them gone. They were noisy as a rookery and ruining my pristine peace of mind. Regrets didn't belong in my beautiful estuary moments alone with God. They were like vultures showing up out of nowhere, feasting on my already lived moments, ruining memories of life gone by. Giving them too much thought was dangerous, like feeding alligators. It made them unafraid and comfortable, to where they might have eaten me alive, devouring me from the inside out.

I didn't want to live life fixated on the past. It was best to keep my eyes constantly moving from the rearview mirror, to the sides, to the view ahead. Mostly, I wanted to appreciate the present, and look forward to all that was ahead.

"Leave me alone," I said to Old Lady Guilt, rearing her ugly head. "I did the best that I could, and I miss those days when my kids were still my passengers."

But in all those years of whizzing about the noisy and chaotic port of motherhood, shuttling them here and there, did I ever once show my kids how to anchor for a moment, drift about with God in prayer?

No. But still, I did the best that I knew at the time, sending each on their way with the necessary skills to navigate life, how to go, go, go, waking to the sound of the fog horn, rowing in the direction of their dreams, full speed ahead through the ports of life, from this goal to that, letting nothing stop them or get in their way. And should they show signs of weakness or fatigue along the way, I taught them to keep going, listen to the beat of the fast-paced world, and go, go, go, just keep going!

But did I teach them how to listen for the wooing of the Holy Spirit calling them near, or the voice of God whispering in their midst? Did I once show them how to nose-dive into the Word? I held my paddle still. It was too late. My children were gone, had left my port, and were off on their own in the hustling, bustling waters of young adulthood, getting caught up in life's entanglements and messes of their own.

Uh oh, where was the group? Hopefully just around the bend. I smacked my paddle to the water, moving full speed ahead, wishing I had taught my kids to drift about in God's presence. Let Him be your refuge—your go-to place in this scary, threatening world.

But don't just drift. Work with God, too. As I had read in Mom's letter, after the ancient Jews returned from Babylon they got sidetracked, halting all work on rebuilding the destroyed temple. God's prophet Haggai urged them to pick up their tools and get working on the rebuild. I should have taught my kids how to get working again—how to move past those sidetracking things halting their growth in the Lord and get working on their relationships with God.

"Pick up your paddles and row, row, row," I muttered beneath my breath. "Pick up Truth and read, read, read. Paddle and pray, paddle and pray, and be swept up by the current of God in your lives!"

If I called and tried telling them that, why would they listen to me—their mother alone in a single-person kayak moving closer to God all by herself? If only I could have pulled them all into my vessel, but they were too big. And besides, I was doing what I had to do, salvaging my own relationship with God, and reclaiming the dreams I tossed out to sea way back when...when they were my kiddies and there was no space left in my boat for anything but them.

I was speeding around the bends in the trail, trying to catch up, when a mangrove appeared in front of me, and it was coming up fast. I didn't want to slam into it. In my minivan, I would have swerved around it, but in the kayak all I could do was crouch low as my body allowed, hoping the branches and aerial roots would comb through my hair without ripping it out. The fender bender wasn't bad. I caught my breath, then reached up and untangled a strand of my hair from a low, overhead branch.

And thank goodness Peter wasn't around to see his wife stuck in the arms of a mangrove. The only ones around were a spiny sea star in the sand below and a black-crowned night heron in the branches above. As I pushed off the twisted limbs, maneuvering out of the entanglement, I declared in the name of Jesus—who came into the world to save and not condemn—enough, no more encroachment of regrets upon the inner sanctuary of my soul!

I was a walking temple of the Holy Spirit, an ongoing beautification project built to the glory of God, and regrets had no right knocking me down...not when I could pray to God about them instead, and when needed, also repent. Once the kayak was pointing in the right direction, I picked up my paddles and with all my strength left the port of stagnant regrets behind, paddling and praying full speed ahead.

There was no way of reversing my days on Earth, no going back twenty years to do things better, do things right. But there was prayer, the only power tool that productively worked on the past, the present, and the future all at the same time.

"I know I'm dramatic," I said to the merciful, gracious, Captain of my soul, "but I hand You my burdensome load, all those things I wish I did better as a mother. And please, I pray, reach my kids...reach out to each of their hearts!"

The distance between me and them felt worlds away, and I tried doing the math. If I abandoned the mangrove estuary tour, left Sanibel and the state of Florida, then paddled a line North, how many months would it take to reach Michigan by kayak?

It was too complicated a story problem for me, but nothing was too complicated for God. He had His own ways of working things out. All I could do was pray…pray, pray, pray…the most immediate way of reaching my kids. As I moved my vessel across the water, I listened to the commands of the Shipmate within, and prayed for Lucy, Mallory, Henry, and Charlie.

At first when my utterances set sail, disembarking from my heart and leaving by way of my lips, they felt like no more than belated birthday wishes, well-intended goods sure to sink before land was even sighted. But the Holy Spirit within encouraged me to continue the course. I did, paddling and praying with gusto.

Soon, my prayers were like precious pearls that my heart was producing, one uttered word after the next, and what greater heirloom in life than a mother's prayers? An old sailor of a woman tossed about the waves of life, a wretched vagabond merely flirting with God all those years, grateful He saved me from sinking, but telling Him over and over again that I'd meet up with Him at a later port…make Him captain of my life then. What better gift did I have to give my kids than prayer?

If only they saw me, their mother, moving across the water sober, no longer drunk on worries, nor wasting away with regrets and unconfessed sin—but praying my requests for each of them before the Lord. Of all my life experiences, it was the picture I wished my kids had of me forever in their minds.

I felt like Queen Isabella of Spain, only I wasn't talking to Christopher Columbus, nor giving anyone the go-ahead to discover a new route to India. I was giving a thumb's up to the Holy Spirit, offering Him not riches nor spices, but freshly formed pearls of prayers straight from my heart. And I was trusting Him with my sacred goods, giving Him the go-ahead to set sail on an expedition, finding the quickest and most direct route to my grown kids' hearts.

When another story problem came to mind, I didn't try figuring it out myself and asked God if He might whisper the answer. "When will my prayers make landfall?"

I didn't get a specific answer, but was filled with the peaceful knowledge that it was all up to Him. He would discover the best routes to reach each of their hearts, and in His timing.

At last, I caught up with the other kayakers as they headed out of the winding mangrove tunnel and into the final stretch of wide-open bay.

"Weren't you the caboose today," Peter said as we reached the shore and my kayak bumped into his. "How was your ride?"

"You don't want me putting it into words. An amazing experience, that's all I'll say."

I climbed out of what felt like a sacred shrine. As Peter went into the shop to sign us out, I walked over to the edge of the dock and stood there, perched like a wingless mother bird. Better wingless than prayerless. My lips curved upward into a huge smile. My prayers for my kids were on their way, aboard the Holy Spirit.

And the USS HS wasn't going to let them sink!

FORTY

Interior Design Tidbits

* * *

*Establish a focal point. Every house needs
a focal point from which all
else flows, and matches up.*

* * *

*Find an item that epitomizes you,
and put it on display in your house.*

* * *

*Create a self-portrait!
Nothing personalizes a home more than a self-portrait.*

After our morning kayaking, I was in the mood to relax on the front porch with Peter. I made a bunch of food to lure him since he also had reports to do. For the fun of it, I brought out the glittery golden bag of sea grape leaves Viv had given to us.

Peter reached in, pulled one out, and read it. "Is she for real? Does she tell her clients to paint their self-portraits?"

I couldn't help but crack up. "What a hoot, we should do it, create our self-portraits, hang them on a wall."

"If you like preschool finger painting. No thanks, I'll pass."

"Well, then," I pulled out another leaf, "how about a self-epitomizing item?"

"Aw, that's easy. For me, it's a tarpon." He reached for his electronic tablet and within seconds an airbrushed fish replica with a wide-open mouth, acrylic teeth, and fire-enameled glass eyes appeared on the screen

"Tell me you're not wanting to hang one of those in Lovely Dwelling," I gasped. "A man cave in Michigan, maybe, or if this place was a lodge."

"Don't freak, looking them up for fun, is all."

I let out a sigh of relief. "So, how does a tarpon epitomize you?"

"Well," he said in between bites of food, "here's what I'll share with you." His eyes turned contemplative. "The world, it sure throws its bait out…at all of us. And there's always going to be those dark shadows lurking on the surface that we have to watch out for, right?"

I nodded, impressed. Peter was sounding more dramatic than me.

"I think you know this," he went on, "but I've made a point, other than TV, to stay away from whatever might hook me alive."

"It's easy to get hooked on things."

"Yep," he looked at me with sensitive eyes, "but thankfully we've got free will. I keep telling the boys, give thought to free will. It's a gift, use it wisely. Keep away from certain things. Don't go near them, and without getting too philosophical—"

"I like philosophical."

"Well, then," his mouth turned upward, "refuse victory to whatever wants to hook us, right? I'd rather battle…thrash about and break free… than get passively pulled through life, jerked around by a controlling thing that hinders me from living my full potential, or hurts me or you or my family." He shrugged his shoulders, when really, he should have stood up and taken a bow for sharing how the tarpon epitomized him.

Grateful to be a part of his tale, a classic tale of a good man and the sea, I got up and gave him the worthy kiss he deserved, although he deserved more than a kiss. He deserved to have a Silver King replica on a wall in our house—any wall of his choice.

Later, after a cat nap, Peter got working on his reports, and I went over to Viv's on a mission—to find out about her self-portrait, or epitomizing item. Of course, I also wanted to know more about her special dinner guest.

I headed down my drive, turned onto the road, then went up her drive. I wasn't prepared and gasped with fright the second I saw it standing in her front yard—a vulturous, acquisitive, opportunistic beast holding threateningly still on its thin, silvery legs.

I would have been less shocked to see a coyote or a bobcat. I had been hearing packs of coyotes howling from the preserve every time sirens blasted down Periwinkle Way, and spotting bobcat paw prints in the silty mud areas of my yard. Even though Viv had told me to be on the look-out, nothing prepared me for the corrugated, 18x24-inch foreclosure sign standing its ground in my friend's front yard.

Holding my breath, I backed up, wishing it was a coyote so I could have thrown my hands up and scared it away in defense of her territory.

After ringing the doorbell with no answer, I opened the door and went in to find her in the great room with spoon in hand, chiseling away at the precious stones embedded in her gorgeous, white fireplace mantle.

"What in the world?" I said at the sight of it, hundreds of shallow gouges.

"They can take my lock and key, my sinks and toilet, too, but they're not taking my precious stone collection!"

I walked over to a crystal bowl on the ground, filled to the brim with colorful stones. "Tell me you didn't dig all of these out yourself!"

"Sure, why not? I glued them in the first place...a creative frenzy in-spired by a trip I took to the Golden Temple in Punjab, India. I love my stones, my precious stones. And you know what? I refuse to leave a single one behind." Her tone was deep and resonant as usual but there was an unhinged look to her eyes, as if a hurricane was coming and she only had so many days to gather what she cared most about.

I felt selfish for having hardly gone there in conversation, and for keeping a protective distance from her impending reality. "When did the sign go up?"

"This morning." She continued scraping frantically. "It went up this morning, and I tried. I tried going about my day...lots of deep breaths, ate a croque monsieur and a bread pudding."

"When do you need to be out?"

"Ninety days...two years...a month...who knows? But it's still my house!" She tossed a turquoise into the bowl, then started on a ruby, first with the spoon, then with her fingernails, which were a chipped mess. "Until it gets sold at a public auction, it's still my house!"

"Oh, for crying out loud," I gasped, stealing her notorious phrase, "where will you go?"

When at first, she didn't answer, I feared the worst, and it was hard to imagine, hard to picture my friend...like a fox without a den, a skunk without a burrow, a bird without a nest, a crab without a shell, a doll without a dollhouse, a woman without a home. I could hardly breathe at life's harsh circumstances. But then, she looked at me with a raised eyebrow. Rest assured, she had a plan—a spectacular plan.

"What?" I insisted. "What's your plan?"

For a second, I suspected she was bluffing. But then, "How's that guest room of yours coming along? Have you and Peter been working on it?"

"Oh, um…" I choked. If I gave her the spare room, where would I flee when Peter's snoring reached monster-storm loudness? And poor Peter, where would he go to get away from us gabbing girls? "Do you mean our storage closet?"

"No, not the storage closet…your guest room."

"Oh," I nervously laughed, "grandiose to think of it as a guest room when it's no bigger than a dorm room. But no, haven't done anything to it, other than declaring it a disaster zone. I was thinking of hanging construction tape, or the Halloween *beware* kind, so no one goes in. You know, keep people safe." When I feared I had gone overboard in condemning the guest room, I circled back. "I mean, it's better than—"

"Addie, my friend," she stopped me as I was about to tell her it was better than her ending up homeless under some bridge. "I'm kidding, I'm totally kidding. No way would I ever move in with you guys!"

I felt like the victim of an embarrassing prank, my lack of hospitality revealed. "Even if you weren't kidding," I tried to recover, "I hope you know, it goes without saying, the room is yours, if you need it." I then sat down—not on the sofa—but where I deserved, on the floor in front of the fireless fireplace. "Seriously, tell me your plan, Viv. I want to hear your plan."

"Fine, I'll tell you everything." She clicked a remote control and the fireplace lit up. "I've put a lot of myself into this house. And not just this one, all my houses. I pour all my love into them. And you know what?"

"What?"

"They don't love me back."

"Of course, they don't. Houses can't love."

"Yeah, and I'm sick and tired of it…of loving houses, then losing them. Put me in a hut in Cambodia, I'd be happier in a hut in Cambodia, than I am here."

"Have you been to Cambodia?"

"Yeah, and I'm not kidding, the people were so doggone happy, I envied them. It had nothing to do with things. They hardly owned anything. When the monsoons came, they had nothing to pack up. Me? Trust me, you don't want to know how much I've spent on airtight containers alone." She made a crazy face. "I kid you not, I've got the biggest storage unit in town to store them all, in case of a hurricane. But when the monsoons came to Cambodia," she leaned over in her chair and picked up a handful of the precious stones from the bowl, "nothing seemed to matter to the people but each other...and the belongings they had inside of them."

"That's beautiful. But tell me you're not moving to Cambodia!"

"California." She dropped the stones into the bowl. "Back to California I go...the Bay Area. Found myself this tiny home, a rental in Sausalito. But I can only take the essentials."

"That's going to be hard."

"I'll survive, you know why?"

"Why?"

"I'm up for the experience...ready to sort through my junk, focus on what's inside of me, leave all darkness behind. I feel like I'm on the brink of a renaissance. Meh, you're looking at me like I'm crazy."

"I am not. I admire anyone who wants to sort through their inner possessions."

She looked over at the charcoal sketch on the wall. "Remember my dream, my recurrent dream of walking across the Golden Gate Bridge?"

"Yep."

"Well, the rental house has a view of the bridge, and I'm going to do it. So help me, I'm going to walk all the way across that bridge!"

"Text me the moment you do!"

"Okay."

"Text me something special." I rubbed my chin. "The bird with the golden slippers...text me that."

"Why?"

"My favorite bird is the snowy egret. And when you make it across the Golden Gate Bridge, it's going to be a golden moment for you. You're going to feel happy as a bird with golden slippers, dancing in the shallows!"

She nodded with a smile. "When you do something brilliant, text me the same...the bird with the golden slippers. We can then call each other later and share the details of our golden moments."

"Love it," I said.

"Me too."

It was then I remembered what I had come over wondering about in the first place. "The sketch of the bridge...is it the focal point of your house?"

She shook her head. "Focal points attract interest. They set moods, evoke emotion. They're the first thing people notice when they walk into a house."

My eyes went to a canvas high above the fireplace. It had caught my attention the first time I was over, and every time since, although I always looked away. I didn't like the painting.

"Yep, that's it alright. You're looking at the focal point of my house. What do you think?"

When I felt the lines on my forehead tightening, I got up from the floor and took several steps back to get a better look at the giant canvas the size of a billboard. "All I see are dark and depressing globs of paint. What is it?"

"'The Great Conversation Piece,'" Viv declared. "And you wouldn't believe the conversations it has sparked. Everybody always asks me about it. I'm surprised you haven't. Back when I was throwing parties, we'd play this game. My guests would tell me what they saw in the painting, and whoever came closest to what it was won a hundred bucks, or a box of chocolates." With an elegant stroke of her hand, Viv maneuvered her chair, rolling it to the center of the room, parking it with finesse. "Sorry, no chocolates, no hundred bucks, but what do you see in the painting, Addie?"

"To be honest, nothing. I'm not a fan of abstract art."

"Come on." She tapped her armchair. "On your mark, get set, go... blurt out whatever you see!"

I rolled my eyes. "Fine...a bird in a cage...or a frail house in no-man's land, I don't know."

"Ah, yes, good." Her voice was dignified, like the elegant hostess of a grand party. "Keep going, it's still your turn, don't be shy...whatever you see in the painting."

"A fragile canary with a broken wing...down on the floor of its cage." I was getting into it. "No, a house all boarded up...covered in graffiti, about to collapse. Or a butterfly pavilion...overtaken by litter. That, or houseboat barely keeping afloat on a stagnant swamp...ready to sink. Yes, it's ready to sink."

"For crying out loud," Viv sniffled, "we have a winner."

Although I won the game, I didn't feel good when I looked over at her face, a mess from tears and mascara.

"Don't feel bad. You nailed it, that's all."

"Nailed what?"

"My self-portrait."

Ouch, I hadn't put it together, that the deplorable painting she deemed her focal point was also her self-portrait. I swallowed hard, then went for a tissue and pulled up a chair next to her. "Close your eyes," I said, the way my girls had to me, back when we'd play salon. It was their favorite activity. I'd open my box of old make-up, then close my eyes, taking in their precious comments. "You're so beautiful, Mama. Do you know that?" In truth, it was being loved by them that made me beautiful. Their make-up application skills had me looking more like a creepy clown.

I glanced up at the perception Viv had of herself—the painting depicting her self-esteem—then back at her face, smeared with makeup. Borrowing the words my daughters spoke to me, I applied them to her. "You're beautiful and strong, Viv. Don't listen to anyone who tells you otherwise."

"You're the only one who knows. Even at my parties, I never told anyone it was my self-portrait. Its real name is *Inner Me*, and you have no idea the hours...no, the years that went into creating it."

Dipping brushes into acrylics, mixing colors into hues that best portrayed her innermost being, dabbing the canvas, stroking the harsh contours of her life had been the easy part. A person's self-portrait was years in the making, and sometimes it was like too many chefs in the kitchen, messing it up. Viv's father tossed in horrible names as she was growing up, and those names were splattered all over it.

As I finished wiping the mascara, Viv opened her eyes and took hold of my arm. "I need your help. I need you to get Inner Me down!"

I didn't have the strength to remove Viv's self-portrait from the wall any more than I did to dismantle her larger-than-life self-contempt, yet wasn't sure which of the two she meant. The first required a team of movers, and the second the supernatural strength and love of God.

I gave her my *no-can-do* look, and in response she gave me her infamous *don't be a boring person, embrace the adventure* look.

"What will do you with it once it's down?" I asked.

"Bubble wrap it, prepare it for the move."

"Do you want to bring it? You're downsizing."

"Yeah, but I can't just all of a sudden get rid of my *Inner Me*. Help me get it down, will you? It's giant, but lightweight. Pull the cushions off the sofa and once you unhook it, let *Inner Me* drop onto them. Oh, and there's a ladder in my guest room, a special ladder."

"A special ladder?"

"The most charming seven-rung vintage ladder you'll ever lay eyes on, I'm not kidding. I got it for a couple of bucks at a yard sale. My plan was to turn it into a bookshelf, a towel hanger, a trellis for the garden. I never got around to any of that, so it rests on the floor of my guest room. Go get it, Addie!"

I went to fetch the ladder, which to her was charming, but to me ladders were ladders, nothing charming about them. I toted the splintery wooden object into the great room, then stood it up against the wall. I pulled the red velvet cushions off the sofa, arranging them on the floor in case Viv's *Inner Me* took a fall.

I stepped up onto the first rung. "Did you know the ladder was this wobbly?"

"Aw, be a daredevil. I wish I could be a daredevil. As soon as my legs are strong enough, I'm going to climb to the top of that rickety ladder for no other reason than I can. I'll text you...the bird with the golden slippers...once I reach the summit."

Despite all of that, I detected a tinge of nervousness in her voice. The higher I climbed, the more responsible she felt for my going through with her dare.

"At least you're doing a good deed, bringing Mr. Ladder out of retirement, making him useful one last time. So," she said, a nervous chatterbox, "what would your self-portrait look like?"

I had already chosen the dare and was making a treacherous climb up splintery twigs assembled into what she considered a ladder. I didn't need to also answer a question.

"I painted mine with acrylics, but you can paint yours with words, you know."

I still didn't answer, but knew the words to my self-portrait. God's Word painted for me a clear image of who I was. *Beloved child, daughter of God, crowned with glory and honor. New creation. Loved. God's precious, living stone. Temple of the Holy Spirit.* Christ was my focal point, and more so than ever, He was setting the mood for my life and the emotional impact of everything around me. I glanced down at the top of Viv's head and prayed for my friend that she'd come to know God's love for her. And that His love for her would change the perception she had of herself.

By then, I was face-to-face with the abstract blotches of woefully colored paint. As I stared into what looked like tiny pupils, I wanted to share light…tell Viv what the Supplier of canvases had done for me. He loved me so much that He gave me a fresh start, a new canvas. And the more I got to know, love, learn from the Master Artist Himself, the more peace, joy, hope, and other traits of Christ filled my blank spaces. Love was flowing, spilling out onto my canvas from an endless supply, and the finger of God was at work on it, spreading it around where He wanted it.

I wanted to share a more laid-back-sounding version of that with Viv, but I had reached the summit and always heard that most people died on the way down. I didn't want to stumble around with words and lose my footing. I kept to the mission, shifting my feet, grasping the corner of the canvas, then lifting it up and off the metal hanger. I eyed the red velvet cushions, where it needed to land, and was about to send it flying through the air in that direction when…crack…snap…pop!

Those three sounds had nothing to do with a certain cereal I ate as a child. Old Mr. Ladder's legs had given out and down I dropped, with the mammoth canvas dropping, too, although it felt more like the sky was falling.

Viv wailed when the corner of the canvas hit smack-dab on my temple. "Are you okay, can you breathe? What should I do, call 911?" She was in my face. My eyes wouldn't open, but she was shouting in my face. "Can you hear me, Addie? You're the nurse, not me, but I think I'm supposed to have you answer something, anything, to keep you awake. Okay, um… what do I write my tidbits on? Yes, what kind of leaves do I write my interior design tidbits on?"

Without moving my lips, I hummed the song to *Jeopardy*, and soon knew the answer—sea grape leaves! I kept my answer to myself, though, and flat on my back on the creaking, singing nightingale floors, the nurse in me went to work. My fingers stumbled their way to the throbbing right side of my forehead. No stickiness, no blood. I rubbed my eyes and looked up at the ceiling, trying to regain focus. "Uh oh."

"Uh oh, what?"

"Uh oh, circles. I see circles and squares."

"That's good," Viv clapped her hands over my face. "I painted them myself, circles and squares all over the ceiling, after my trip to Beijing where I visited The Temple of Heaven. I sent you a postcard, remember? It was a Taoist temple, and everything in it representing Heaven was circular. The ground levels, representing Earth, were square." Viv let out a nervous, miserable laugh. "Listen to me rambling. I ramble in moments of crisis. I'm trying to keep you awake, that's all I'm doing."

She was leaning so far in her chair, I feared she'd fall out and land on top of me, like her self-portrait had. I tried to roll onto my side, but gave up.

"I'll be right back," she declared. "I'm calling Peter."

"No, no, no, rambutan," I managed to say, only because she needed to stop panicking, "get me a rambutan, please."

"A rambutan? Oh, for crying out loud, that's not normal coming from you."

"Ice. Do you have ice?"

"Of course, I do."

"Good. Get me ice." I touched the throbbing spot on my head, and lay there, feeling relaxed.

"Open your eyes!" Viv put what felt like an iceberg in my hand. "Keep them open and gab...gab!"

"I don't need a cab."

"Not a cab...gab. Pick a topic, any topic, and blab!"

The iceberg was too heavy to hold. I let it drop to the floor, then squirmed my body until my temple touched its frozen tip. "I don't want it to melt," I mumbled, worried about her wooden floors. "It might melt."

"I'm worried about that, too. We all are," she said, as if she thought I was talking about global warming. "Pick another topic...that doesn't worry you."

By then, I was feeling better, but went ahead. "Spirituality for a hundred bucks, please."

"You know I don't have a hundred bucks. But sure, if that's the topic you want, anything to keep you from falling asleep. Go ahead."

Keeping a mumble, I talked about my fall in the kitchen, back when Peter and I first moved to Sanibel, and my moment down on the floor when I opened the box with Mom's Bible, then found and read her letter to God. Even as the ice melted around my head, Viv didn't seem concerned about it ruining her wooden floors, so I went on gabbing about the ever-present, sovereign, loving God, and who I was to Him, according to the Bible.

I no longer needed to mumble, but since Viv was paying extra special attention to my mumbling, why talk outright? "I was reading this article about birds and hurricanes." I was on my back, eyes partially opened, gazing up at the circles and squares painted across her ceiling. "Birds have been spotted on radar, flying in the calm eye of the storm. In the midst of life's storms, I want God to be my calm center, my special go-to place."

"You're feeling better now, aren't you?"

"No. Can I pick another topic?"

"Sure, whatever."

"Interior Design of temples. God as the interior designer."

I went on gabbing all about God's details in putting together the tabernacle, that place on Earth back in Old Testament times, where He put His Holy presence.

"He was so particular about it, and no wonder…He filled it with His glory," I said. "But then, Solomon's temple replaced the tabernacle, and later the temple was destroyed, but then rebuilt. And Jesus showed up at the temple…a greater glory than ever," I mumbled with great refrain when really, the glory of God warranted declaration. "But that's God. When He restores, He doesn't return things to the original, but to something greater."

"Okay, are you all better now?"

"Getting there, but not quite. So now, there's us…those of us who believe…we are God's temple on Earth, with Jesus as our focal point. Everything we believe revolves around Him, who took on our sins and died, rose from the dead, and is seated in Heaven with God, present in us through the Holy Spirit, and who one day will return."

I turned my head on the floor, opened my eyes fully, and looked at Viv. "You love your precious stone collection. Well, God loves us. We're the living stones that make up His spiritual house here on Earth—and He fills us with His glory. If God cared so much about the particulars of that tabernacle—where He put His presence on Earth back then—and later, the temple, no doubt He cares about us—our particulars—as He fills us with His Glory."

"Yeah, yeah, yeah," she stopped me, "enough blabbing. You're fine. Whatever you do, don't pursue acting. I know you've been fake mumbling. I'm glad your topic wasn't politics. I don't know what I'd have done if you picked politics as your topic."

I sat up, letting my mouth close shut like the bill of a black skinner. I had seen one at the beach. The bird had been flying along, its lower mandible in the water, when all of a sudden it slammed its bill shut above the water. I didn't know whether it had caught a fish or not.

"Now that you've shared a piece of your mind with me," Viv said, "let me share with you something that drives me bonkers. I took my car in for an oil change...before I owned my Jag. The guy told me I needed wiper fluid. Sure, change my oil and give me wiper fluid, no big deal. But then, on top of the oil and the wiper fluid, he tried convincing me I needed a brand-new engine, too."

I scratched my head, like I didn't understand the point she was trying to make.

"Listen Addie, who doesn't want God? I want God. And if I knew where to go, I'd go there to the God-shop to get me some God. Now if they tried telling me at the God-shop that I need the Holy Spirit, too, sure, fill me up, that's fine. But they don't stop there." She put her hands up. "No, they try upselling. They tell me I need Jesus before I can get what I want, which is God. And by now, it's getting costly."

"It's not an upsell. It's more like a three-in-one deal—Father, Son, and Holy Spirit, all for the price of one. They throw in a new heart for free, and you get to hand over your junk, your sin. And you're also getting life out of it—eternal life, and God's inexhaustible love for you."

Viv said nothing in response but looked over at her dented canvas. It was probably my imagination, the look of anticipation filling her eyes and the exhilarating silence overtaking the room. I wanted to believe that like a death-defying tightrope walker, she was ready…to point her toes and take those first colossal steps onto thin wire. Her eyes sparkled with adventure, like it was her turn…Truth or Dare of a different kind. And she was considering choosing Truth, and along with it the dare of stepping out high above her problems, her low self-esteem, and setting her mind on things above while walking the straight and narrow line leading to Eternal Life. Even her posture seemed to respond to the moment of possibility in front of her as she straightened her back then tilted her chin upward.

Not wanting to make the slightest sound of distraction, I held my breath, praying in the name of Jesus that the trustworthy ringleader, the Holy Spirit, was there in front of her, guiding her steps, whispering to her the way, and giving her the assurance that He would never let her go… catch her if she fell. I didn't know why the silence was lasting so long. Maybe He was whispering to her, convincing her heart, soul, and mind of who she really was—the most spectacularly loved Vivienne Watts that ever was, and loved by the one and only, everlasting, unchanging, larger and stronger than anything in the world, sovereign God.

I opened my mouth, about to cheer her on, tell her it was real…not some grand illusion. But then her demeanor changed, and with a sigh, she slouched down into her chair.

"What's wrong?" I asked.

She shook her head, then looked at me. "Nothing."

"Oh, come on, you looked so deep in thought."

"Meh," she said, but pleasantly.

FORTY-ONE

"If then you were raised with Christ, seek those things which
are above, where Christ is sitting at the right hand of God. Set
your minds on things above, not on things on the earth."
—Colossians 3:1–2

"Finally, brothers, whatever is true, whatever is noble,
whatever is right, whatever is pure, whatever is lovely,
whatever is admirable—if anything is excellent or
praiseworthy—think about such things."
—Philippians 4:8

To the One who gives me all kinds of good things to set my eyes on,

*Here I am, toes in the sand, sitting on my favorite bench—where I sat when I
first arrived on Sanibel and started writing You these letters. In front of me is a
patch of scruffy beach plants. And dune daisies galore are covering the ground,
all of them turned on their stems and facing the rising sun. I have a wide-open
view of the Gulf of Mexico, and when I turn and look over my left shoulder, I
see the tip top of the lighthouse.*

*I snuck out before dawn, before anyone else was awake, and biked out here
to see the sunrise. That was a good hour ago, and here I still am, sitting with
You, savoring the brilliant effect morning's sun has on everything it touches.
Your Word has a brilliant effect, too. When I read it, I feel like a bee feeding
on golden, glistening honey. It affects the way I look at things.*

*A little while ago I rolled my pant legs up, then stepped into the glistening
water. I had never held a sea star before, so when I saw one I reached in and*

pulled the brownish, purplish creature up into my world. Holding its round body flat in the palm of my hand, I discovered the poor thing was missing an arm…instead of five, it had four.

Only You know its story, although I'm guessing its arm fell off when it got threatened by a predator. But as I stared into the purple eyespots on the end of each of its arms, I knew there was hope for the sea star. You designed it to house most of its vital organs in its arms, so from one arm, and a portion of its central disc, that sea star can regenerate its lost arm. I flipped it over in my hand and its hundreds of feet wiggled back at me, then I gently returned it to the mushy floor of the sea.

So here I sit now, back on my bench, hoping to remember that sea star, and never forget that You are Your Word, and Your Word is within me. Parts of me broken or hurt from this world can be made whole again, thanks to the way in which You designed me—and housed the Holy Spirit inside of me. But if I let parts of me get infected with sin, I must break off my connection with the sin. Then, from the palm of Your hand, I can look forward to the regeneration that occurs in that particular area of my life.

This gift I've been given—these couple of hours alone with You each day on Sanibel—is a once-in-a-lifetime thing. I'm soon going to get busy again, but it's okay. I'm recharged and ready. I just hope as I go to bed each night that my thoughts set on You, and come morning, they rise to You—the Light of the World, the light in me that never goes out.

I'm seeing Your wisdom and creativity in the sunrise, the sunset, and everything from a sea star to a sea oat, but it has nothing to do with being on an island. I've always found that when I read even a little of Your Word each day, it makes me more receptive. It's like putting on special sunglasses, and wearing them all day, seeing life through a lens You've designed.

I don't want to take these sunglasses off. I want to wear them back home when I'm doing dishes in the rental. The carpet is old and stained, the walls need a painting, and the kitchen cabinetry is dark and depressing. I haven't the money to change anything, and it depresses me that I can't give my kids a more beautiful home. Help us focus on You, as the center of our family. Like three pillar candles bringing everyday fragrance—Father, Son, and Spirit—be our centerpiece, right there in front of us, spanning not the length of the wobbly table that came with the place, but the length of our lives.

Please set the mood for everything I do. I don't want to overlook You as I have before, or replace You with a gaudy, oversized something that the world tries putting down in front of me, blocking my view of You.

I want to get us back to church, join with others, and pack the pews. But more so, I want us to sit in the palm of Your hand. I pray that Adele and Luke's names are engraved in the palm of Your hand, and they may know what it's like to sit in Your presence. It's hard to step away from the rat race, but I pray they can do that—step away and acknowledge You as their ever-present father, their comfort, and their strength.

If only they knew how I pray for them! Both of them gave their hearts to You, but Adele doesn't like talking about You anymore, and Luke...he's angry over the loss of his daddy. I won't write about that, and don't need to. You hear my cries and theirs. I pray that like two dune daisies tilting on their stems, facing the morning sun, their faces turn toward You, and receive the warmth of Your love. And may they stay close. When they grow up, I pray the two of them stay close, look out for each other in life.

Well, I need to get up from this bench and get back to the kids. They got way too much sun yesterday and will be hurting when they wake up this morning. They wanted to go back with great tans, even though I keep telling them a tan lasts a week and then fades.

But isn't that the way it goes? So much in life lasts only a short time, whereas Christ's righteousness in us is eternal. And for that, I thank You!

Love,
Finley (who wants to set her mind on things above)

FORTY-TWO

*The focal point you pick for your house will keep you
from going off into a million mismatched directions and
stop you from collecting hodgepodge here and there.*

Peter and I fixed up the front porch. We bought cans of polyurethane-reinforced porch paint and bathed the wood floor in white. He found a vinyl floor remnant rolled up under the house, and I turned it upside down, then painted turquoise, teal, and aqua stripes across it. Since the screen around the porch was ridden with holes, Peter put in brand-new black aluminum screening, which not only kept bugs out, but minimized the sun's glare.

After all of that, the front porch still wasn't finished. The door that banged in the breeze needed replacing, as did the broken overhead ceiling fan, and the hodgepodge wicker furniture pieces. Peter and I enjoyed our cozy nights squished together on the loveseat, but it didn't match the other pieces, and its natural wicker was falling apart.

Even with its imperfections and pending projects, the porch was our favorite spot, and we spent much time there, roosting high in the treetops. It was like our own café where, in the ambience of nature, we'd drink coffee with the cardinals in the morning and tea with a family of raccoons at night. Of course, the cardinals didn't drink coffee, nor the raccoons tea. They preferred feasting noisily on the small black berries in a nearby cabbage palm.

What I loved most about the porch was that reservations weren't needed, and there were never lines to get in. All we had to do was show up in our pajamas, then talk for hours about everything under the stars. But with all that was happening in our country—violence, political messes, natural disasters, and more—I didn't always like talking about things under the stars. We made sure to talk about things above the stars, too.

Sometimes when Peter arrived at the porch after me, he'd find me sitting there with my nose in the Bible, or with one of Mom's letters to God opened in my lap.

"Reading anything good tonight, anything worth sharing?"

"Oh, it's always good." I folded up the letter and slipped it back into the pages. "Mom was writing to God about Luke and me, hoping we'd keep Him center and surrender our lives to His will, that's all." It wasn't all, but it was all I said. As usual, I didn't want to overdo things.

It felt nice to relax, squished together on the wicker loveseat, listening to the frogs that played nightly, belting out song after song with upbeat tempo. We were their biggest fans, and I almost got up and danced when I heard the branches of the gumbo-limbo trees waltzing in the breeze, brushing up against each other.

But then Peter cleared his throat, making way for his burning embers of thought to ignite into conversation.

"What's up?" I asked.

"Ah, thinking about what you said...about your mom's letter to God. No doubt He should be at the center of things. I won't argue with that. But here's where I struggle." He thought for a moment. "It's good to be strong. I was raised to take pride in strength. Weakness is bad. I'm just saying, surrendering...even to God...sounds like a bad thing."

Oh, how I loved our porch talks—and agreed with Peter, it was good to be strong. "I want to be strong, too. But when I'm not...when all the woman power in me isn't enough, and I can't solve or figure things out, these days I'm wanting more and more for God's strength to kick in. I'm desperate for it."

I stared through the branches at the stars in the sky. "I think His strength is like those stars...always there but more evident in the dark. I notice it more when I'm weak, which oddly makes me appreciate my weakness, so I can experience His strength, if that makes sense."

"I get what you're saying." Peter leaned forward, indicating he wanted a massage. "Still, I'm not gung-ho about surrendering one hundred percent of myself over to anyone, even to God, no offense. I mean, why?"

When Peter hinted for a massage, and at the same time asked such questions, what he really wanted was for me to get lost in my answer, while endlessly rubbing his back.

"Well, think of the home makeover shows." I worked my fingers across his shoulder blades. "In some episodes, just one room of a house got redone, and in other episodes, an entire house...a total transformation. I would think most people wanted the total transformation but for whatever reasons...budget, probably...they got the partial."

"Oh, yeah, right...my neck, right there...keep going!"

"Okay, so what if the interior experts were willing to work on the entire house, but the homeowner refused to hand over three of the four rooms?"

"They'd miss out on getting all they could have gotten."

"Exactly," I said, still rubbing his neck. "One room fixed up, and the rest of the house left as is, not matching the new fixed-up room."

"It takes a lot of trust, handing over your entire house, trusting they'll fix it up the way you like it."

"Yeah, no kidding. But if you know the one doing it...their promises, and the kind of work they've done before, and what others are saying about the work done for them, you can be excited, not scared."

"I see what you're saying," Peter said. "But I'd still be careful. Before you know it, you'd hand over every square inch of yourself, and end up with nothing recognizable left. I like who I am, and I like you. I married you, didn't I? What's wrong with not wanting an unrecognizable wife? I like my old wife."

I wasn't sure what to think of that, or even what to say, and it was bad timing for the frogs to go on break, the trees to stop waltzing, and the breeze to leave. "Are you for real worried about that, or do you like me rubbing your back, so you want to keep the conversation going?"

He shrugged his shoulders nonchalantly. "I may have a few what-ifs of my own, sure. Every so often, it happens, when I have good reason. I see you getting more and more into what you're reading, and I'm not against that. I've been saying more prayers myself lately, especially for our country. I'm interested in the big picture...God's response to it all, how He uses things for His purposes. But on a more personal level, what do you think

He's doing in you...and what if you don't like it? I'll speak for myself, what if I surrendered every part of my life and myself and no longer liked my life or the guy He turned me into?"

Oh, thank goodness for the frogs who returned from their break, playing louder than before and causing me and Peter to crack up. Then, in a lighter tone of voice, he went back to what he was saying before. "You seem to like the charming old me with all my nicks and flaws, and I'm sure you wouldn't want God stripping me of my charm, would you?"

I couldn't imagine God stripping anyone of their charm, not even the frogs, making them chirp like nightingales instead. It was hard to think, what if in the lifelong process of transformation, God stripped us of our charming individuality and eccentricities? And Peter, what if he handed over one hundred percent of himself and there was nothing recognizably left of the man I loved, and all those things that differentiated him from every other man on the planet?

What if God churned us both into walking-talking, prim and proper, perfect and polite Jesus freaks? And what if we didn't like our transformed selves, and missed the old? In the world of interior design, it happened— Viv told me so herself. She had clients who preferred the way things were before all the changes were made.

Even if I wanted to say something, I couldn't. The high-pitched maria-chi band had moved to a branch right outside the screen and were playing in our ears. They weren't dressed in handsome silver-studded *charro* outfits with wide-brimmed hats, but the frogs were singing about things that mattered, about love.

I rested my head on Peter's shoulder and let Truth move about my mind, butting right into mine and Peter's what-ifs, knocking them over.

"Find me one person," I said above the frogs, "who doesn't like the work God has done in them...one person who says, 'I let Christ into my life to do His work, have been reading God's Word, renewing my mind, and am miserable because of it. From my new view of eternity to my fresh outlook on life, to the gunk removed, the nicks and gouges repaired, and the housewarming gifts...I'm unhappy with it all. So I've called another guy...the devil, to come and redo it all for me."

Peter gave me a nice laugh for that. "Point well made."

I just hadn't ever heard of anyone disliking the work God did for them in their life. "What's not to like about Him rediscovering our bones and breathing new life into us?"

I couldn't help but think of our house on stilts, how we loved it, made it our own, and even changed its name from Hidden Potential to Lovely Dwelling. Sure, it had charm when we first moved in, but that charm was covered up under layers of musty carpeting, wallpaper, unnecessary walls, and grungy cabinets. Getting rid of all of that, opening up the ceiling, and exposing the rafters brought out the hidden charm.

I leaned into Peter. "God would never strip you of your charm. If anything, He gives purpose to our uniqueness and puts it to use."

When Peter didn't reply, I turned my head and sure enough, his eyes were closed. He was snoring, but it didn't matter. His snores blended with the sound of the frogs. I stared at the contours of his profile. Who did he think gave him his charm in the first place? If anything, we stripped ourselves of charm when we focused on the self-centered things of the world rather than focusing on Christ. Christ's work in us revealed more charm—charm obscured by sin.

My sweetie pie Peter had fallen asleep on our porch date, but creation was wide awake and ministering in a way that I needed, insisting that the Creator of astounding charm wasn't a character-stripper, but a character-builder. Even the branches of the gumbo-limbo trees were reminding me to surrender to the breeze, enjoy the adventurous triple-time dance God had for my life, around and around the dance floor, progressing in sync with His will.

I closed my eyes and praised God for the ways in which He worked. He didn't mass-produce people. Fingerprints, snowflakes, even granules of sand under a microscope—no two were the same. And his believers weren't sugar cookies, all from the same giant batch of dough, shaped with cutters and baked to perfection on giant silver trays. Sure, there were similarities among us. He made us in His image and Christ was our main ingredient. But no two of us were the same.

Yet still, He knew everything about us, down to the number of hairs on our heads. What baker in the world knew His cookies down to the number of sprinkles on top? From the palm of His hand, God went about determining individually: more salt, less sugar, more peace, less fear, and so on. All through our lives His rolling occurred, intimately and exclusively shaping us while bringing out more of our Christ-like character.

When Peter's nose made a trumpeting noise louder and stronger than any frog sound, I feared they'd want him to leave me and join their group. "Bedtime," I announced, then blew out the candles.

As we went into the house and up to our room, he held his achy neck. "Could it be this?" He held up his flat pillow. "My head has smashed the life out of it. Should I get rid of it?"

I took the pillow, and like playing an accordion, only faster, gave it a good fluff. Mom was adamant about fluffing pillows, even tossing them into the dryer with a couple of tennis balls once a month to beat the clumps out of them. But it was too late for that kind of noise so instead, I put Peter's pillow on the end of the bed and hit the sides of it simultaneously.

"No need to get rid of it. This should do the trick, and really, we should be doing it daily, so they can breathe." I returned it to its spot. "It keeps them like new."

Peter's eyes closed the moment his head hit the pillow. "Thank you," he mumbled. "But too much effort to have to do every day to a pillow."

I settled my head down onto my own unfluffed pillow and thought about Mom, always so into fluffing. A smile spread across my face, wishing I could thank her for the things she taught me. If only she knew the freshening effect the Bible was having on me, fluffing me from the inside out.

God didn't have to beat clumps out of me. That wasn't how He worked. His Word had a way of quietly, peacefully smoothing things out.

FORTY-THREE

I woke up missing my mom and wishing to do something special for her and for me. I tiptoed across the house, left before sunrise, then drove to the east end of the island, to Sanibel's Lighthouse Beach. I needed to find that favorite bench of hers, the one with the lighthouse over her left shoulder, the view of the Gulf in front of her, and the dune daisies galore at her feet.

Leaving my flip flops in the car, I followed the first sign of morning—a great blue heron promenading along the wooden plank and heading for its breakfast buffet of all-it-can-eat fish and crabs down by the shore. Up and out so early in the morning, barefoot, and with uncombed hair as messy as the wire-thin, billowy plumes of muhly grass had me feeling like a carefree child playing follow-the-leader with a bird.

But Mr. Great Blue Heron and I weren't the only early birds up before dawn. Sanderlings by the dozen were chasing waves up and back, lightning whelks building egg cases, and hermit crabs house-hunting for shells near the shore. Watching the crabs was entertaining, especially when a giant red hermit crab checked out three modest spiral shells before moving into its new residence—a mansion of a horse conch with more than enough room to grow.

I stepped ankle-deep into the water, trying to spot a sea star like Mom had, but when something brushed past my foot, once, twice, three times, I let out a scream. I didn't have to see the eyes on the top of its flattened body to know it was a stingray.

At least I wasn't wading the waters of Australia where Luke lived, and the world's most lethal animals lived, too. Oh, Luke, we hadn't called each other in a while, and I missed him, not to mention it was Mom's wish that we stayed close to each other and to God. I didn't know if he was keeping in touch with God or not. It wasn't something we talked about. We knew little about the inner details of each other's lives, and kept our talk mostly to what was going on in the outer courts. I needed to call him, let him know I had taken his advice…set sail to a kingdom with treasures for the taking. And remind him, too, there was someplace brighter than the bright side of the moon…a go-to place I knew he'd love!

I headed east along the shore as the waking sun painted the sky crimson, like a dramatic curtain at a theater. I couldn't help but wonder if Mom was up there, peeking out from behind the crimson curtain, cheering me on to go sit on the bench and call my brother…if anything, just to tell him I loved him. Mom was a cheerleader like that.

"Did you tell him," she'd ask over and over when she first moved in with Peter and me. "Did you tell that husband of yours how much you love him?"

"You asked me that ten minutes ago, Mom. I haven't yet, but I will."

And then ten minutes later, "Did you tell that husband of yours?"

"Yep, I told him."

"Good, tell him before it's too late, tell that husband of yours how much you love him."

Peter heard it a record number of times the first few months I was caring for my mom. We'd be rushing around, making dinner, helping the kids with homework, folding laundry, and hardly looking at each other, but from across the room, every time Mom repeated that, he'd get the shout out from me—*Love you*. We'd laugh because two minutes later, in the midst of it all, Mom's voice, "Have you told that husband of yours?"

I pulled out my cell phone and texted Peter.

Have I told you, my husband, how much I love you? Xoxo.

As I continued along the shore, I passed an impressive home being built past the line of sea oats. It got me thinking about Peter's concern from the night before regarding charm and uniqueness. The home was being built according to a blueprint, but as walking temples, our blueprint was Christ. We who loved Christ weren't changing to be like others but like Him, so there were going to be in us matching, complementary interior features recognizably evident as the workmanship of the Trinity. But also, God put into each of us our own intricate and elaborate details and we were nothing like stock homes.

"Oh my Lord, I'll bet that home is worth millions," I muttered out loud, "But it's nothing compared to the value You place on us…we're priceless to You."

There were a few other people on the beach then, and their faces were turned and staring at the all-consuming sky. The clouds were changing, going from what looked like freshly fluffed orange and white pillows to stretched-out yellow blankets. They weren't changing to be like all the other clouds but changing based on their individual proximity to the sun. The ones closer to the sun were ablaze, reflecting the light.

"I don't want to change to be like other people. Whatever happens from walking closer and closer with You, the risen Christ, that's the change I welcome."

There had been times in my life when I changed in hopes that a certain someone might like me, and times when I changed according to the behaviors and patterns of those around me. The only kind of change I wanted was the kind that happened naturally and gradually from living in close proximity to God and from keeping Christ at the forefront of my being, my focal point within. I welcomed such change—change in my outlook, mood, perspective, and focus. And should the upside-down world knock crooked my focus, then may Truth get to work in me…recognizing uncomplimentary actions or mismatched thoughts within!

Before I reached the rounded tip of the island with the towering lighthouse, I saw the scruffy beach plant area Mom had described in her letters. And sure enough, like an old wooden pew dropped from Heaven, there was her favorite bench.

I left the shore and followed a trail, then sat down on the toasty wood, putting my toes in the sand where dune daisies galore carpeted the ground. Glancing over my left shoulder, I winked at the lighthouse, which through the tip top of the trees winked back at me. Sitting on that bench, staring out at the sparkling water in front of me, I wasn't alone. God was present, and so was Mom's love. She loved me enough to share with me a view… the view of Eternity. I wanted to watch not just the news, but the sunrise, too, and remember Eternity's ever-present light was in me.

And even though I still struggled at times—brooding over things— my wings were getting stronger every time I brought my worries to God. I just had to keep telling myself, "When the outside chaos intensifies, when the storms get louder and closer together, when the ground shakes and the waters spin out of control…fly birdie, fly to the eye of the hurricane, the center of the storm. May God's presence be your go-to place where it's quiet and calm and your inner bells of praise ring louder than the chaos outside. And when the storm is over, go watch the sunrise because every morning it rises and every evening it sets. Open your eyes to Christ and close them with Him at night. He is your stability in the unstable world!"

FORTY-FOUR

INTERIOR DESIGN TIDBIT

* * *

*When it comes to picking out wall colors, go with the colors
that move you. Make it a personal experience and have fun. If
you can't do that, consult a certified color coach to help you.*

When I got home from the sunrise, Peter was giving the bedroom
floor a facelift, staining it in the first of three coats of dark ebony. I
had already, over the course of several days, helped sand it by hand, vacu-
um, clean it with mineral spirits, and apply a wood conditioning base—all
of which proved to be the workout of my life—and therefore dismissed
me from doing more until my muscles recovered.

I took a shower, threw on shorts and a t-shirt, then grabbed my binder
and a pen. Wanting to be in the same room with Peter as he worked, I
flopped down on my stomach onto the bed.

"How's your writing coming along?" he asked the moment I opened
my binder.

I looked down at the floor, to make sure he was still stroking the stain
in the same direction as the wood's grain, which he was. "It's going," I
said, but wondered—should I tell him I was still writing about the work
we were doing on the house, and the supernatural details occurring within
the infrastructure of my being?

"Any formalized story yet?"

"Formalized story!" Pouring the contents of my mind onto paper was
easy. But whenever I read it later, my words seemed like nothing more
than chicken scratches. If ever it was going to become a formalized story,
I'd need to go over it with coat after coat of editing, polish every word,

walk away from it to let it dry, then return to look at it freshly. "It's not that easy, Peter. We're talking even more laborious steps than staining the floor. Writing is a process...that's what I'm finding. And once it's out there, it's a permanent thing, just like stain. I have to do it right."

The bedroom floor would be done and dry long before I even finished one page of writing. I couldn't wait to place a seagrass rug on the finished floor, then push the old weathered pine chest to the foot of the bed and see whether my vision for the room was going to work or not.

A few minutes later, Peter's voice interrupted my writing, like a chair scratching across a floor. "So, where are you at with picking out wall colors?"

Uh oh—I held my pen still. "How about streaks of crimson, orange, and pink for here in the bedroom?"

"Funny, you're joking, right?"

"It looked good in the sky this morning." Then again, Florida's sky was every bit as indecisive, never sticking with one color very long. "How about light blue, or bluish grey throughout the whole house?"

"What else do you have in mind?" Peter had every right to hound me about colors after already canceling the painter four times in the last couple of weeks. The painter didn't want to deal with us. But like Lucy had trouble picking out ice cream flavors, boys, and rings, I had trouble picking out colors.

It was easy for me as a kid, though. As a kid, I liked pink...plain and simple, pink. Oh, and green...pink and green together. Also blue...the Blue Moon ice cream color. "I don't know why it's so hard for me," I told Peter. "You think it's a symptom of something bigger going on in my brain?"

"What do you mean?"

"You know." I closed my binder and sat up to better see him down on the floor. "Things in my brain tangling."

He stopped moving the stain-drenched rag and shook his head. "Wall colors—that's all it is, Adele. You're having a hard time picking out wall colors—don't make it into more."

I looked over at the naked walls. No colors came to mind. "I don't want to ruin the place. Should I ask Viv?"

"Don't you dare ask Viv. Every wall in our house would be gold, or something odd like that. Listen, I don't mean to sound mean, but if you don't figure it out...and I mean today...I'm going to pick for us, and that's not good. We'd for sure have an ugly situation on our hands if I came up with the colors…the colors of my favorite teams." He applied more stain to the rag and started back up again, working it into the floor. "It's not brain surgery. It's wall color. Worst case scenario, we can change it ten years down the road if we don't like it."

I closed my binder, slipped off the bed, and hopped across the dry parts of the floor to the driftwood-framed mirror I had hung the week before on the undone wall. As I adjusted it, I didn't dare tell Peter I liked the mirror on the unfinished walls—sort of an organic, island, industrial look.

The unfinished walls made Lovely Dwelling feel like a productive warehouse with all kinds of creative work happening. It felt like the kind of place you brought raw ideas after walks on the beach, and those ideas were then stored and soon processed…and one day, manufactured and even exported into the world.

Peter got up from the floor, walked over, and took the driftwood mirror I was looking into right off its hook.

"Nincompoop. I can't believe you did that."

"I've got yet another painter coming out Tuesday. That means you've got a deadline, your final deadline. I'm not asking. I'm urging. Figure it all out, and go buy the paint, please."

"Fine, but look at me. What am I wearing?"

"Black shorts…white t-shirt, why?"

I went to my closet and opened the door. "What do you see in there?"

"Black and white."

"Exactly, that's all I wear. I'm like a character from a black-and-white movie. If I were a bird, I'd be a black-and-white warbler."

"Listen, you're turning this into bigger than it is. At the end of the day, wall color. That's all it is, and I'm good with anything…just no crimson, pink, orange…no neon. No crazy creative frenzy, please."

After breakfast I put my flip flops on, gave Peter a wink, and headed out the front door, hoping for the lights to go on in the color-picking department within me. It didn't matter I had already walked that morning. There were countless places to walk on Sanibel, and not just beaches but preserves.

I especially loved walking and talking with God through the preserves, and a trail not far from our road was my favorite. I went there often, listening for the resonant *whoo whoowhoowhoo whoo* of the great horned owl, the *ooah, woo, woo, woo* of the mourning doves, and the whisper of the still, small voice within. But to hear the still, small voice within, I had to block out the persistently loud chatter of the squirrel tree frogs, and the even more persistent chatter in my mind.

I wished it was, but it wasn't my day to just walk and pray. As I passed by a tree of wild coffee berries, I thought how elegant the rich, dark green glossy leaves might look on pillow fabric, with walls the color of coffee berries!

I had once read that cavewomen used berries to paint the walls of their caves. Those cavewomen and I would have had a blast walking through the preserve together. There were beautiful berries everywhere, and I stopped to take pictures of them with my cell phone. How could I not paint something—our bedroom ceiling, perhaps—a striking magenta, like the berries? Of course, if I did that, for Peter's sake I'd have to add lots of dark wood and burlap textures to counter it.

I walked further, then stopped to take pictures of Indian hawthorn berries. My, did I want to paint one room, or one wall, the intense purple-black of those berries! If I were a cavewoman, I'd have pulled off the berries and carried them home with me, squeezing out their color, rubbing it onto the walls with my hands. But I wasn't a cavewoman and would bring my pictures to the paint store instead, and match everything up there.

As I followed the meandering trail deeper into the preserve, the colors of nature were a gift, packed perfectly like crayons in a box. I stopped in my tracks and stared—not at a green pointy piece of wax—but right into the eyes of a bobcat. Should I paint the walls of our guest room green, like the iris of the bobcat?

The feline went its way and so did I, pulling a wax myrtle berry off its branch. Should I paint the kitchen *its* color blue, or the colors of the indigo buntings perched high on the overhead branches? Or should I go with a purplish maroon, more like a little blue heron's plumage? I was about to decide when an osprey flew overhead with a reed-like leaf of muhly grass dangling from its beak. That bird knew what it was doing color-wise! The lavender muhly grass was going to look gorgeous on the walls of its nest, and I should paint a room that shade of lavender, too.

There were endless colors to choose from, and it didn't help my indecisiveness when the indigo bunting took flight. The most colorful bird in Florida made me want to paint a room like it—one wall blue, a second wall lime-green, third wall red, and fourth wall gray. If Lovely Dwelling ever turned into a bed & breakfast, it would be called the Indigo Bunting Room. Then again, indigo buntings were known as fierce fighters, pecking and beating each other up with their wings. Peter and I would fight alright…he'd fiercely quarrel with me if I painted any room in our house blue, lime-green, red, and gray.

I walked further, leaping over lizards. Most were emerald-green, but some had changed from green to brown, or tan, or gray. I tried not to let it overwhelm me that the color possibilities in my mind were changing ever more quickly than the colors of a lizard.

I stopped walking and held my head back. How did God do it? How did the Creator and Master of Colors decide which colors to put in the rainbow? And that the laughing gull should don a black cap? The pileated woodpecker a bold red crest? The American oystercatcher a red bill? And all the billions of tiny coquina shells that washed up like colonies on the shore, how in the world did God make each one of them a different color to where no two coquina shells were colored the same?

I shook my head in awe, praising all the way home the awesome connoisseur of colors, for there was no greater color coach than He.

"Hello, there," I said to Don Juan Cardinal sitting on our car, admiring and pecking at himself in the window. "You sure like the color of your breeding plumage, don't you?"

But I gasped when, halfway up the porch steps, I saw yellow wrapped around our door handle, when nothing yellow should have been there.

Where was Peter? He was the one, not me, with an intense fear of snakes. I would never have owned a snake as a pet or let anyone put one around my neck at a carnival, but finding a yellow rat snake wrapped around our door handle wasn't a scary moment for me. Peter, though, struggled even hearing the word *snake*. A picture of one, or even a belt left out on our floor elicited embarrassing emotional reactions in him.

I went into the yard and called up to the bedroom window. "Peter, are you up there?"

I reached into a bucket and chucked a few Atlantic calico scallops up at the screen. They were beautifully colored, some yellow, but mostly white and splotched with patches of bright red, maroon, and lavender. I tossed one at a time, until he appeared, nose to the screen.

"Why not come up?"

"Trouble getting inside, that's all."

"Inside the house?"

"Yeah, this adorable, not scary at all, yellow, um…" I hesitated, contemplating a less scary word for snake. I couldn't think of one, and wasn't going to use the word serpent, so trying to avoid the word altogether: "…creature that wished it had fur and was fluffy, cute like a puppy, so it can be man's best friend, is blocking my way into the house."

"Huh, what are you trying to say?"

"I don't think we should be afraid of the yellow creature affectionately hugging our front porch door handle."

Peter cleared his voice, then gagged. "Are you ssserious—a sssnake? Is this a p…p…prank?" His pitch skyrocketed high as a soprano. "A sssnake at our front door?"

"A cute, friendly snake. And silly, too, all wrapped around the handle."

Peter's face turned an eerie, glow-in-the-dark white. "W…w…wait a minute." With his mouth and his nose pushed to the screen, his words came out muffled. "It's not red touch yellow, k…k…kill a fellow, is it? Tell me it's red touch black, friend of J…j…jack."

"I already told you, Peter. It's yellow…a gorgeous yellow rat snake, harmless."

"How big? A big sssssssss, or small sss?"

He had already turned into a damsel in distress and didn't need to hear it was a good seven feet long, and thick as my wrist. "Listen, Peter." I put my hands on my hips. "This is an opportunity for you to get over your phobia. I'm hardly afraid of frogs, thanks to the ones that play music for us every night. And I'm getting over my color phobia, too, picking colors for the house."

"Sweep it away," he grunted. "Get the broom and sweep it away."

"I would never. But here's what I'll do. I'll go around to the porch steps and keep an eye on it. All you have to do is keep yourself busy, be productive, okay?"

"How?"

"The bedroom floor, Peter. If you haven't already, remove the extra stain with a rag, apply the top coat, let it dry a couple of hours, then apply a second coat. In other words, finish the floor! I'll be on watch and let you know the moment it slithers away."

No sooner had I gone to the front of the house to see that the snake was still there and to research severe snake phobias on my phone, when I heard Peter belting out my name from the window.

"It's hot in here," he groaned.

"Then close the window and lower the air."

"I don't know, I'm having trouble breathing."

"It's one of the symptoms, sweetheart. *Ophiophobia*—abnormal fear of snakes. But you know what? You're brave, and you need to tell yourself that…you're brave…you are!"

He didn't choose a fear of snakes. The fear chose him. I wanted to help, to be the heroine that rescued him from his dire predicament, but had to figure out how.

His face disappeared for a good minute, then reappeared. He was breathing into a paper bag. "C…c…call someone, a wildlife removal pro…trained for this k…k…kind of emergency."

"Oh, for goodness' sake, no, no, no! No need for that. Let's wait it out…let the snake finish its nap and be on its way."

When he left the window, I went around to the gorgeous yellow snake and did a photo shoot, but it refused to strike poses. It showed no signs of moving, so I abandoned post, taking off into the yard to check the lemon tree. Still no lemons, but if ever there was a day in which Peter deserved to bite into a comforting lemon bar, it was then.

At the sound of a vehicle speeding down our drive, I left the fruitless tree, my mouth dropping open at the sight of a police car. "Officer," I said apologetically as he got out of his car. "Did my husband call?"

"A man by the name of Peter called 911, said he's trapped in his house, something about a snake at his front door. We lost connection after that."

My hands were on my cheeks and I was shaking my head. "He's got this deathly fear of snakes."

"We get calls like this all the time. A good day for it, though…no one's falling asleep at stop signs or taking live shells from the beach."

With a grin, he went to the porch steps and nodded. "Yep, a harmless rat snake."

"A beautiful color, isn't it?"

"Oh, yeah. And these guys seldom bite."

"Officer!" Peter's voice came not from the window on the side of the house, but from the porch itself.

Putting a hand over my eyes like a visor to shield the sun, I spotted him at the opposite end from where the door was, standing behind the wicker loveseat, which he had moved and set up like a fort. He had on his old red and black checkered flannel robe the kids got him years ago for Christmas and was twisting the ends of its belt in both hands.

"How are you doing up there, Peter?" the officer asked.

"I don't like what they do to me, officer. I don't like how I'm feeling right now. I'm not afraid of much. My wife will tell you that." He pushed his nose to the screen and peered down at us.

"It's alright, you're not the only one. I've been on more snake calls than bank robberies." But when Peter crouched down in the corner and held his head with his hands, the officer lowered his voice, and whispered to me, "Worst case I've seen. You might want to seek help for him." He then looked back up at Peter. "If it makes you feel better, the snake is socializing with your door handle. If I were to guess, it'll get bored real soon and the playdate will end."

"Then what?" Peter asked.

"It'll head back out to the preserve."

Peter hurried inside and closed the door, and I thanked the officer, assuring him I already had a desensitizing activity in mind that might help Peter overcome his irrational fear.

I started it later that day, after the reptile unwrapped itself and slithered up onto our roof. I took my pictures to the paint store and had them whip up a can of paint matching the snake.

"First color decided," I told Peter as I opened the can. "We can save money. You can paint the guest bathroom yourself...this gorgeous yellow. You spend a lot of time in the guest bathroom, what do you think?"

"Um," he scratched his head. "G...g...good, I think. I'm not so sure."

"Give it time. You'll get used to it, and soon enough, start liking it, too."

FORTY-FIVE

INTERIOR DESIGN TIDBIT

* * *

*Identify your favorite go-to store and frequent
it often. It's that one sure place where
you find what you need, and also what you don't.*

I was sitting in my pajamas on the bottom porch step, drinking coffee and going over the beautiful names God calls His sons and daughters from the Bible, when I heard a dramatic sneeze coming from Viv's yard.

Having forgotten I made plans with her, I hurried into the house, threw on my t-shirt and shorts, then rushed over. "What in the world are you doing with that?" I asked when I saw she had wheeled herself down the ramp and was waiting for me at the end of her drive with her enormous self-portrait sitting on her lap.

"Saying good riddance to it, that's what I'm doing." She had on a fitted charcoal-gray dress with a draping cowl neck, and whether intentional or not, it matched the colors in the painting and the gray, foggy morning. "Today's the day, I kid you not. I'm getting rid of *Inner Me!*"

"That's wonderful," I said in a congratulatory tone, then glanced over my shoulder to see if the trash collectors had come. "There's still time. Want me to haul it to the trash?"

"Nope, I've got a better plan, but I need your help. There's this thrift store on Periwinkle, hidden behind a church. It's not your ordinary thrift shop, but a famous one that everybody loves. I used to frequent it back when I was still working, searching for vintage finds. Take me there, will you?"

"You mean you and your painting?" I put my hands on my hips and stared at it. "You want to give your painting to the thrift shop?"

"They might not want it, but we could drop it there and run…take off before anyone has a chance to tell us otherwise."

It was a cringy plan, and I felt the lines on my forehead deepening. "It wouldn't even fit in my van, Viv. I'd have to strap it to the top."

"No van," she insisted. "I'd hold it like this…make it our morning stroll."

I rolled my eyes, giving in to her as usual, hoping it wasn't something I'd regret. Her fingers were clinging to the wiring on the back. I adjusted the canvas, wedging it between the corner of her chair, so it balanced more at an angle.

"Sorry I was late," I said as we went down our road. "Would you believe I forgot?"

"Ouch, glad I'm so important to you."

"No, I've been forgetting a lot of things. And it's driving me crazy…I go there."

"Where?"

"Wondering if the same thing that happened to my mother is happening to me."

"What else have you forgotten?"

"I forgot to set my coffee maker last night. I set it each night to go off in the morning, but I forgot. A couple nights ago, I forgot to put water in it. I put the grinds in it, but no water. Oh, and I forgot to put my hair up in a ponytail this morning. I don't even think I combed it." It felt good telling someone other than Peter, who was tired of hearing it. "I forget things like that all the time."

"Brain fog, my friend, that's all it is. We all experience it, bouts of brain fog."

I appreciated her nonchalance, but swung around to the front of the chair to see if the look on her face matched her *no big deal* tone of voice which, it did. "So what exactly is brain fog?"

"Brain fog," she repeated with an official voice, as if for a vocabulary competition, "a common condition that forms within the nooks and crannies of brains like ours that are saturated."

"Saturated with what?"

"It's different for everybody. I can't list all the things we saturate our brains with. For me, it's the mean stuff people have said or believed about me. For others, maybe it's one too many regrets, or worries, or stuff that has to get done."

By then we had crossed over San-Cap Road and were heading east along the pedestrian path, with the wildlife refuge on our left and cars going by on our right. I didn't want brain fog, but was glad for the morning fog because Viv's self-portrait was the size of a billboard, and billboards weren't allowed on Sanibel. I didn't want a citation, especially from the nice officer who handled Peter's snake call.

We passed the Ding Darling Wildlife entrance and a car filled with people slowed. The driver shone the high beams, making us the show. "We look ridiculous, Viv, a couple of ding-a-lings, toting this giant canvas."

"Don't kid yourself. I guarantee they're ding-a-lings, too. We're all a bunch of ding-a-lings. Who hasn't done foolish stuff in their lives? I sure have, and to tell you the truth, it's comforting to admit. Try it, my friend. Tell me ding-a-ling stuff you've done, other than this."

A river otter bounced across the path in front of us, disappearing into the thick preserve. I'd have rather followed it into the wild than rattle off the harebrained things I had done.

"Let me ask you," Viv said when I didn't answer, "and I want your honest opinion, okay?"

"Sure."

"After marrying two yahoos in a row, was it ding-a-ling of me or daring to tie the knot the third time? And remember, my third…he's a great, great person. You can't find a better person!"

"You're asking something monumental, beyond my qualifications. I'm not sure. I don't know."

She twisted in her chair, pushing her face around the canvas to see me. "When love fails us once, twice, then shows up a third time," she said, restating her question, giving me another chance to answer, "do we cower from love, or chase after it like daredevils?"

"I wouldn't chase after it like a daredevil, no."

"You wouldn't?"

"No, not like a daredevil."

"Why not?"

Her persistent questioning confirmed there was a love interest in front of her, and she was considering whether to pursue or run. "If I were you,"

I sounded like Peter giving me advice, "I probably wouldn't enter into another relationship until I had something new to bring to the table."

"New, like what?"

"Inner assurance of a fresh start."

"What do you mean?"

"Think of it like a new canvas to paint on."

"Yeah, yeah, we can see if they have blank canvases over at the thrift shop. You can find all kinds of things in thrift shops."

I opened my mouth, wanting to tell her God was the go-to for that. He was the supplier of new hearts and fresh starts, but then came a burst of thunder, and a second later, rain. And not just rain, but a torrential downpour that had us both screaming.

"Hold on tight!" I went from a power walk to an all-out sprint for fifty yards, and when we came to a gazebo on the side of the walkway, I made a sharp turn at full speed, pulling her ride to a screeching stop once we were under its roof.

"What a thrill," Viv screamed, "like riding a cable car."

I took *Inner Me* from her lap, propped it up against the wood, and with my hands on my hips stared at the smeared and smudged mess of a painting. "I hate to say this, but what if they don't want your artwork... look at it, it's ruined."

"I don't care." She shook the rain off her arms, then wiggled into a comfortable position, stretching her legs onto the bench. "I just want to leave it somewhere. I'm sick and tired of it. Wouldn't you be? Wouldn't you be sick and tired of your own self-esteem if all it ever told you was to not believe or trust anyone who claims to love you?"

I sat down on the wooden bench across from her. "Don't listen to it."

"Yeah, right. Come on, Addie, we all carry on dialogue with our inner selves. And low self-esteems are the loudest. It's hard to block mine out. You want to know what it tells me every single day?"

"What?"

"I'll never be good enough, but you know what?"

"What?"

"I'm not a bad person."

"You're a great person!"

"Let's not overdo it. I don't deserve a halo or golden stars above my head. I'm no Mother Teresa. Others in the world are doing way more significant amounts of good and random acts of kindness than me. I mean sure, I did keep dollars in my purse, to drop into the hats of people who were homeless. Never bought one sandwich…always two, so I could give one away. And Girl Scout Cookies…no wonder I have no savings. I helped the girls out…bought up hundreds of boxes, then handed them out to anyone living on the sidewalks. They need cookies, too." She paused, then shook her head. "Guess how many goats I've bought?"

"Goats, why on earth would you buy goats? Let me guess, goat yoga?"

"Nah, did that for a while, but I bought them for families…in third-world countries. No wonder I'm broke! But my point is, I'm not a bad person."

"You're a big-hearted, generous person…that's what you are, Viv!"

"Aw, thanks, but enough about me. I didn't mean to go off on a monologue. What about you, are you cold?"

It was a ridiculous question. Drenched as I was, Florida's humidity had me feeling like a person lounging on the wooden bench of a sauna. I could have sat there all day.

Viv looked at me intently. "So, where do you go, my friend, when searching for vintage finds? I love the thrill of it…the thrill of searching for anything vintage."

"I don't know. I've never gone vintage shopping before."

"Deprived," she said in a spasm of pity. "Deprived and don't even know it."

"I search for other things, like Truth. Ask me where I go for Truth. Truth is vintage, right?"

"What do you mean?'

"Truth about myself, my true identity…from where I came and where I'm going."

"Okay," she said, as if I was the strange one, "where do you go for all of that?"

"Well," I gave her a wink, "this morning, I was sitting on my bottom porch step, perusing through God's Word. I do that often…my go-to place when searching for who I am."

Her face cringed. "Good for you, if it fits, put it on. I don't think any of it would fit me."

I should have asked what she meant by that. Or told her it didn't fit me at first, either, until God went to work in me, making His adjustments. Unlike a seamstress with clothing, though, He didn't change His words to fit me. He changed me to fit His Words. I didn't mention that to Viv. It was personal. Inside-out changes were like being in a fitting room alone with God, then stepping out wearing perfectly fitted words. Not boring words, but beautiful words God designed for me to wear. I was grateful for the private fitting, and the beautiful words He dressed me in.

As personal as it was, I tried to continue the conversation the best I knew how. "The Bible is fast becoming my go-to place for everything I need. Even things I didn't know I needed...once I catch glimpse of them...I need and want them, too."

Viv scrunched her nose. "What do you mean, what are you finding...a bunch of old, outdated stories? I mean, vintage is one thing, antiques another. I'm not big on antiques. Some people are."

"Truth," I said again. "I'm finding Truth. It may be old, but never outdated. It's timeless, relevant, and more valuable than the most priceless item in a history museum, antique store, or thrift shop on Earth. It's not just reading old stories. It's like window shopping...no, better. It's like peeking into the mind of God, and catching glimpse of all the things I want for myself...things God wants to give me."

"Like what?"

"Oh, let's see...love, forgiveness, justice, mercy, grace, righteousness, comfort, peace, joy, patience, relationships." I could have gone on and on, but stopped myself there.

Viv put her hand out the gazebo and let the rain splash off it. "You like trivia?"

"Sure."

"There's three braking mechanisms on a cable car."

"Thank you for telling me that."

"Did I tell you I once dated a grip?"

"No."

"Well, I did. And I kid you not, he told me everything there was to know about cable cars. One day, we were careening superfast down this enormous hill in the financial district. I was scared out of my wits that we weren't going to stop. That's when he told me all about how cable cars stopped. He said there were three main track brakes, front wheel brakes, and rear wheel breaks."

"Hm…" I was curious as to where she was taking me with the cable car trivia, and hoping somewhere special.

"After a month of me hanging off the sides, and us flying down hills at thrilling speeds, narrowly missing other passing cable cars, we broke up. Don't ask why I brought all of that up…other than, who knows? Like the cable cars, there's different kinds of braking mechanisms on the ride of life, too."

"What do you mean?"

"Storms," she whispered, as if saying it out loud might rouse one. "Things show up out of nowhere…illnesses, layoffs, stock market crashes…and life as we knew it stops…stops in its tracks. And what a bummer, not making it to our destinations."

"Unless," I remembered what I once heard from a nurse friend of mine who took a three-month leave of absence from the hospital to care for her husband after his car accident, "those sudden, unscheduled stops drop us not where we planned or wanted to be, but for reasons unbeknownst to us, put us where we're meant to be."

I didn't tell Viv, but my friend had told me how the entire experience, tragic as it was, catapulted both her and her husband into God's presence. They both began praying, crying out to Him like never before.

"Philosophical of you, Addie, but where are we meant to be? Maybe wherever we are is where we're meant to be, but what do I know?"

"I don't know, either. But remember when you saw me in my yard crying that morning?"

"A scene I'll never forget."

"Well, I was going about my morning, and like an internal breaking mechanism operating within me, I felt an urge to stop. I believe it was the Spirit of God urging me to stop…stop and cry out."

"That you did."

I laughed. "I know, I sounded like an osprey. But my point is, that wasn't one of those forced stops in life. I could have kept going…could have gone up into the house, carried on with my day. But I'm glad I stopped. I'll never regret stopping in the yard that morning, crying out to God."

Viv stared out at the rain. Blame it on my overly active imagination, but her eyes reminded me of boarded-shut windows that suddenly opened a crack. "I wonder what I'd sound like crying out to God. Probably like a Pier 39 boisterous sea lion. You should hear them, my friend. Come visit the Bay Area, and I'll take you to Pier 39 so you can hear the sea lions." She let out a wonderful laugh, then slapped my arm. "What do you think…for the sake of fun conversation…what do you think I'd sound like crying out to God?"

I wanted to tell her something beautiful, like a mourning dove with its soft, drawn-out lamenting calls, but how was I to know? Maybe she'd sound like a groaning cable car, all worn out from making its way up and down the grueling hills and from careening around the same crazy track one hair-pulling day after the next, year after year, on the ride of life.

"That's between you and God. All I know is we don't have to sound all dignified when we cry out to Him."

The raindrops falling on the gazebo were making a beautiful sound, like a song. Viv and I were quiet, listening to nature play its elaborate piece of music for us. I was so moved by the sound of the rain on the wood, that when the spirited finale—filled with bolts of thunder—ended, I would have jumped up and given a standing ovation, had it not been for the dismal look on Viv's face.

"What's wrong?"

"Brain fog," she said miserably. "And it's thick. Mine is always thick."

"Thick from what?"

"If you want to know…one too many doom-and-gloom memories, childhood incidents that never lifted from my subconscious. I wish I could sit here and enjoy the rain, like you. Sometimes, I can. But the memories are always in me—condensed into other forms, but still in me. They come out at the worst times, like a gloominess that settles into my soul, some days thicker than others. To tell you the truth, I don't mind your god-talk.

I just don't see what you see, but you know what? It is what it is, and I'm used to the way I see things."

I was no meteorologist but got the feeling she wanted me to forecast a hint of sunshine. "Have you anywhere in your life, Viv, ever caught even the slightest glimpse of God's love for you?"

Her mouth dropped open and she looked at me like I had read her mind, which I hadn't. I read the wanting in her eyes. "Crazy you ask. I swear I couldn't make this up if I tried. Last night, in the middle of the night, I couldn't sleep and was up thinking about what you just asked me."

"No!"

"Yes, when I was seven, my Aunt Christi came to visit. She was Ron's sister and they hardly spoke, so her coming to see us from all the way out of state was a shock. She showed up at our front door with this giant bag of craft supplies…wanted to teach me how to make heart-shaped pillows."

Viv stared into a puddle outside the gazebo, trying to pull out the details. "Aunt Christi and I were sitting on a swing chair in the yard. I was crying, and she pulled out this handkerchief." She paused. "You know what a handkerchief is, right?"

"Of course, I do. Why would I not know what a handkerchief is?"

"No one uses them. Ask anyone under the age of ten, and they couldn't tell you. But this one was embroidered with flowers, and scented like the perfume Auntie wore." Viv closed her eyes and a bittersweet expression overtook her face. "She let me bawl my eyes out into that gorgeous hankie."

"Why were you crying?"

Viv's eyebrows squeezed together. "I had been carrying Ron's plate of food from the kitchen to his armchair and dropped it. Long story short, in his usual drunken rage, he called me a clumsy, no-good kid, told me I was a danger to others, and should lose my right to walk." She opened her eyes, and with her hands in fists, hit the arm of her chair. "I kid you not, Addie, my own father told me I had no right to walk."

No wonder, after the golf cart incident she was most ashamed of, Viv had refused to listen to the doctors telling her she'd walk again, and instead listened to her own self-esteem telling her she screwed up so badly, she didn't deserve to walk again. And no wonder, if I told her I was a walking temple of the Holy Spirit—and that thanks to the work of Jesus on the cross, God would make her a walking temple, too—no wonder she'd roll her eyes in disbelief, like yeah, right.

A tear dropped from my eye, and one second later, a tear dropped from Viv's eye, too, which caused another to drop from my eye, and soon hers were coming out faster than mine, but mine caught up. As she tugged on the draping cowl neck of her dress, and was wiping her nose with it, I was using my arm like a windshield wiper across my face.

"I wish we had hankies," I said into my slobbery arm. "What happened to that era…of ironed and embroidered hankies?"

"I'll tell you what happened," Viv sobbed. "We entered the era of disposable everything…toss-a-way tissues, disposable diapers, to-go cups for coffee. Heck, most of us use toilet paper to wipe our eyes, and you know why?"

"Why?"

"The rush-around era, that's why. Even when we cry, we're in a hurry. We grab whatever we can to dry our faces, get on with our productivity."

"Well, I'm in no hurry today and I could care less about productivity," I said like nothing else mattered. "We can sit here as long as we want, enjoying the lost art of weeping."

She sniffled, then cleared her throat. "I never got to the God part of my story you know. You asked if ever in my life I had caught glimpse of God's love."

"Oh, yes, yes, yes…we went off on a tangent, which we tend to do."

"So, there I was," she nodded, "crying into my aunt's hankie when she sang this song for me."

"Do you remember the song?"

"Yeah, one of those silly childish songs…Jesus loves me, this I know."

I loved that song. Mom and I used to sing it together as we made our Sunday morning pancakes, and we were always singing it in Ms. Viola's class. "You mean this song?" Even though I was a horrible singer, I began, "*Jesus loves me, this I know, for the Bible tells me so.*"

Viv closed her eyes, and when I finished, she opened them. "Yep, that was the song alright. I don't know why I mentioned it. It was just a song. But what I remember is the rainbow that showed up while she was singing it. Was that God, putting up a rainbow for me? Meh, enough. Enough about all of this, if you don't mind…enough."

By then, the sun was peeking through the parting clouds. I got up from the bench, returned the painting to its spot, then pushed Viv down the wooden ramp.

"You know what I think?" I said once we were back on the path, making our way along the final stretch of San-Cap Road. "God works through people. And for whatever reason, your aunt had it on her heart to sing you that song about Jesus. I'll bet the Creator of the Universe has been reaching out to you every single day of your life in one way or another."

All of a sudden, a rainbow appeared in the sky, and surely God's signature was on it. Who, but the God of intelligence and intricate detail, of order and beauty, the God in control of the powerful forces who used His creation as He liked, giving purpose to His workmanship, revealing Himself in one way or another to every person on the planet, could have put that rainbow in the sky at that exact moment?

"You think it was God?"

"He can work through anything, Viv, through flowers and songs, seashells and rainbows, and through circumstances, too…not causing the bad, but using everything for His purposes."

"I should tell you the rest of the story," Viv said as we turned onto Periwinkle Way. "Long story short, Ron gave her the boot…kicked Aunt Christi out."

I gasped.

"It is what it is, welcome to my life. And that's not all. She left me her pillow-making supplies. After she left, I was doing what she taught me… drawing my heart onto a piece of cardboard, cutting it out, tracing it onto pink fabric…singing that song when Ron barged in."

I slowed my pace but kept going, and we looked like the lost float in a broken-up parade as we headed down Periwinkle Way, passing restaurants and gift shops.

"It's no exaggeration, he was ranting and raving how his sister was a ding-dong. He told me never to sing hogwash again. And from there, he rattled off a bunch of stories about big-name Christians who did as many ding-dong things as non-Christians, and how they were no different from each other, except the Christians believed ding-a-ling stuff."

I swallowed hard, wanting to tell Viv I had done all kinds of idiotic things in my life, but also, I believed in a holy, loving, forgiving, merciful God who loved me and made a way to be close to me, despite my sinful nature. Even on the cross, when they were persecuting Him, Jesus cried out to His Father on behalf of the ones persecuting Him, "Father, forgive them, for they know not what they've done."

What a vulture Ron was, snatching the truth right from Viv's hands, tearing her God moment to shreds. All the sharp-edged words used on her as a child were like scissors cutting into the lines of her heart, messing up the perfectly laid-out pattern of love, and the way things were supposed to be. No wonder when she tried pinning together the fabrics of her life, with the God moments that she had, things didn't seem to match up. Yet she did the best that she could, all by herself, sewing her imperfect heart inside out, leaving a section open for stuffing.

When we reached the church, Viv directed me to walk around back, to where the thrift shop was hiding. I felt sadder than ever for my friend parading a dark and depressing self-image wherever she went, and for the moments of her past beating on her insides like a death march, telling her it was a foolish thing to believe in a God who loved her.

The doors of the thrift shop were open. *Oh, please, Lord. Please help Viv!* I prayed as I pushed her chair up the ramp and into the busy shop, full of chatter. *You know what she needs—to be made righteous through Christ alone, and a new heart, stuffed and bursting at the seams with Your love for her, and her love for You.*

Heads turned and eyes became quizzical as I lifted the painting off Viv's lap, then rested it against a kitchen table that was for sale. Viv paid no attention to anyone and was quiet, but for the cracking of her knuckles. I feared she was having second thoughts about saying farewell to *Inner Me.*

Once her knuckles were cracked, she reached over to a counter of jewelry and picked up a bracelet with a dangling solitary pearl. "I know what I'd sound like." She clenched it in her fist.

"What do you mean?"

"I'm not saying I'm going to, but I know what I'd sound like if I cried out to God." Even when Viv thought she was whispering, her deep, raspy voice didn't allow for it, and an old lady, browsing through a pile of vintage handkerchiefs of all things, looked over at her.

"What would you sound like?"

"A person requesting an appraisal." Viv was unphased by the old lady shopper listening. "I'd sound like a person requesting an appraisal, wanting to know if I was of value to Him."

The eavesdropping lady, dressed in a shimmering pink jacket and sheath dress with a fancy beaded neckline, hair in tight, silver curls, tossed the hankies down, picked up her cane, and waddled over toward Viv. "I saw you come in with that piece of art over there." She tilted her head toward *Inner Me*. "Are you the artist?"

"She sure is," I answered on Viv's behalf, like a protective mother, ready just in case she was about to dish out negative reviews of it that Viv didn't need. "It's her self-portrait."

As Viv rolled her eyes at me, the lady announced, "I want it. I want to buy it, whatever it costs."

I was about to butt in again, but this time on behalf of the old lady. Surely, her eyesight was off, and I didn't want us taking advantage of anyone throwing away money on a wet mess of a painting they couldn't even see.

"I want that painting!" She looked back and forth at Viv and the artwork, her eyes sparkling like aquamarine gemstones. "I'm for real, girls. You're both looking at me in disbelief, like I'm a fairy godmother. But when I say I want the painting, I really do want it!"

"Why on earth?" Viv said, stealing my phrase, and also my thoughts, "why on earth would you want it?"

"I have to agree," I said to the woman. "What do you see in it?"

The old lady looked offended, as if we were questioning her ability to see beauty. "I'll tell you what I see." She took two steps back, then eyed the painting up and down. "I see a woman." Like Viv, she wasn't good at whispering, and already her voice carried above others in the shop. A few shoppers had come over and were hovering around, curious to see the painting she was talking about. "I see a woman in this painting," she said again, and the nosy shoppers all nodded, like they did, too.

"But the woman that I see," the old lady continued, "doesn't see how beautiful she is. She sees herself as no more than a grain of sand, scarred and scratched. And like a micro-mollusk, the woman in this painting has fallen to the bottom of the ocean." By then, shoppers lost interest and wandered off.

When Viv shooed me away with her hand, I wandered off, too, over to an acrylic tarpon with one eye. On Peter's behalf, I considered buying it, gluing in a marble for its missing eye.

"My self-portrait doesn't depress you?" Viv whispered loudly from across the store.

"No, my child. Listen to me, I'm a poet. I've written thousands of poems in my life, and your painting inspires me. It doesn't depress me, and here's why. The woman I see in the painting can be twenty-five-thousand feet under—as far down as Mount Everest is high. But there, in the cold darkness and enormous pressure of the deepest depths of the sea, the vital signs of her fainting heartbeat are still heard—heard by God. I look at this painting and know, darling."

"What…what do you know?"

"Something good is about to happen…between God and you."

I wanted to hear more, but couldn't. I picked up a toy snake that happened to be yellow. Should I buy it—a therapy tool for Peter? But when Viv let out the loudest, most dramatic one-syllable sob that sounded like my name, I dropped the snake and hurried over. She had the pearl bracelet on her wrist and a vintage hankie to her face. The old lady was gone, and so was *Inner Me*.

"I tried telling her she didn't have to," Viv's eyes were blinking, processing. "She bought me this bracelet, and hankie, too."

Our stroll home was pleasant and carefree without the burden of *Inner Me*. The trees were fervently clapping their leaves, the birds spiritedly singing, and all of creation was acting like it knew the something good going on between God and Viv. I wasn't going to bring it up, but every so often I'd swing around to the front of her chair to appreciate the fresh expression of anticipation on her face.

"You know how pearls are formed, right?" she asked as we went down our crunchy seashell road.

"No, how are pearls formed?"

"An exterior object puts pressure, crushing the shell inward, causing a piece of the shell to fall off into the mollusk. And if all of that happens near the mantle, the mollusk secretes this protective coating around the piece of shell that has broken off."

"Thank you for the interesting pearl trivia."

It wasn't until we turned onto her drive that she added another precious piece to that strand of conversation. "That lady told me to consider someone."

"Consider someone, who?"

Viv shook her head, and half-laughed. "Him."

"Him…who?"

"You know who…the taker of old hearts, the giver of new. I told her it seemed like everybody was talking about Him, and you know what she said?"

"What?"

"God does that, He uses the pressures of life for His own purposes, and also the pressure of conversations. And through them, nudges us toward Jesus. I kid you not, that's what she said when I told her everybody was talking about Him." By then, we had made it into her yard and were at the bottom of her ramp.

"Wow," was all I said. I didn't want to overdo an already significant moment.

As I went up my front porch steps, I thanked the One who was at work. He was making right the conditions, preparing to replace what Viv thought was no more than a worthless trinket of a heart…with a brand-new, priceless pearl.

FORTY-SIX

"By wisdom a house is built, and through understanding
it is established; through knowledge its rooms are
filled with rare and beautiful treasures."
—Proverbs 24:3

My Dear, Sweet, Heavenly Father,

The sun seems to be getting stronger here by the day, and I fear it's going to bake me like a Shrinky Dink if I sit for too long. When it comes to sitting in Your presence, though, I pray for that—less of me, more of You. May You get bigger in my life!

So, here I am, sitting in a gazebo on Periwinkle Way, just past a street called Martha's Lane. I happened upon it while biking, and love when that happens. I love when I find special spots like this to meet up with You. It has two entrances, one leading back to the pedestrian path, the other out into a secluded preserve, and the smell of its fresh wood, mixed with the scent of the wildflowers, and the chorus of birds make me feel like I've wandered into a chapel in the wild. It's filled with Your presence, and granted, I showed up with great expectations, and room in my heart to meet up with You. And I've been sitting here praising You. According to Your Word, You inhabit the praises of Your people.

As I've been reading Your Word, I've been especially receptive to everything temple-related, and yet temples of the Holy Spirit are only one of the many things that we as believers are called. Next time I read the Bible in a year, something else might pop out at me, and I'll focus my letters to You on that. We're Your sons and daughters, Your beloved, Your blessed, too. And so much more!

For now, here's a summary of the temple history I've read so far, and also learned before:

Solomon built the temple in 949 B.C. After Israel turned away from You, Your presence left the temple and the temple was eventually destroyed by invading armies (2 Kings 25). Some one thousand years later, on the same hill as Solomon's temple and overlooking the city of Jerusalem, the people returned to rebuild the temple (I read about this in the little Book of Haggai). But then they got distracted, putting all work on the temple on hold. After being put on hold, the temple was rebuilt, and Herod the Great had it enlarged and remodeled.

The enlarged and remodeled temple wasn't the end of the temple saga, however. It wasn't the high-water mark, so to speak. You are a God of greater ideas, and bigger plans! Knowing what was coming, or I should say Who was coming, my eyes keep speed reading along the lines of the Old Testament scriptures like a train on a track, heading somewhere exciting. The temple anticipated Jesus, the coup de grace, who took on the sins of the world and ended the suffering that comes from living as slaves to sin.

Thank You for moving Your only begotten Son, who was with You in the beginning, from His perfect spot in Heaven down to Earth, putting Your love on display in an unmeasurable way. Jesus, the high-water mark, in which the body of Christ can rise over the land, flooding it with Your love.

When I go over the before Jesus and after Jesus pictures in the Jerusalem temple, and in my life, I want to stay put in this gazebo praising You all day. The complex details of both the Old and New Testaments, and Your overall plan keep coming together like beams of timber in an extraordinary building project, aligning me with You.

I praise You for Your holiness, Your justice, Your mercy, Your never-ending power, and for loving me. Just as the enlarged and remodeled temple wasn't the end of the show, there is no end to Your love. Thank You for loving me as I was—a sinner—but seeing my potential, and doing Your work of salvation in me, making me not just a walking of the Holy Spirit—heart, soul, and mind filled with rare and beautiful treasures—but also Your daughter, Your beloved, Your blessed.

I pray for more spots like this where I can meet up with You. Even if it's a corner in my closet back home, I hope that when I close my eyes and pray to You, it can be like I'm sitting in a gazebo, filled with Your presence, and surrounded by wildflowers.

Love,
Your ever-praising Finley

FORTY-SEVEN

Despite the colors of nature inspiring me on my walk that day, I went with a white-on-white palette for the interior walls of Lovely Dwelling. From the baseboards to the rafters, I had every room coated, except for the guest bathroom, in gallons of pearlescent white paint, and to capture the sunlight on the surface, I chose luster instead of matte.

"Time to figure out our furniture situation," Peter announced before the walls had even dried, and while eating his breakfast at the wobbly, weather-beaten bistro table that came with the place. "I can't wait to get rid of this table! If I pour too much cereal into my bowl, it'll fall down."

For days we had been debating furniture options. Peter wanted our stuff from storage brought down. But out of sight, out of mind, I wasn't missing it. And there was no way that our chunky mahogany furniture sets from the 3,000-square foot house up north were going to fit in the 1,800-square foot bird house ten feet off the ground!

"I agree, that table belongs in a dollhouse," I told Peter. "Let me go for my walk and I'll think about it. We need places for people to sleep."

"Places for people to sleep?"

"Our kids, their spouses, and our grandchildren."

"Grandchildren!" Peter shrieked, "The kids aren't even married yet. Don't worry about where our grandchildren will sleep…worry about us. I miss my California King bed."

As I went out the door and down the steps, I glanced over at the ospreys in their nest, wishing certain things were as simple for us as they were for them. I wanted to make Lovely Dwelling guest-friendly, but unless we wanted to sink the cockleshell we called home, Peter and I could never sleep on our California King bed ever again. It was too big for our little house on stilts, and I needed to figure it all out.

I had already stripped and painted white the iron twin beds that came with the place—the ones we had pushed together and were still sleeping on—but I wanted to move them to the guest room and buy us a queen bed instead. And we needed a trundle or day bed. In the great room, a sleeper sofa, along with another matching sofa/ottoman combo, the kind that formed a queen-size bed. Oh, and for the front porch, so more family could sleep there, a durable, weatherproof swing bed.

My mind was so in a whirlwind with furniture configurations that it wasn't one of those walks where I blocked out the noise and distractions of the world and prayed, although I wanted to. Those were my favorite walks, and like Mom did in her written prayer to God, I wanted somewhere in my day to take a moment to praise the One who deserved to be praised.

I made it to the end of the crunchy seashell road when six 1950s Thomasville chairs left curbside with the trash stopped me in my tracks. I took a few steps closer. Was sparing them from their doom the looking-out-side-of-the-box adventure Viv suggested when it came to furniture hunting?

Along with the chairs was a thick slab of pinewood wedged between two trash cans. It was partially burned but I saw the strong and sturdy dining table it could become. Like a cautious bobcat, I sauntered toward the trash, and could almost hear Viv cheering me on. Peter would have been shooing me away, telling me only termites were drawn to burnt slabs of wood.

I walked away, wanting to forget about it, and praying instead. "I was drawn to burnt wood," I muttered beneath my breath. "But You, You're drawn to hearts scratched, damaged, burned by the world. It's Your passion, and what some deem trash, You declare treasure." I went on thanking God for bringing me into His kingdom, and asking Him to continue His work of stripping me down, reimagining, repurposing, and reclaiming. "And not just that, but apply Your imaginative finishes, make me purposeful, please!"

I made it so far down the road when I heard the waste management trucks in the distance. I could hardly stand to think about them dumping those Thomasville chairs and burnt slab of wood. "No time to explain," I said frantically into my cell phone as I turned and hurried back to the pile of potential, "Come get me with the van, fast as you can!"

"W…why, are you okay?"

"Fine, found us a table and chairs. Bring a rope!"

"W…w…where are you?"

"The first house on our road. But hurry, the trucks are coming!"

He cleared his voice but said nothing.

"Peter, are you there?"

"Y…y…yeah, I'm in the y…y…yellow bathroom, installing the sh… sh…shiplap paneling, like you wanted…halfway up the w…w…walls, right?"

"Aw," I said. Unbeknownst to him, he was in the midst of rat snake desensitization therapy. I wasn't trying to be sneaky. I wanted him to conquer his fear and feel like the captain of a ship, confident and in control whenever he used that yellow lavatory, or saw a rat snake in our yard. "I'm proud of you, Peter. But putting up shiplap is a lengthy process…short bursts of time at first, until you get used to it. For now, I need you to drop everything. Leave the house and come get me!"

Thanks to watching *Price is Right* in my younger years, I knew how to work it. The moment Peter pulled up I waved my hand in a showcasing manner toward what was going to be our new kitchen dining set.

"Tell me it's April Fools." Peter stuck his head out the window. "Even though it's November, lie to me, will you? Tell me you're not serious about bringing someone else's junk up into our house!"

I put my hands on my hips. "I've got plans for it, good plans, you'll see."

He looked in his rearview mirror, to see if anyone was coming. "Don't you feel embarrassed, prowling through people's trash? Isn't that illegal?"

"I don't know, but I wasn't prowling. I was walking on by and there it was." I ran my fingers across the damaged piece of wood, so full of potential. "Trust me, let me have fun, let me try!"

In the days that followed, I experienced delight in making old things new. I sanded down the burnt slab of wood and picked out the most beautiful legs for it at the home improvement store in town.

"So, what exactly is worry-free fabric?" Peter asked as I was using a staple gun to attach new teal-blue fabric to the chairs. "Does it mean that whenever you sit on one of them, your worries go away?"

"You're funny, Peter, and your humor reassuring. I take it you like what you're seeing, this lovely dining set coming together?"

For the first time ever, I didn't bother making a turkey for Thanksgiving. Instead, I baked homemade crusty Cuban bread in the oven and a simmering pot of Florida grouper chowder on the stove. I had wanted the kids to come, but they didn't have enough time off work, so I invited Viv. Peter was more than willing to help her up our porch steps, but she had already made plans with someone else. Who? I didn't know. She was still tight-lipped about it.

When the feast was about ready, I went down into the yard and picked hibiscus for our table. I was in a great mood, happy with the progress Peter and I were making on the house, but also at peace with the work God was doing in my life, and the restoration of my marriage, too.

"You're a good God," I whispered as I went up the porch steps with gorgeous orange and hot pink hibiscus. "I can't help it. I want to praise You every spare moment I get. How can I not when everything on this island from the strangler figs to the osprey, the curbside trash to the dune daisies, and even these trumpet-shaped flowers in my hands has my eyes and ears turning toward You—I want to sound a trumpet, I love You so much!

I dropped the showy flowers into a glass bowl filled with water and placed it as our centerpiece on the old wooden slab-turned-table. Peter sat down and when he offered to say grace, I saw it in his eyes, then heard it in his prayer that he was a believer, too...a believer in renewal, and in old things made fresh.

"That was a nice prayer. Thank you for saying one."

"I meant it. I like the something different that I'm noticing about you. It's nice seeing you at peace...not all wrapped up in a mental fluster, driving yourself crazy, that's all."

I dipped my bread into the chowder, thankful for the decluttering expert at work in me. I was no longer hoarding my worries and regrets but handing more and more of them to God in prayer. Praying about worries and regrets, instead of just thinking about them, was like putting them in a recycling bin, and trusting that God was doing something new and good with them, according to His will.

If anything, that's what Peter was noticing about me—the work of God freeing up my insides and furnishing my mind with new things to think about that were pure, lovely, admirable, excellent, and praiseworthy. And although I would still be a work in progress for the duration of my life on Earth, the worry-free fabric of Truth was wrapping itself around the dimensions within me, replacing my old ways of thinking.

"So, we keep putting it off," Peter said, "but regarding our furniture in storage—"

"It's not healthy to talk about stressful things while we eat. Sure you want to bring that up now?"

He looked at me from the side of his eyes, then put his spoon down. "You'll like what I'm about to say. I've come to a conclusion."

"Oh?"

"We live ten feet off the ground. It would break my back hauling it all up here. So..." He lifted his bowl to his mouth, and sipped the last drops to keep me in suspense. "I think you should go ahead furnishing this place in whatever out-of-the-box way you like. Pure creative freedom, that's what I think."

I got up and did a celebratory dance, then wrapped my arms around his neck. "Thank you." I kissed him on the cheek. "A brilliant plan, and we'll make it fun. You know we'll make it fun."

Making it fun was an understatement. Over the next several days, I went for walks, combing the curbs for treasures and things to salvage. I frequented estate sales, yard sales, garage sales galore, and even crossed the bridge into town, perusing flea markets. All the while I was rediscovering the art of junking—something I loved doing as a kid with my allowance money.

When Peter saw it bringing out a younger side to me, he got into the sport of it, too, and bought a 2001 platinum silver Ford Mustang convertible for dirt cheap. With tons of miles, scratches, and rust, it was a real eyesore, but none of that mattered come night as we cruised around with our noses whiffing the salty air. We were like two wild bandits in the moonlight, roaming the dark in a frenzy, and when we saw signs, *take for free*, we grabbed a wide variety of fare with lightning-quick hands.

One night alone, we came home with a bamboo chair, a reclaimed wooden coffee table, and a chest of drawers—all of it put out by the house at the end of our road. None of it was in horrible condition, but most of it needed a touch of paint, or a knob, or a new leg.

"I'm loving this," I shouted our second week into it, with the tropical air hitting us in our faces as we turned onto Periwinkle Way. It was night, and the trees were glistening with strings of festive holiday bulbs, making me feel like I was living in a magical, charming snow globe of a world, without the snow. It felt like someone shook both Peter and me up and our vim was back, and along with it, we were laughing and having fun. "I love this so much, love having our vim back, Peter, don't you?"

"I'm not sure," he grinned, "What do you mean by *vim*?"

I put my bare feet up on the dashboard. "*Vim*," I said, as if he and everyone else in the world should have known what vim was. "It's a noun, Peter. She's so full of vim and vigor."

"Not a word I've ever used before...never heard anyone else use it, either."

"You're kidding me, Peter. Lively or energetic spirit...enthusiasm... vitality. I'm so glad to have my vim back!"

"Okay, so your vim is back," Peter said like a schoolboy learning a new word. "But when it left you, where did it go, and why'd it leave you in the first place—your vim?"

"How should I know?" I laughed. "It's a mystery *where* our vim goes. All I know is it's sad when it's gone, when we lose our oomph, our pizzazz, our get up and go. Have you ever felt that way, like something about you was missing and you wanted it back, that part of you, the good old energy you once had when you were young?"

"Yeah, I know what you mean." He gave me a casual smile. "I guess we take it for granted until it's gone, and then we miss it. Glad yours is back. It's nice seeing you so full of vim and...and..."

"Vigor, Peter. So full of vim and vigor."

We were only going thirty-five miles per hour, but I released my hair from its ponytail, letting it whip about in the breeze the rest of the way home. Whether he knew what to call it or not, his was back, too. Peter had caught that second wind in life, and his mojo was back. He proved it when he came home with the beat-up convertible and invited me out for our first moonlight madness ride. I was glad our vims were compatible, and we were having fun together.

As Peter turned onto our road, he shined his lights and we were forced into action. The lady in the first house had set out another treasure—a small antique armoire. If we didn't save it, come morning, it was going to meet its demise. We pulled over and did our thing, putting it in the backseat, then taking off.

"Let's hope she doesn't run out of butter and come over to borrow some," Peter said as we heaved it up our steps, leaving all her other stuff outside under the house, waiting to be worked on.

"Nope," I assured him. "People don't do that. First of all, who uses butter? Olive oil, maybe. But still, no one runs next door to borrow anything anymore."

"I'm just saying. How humiliating if she happened to come over and see all her junk we've taken."

"Well, if anything," holding my end, I kicked open the screen door with my foot, "we've rescued it, spared it from destruction!"

"Still, you're answering the door if she does." We parked the armoire not far from her old wooden slab-turned-dining-table. "I'll be hiding in the closet."

"No need," I assured him. "When I get done with it, you just wait and see, it's all going to be like new!"

FORTY-EIGHT

INTERIOR DESIGN TIDBIT

* * *

Scrutinize before bringing items into your house. Some things will add, and others take away from the overall atmosphere you desire.

It was around five in the morning when I dropped Peter at the airport. A series of mandatory work meetings popped up in Michigan, but also, he wanted to offer the kids our furniture from storage, then begin the process of clearing out whatever wasn't sentimental.

It happened to be Thursday—trash day—and the first house lady put out even more stuff, and not just stuff, but irresistible stuff, including end tables, bookshelves, lamps, cobalt bottles, and Christmas decorations. I wanted to pull over on my way home and toss the goods in, but since Viv and I had plans to go for a morning stroll, I picked her up first.

"No time for chit-chat." My mind was going sixty-five thoughts per minute, and I had to bend over to catch my breath from all the dizzying adrenaline. "It's like a flea market at the end of our road!"

"Flea market?"

"You'll see." I took hold of her chair and took off at full speed, wanting to get us there before anyone else, especially the trucks.

"First off," Viv said once we approached, "why would anyone dump all of this and not donate it?"

I pointed to her sign, *take for free.*

"Yeah, but what if no one sees the sign? She should bring it to the thrift shop. And second, are you alright?"

"Fine," I gasped, "it happens when the junking fever comes on."

"Junking fever? Addie, you ran a two-hundred-meter sprint in like twenty-one seconds."

I had told her about my thrill for salvaging whatever the dump trucks were about to take, but nothing prepared her for my behavior. I acted like a contestant on a game show rushing against the clock, ignoring her shouts of what to take and what not to take, doing my best not to drop anything. I piled seashell books, vases, a Christmas wreath, wicker baskets, and more onto Viv's lap, squeezing items into the spaces around her as if her chair was Santa's sleigh. Soon, she was so covered with stuff that the knee-length, light blue silk dress she had on was hardly visible.

"Don't you dare," Viv scolded when I tried wedging a giant round wall clock with Roman numerals between the seat and her back. "You want your house looking like a classroom? And put these broken clay pots back," she insisted, lifting them from her lap. "You can buy new pots dirt-cheap."

I put the clay pots back, then swiped up a mermaid statue, which she approved of. Her lap was full. I set a small Christmas wreath on her head, like a visor, shading her from the morning sun.

"Let's get this show on the road," she ordered when we heard the trucks one road over. "Grab that rooster lamp, and we'll call it a day."

"Nah, rooster lamps are for country homes. Mine is a beach house."

"I mean it, grab the rooster lamp. Trust me. Every house needs a quirky item that seems off—adds a peculiar element of interest. It'll be a fun conversation piece in your home."

A fun conversation piece until asked where I got it. Viv was already using her free hand, wheeling herself away from the site, like a trash robber fleeing the scene. I caught up with her on the road and when I put the rooster lamp on her lap, she let out a crow-like laugh so loud it sent a pair of nearby doves into flight.

"I should have put a basket on your head instead of that wreath." I glanced back at the trucks turning down our road. "Then I could have taken more!"

"More is not better, my friend," she said through pressed lips, hardly moving her head. If she moved, things would drop. "And I don't mean to be mean, but if you don't learn to scrutinize, I'll never go for a walk with you on a Thursday again. Look at me, I look like a traveling clown, balancing all these knick-knacks."

"I got carried away," I admitted, but when I looked back at the precious items getting tossed into oblivion, I wished I took more.

"You wouldn't eat five meat lover's pizzas because they were free, would you?"

"I don't know, who doesn't love an all-you-can-eat pizza buffet?"

"Me," Viv said. "I wouldn't eat one free pizza, you know why?"

"Why?"

"Pizza makes me lethargic, turns me into a zombie. My point is, Addie, just like we scrutinize what food we allow into our bodies, we need to think about what we let into our homes. I'm serious, don't underestimate the importance of scrutinizing."

It made sense. I didn't want all of my stuff from storage hauled into Lovely Dwelling. It was too much, and didn't match the atmosphere of a beach house. Same thing with my mind. If I wanted an overall atmosphere of peace, well-being, energy, for instance, I needed to inspect what I allowed into my mind, and what was accumulating there.

"Whoa," Viv hollered, "hold the reins!"

I pulled her chair to a careful halt. "What's wrong?"

"Salad plates. Do you need salad plates?"

"Too late." The treasure monster was at our heels, breathing on our backs, digesting the precious items it devoured. "Whatever we left, the truck has already swallowed."

"No, I don't mean salad plates from back there." Viv waited for the truck to go around us, then pointed the mermaid statue she was holding toward the side of the road. "Sea grape leaves, look at all those fallen sea grape leaves on the side of the road, like multi-colored salad plates, gorgeous. If I were staging a home today, or throwing a party, I'd be setting the table with them, for sure!"

I came around to the front of her chair. "How many do you want, a set of eight, ten?"

"*Argh*, why do I need salad plates? I don't entertain anymore." With a look of scrutiny on her face, she was quiet for a moment. "Then again, you know what? A person can never have too many sea grape leaves, salad plates, whatever. Sure, get me as many as you can."

Lots of the leaves were large like dinner plates, and others small like dessert plates. I collected an entire set of sea grape leaf dinnerware for my friend in case one day her vim for entertaining, or even staging homes returned.

"All I have to do now," she said with a satisfied nod as I placed them within the pages of a giant seashell picture book, "is wash them, one-part bleach, to ten parts water, then rinse and lay them out on my deck to dry."

"Is that what you do to them, so they stay so nice?"

"Yep, whether for salad plates, or as paper to write my tidbits on, that's my secret with the sea grape leaves. Then once they're dry, I plop them onto a cookie sheet lined with parchment paper, bake them at 200 degrees for about twenty minutes."

"I want to do that, too…make sea grape leaf paper to write on!"

"As long as you write something special on them. They're so special, they deserve something special written on them."

By then, I had started back up, gained my momentum, and was pushing her at good speed down the road when she asked me to stop again. "Park me right there, will you, under that banyan tree? I want to ask you something."

Her tone of voice told me it was important, so after parking her under the awning of the banyan tree, I took the mermaid statue from her hand, the rooster lamp off her lap, the Christmas wreath off her head, then sat down on a tree root, which Mom would have loved. It was the size of a bench.

"I thought of another God moment," Viv announced in a rehearsed voice, as if she had been up all night preparing what she was going to tell me. "But maybe it wasn't God, I'm not sure. Tell me what you think, and don't hold back. I mean, at the end of the day, it probably wasn't…but who knows…maybe it was."

"Tell me!"

"Okay, long story short," she wiggled in her seat, "I was in this Bay Area hotel…an old, luxurious art deco with exposed brick walls, mosaic murals, and opulent moldings…floor twenty-nine, room eleven, to be exact. That's an important part to my story, but first, I have to say how hideous the rooms were, which was why I was there—competing with a few other designers for the job. We all had one afternoon to create floor plans, then present to the group of owners, who would then hire whichever one of us they liked best."

She was pulling apart a leaf in her hands—one of the smaller salad plates. I didn't say anything, didn't want to interrupt her story.

"The oversized furniture dominated the tiny rooms. I'm serious, the nightstands alone robbed half the space. Who does that?"

"Me," I said with a laugh, thinking of my overbearing furniture sets back in Michigan, "but not anymore."

"Well, it's a pet peeve of mine. Don't get me started."

"I won't—stick to your story."

"Fine, there was a Bible in the drawer of the nightstand. I never thought literature like that should be in a hotel room, but here's what happened. I pulled the Bible out, put it on top of the bureau, then went to the window where I stood there staring out at the theaters and galleries below. Ideas for the rooms…winning ideas that later got me the job… kept coming." She dropped the tattered leaf, then dusted its remnants from her lap.

"What were your plans for the rooms?"

"Fuse contemporary with classic San Francisco, put in platform beds with custom-made, tufted cream headboards, six-hundred-count luxurious bedding, dark wooden desks, velvety chaise lounges. Tiny nightstands—no drawers for religious literature whatsoever."

Her hands were working on another leaf—a dinner plate, crumbling it to nothing. Soon, she'd have no dinnerware left, nor paper to write on. She dusted her lap, then handed me the seashell book.

"So, here's where I'm going with this. As I was staring out the window, brainstorming," she went on, "there was a loud smack, like thunder I've heard once, twice in my life…early in the morning. Do you know what I mean, thunder so loud it's unforgettable, to where you remember forever how it woke you, made you feel? How it woke you from sleep and had you sitting up in bed, heart shaking, feeling so small in comparison to how powerful the noise of it alone was?"

"Yeah, I've heard thunder like that."

"Okay, well, it was like that." She looked me in the eyes. "But it wasn't thunder. I kid you not, it was the Bible."

"The Bible?"

"Yep, dropped off the bureau, hit the wooden floor so hard, it terrified me. And sure, any sound when I'm brainstorming is loud. But here's the part I wanted to tell you…it landed, open."

"Oh, okay. Did you read it?"

"Sure, I had never looked inside a Bible before, so I went ahead and read a few lines."

"Do you remember what you read?"

"I wrote it down in my sketchbook, yeah, I remember. And last night, would you believe I was cleaning through my junk, getting ready for my move, and there it was…my old sketchbook with the verse I copied down that day."

"So?" I asked on the edge of my tree root, eager to know.

"First, are you ready for the crazy part?"

"Sure, tell me the crazy part."

"Okay, so, the Bible opened to Jeremiah twenty-nine." She stared at me, as if that alone should have meant something. "And the first thing I read, Addie, was verse eleven."

"I don't get it. What's crazy about that?"

She tapped the arms of the chair with her fingertips. "Um, I was on the twenty-ninth floor, room eleven."

"Oh."

"Yeah, if this was one of those supernatural shows, it's where the music would play and the host would say, 'what do you think—coincidence, or God?'"

She went quiet after that, and looked away, giving me time to think. But soon, she was going to expect an answer, so there I was put on the spot, expected to discern what from what—coincidence or God. I looked across the street at a small treetop weighed down by giant birds with large, angelic-looking wings. How in the world did so many big birds stand on the top of a tree like that without breaking its branches? There were lots of things in the world that seemed impossible but weren't.

"It could have been God. Maybe He didn't knock the Bible off the bureau, but it was God who put those words in the Bible, and who speaks to us through the Bible, and God who put that certain something inside of you."

"What certain something?"

"Whatever it was that had you down on the floor, curious and longing to read what the Bible opened up to."

"You think?"

"Sure." I pulled out my cell phone and looked up the verse. "Oh, I like this verse. Maybe I'll memorize it."

"Why?"

"Part of my cognitive training, I've been memorizing verses." It wasn't just for the sake of cognitive training, though. Putting more of God's Word in me was like stocking the drawers of my mind with good and practical things.

"Well, what are you waiting for?" Viv said. "Read me the verse."

I squinted. "'For I know the plans I have for you,' declares the Lord, 'plans to prosper you and not to harm you, plans to give you hope and a future. Then you will pray to me and I will listen to you. You will see me and find me when you seek me with all your heart.'"

Viv's eyes were like petrified rocks. "Do you think He was reaching out to me that day?" She put one hand on top of her other, resting them on her lap, waiting for a formal answer.

"I believe He reaches out to us every single day of our lives, through one way or another. And longs for us as we long for Him, that's what I believe. He speaks to us through His Word, and there's a lot He's telling you in those words."

With her pinky finger, she wiped a solitary tear from the corner of one eye. "Words written thousands of years ago…how can they be meant for me?"

I was no preacher, and didn't know how I was supposed to answer such a thing. "All I know is this. God is the same yesterday, today, and forever. His Word is living and unchangeable. I believe that with all my heart."

Viv had a look in her eyes, like a beachcomber spotting a one-of-a-kind living shell she had only heard about. It looked like she wanted to take hold, but then, the next wave of thought washed it back out to sea, and the look vanished. "Even if it was God, I don't see how with all the junk He has to deal with in the world today, He'd have a plan for me. A plan for the world, sure. But a plan for me?"

"Well, He does. He has a brightly lit floor plan for your life, and open, so wherever you are, you can be in His presence."

She looked up at the intricate branches of the banyan tree, then squinted from the sun reaching through. "I like bright and open floor plans. I'm sick and tired of being in the dark."

I wanted to tell her the world had its floor plans, too, with walls master-crafted by the enemy himself. And every time we fell for one of the worldly lies, brick by brick, more walls went up, blocking us from Truth. If she didn't like living in the dark, she could surrender that floor plan and every square inch of her being to the One offering the bright, open, airy floor plan, full of light.

"Enough lollygagging. We're burning daylight," she said then.

"Nothing wrong with lollygagging…with doing nothing but sitting under a tree, chit-chatting about God and stuff. Seriously, how often do we do that?"

"True, but I do have to get going. I have a meeting today, I'm not lying. I do!"

"Okay," I said with a smile. "I believe you, Viv, I do."

FORTY-NINE

* * *

Turn junk into treasures by repainting and applying imaginative
finishes—linen, ruffles, tulle, glitz.

* * *

Stay open-minded when placing furniture. Maybe you always put
the desk in the office, when the desk serves better purpose elsewhere.
Move furniture into different rooms, letting it be useful in new ways.

I took the goods off Viv's chair and added them to the other random
furnishings I had been collecting and storing outside under the house.

"You know what you've got to do next, I hope," Viv said of my hodgepodge collection.

"I have no idea, what?"

"Custom mix paint, produce your own hues, give everything a new
look. As for that over there," she pointed to an old ottoman with mahogany legs, "put tropical fabric on it, paint its legs gray."

I folded my arms and shook my head. "Custom mix paint, produce
my own hues? I'll ruin stuff."

"What are you talking about? Be dramatic with color…have fun," she
insisted, her vim for interior design all fired up. "Take whatever drama
is in you, use it in new ways. Indulge your imagination, let loose. Don't
be timid, and don't make it more serious than it is. It's not brain surgery.
You're adding color to furniture, fun stuff. What else can I tell you?" She
looked at her watch. "I've got to scoot!"

If she were an art teacher and I her pupil, I would have nominated
her for the Golden Apple Award. She inspired me to have fun, and over

the next several days, I worked on the knick-knacks under my house like an elf at the North Pole. I even put on Christmas carols, and as I went about dipping rags in soapy water, giving the newfound treasures a good cleaning, I hummed along. I then primed the items, using a water-based paint for a chalky matte finish, water-based enamel for a semi-gloss finish, and oil-based enamel for a deep glossy look.

After buying several packs of budget brushes, I painted the bamboo chair a beautiful black, the chest of drawers the color of a Blue Crab, and the early twentieth-century child's armoire a different sort of blue, like the head, neck, and wings of a tricolored heron I had seen on one of my walks along the mangrove-lined tidal flats. For the front porch, I unrolled a large outdoor carpet that I found beneath our house and painted it white, then added blue and green stripes of varying widths.

When there was no paint left to play with, I laid the finished products out to dry on a tarp alongside my house, and couldn't wait for Viv to see them. She was going to fall out of her chair at the sight of it. Peter was going to be impressed, too. And the woman at the end of the road, if ever she came by, wasn't going to recognize any of it.

I had heard that the lighthouse was all decked out with a wreath for the holidays, so while the last of my items were still drying, I hopped on a bike I got from a thrift shop and headed east to go see it. But while pedaling down Periwinkle Way, the strangest thing happened. It looked like it was snowing on Sanibel. Although riding a bike while looking up at the same time wasn't a wise thing to do, they were feathers, not snow, falling from the sky, as if the clouds above were engaged in a celestial pillow fight.

I should have watched where I was going, but there was no removing my eyes from one of the most amazing sights happening above: at least seventy-five white pelicans with majestic nine-foot wingspans and large, heavy bodies flying in a V-formation, all of them moving westward as a group, toward the refuge. I had no idea how, with the improbable proportions of their huge bills and pouches, it was even possible for such creatures to fly, let alone so precisely spaced.

"You are more than genius," I gasped with praise to the One who surpassed the impossible and designed them not only to fly, but to gracefully fly, and in synchronized flock. "Every single day, You amaze me in one way or another!"

My mind fixated on God and my eyes on the sky, I didn't see the bend in the trail, nor the palm tree that I hit head on. I only saw the dirt, as I dropped down into it like a disoriented palm rat fallen from a tree. The show was still going on and from my new ground-level seat in the soft patch of dirt, I watched the blue stage of sky until I could hardly contain my excitement and had to tell someone.

"You'll never guess what's playing not on Broadway," I said into Peter's voicemail, "but on Periwinkle—the spectacular, awe-inspiring monstrosities that up until now I've only read about in my nature books—an entire cast of *Pelecanus erythrorhynchos*—one of the largest Northern American birds, wintering on the island, performing for us all. Miss you and wish you were here to see it with me. Other than that, there's not a whole lot going on. I had to call and tell you."

Okay, I was dramatic. But a fan of creation, I was thankful to God, the all-knowing ticket master for giving me the opportunity to experience such sights.

I couldn't wait to write my review of the culture on Sanibel. How could I not ravingly write when walking the beaches, watching the sanderlings at the water's edge skittering after outgoing waves was nothing shy of comedy! And opening my front door, hearing the extraordinary vocal abilities of the mockingbirds was every bit a symphony. One talented bird in particular had at least two hundred songs in its repertoire. Wading ankle-deep, looking for seashells, holding in my hands the works of art so elaborately sculpted by the talents of time and weather was like being at a hands-on art museum.

Oh, and I already had my tickets for spring, to see the courtship dances of the mating birds all dressed up in their colorful plumage!

The white pelicans with dramatic jet-black wing tips elegantly spread, soared and wheeled in unison, their bodies gliding, forming semicircles as they moved forward like synchronized ballerinas in the sky. When the show above me ended, I jumped up from my seat in the dirt, giving the choreographer of those majestic creatures a standing ovation.

I then picked up my dented bike and was about to continue onward to the Lighthouse Beach when I heard a light ruckus coming through a line of trees. Through the branches and across the street I saw more flocks—not birds, but people—moving in unison from the outside courtyard, up the wooden steps, and into the doors of a church. From where I was, their voices sounded like chirping birds.

"No thank you," I muttered beneath my breath when deep in my heart I felt the finger of God nudging me to cross the street, join up with the flock. "You're so good at putting things where they go, but don't try putting me there. Put me at the dentist, the hardware store, in bumper-to-bumper traffic. But please don't put me at church!"

Why would I want to go to church when I was already content alone with God in my own time-out corner of the world, a cozy experience.

The deep-seated chair in the corner of our great room used to belong to a collection—its matching pieces still out there in the world—but separated, it was still a fine chair all by itself.

So why the nudge when already, I had returned to God and His Word, and that alone was more spectacular a return than even pelicans to the refuge. God was my refuge, His Word my source of nourishment. My hungry soul was more than satisfied.

Besides, there were so many different churches, who knew which one to go to? Good for the birds. They didn't rely on reason and intellect when it came to choosing where to go. It was instinct that led them to wetlands, coastal estuaries, and all those other places they were dependent upon throughout their life cycle. My God-given instinct played a role in my return to Him, but when it came to flapping my wings toward any particular church or denomination, I needed more than mere instinct.

"Please, God," I prayed as I looked through the branches at the people going inside, "You know I love being alone with You, meeting up with You backstage, just the two of us…me out of costume and no audience. I don't want that to change. Let me sit in the corner longer, in the deep-seated armchair, singing my solo with no one to hear me but you."

It wasn't like there was one can of Christianity, but two, and even then, countless shades and types to choose from. Like varied finishes of paint, there seemed to be the duller, understated, matte-like churches that didn't reflect light, as well as the high-gloss churches reflecting light in a spectacular way. Low-sheen churches with easily cleanable services, hid their imperfections. High-gloss churches offered a dramatic shine effect, sparkling from within, but their imperfections were magnified. There were churches with subtle shine, but when reflecting the light, they were glaring. And there were low-gloss, in-between options as well.

Some preferred a glistening charisma, while others a matted comfort. And even when people did try settling on one, there was variation and inconsistency within that one, as when looking inside several cans of say, red paint. I needed to cry out to the Consultant, ask Him whether variations were matters of personal taste or matters of Truth. And also, I needed to continue reading and studying His Word to know the blood of Jesus in true form, and recognize when and where it was being tainted by untruth. The birds spent more of their time foraging than doing anything else, so why not spend more time foraging for Truth in the Gospel?

Peering through the branches, I tried telling myself that falling off my bike across the street from church on Sunday morning, as people were going in for the service, was all a silly coincidence. And the small, still voice, encouraging me to cross Periwinkle Way and join them, was only my imagination. After all, I once heard what I thought was a cardinal, and it turned out to be a mockingbird instead.

Still and quiet, I stood there, waiting to hear a simple chirp of confirmation from my pristine inner enclave, that safe and protected habitat for the Holy Spirit tucked within me. And then a medley rang forth from my *sanctum sanctorum*—a medley of things I had been taught from childhood on, reminding me God's church was a magnificent building project made up of those who loved the Lord their God with all their heart. Jesus was the cornerstone, the capstone of the church, and salvation made us its living stones. We made up the temple of the body of Christ, and when we, the living stones, came together, we brought glory to the One who deserved all glory.

I brushed off my dirty knees and with a limp, crossed the street. I still wanted my time alone with Him—on my walks and talks, on the bottom porch step, and while sitting in the corner of my great room—but I was also part of a collection, and it was time to rejoin the set.

No sooner had I arrived at the courtyard when a familiar voice called out to me. "Hello child, how are you?" Of all people, it happened to be Marita, her eyes large as avocado pits when she saw me. "It is so good to see you, how is everything?" She took my hands and squeezed them.

"All is good, how about you?"

"I am good, too. I found another job, and love it!"

"I'm so happy to hear. Is this your church?"

"No, no, no, I'm working for this old lady. It is her church. I drive her here, make sure she gets inside, finds her seat without falling. She is in there now. I sit in on the services, though, and enjoy them very much, but already have a church I go to."

"So many churches to pick from," I said with an overwhelmed expression.

"Yes, but let me tell you," she took hold of my arm and walked me through the courtyard, "this is a good and humble church. It is about Christ here, walking in sync with and knowing Him." She looked around, waved at someone, then focused on what she was saying. "God's church is more than the address we drive to on Sunday. It is bigger than any one building, and this church knows that. I like to stand out here and chit-chat until it is time to go in, and let me tell you, I've asked people why they attend this church, and you know what a lot of them say?"

"What?"

"It wasn't about curb appeal, or going with the latest trend. But rather, they wanted a Bible-teaching church, and one that teaches how to love more deeply, know more intimately, and fear more reverently the Lord God with all their heart, soul, and strength. That's what I like, too, in a church." She pointed her finger in the air. "And the door must be Jesus. It's Him we must go through."

All that time, the doors of the church had been open, but suddenly, they began to close.

"Tell me quickly, how is she?" Marita insisted as up the wooden steps and into the brick-and-mortar structure we went, the salt-filled breeze following us in. "How is Vivi?"

"Headed back to California soon, but doing okay."

"I still pray for her," Marita told me, "You know I can't help it. I pray for people, it's what I do. I pray that God will remove her heart of stone, give her a new heart, and put a new spirit in her."

The service hadn't yet started, but the place was packed and seats were hard to come by. I slipped into the first open spot near the back, next to a woman in a purple dress with a head full of tight silver curls. Marita found a seat on the other side of the church, then waved over at me.

"God Rest Ye Merry Gentlemen"—one of my favorite Christmas carols—was playing on the piano, and along with it, I heard a few coughs, and the clearing of one's throat. The old woman next to me pulled out a piece of candy and made noise, struggling to open its wrapper. At the sound, a girl in the row in front of us turned her head like an owl, and with entertained eyes, watched the woman trying to unwrap the candy.

The old lady twisted in her seat and looked at me. "I don't remember candy being this hard to open." Her eyes narrowed and her brows came together. "What's happening in the world today?" Her whisper was so loud that it turned a few heads and a man chuckled. "Security measures, that's why they wrap them so tightly now. Can't even trust candy."

"Let me help you." I took the butterscotch from her, but my midlife eyes made it hard even for me to open. As I reached into my purse and pulled out my reading glasses, the pianist started playing another familiar hymn. It happened to be one of Mom's favorite hymns: "I Come to the Garden Alone."

Mom sang it so passionately while doing housework that once I poked my head into the laundry room, to see if it had miraculously turned into a garden. Nope, it was still a laundry room, but Mom was singing and picking dirty socks off the floor as if they were flowers.

And He walks with me, and He talks with me.

My tear-filled, blurry eyes made working on the candy wrapper harder. I looked away, over at the piano player, and when I saw it was Daniel—our landscaper—a couple of the tears I had been holding in, dripped out. He sat as comfortably on the wooden piano bench as he had up in our tree branches, and there was the usual look of contentment on his face.

I wasn't going to give up on getting the wrapper off, but the song was still playing, striking a chord within me. I felt it coming on, and if I didn't stop my tears right then and there...*drip, drip, drip*...just like what happened to our master bathroom sink, no warning signs leading up to it and *wham*, water poured out for an entire hour, flooding the floor.

The lady waiting for her butterscotch rummaged through an enormous bag parked at her feet, then pulled out and waved in front of me an embroidered vintage hankie, as beautiful as Viv's.

With the still fully wrapped candy in one fist, I took the fresh, powdery-scented cloth with my other and used it to blot my eyes. "I'll get your candy open. I won't give up."

"Take your time. The music goes on for a while, gives all the latecomers time to get in. I've never seen you here before."

"First time...first time to church in a long, long time."

"Oh?" she said in a questioning tone. "There are churches everywhere, dear."

"I know, so many to choose from."

More people must have come in, squeezing themselves onto the other end of the wooden bench, pushing her and me together. It was like sitting in a patch of gardenias, her perfume lovely.

"I remember when there were only a few cereals to choose from," she whispered loudly. "Now, there's new cereals popping up daily, and I stand there so long trying to find the one I want. I have to look at the ingredients, ask myself a simple question." She put her hand on my arm and held it there. "If my grandmother were still alive...she'd be older than St. Augustine...would she recognize the ingredients?" She licked her lips. "Would she even be able to pronounce all the new stuff?"

"Have you tried any of the new wholegrain flakes? They're pretty good." I placed the unwrapped butterscotch into the palm of her hand.

"No, child. I was talking about church, using cereal to make my point." She pressed the candy into her mouth. "Too much sugar, no mention of sin...not good. The Father, Son, and Holy Spirit—the three main ingredients, and in Biblical proportions. Oh, and don't attend a church that tries to remove God's holiness. Make sure that what you experience is in the Bible, no artificial additives. You want a piece of candy?"

"No, I'm fine. Thank you."

I didn't have it in me to unwrap another. And besides, I already had a sweet taste in my mouth. Sort of like Viv had in the thrift shop that day, I was having my own fairy godmother-like moment. It wasn't like anyone was waving a wand in my face or transforming me out of my t-shirt and shorts into church attire, but first Marita, then the old woman appeared at the right time, waving words of wisdom I longed for.

I blew my nose into the hankie so loud it sounded like a trumpet.

"You can keep the hankie, sweetheart. My gift to you. Oh, and by the way, I cry, too. Every so often, I curl up in bed and cry my way through the lamenting section of Psalms, wetting my hankie as I go. You should try it. Grab your hankie, climb into bed, and read the book of Psalms. It's how I spend my Friday nights. And every Saturday I wash then iron my hankie."

The people stood up, and when we opened our mouths to sing, we sounded like a rookery. Together we clapped our hands and produced a racket, like pelicans pummeling the water's surface with their wings, herding the fish into a circle. Only we were ushering in the presence of God.

I peeked around at the differing faces. The little girl in front of me looked new and fresh. Others, like the woman next to me, were old with the patina of age. The distressed ones with aged appeal lent history and authenticity to the place.

I couldn't help but think—I was filling my house with new and old furniture pieces, and God was outfitting His kingdom by gathering all kinds of people. The items drying out under my house were random and mismatched, and so were the people in God's church. They had their own hodgepodge backgrounds, and even clashing experiences, but from the beginning the one thing in common was their fallen short of His glory. To the pieces going into my house, I added lots of imaginative touches, giving them a cohesive and complementary consistency. God's people were disparate beings until coated with the redeeming blood of Jesus.

As we sang praises together, it was His redeeming effect—His work in us and not our own efforts—that made the before and after difference. The love of God, the work of Christ had us all belonging together in His house, under one roof.

Alone, I was a walking temple, my light shining brightly. But together with the people around me, I was part of a high-watt kingdom reaching the far corners of the Earth, bringing glory to God in the dark world.

FIFTY

* * *

"Do you not know that your body is a temple of the
Holy Spirit who is in you, whom you have received
from God? You are not your own: you were bought at
a price. Therefore honor God with your body."
—1 Corinthians 6:19

My Dear Loving God,

*I may be sitting on a bench outside the island general store sipping my coffee,
nibbling on a donut, but my real dessert was what I read this morning—Jesus
walking into the temple courts! Your Word is like a seven-course meal, and five
centuries after the Jerusalem temple was rebuilt and made bigger, Your presence
returned to it in greater splendor than ever as Jesus walked into the temple courts.*

*After hundreds of years of Old Testament temple history—course after
distasteful course of people turning from You, being ruled by enemies, having
bad kings rob the temple of its treasures, letting idols in, restoring the temple,
then letting it fall back into brokenness and decay, then rebuilding it—Jesus
showing up there was like scrumptious dessert to my soul.*

*But I'm still digesting all that happened next—what Jesus found when He
went into the temple courts.*

> *"In the temple courts He found men selling cattle, sheep and
> doves, and others sitting at tables exchanging money. So he
> made a whip out of cords, and drove all from the temple
> area, both sheep and cattle; he scattered the coins of the mon-
> ey changers and overturned their tables. To those who sold*

doves, he said, 'Get these out of here! How dare you turn my
Father's house into a market?'"

—*John 2:14–16*

At first when I read it, I rolled my eyes. Duh, didn't they know by then
that the temple was supposed to be that place of worship and connection with
You? But as a temple of the Holy Spirit myself, I'm not one to judge. All I can
say is, do with me as You did in those temple courts. Walk the outer corridors
of my life, the inner corridors, too, and be the table-turner in me! Expose in
my heart behaviors and practices that dishonor or take away glory from You.

I have a friend back home who says moderation is key, and I agree. But
when it comes to spirituality, more often than not we err on the side of scanti-
ness. Why do we tell You to stop halfway and not fill us to the brim with Your
presence? And if You offered us a blessing to go with it, why would we tell You,
"Just a small one, please." Then if You offered a second, "Oh no, one blessing is
more than enough. Let's not overdo things."

Your love for me isn't moderate. I think of that Psalm, "How precious are
your thoughts about me, O God! They are innumerable! I can't even count
them; they outnumber the grains of the sand!"

If Your thoughts for me are innumerable, and I can read about them in Your
Word, why would I want to read only a passage from Your Word, or a page and
no more? That would be like going to a beach that has only one granule of sand...
when instead I could be going to a beach with innumerable granules of sand.

I don't ever want to handle Truth like a box of donuts—only allowing
myself tastes of it here or there. Please turn those tables of spiritual scantiness in
me. Show me my sin and scatter evil attitudes, thoughts, or intentions forming
within. Overturn false doctrines or teachings that aren't from You and toss far
outside my temple courts the bitterness I tend to hoard.

The religious leaders were offended by what Jesus was doing and they de-
manded that He give them a sign, proof of His authority to come in and drive
such behaviors out of the temple.

"Jesus answered them, 'Destroy this temple, and I will raise it
again in three days.'"

—*John 2:19*

They thought Jesus was talking about the physical, man-made structure that was the Jerusalem temple. They thought He was saying the imposing structure could be torn down and rebuilt in three days.

> *"The Jews replied, 'It has taken forty-six years to build this temple, and you are going to raise it in three days?'"*
> —John 2:20

But Jesus wasn't talking about that temple. He was talking about His body because in Him were Your divine attributes, and the fullness of all that You are. He was Your temple on Earth, and far more perfect than any wood or stone structure made by men. But soon, His body was going to die on the cross and be raised three days later. That's what Jesus was talking about.

After Jesus cleansed the Jerusalem temple that first time, certain behaviors in the temple started back up again and the behaviors were once again interfering with worship. So, three years later, at the end of His ministry, Jesus again drove it all out.

> *"It is written," he said to them, "'My house will be called a 'house of prayer,' but you are making it a 'den of robbers.'"*
> —Mathew 21:13

During the first cleansing, Jesus referred to the temple as being His father's house. Now, during this second cleansing, He refers to it as being His house. The religious leaders didn't like this, but praise Jesus for declaring His true identity. Even as He went on teaching in the temple, they went about trying to kill Him.

As I sit here, listening to the birds chirping from their home in the rafters above me, I hear Jesus' words engraved in the rafters of my mind, echoing through the corridor of my soul.

My house, my house, my house. House of prayer, house of prayer, house of prayer.

I want to be filled with prayer, and to walk and talk with You every day of my life, from here into eternity! But I need help with the distractions. How many times has it happened? I'm walking along, heading to the water, when

I step on a burr. There are so many things that show up, stopping me in my tracks and from walking and talking with You. Often, I drop down into the sand and spend who knows how long trying to pull the burr out, pricking my fingers in the process.

It's not a burr-free path on our walk from here into Eternity, but help me avoid them, please. Or when I do step on one, help me pull it out right away so I can get on with my walk. They're hard to pull out myself, but no burrs are too prickly, nor burdens too heavy, nor situations too tricky for You.

Love,
Finley

P.S. People from all over the world are coming out of the general store with bags of groceries for their stay here on Sanibel. It took some of them multiple flights, exhausting layovers, and grueling car rides to get to this tropical island paradise.

I'm so glad the route to You is immediate! My slightest groan makes its way—not slow like the United States Postal Service—but in no more than a split second, my thoughts arrive to Jesus, seated to the right of You, at Your throne. Even before a prayer departs from my lips, You've already received the intention of my heart. My words reach paradise before my lips even form them. Thank You!

FIFTY-ONE

INTERIOR DESIGN TIDBITS

* * *

*Before moving furniture around, try visualizing the three-
dimensional effect in advance. Rearranging is the simplest,
quickest way to update and improve the look and feel of a room.*

* * *

Repurpose items in your house for greater impact.

A steady line of traffic—big-headed, small-waisted ants toting relatively large specs of goods, three times their weight—inspired me. I got to work myself—up and down the wooden steps, carrying the finished items into the house.

Once most of it was inside (the heavy stuff was kept under the house for when Peter returned), I stood there with my hands on my hips, figuring where to put everything. I pushed the sofa from the wall it had been on all along, to another wall, then another, and another. After it still didn't look right on the fourth wall, I moved it back to the first wall, where it blocked part of the window.

Obviously, visualizing three-dimensional effects in advance didn't come easy to me. I sat down to write instead. Writing was a form of rearranging. It was moving whatever I had on my mind out into the world, although some things were best left where they were, in my mind.

How on earth did God do it? How'd He know where to put the moon and the planets, how to group the stars in the sky, how far to stretch the boundaries of the sea, and where to scatter the granules of sand? I couldn't even figure out on which wall to put my sofa.

I saw in part, but the One who held the floor plan of my life saw in whole, and not only the big picture, but all the random details. He was an expert mover, and He knew me, loved me, and cared—all the more reason to trust when His nudging. Sometimes I felt Him wanting to help me with the rearranging of priorities, the moving over of certain attitudes, or with finding the right spots in which to display my gifts, so they might best be used for His purposes.

After writing for a while, I moved the sofa back to the third wall, where it looked good enough. I put more of Viv's nifty interior design tidbits regarding furniture placement into action. Instead of putting the chest of drawers in the bedroom, I pushed it near the front door to function as a console. Instead of filling it with clothing, I filled it with flashlights, sun lotion, and umbrellas. I put a silver beach pail on top, for Peter to stash those items he notoriously misplaced. And I moved the child's armoire—painted an icy periwinkle blue—into the kitchen.

My thoughts kept moving to God. Whereas I was stocking the drawers of the armoire with handy tablecloths, napkins, and candles, reading the Bible was like stocking myself full of essentials. God loved me—what greater essential than that! He was His Word and His Word was in me. I had been reading about His love, but it was Him who put the knowing in me, how much I was loved.

I liked thinking such thoughts, but as I went outside and down the front porch steps to get a brand-new slipcover I had bought for the sofa and left in my van, my thoughts moved to unpleasant things. If forgetting wasn't a fear of mine, I would have preferred to keep the unpleasant things like forgotten statues on the back shelves of my mind. "Made my life miserable," I mumbled beneath my breath about the rude someone I used to work with. Petty as it seemed, her chronic silent treatments, glares, and automatic, uninterested singsong replies of "Uh-huh," to everything I said had, like a migraine, ruined one too many days for me. Behind my back, she twisted my words and intentions, once telling others at work that I screamed at her, when all I did was tell her I wasn't able to cover the weekend she wanted me to. The others comforted me. They knew I wasn't the screaming type. But she had a distorted notion of things.

Mom had always said, "There'll be people who don't like you, for whatever reason. Don't over-exert yourself convincing them to like you. Even an entire public relations firm, working on your behalf, wouldn't do a thing. You'll feel like a failure if you try getting them to like you or treat you kindly. You'll drive yourself crazy."

It did drive me crazy. I poured valuable energy into trying to understand her dislike for me. Over time, I developed a resentment, which even as I lived several states away, was flaring up like an allergy just thinking about her.

She wasn't the only VDP—very difficult person—in my life. I had a small list of names, and thinking of one got me thinking of another and soon, it was like a cold sleet coming down, dampening my spirits. Certain VDP memories had a way of dictating my mood, and pulling me into battles in my mind that I didn't want to engage in. So and so took my well-intended words and turned them into bombs, throwing them back at me, immobilizing me with undeserved guilt!

I didn't like the convoy of VDP memories, like artillery making its way from my past into my present moment. And maybe it wasn't the memories that bothered me, but the resentment attached. Even though I had created protected buffer zones back then, I still gave the villains my life power. I let them change me in negative ways. When around them, I became a villain right back at them. I let innuendos slip out, even though I disliked using them. I turned myself into a VDP and was probably on their lists as well.

I carried the bag with the slipcover up the porch steps, but where were the ants carrying their stuff to? Hopefully somewhere important, from point A to point B, then continuing load-free. I wanted to be load-free, but where was I carrying my resentment to, other than around with me in my thoughts! The more I festered over it, the heavier it got…three times my weight. But where was I carrying it to…all the way to my deathbed someday?

I pulled the loose-fitting, toss-in-the-wash, wrinkle-free slipcover from its package and laid it over the sofa that came with the place…the sofa with stains. As I tucked it into the creases, then beneath the cushions, I tried tucking away the unpleasant memories, but they kept coming out, revealing stains of resentment all over my heart.

I dropped onto the sofa, like a soldier down, but still hearing the attacks all around me, hitting from every which direction. I longed for letters from home—from Heaven—to know that I was loved, despite the VDPs in my life. "Help me, please," I prayed to the One whose blood was shed for me. "Do you hear my battle cry?"

It was out of love—God loved the world so much, including my list of very difficult people—that He moved Jesus from Heaven to Earth. He knew in advance the multidimensional effects of moving His only begotten Son to Earth.

That strengthened me. I slid off the sofa, onto my knees, like a behind-the-scenes warrior, surrendering, handing over my bulleted list of grievances. I wasn't going to change another person's view of me, and no longer wanted to listen to VDPs dressed up in uniforms attacking my peace of mind. I didn't need to carry resentment all the way from A to Z, not if I stopped at J—Jesus. Why continue carrying it when He already carried it for me? The One I wanted calling the shots in my life, the One who carried the weight of my sin, never promised peace on Earth, but peace in our hearts. Sometimes, the only peace treaties to be made were in our hearts.

I got up from my knees and sat down on the sofa. Nothing ironed out the wrinkles in my thought process better than the love of God, the Word of God at work in my life.

FIFTY-TWO

I covered one wall in our bedroom with golden seagrass wallpaper, and was hanging white coral sconces, when through the opened windows came a crisp winter breeze and along with it, laughter, singing, and a fiasco of sorts coming down our normally quiet road.

Hurrying to the window, I looked out at the treetops, in search of a mockingbird singing like Tony Bennett. But even the most talented mockingbird wasn't capable of singing the old classic Bennett song, "I Left My Heart in San Francisco."

As the singing grew louder, I went outside, to the end of my drive. A Surrey bike, festive as a parade float with its red and white striped canopy, was making its way down our road. The well-dressed man behind the wheel, belting out that song, had salt and pepper hair, freshly styled as if he had just walked out of a barber shop. Of all the people, Viv was seated on the single bench next to him in a strapless floral dress with a black vintage belt and drop earrings. She was singing along, and I knew in my gut he was the one she'd had over for dinner, was meeting up with, and spent Thanksgiving with. But she had kept him a secret from me, and I wanted to keep my nosy spectator self a secret from them.

I darted into the low-lying branches of a rubber tree plant not far from my mailbox. As they approached, Viv's feet were resting on the footsteps while her Mr. Somebody Special pedaled with one hand on the steering wheel and the other around her shoulder. My curiosities were so tightly packed I was ready to go off like a firecracker. I had to pull down on a branch of the rubber tree, bar my mouth shut with a leaf to keep my questions from going off.

"So where should I take you, darling?" His voice was sultry, actorly, like a character in a black and white movie, or belonging to a fictitious era, when life was rosy and people had nothing better to do than spend their afternoons singing and strolling around on Surrey bikes.

"Take me to Philz Coffee on Folsom Street, in the Mission District," Viv said like a city girl in a cab.

Her driver stretched his neck outside the Surrey, examining the road ahead. "I don't know, darling. Depending on traffic, going all the way to the Bay Area for coffee might take a while. Are you sure?"

"Love their strong coffee with the mint leaves, yes, I'm sure. Take me there, will you?" Viv played along in a stagy voice of her own. "And take me to the Roxie after that...my favorite theater. I wonder what's playing." She twirled a strand of hair, then dropped it with a sigh.

I felt guilty eavesdropping and wanted to step out onto the road, insist that she introduce me, but I didn't want to interrupt their great show.

"*Oh, darling,*" his low-pitched voice went back to singing, making up lyrics as he went, "*I know where you want to go...anywhere in that city of fog.*"

Viv leaned into him on the bench. "The place we first met. I would like that very much."

"*Well, I'll take you there, darling,*" he sang, "*so you can walk those hills to your heart's content.*" His feet pedaled with ease and he gracefully steered the Surrey bike in a circle on the road, as if the Surrey was dancing. "*Are you ready?*"

"*Ready for what?*" she asked.

"*To cross the bridge over the bay.*"

"*You mean the Golden Gate Bridge? You know I'm ready.*" She planted a kiss on his cheek. "*Let's do it. Take me over the bridge and into the city where I left it.*"

Where she left her heart, I assumed. They were making up lyrics as they went, but still singing to the tune of that song, so what she meant was she had left her heart in San Francisco.

Neither Judy Garland nor Tony Bennett would have been disappoint-ed, and when the Mr. Somebody Special lifted his hand from the wheel, snapping his fingers in the air in a jazzy sort of a way, I wanted to shout out a much deserved, "bravo, bravo!" But then, he forgot to return his hands to the wheel, and the Surrey took on a mind of its own. Careening across the edge of the road with both of them hooting and hollering, it skidded across the bumpy seashell-ridden gravel, right into the arms of a Brazilian peppertree shrub across the street from where I was hiding.

"You're not allergic to Brazilian peppertrees, darling, are you?" He climbed down and went to the back of the Surrey.

"I don't think so," she said with a sneeze. "You're not allergic to fire ants, are you? Watch where you step."

"No worries, darling." But then, he hopped on one foot, while brush-ing his pant leg. He'd already been bitten. After all of that, he tried push-ing the Surrey onto the road, but it barely budged.

Uh oh, they needed help, which meant I couldn't in good conscience stay like a fly on the wall. I emerged from my exotic wall of greenery and stepped out onto the road. "Hello," I said, like a person going for a walk.

"Look who's here!" Viv twisted in her seat.

"Why hello, Addie." Her mystery man shook my hand like he knew me—knew everything Viv imparted to him in one too many of her "long story short" summaries. "What a wonderful thing, the two of you long-lost friends crossing paths again, and although I haven't seen it, very im-pressed with all that I hear you've done over there...to that property of yours!"

From his introduction alone I learned he was a talker, a man of many words, but genuine. "Thank you," I said, "a real work in progress."

"Yes, I'm sure, isn't everything in life? It's a pleasure to meet you. I'm Frank"

Towering over him, I glanced down at the ground to see if I was stand-ing on a mound. But nope, even on level ground, the tip of his head hard-ly reached my shoulders.

"Enough small talk," Viv chided, "let's get to the point. It's him...my third husband, although I'd rather call him the one and only good man I've ever known. And yep, it is what it looks like, Addie, it is!"

"Wow," I said with gusto. They were in love—that's what it looked like, and I let my face react however it wanted to expression-wise.

"You're probably thinking we're both crazy, but I kid you not, my friend, us getting back together is the sanest thing I've ever done."

"Me losing control of the Surrey...that was crazy," Frank said, and what he lacked in height he made up for with a robust voice. "But I agree with Vi, the two of us returning to each other...this relationship...it's *compos mentis.*"

"*Compos* what?"

"*Compos mentis,*" he said again. "Latin, for the most sensible thing. Despite all the chaos, we never stopped loving each other, so it's a good return...not to the way things were, but better."

Carefree as a schoolgirl, her hair flapping in the breeze, Viv stretched her legs out across the bench of the Surrey bike. "In a nutshell, he emailed me a few months ago, and that's what kickstarted it."

"I had to reach out," Frank added. "There was a burden in my heart. I loved her...never stopped." He hesitated, then looked at Viv.

"Go ahead," she said, as if she knew in his pause that he was asking permission. "Addie already knows my issues."

"Then you know how she builds protective forts around herself. And when she kicked me out, I felt like I failed, like my love wasn't enough...it wasn't enough to mend her heart, which to be frank, was damaged pretty early in life."

"I told you," Viv threw in, "Frank's a heart surgeon."

"Retired," he added, "and although I operated on physical hearts, you can imagine the frustration I felt when unable to fix my own Vi's emotional heart. When she left me, I felt responsible, like I didn't do enough. It took me time to realize, I'm not the one...as much as I love her...it's not my job to make her heart new. It would be impossible. But what I've come to know...there's someone who can. I've referred her to Him, but it's up to her if she wants to go."

I was pretty sure he was talking about God, the Great Physician and Heart Specialist known the world over for His work on people's hearts, and for giving new ones, too. I wanted him to continue, but he shook his head in a self-aware way, as if he knew he was a man of many words, and didn't want to overdo it. "And so?" I asked, giving him the floor to continue.

He scratched his head, trying to remember where he was in his story. "Oh, yes…so after she left me, I went through a series of personal encounters, which I won't get into right now. But I was left with a burden that wouldn't go away. I had to make peace with her, or try, and so you know what? I reached out…to make peace, and nothing more. I sent her an email, which brought me peace."

"And I replied to his email," Viv said. "Then he replied to mine, and before we knew it we were emailing back and forth, and soon texting a thousand times a day, I kid you not, for weeks on end."

"We found ourselves saying things in writing that we weren't able to say in person." Frank cleared his voice. "I never expected this, but you know what they say…anything is possible with—" He glanced up at the sky, then back at me.

"Wow," was all I said, but using every muscle in my face.

"Frank's helping me get back to California."

"Where she says she left her heart," he added with a chuckle.

"Tell her where you left your heart, Frank!" Viv shook her head and laughed. "It's like the running of the bulls…mass herds of people, four that I know…Marita, you Addie, my physical therapist, and now him."

"What do you mean?" I asked.

"Everybody it seems, running for dear life…okay, not from bulls but from the bullies in this world and bad stuff…and to where…where is everybody running to?"

"I don't know," I said. "You tell me."

"Argh, don't play games. You know who I'm talking about. It's like He's some destination hot spot, or something."

"I wouldn't consider Jesus the hot spot, darling," Frank chimed in.

I laughed, but Viv continued her rant. "Whatever it is, if one more person tells me they went to Him, gave their heart to Him, guess what?"

"What?" we both asked.

"I might go there myself, for no other reason than to find out if you guys are the crazy ones, or if I'm the crazy one. No joke, I might, just to see."

The birds had been singing all day, and were always singing on Sanibel, but after she said that, their song seemed to joyfully intensify. If anyone asked what they were singing about…words to go with their chirps— *"Let the sea resound and everything in it, the world, and all who lives in it. Let the rivers clap their hands, let the mountains sing together for joy… "*— I'd have recited the latest Psalm I was memorizing.

By then, Frank had gone around to the back of the Surrey, but when he tried once more to free it from the arms of the Brazilian peppertree shrub, it hardly budged. "Hmmm," he said with a look of optimism in his eyes, then took hold of his ankle, pulling, stretching, warming up for the task ahead. He was going to need help. I stretched as well, putting my arms out wide, then hugging myself.

Viv scooted herself across the bench and took hold of the steering wheel. "Do you hear those crazy birds? What are they all worked up about?"

"They're singing," I said, and if I had to name their song, I'd have called it, "Ode to Restoration." By then, Frank and I were pushing with all our strength and maybe he was singing in his heart like I was, along with the birds and all of creation, praising the Great Physician, the almighty resuscitator of distressed hearts. He looked so filled with joy.

Viv kept turning to look back at us—two people who just met, but what a small world! Frank and I were brothers and sisters in Christ. It shouldn't have surprised me. It happened all the time. When people got talking long enough, there was always a connection. Either they found out they went to the same school, or grew up one town away, or were cousins with so and so. God's family was big and always growing. Bumping into brothers and sisters in Christ should have been an everyday thing.

We maneuvered the Surrey up and onto the road and were walking behind, pushing as Viv steered. "By the way," I whispered to Frank, "I pray for Viv, and so does Marita. She prays all the time, just so you know."

He was about to say something back when Viv twisted in her seat and looked at us. "I knew you two would hit it off. The two of you are always raving. I hope, for your sakes, it's not bologna, a temporary high you're both experiencing, façade restoration."

The birds changed song, and if anyone asked what they were singing about then, perhaps it was all the burdensome hearts ravished by the world. But such were the treasures that God went searching for in the shipwrecks of life. And whether sunken to the bottom of the ocean, held down by sin, buried beneath rubble, or entangled in nets, God wanted to salvage them all. It's why from all the way up in Heaven, He sent His son diving deep down into the darkest depths.

Maybe it was my imagination and they weren't singing about that. But if I had to write lyrics to go with their chirps, I would have written along those lines.

"Okay, we're good now, hop aboard, you two," Viv said, "let's take off somewhere fun!"

The words...take off...reminded me that Peter's plane was landing soon, and the only place I needed to take off to was the airport, immediately.

Our farewells were briefer than I would have liked, but I didn't want to be late in picking up Peter.

FIFTY-THREE

Do not neglect your front door—the entry point of your home, where
energy, abundance, and opportunity meet and welcome you in.

Over the next few days, Peter and I worked on random projects in and
around Lovely Dwelling. We painted the shelving of the walk-in
pantry white, and since the pantry was a room of its own, and there was
no such thing as too many spots to write, I set up another spot for myself.
Around noon, I was still in my pajamas, writing away in the pantry as
Peter was hanging rustic wooden shutters on the master bathroom window, when we heard a knock at the front door.

"Uh oh," Peter called out, "what if it's her?"

"Who?"

"You know who, the one whose stuff has outfitted our place."

"Well, if it is her," I rushed into the bathroom and helped him set the
shutter gently onto the floor, "she'll witness a miracle...her trash turned
into treasure."

As the knocking continued, I hurried into my closet and got dressed,
then headed for the door, detouring into the pantry to grab the still-recog-
nizable, white-washed rooster lamp from my writing area, stashing it in
the front hall closet instead. I opened the door, and gasped.

"Who is it?" Peter said from the bedroom.

It wasn't her from the end of our road. If only there were news crews,
photographers to capture the look on my face in that monumental moment. It was Viv, all dressed up in a shimmering pink boat-neck tee,
loose-fitting white linen pants, and hair tied at the nape of her neck,

standing on her own two feet, staring past me into Lovely Dwelling. The sight of her there on my porch surprised me as much as seeing a roseate spoonbill on the beach one morning. The pink birds were usually at the wildlife refuge, and Viv perched in her chair.

"Yep, it is what it is," she declared with the face of a determined trekker who had made it over the most rugged terrain in the world—my yard—and after that, climbed to the top of Mount Everest—my porch. "I made it up here. I did it, you know why?"

"Why?"

"I'm here for my tour. I want to see your…your fish shack turned castle…your tiny castle by the sea!" She gripped her shimmery pink cane that looked more like a fashion accessory than a reliable necessity.

I was at a loss for words, and so was Peter when he joined me in the doorway.

"You guys," Viv laughed, "if you could see the looks on your faces!"

"I can't help it, I'm flabbergasted." I held my cheeks, shaking my head.

In the whirlwind of commotion that followed, I scolded her for making it up my steps. Peter congratulated her for the feat. Our hoopla was interrupted by whistling coming from the far end of the porch, and when we poked our heads out, there he was—Frank, like a guardian angel, sitting on the swinging daybed that hung from the exposed beam. His presence put me at ease. It meant Viv had help in getting up there and wasn't planning on sliding down the railing to leave.

"Love, love, love that swinging daybed," she declared before I could even introduce Peter to Frank.

"A real flea market bargain," I said, thrilled to be showing it off to a friend. "I bathed it in gray, replaced its rusty chain, and Peter used a marine grade nylon rope to hang it. So fun, adding all those comfy striped pillows!"

"It was in bad shape," Peter admitted, "I didn't want her buying it. Now it's where I take my power naps." By then, he had already made it out onto the porch to shake hands with Frank, but the handshake turned into more of a rescue mission…Peter pulling Frank up and off the swinging daybed. His legs were nowhere close to reaching the ground, and he was struggling to stand up.

"Whew, didn't think I was going to get out of that thing."

"It's happened to me, too," Peter assured him, like it was no big deal. "More than once I've had to roll out of it and land on the floor."

"Love it," Viv said again. "Love what you've done with this porch, turned it into a room of its own. And not just a room, but a room suitable for a guest to sleep in if they wanted to. And who wouldn't love the experience of sleeping out here!"

"Would you believe," I lowered my voice as if confessing a crime, "the whole porch cost me no more than a hundred dollars?"

"I told you. Nothing short of a miracle what a couple cans of paint can do." Without moving her feet, Viv twisted her upper torso, letting her eyes buzz around the porch, landing on each of my turquoise pillar candles, then over to my silver pail filled with shells. Next, her eyes hovered overhead near the ceiling I had painted a light shade of blue. "Love, love, love it all so much. I'm feeling woozy."

No sooner had she said that when her cane dropped from her hands, and like a flower wilting on its stem, she drooped forward at the waist all the way into what looked like a yoga pose. Her hands landed on the floor with her buttocks in the air. In a split second, Frank was there and both he and Peter took hold of her elbows, steadying her upright.

"Take it easy," Frank said. The look of relaxation on his retired face had vanished, and he wore the high alert expression of a guard on special duty. His assignment—not to let his Vi fall, or her spirits be defeated. "You can do it, Vi, but a little at a time, and a little more each day. And remember, darling, the cane doesn't hold your weight. It's for balance."

Peter handed it back to her. "Cool cane."

"You should see my cobalt blue one with the rhinestone collar! Have to find the right outfit to match it."

Frank shook his head. "She's supposed to be using her walker, until she strengthens that leg more, but she wanted to tour this place in style. I don't want her overdoing it."

I had been holding it in, but had to tell Frank, "Hey, that day on the road...I heard you singing and you're as good as Tony Bennett, you know."

"You should hear him sing Sinatra!" Viv said. "His name fits him."

Frank laughed heartily. "Don't hand me a microphone. I might take it." He then looked at Viv and turned sensitive. "Are you alright, darling?"

"I don't know, it depends."

"Uh oh, what?"

"Will you fly me to the moon, please? We can ride there on my cane." She laughed hysterically, and her laugh was so contagious that we all joined in. Then she lifted her snazzy, silvery pink, metallic cane in the air and pointed it at a box on the far end of the porch. "It's for you guys. I brought you a gift."

"A gift," I said. "You making it up here is gift enough."

"Oh, for crying out loud. I got you a housewarming gift, something you've been wanting…in your yard."

As I went for the box, Frank picked up the raffia-upholstered ottoman with freshly painted legs and positioned it behind Viv. "Here, darling. I'm parking this behind you. Don't be afraid to plop down, if you need to."

"Stop, I'm fine." She tapped her cane on the wooden floorboards, then directed her attention to the box in my hands. "I wish it was more, my friend. If my cane was a wand, I'd turn it into more. Consider it a sneak preview of what you'll have soon enough."

I read out loud the words on the box. "Fruit, a medley of citrus. Deep red, ruby red, and white grapefruits. Tangelos, rare navel oranges, freshly picked from a Florida grove." I stopped reading, not expecting to get choked up. The guys thought I had a bug in my throat, but Viv knew. She had witnessed me from her window, stealing the mango, then dropping to my knees in the dirt all because there was no fruit in my yard.

But whether she knew it or not, it was the other fruit I longed for the most—fruit not produced by rain, sun, or healthy soil, but the works of the Holy Spirit. That fruit, too, required time, going through the seasons, knowing, loving, walking and talking with God, serving, and obeying Him.

I looked up from the box and smiled with more emotion than a person gifted a box of fruits should have. "Thank you, my friend, the perfect housewarming gift in more ways than one!"

With one hand on her cane, she gripped my arm with her other. "It's more of a thank you, than a housewarming gift. You have no idea how you inspired me that morning."

I looked at her strangely. "The morning I stole your mango?"

"No silly, the morning you helped me take that first step in the sand. I already told you, I needed to take a step…anything to change up my routine, get me out of the rut I was in."

By then, the guys had launched into a lively conversation of their own and were looking through the screen out into the yard at the cabbage palms, discussing whether it was good or bad to go about pruning Florida's state tree.

"So, we went ahead and had a bunch of our trees pruned," Peter was saying to Frank, "but not the cabbage palms."

"No need," Frank agreed, "Not when they're capable of self-pruning. I'm sure they'll be dropping those fronds soon enough on their own."

"Wish I was like the cabbage fronds," Viv whispered to me with a laugh. She then plopped down onto the ottoman parked behind her. "Wish I could drop stuff, but I can't. You know I get upset when I think of things. Madder and madder as time goes by, and I can't seem to drop it…how mad I am."

We weren't trying to listen to the guys' conversation, but their voices were loud. "It was so bad," Frank was saying to Peter. "I hired this guy once, and he ended up over-pruning all the good old stalwart natives in our yard, as if they were bonsai."

Viv signaled me closer. "I'm the one," she whispered into my ear. "I told the landscaper to do that, paid him to prune all our cabbage palms to look like bonsai. You know I love bonsai." Her face turned regretful. "Wish I hadn't done that, hadn't told the landscaper to over prune our trees like that."

"He shouldn't have listened to you. A good landscaper would have done what was best for the trees."

"Gets me thinking," Viv said.

"How so?"

"All the stuff I've gone through, good and bad, it has shaped me into who I am. And even if I don't always like who I am, I don't want to lose who I am, if that makes sense."

"Of course, it makes sense."

"I've given a lot of thought to it. My life experiences—even the bad ones—have all grown together. I fear that if I let go of the heaviness attached to them, I'd be losing parts of myself. I don't want to lose parts of myself, as crazy as it sounds."

"Doesn't sound crazy at all, Viv. Your experiences are yours, and you should never have to forget. But you can remember all you went through, and still drop the attached heaviness."

I wanted to go there, at least mention God...tell her that if ever she decided to work with Him, He was good at what He did, and wasn't an overzealous pruner. The Landscaper of her soul knew and loved her better than she knew her own self, and out of love and respect, pruned only where needed, shaping us with great purpose in mind. We were nothing like self-pruning trees. We didn't have to rid ourselves of the stubborn stuff. But even with God's help, not everything we wanted gone would do so with a quick snip. Many things required working with Him on a daily basis, going through the seasons, accepting that which couldn't be cut from our lives, relying on Him for that which needed to be, and asking for wisdom to know the difference.

Frank and Peter were still discussing the trees, but Viv's attention had turned elsewhere. She stood up from the ottoman, and with a bothered face, glared at my chipped and peeling eyesore of a front door.

"I know," I said. "I read your tidbit about front doors, but haven't gotten around to it yet."

"Oh, man," she said like I was negligent, "never, ever, under any circumstance, neglect your front door! It's true, our front doors matter more than just about anything else in our lives."

"I hope you don't mean that seriously." *The door of one's heart is of critical significance*, I thought but didn't say. The door of a house was just a door.

"I do mean it, and the color you paint it is important. Green doors, for instance, do you know what they bring?"

"No, what?"

"Balance, growth, renewal, harmony, and stuff like that. So hear me out, before you decide what color to paint your door, ask yourself, what do you want showing up at your front door?"

Oh, her games, and her efforts to enlighten me. I didn't have to think for long about what I wanted showing up at my front door. Another Bible verse I was memorizing was fresh as wet paint in my mind.

"Here I am! I stand at the door and knock. If anyone hears my voice and opens the door, I will come in and eat with him, and he with me."

—Revelations 3:20

"You're going to think I'm nuts. If I could have anything, anyone at all, showing up at my front door, it would be Jesus."

Although really, Jesus had already shown up, knocking at the door of my heart. And I opened, welcoming Him in, along with the Holy Spirit who brought all those things Viv hoped for from a green door, and more. Talk about housewarming gifts—love, peace, joy, and other fruits still ripening within me! But I wasn't going to say all of that. She'd have rolled her eyes and shook her head at me if I tried.

"Did you know I once had a purple door?"

"Had no idea," I said.

"Yep, it made giving directions a cinch. 'The house with the purple door,' I'd tell people. But you know why I painted it purple?" She paused, waiting for me to guess. "Purple doors symbolize energy. And when you paint your door purple, you invite opportunities into your life."

I rolled my eyes, "says who?"

"They."

"They who?"

"I don't know." She shrugged her shoulders. "They."

"Hey," Peter butted into our conversation, "don't get hokey ideas over there. I don't want a purple door."

Viv swatted her hand through the air, swatting away his words. "Your front door is an atrocity, and I'm giving her advice. Frank knows, I paint my front door a different color every year."

"Yes, she's trendy like that. Whatever the current trends are, that's what she goes with. I think last year it was a light shade of green."

"Like seagrass," Viv nodded. "If I wasn't vacating my place, I'd go with light blue next. They say it brings positive energy into a house, and to tell you the truth, I could use that."

I exchanged looks with Peter and Frank, and when Viv saw it on our faces—that all we wanted was a door that looked good with the house—she gave up trying to enlighten us and walked inside. I picked up the ottoman, and followed her in.

"Wow." She looked up at the whimsical frosted bubble chandelier in the entryway. "It illuminates your entire great room."

Blame it on her putting faith in the color of a door, but as she went about complimenting things I had done in Lovely Dwelling, my insides couldn't help but praise God for the work He was doing in me. The chandelier was lighting up the great room, but the installation of His Word and Spirit were the illumination in me.

"Love the open space you've created here." She pointed to where a wall used to be. "Did you tear that wall out yourself?"

"Peter and I, and our noisy sledgehammers."

If it was a different kind of a tour—not of my beach house, but an intimate walk through the corridors of me, a walking temple of the Holy Spirit—I would have pointed out the praiseworthy handiwork of God, and a few projects He was currently helping me with.

There were walls of a different kind that needed to come down in me, but God didn't use noisy sledgehammers or heavy-duty equipment. The Holy Spirit riding on the Word of God was far more powerful than a bulldozer, and way gentler. Although sometimes it took longer, thanks to my getting in the way, or perhaps God wanting to spend extra time with me.

Viv's eyes made their rounds, searching for something specific. Sure enough, "The rooster lamp…where's the rooster lamp?"

"I thought you were her, so I hid it," I said, then went to the closet and pulled it out.

"You should put it over there." She pointed to the circa-1900 writing desk. "Trust me, the rooster lamp belongs on that desk!"

I wasn't so sure. The desk, freshly cloaked in black and paired in the corner next to the once-isolated, deep-seated armchair with blue cabana-striped cushions, was already gorgeous and whimsical enough topped with the mermaid statue. But I did as she suggested and put it there.

"I told you." She wailed with laugher. "Just wait, you won't believe the conversations it's going to strike! So, is that where you write?"

"Sometimes, yeah, at the crack of dawn, that's where I go. But look around, you'll see. I have a fetish for desks…no such thing as having too many places to write. I don't even need a desk. I'll write wherever, even the bottom porch step."

Her eyes honed in on my binder in which I had both scribbled out thoughts, and also printed pages I was writing on my laptop. "We talked somewhat about it, but tell me again, what exactly are you writing?"

My mind went blank. I panicked, then opened my binder to catch whiff of all I had been writing about since moving to Sanibel. An overwhelmed sigh slipped out. My relationship with God was bigger than the binder, more permanent than ink, and greater than any descriptive words. Everything I had written was a gross understatement for how I felt about God.

"What's wrong?" she asked.

"I'm not sure how to describe what I'm writing, that's all." I closed my binder, then stashed it away in the desk drawer. I'd set up a booby trap later. It was insecurity—not regarding the topic, but my ability to write about it. I didn't want Viv, Peter, or anyone going in for a peek, gasping behind my back. "That's it? That's all she's been writing all this time? We should get her help."

I relaxed when the guys came in, and the attention moved to the new solar and blackout shades. It was Peter's project—he put them on the floor-to-ceiling windows of the great room, in hopes of controlling the sun's glare during the sweltering summer months.

"Love, love, love what you did here." Viv's eyes were wide with enthusiasm as she walked over to the wall where I had put a coffee table with two oversized, comfy linen slip-covered chairs. "Sweet grouping, and the capiz-shell chandelier definitely adds a soft beach vibe to it all. I like the pillows—sky-, sea-, and sand-inspired cabana stripes of watery blues and cream, nice! And your built-ins, how you doused their backs with that burst of vibrant turquoise, brilliant!"

I couldn't wait to show her the seagrass rug in our bedroom, and the hand-woven window coverings of sustainable natural fibers, but feared she was overdoing it. Leaning forward on her cane, her steps were no longer lining up. The cane was supposed to follow along with her weaker leg, but instead, it was touching the ground before it. Frank came over to steady her down onto the oversized chair.

"Would anyone like coffee?" I announced.

"That depends," Peter walked over and kissed me on the cheek. "Are we talking café Cubano?"

"Sure, a café Cubano for everyone!"

"Um…" Viv raised her hand in objection. "Does anyone know what time it is?"

"Sunset is several hours away yet," I smiled, "that's all I know. And it's morning somewhere in the world—coffee-drinking time in Japan. Why, are you thinking it's too late in the day for coffee?"

She cast Frank a gloomy look, as if the two of them were holding back news. "What?" I asked.

"Oh, for crying out loud, if I drink a café Cubano now, I won't sleep on the plane tonight, and I want to sleep on the plane tonight."

"Wait a minute." I swallowed hard. "Don't tell me you're leaving for California tonight, are you?"

Viv pressed her lips together, holding in her emotions. Frank got up from the sofa, crossed the room, then picked up the hourglass I had bought at a local gift shop. He inverted it, then sat back down. The party was quiet as Sanibel's white, powdery sand dropped from the upper bulb into the lower.

"C'mon." Viv clapped her hands. "We knew it was coming, and besides, I don't belong here. Me here is like," she cocked her head toward the desk, "that rooster lamp in a beach house. No offense to the Sunshine State, but I belong in the Golden State, I do."

I was happy for her, but sad. Our time together—chit-chatting, laughing our heads off, strolling around the island, cajoling and consoling each other, acting like fools—flew by so fast, and was over.

"I should have told you right away," she said, "but I'm no good at goodbyes. Don't feel bad if I show no emotion when I leave. You know I'll be waking up in a middle-of-the-night insomnia mode, bawling my eyes out, missing you, my friend, wishing we still lived next door to each other."

I went over to my writing desk, opened one of its drawers, and pulled out the vintage hankie I got from the old lady at church. "You already have one, but it's good to have two. Keep one under your pillow, for those middle-of-the-night moments." I handed it to her, expecting her to stuff it into her pocket, but instead she sobbed.

Like an emergency responder, Frank was already en route. But when he arrived, there wasn't much he could do as she wiped each of her nostrils with the hankie. Granted, the hot cycle on the wash did wonders, but after witnessing it, I had newfound appreciation for whoever it was that invented throw-away tissues.

Frank cleared his voice in a take-charge sort of a way. "It's about quarter to three now. We leave here within the hour."

My eyes went straight to the hourglass, and time running out. "I wish I could break the hourglass; wouldn't that be nice?"

Viv looked up from the hankie. "It wouldn't do any good, Addie. Can't stop time. All we can do is make the most of what we've got left."

So true. Regarding the present moment, and our lives, all we could do was make the most of the time we were given, that portion of time that was ours. Once it was up, there was no inverting the hours, days, years of our lives, no starting over, no going through it again.

But just as there were factors that played a part in slowing down the rate at which sand traveled through the hourglass—sand quality, the coarseness of each granule, the neck width between the two bulbs, or an unexpected seashell in the way—so were there certain things that seemingly affected time intervals in life, too. The super busy and the spectacular moments seemed to slip through quickly. The less busy and difficult ones often pushed through slowly. Viv and I living next door to each other on Sanibel was one that slipped right through, a quick speck of a moment in my life.

Frank was saying something about serendipity when I glanced over and spotted a small cross necklace peeking out from the top of his collar. What a baton hand-off...he was going to do better than me, picking up where I left off, sharing God's love with Viv. Marita got us started, and thank goodness for the relay races in life. Even when it seemed like we were falling behind, running that stretch all by ourselves, really, we were part of a team.

When the top bulb of the hourglass was almost empty of its sand, I got up from where I was sitting, went over and inverted it. "Who wants a café Cubano?"

Frank looked at his watch again. "I would love one, thank you."

FIFTY-FOUR

As I was in the kitchen, mixing the Cuban-style coffee with raw sugar, I didn't look up, but heard Viv making her way in. "Would you believe I haven't had a café Cubano since my last trip to Cuba?"

"Your last trip to Cuba?"

"Yeah, way back when I negotiated with Castro over a parcel of land." She perched herself on the rattan wicker stool, then put her legs up, resting them on another. "I don't think I told you that story. There was this old building I wanted to buy and convert into a bed and breakfast. I wanted to live there and work, drink café Cubanos all day."

As I poured cold water into the bottom of my moka pot, then inserted the metallic filter and filled it with the coffee-sugar mixture, I waited, but she attached none of her notorious phrases like *I kid you not, I'm not lying, I'm serious, I'm not exaggerating*, so I called her out. "You did not."

She laughed. "You're right, but you saw *Mamma Mia*, didn't you? Who didn't want to buy a bed and breakfast someplace in the world? I just never got around to it. All kidding aside, my last café Cubano was back when Frank and I were still married and we took the high-speed ferry to Key West for the weekend."

"That's way more believable," I said, waiting for the stove to heat. "And you know what else is believable?"

"What?"

I looked her point blank in the eyes. "How much you love him, that good man of yours in the other room. And how much he loves you!"

With elbows on the counter, Viv rested her chin on her clasped hands. "Yeah, but you know me. I'm working on things, working on all kinds of things."

"Aren't we all?"

"I'm starting to believe, though."

"Believe what?"

"That it's true. He loves me. But what do you think, Addie…you think pretty much everything in life can be repaired, or some things just can't be?"

"Like what do you mean?"

"A part of me wants to marry him again, make my third husband my fourth…and final. But this other part of me thinks, no, I ruined things. I could go on living in the ruins."

"I wouldn't let living in the ruins become your comfort zone."

"Point taken. I'm figuring it all out…myself out. It's my glitches. My broken relationships are because of my glitches. Should I walk away from him because of my glitches…so the same thing doesn't happen again…or can glitches be fixed?"

I was no expert, but had read in the Bible that anything was possible with God. Restoring relationships was always an option worthy of consideration, and a beautiful process, as was working with God on one's glitches.

"Well, I already told you Peter and I…both of us filled with glitches… have been repurposing, remodeling, reimagining our own selves and our relationship. It hasn't been easy, and it's ongoing. We're never going to wake up one day and say our marriage is perfect, and so are we. It's a continuous work-in-progress, but I'm glad to be working on something significant."

She smiled, content with my answer, then hung her head back and studied the brushed nickel and chrome pendants hanging above the kitchen island. "Why not go with red?" she said out of the blue.

"Huh?"

"Your door, go with red." She looked at me with giant eyes. "I think you should paint your door red!"

"Only fire trucks should be red."

She rolled her eyes and made a face. "When I get to California, I'll send you a book on colors. Red doors mean 'welcome.' It's true, back in the days when horse and buggy travelers came to a red door, they knew they could stop, stay the night. Don't you love that?"

"No, Peter and I wouldn't want tourists from around the world knocking on our door, thinking they can stay with us."

"Speaking of," Viv hushed her voice, "do you hear them in there? Instant best friends. What are they even talking about?"

We held our breaths to listen.

"So, I asked my lovely Vi the other day," Frank was saying, "how much time do you spend researching a multi-vitamin before taking it?"

"Here we go again." Viv made a face. "He's not talking vitamins. Trust me, he's making a point."

"And you know what she said? Skims the label...that's it, which I don't get. I don't get how people spend ten seconds skimming the brief marketing statement on a jar of vitamins, then trust it enough to put into their bodies every day for years on end. They don't care whether it's backed or not by the FDA or other reputable sources. The fine print claim on the jar is enough."

Viv grabbed my arm. "Oh boy, here it comes. Here comes what the chit-chat is all about."

I tiptoed across the kitchen and repositioned my ear so I wouldn't miss it.

"We got into a debate, and she called me a fool for believing what I believe. I tried telling her we have more than a brief label to skim," Frank went on. "We have the inspired Word of God, which I used to think was bologna myself. Then, after she left me, I went soul-searching...got a cabin in Tahoe and during a snowy winter, I read the Bible. I couldn't put it down...read all of it."

By then, the coffee had reached the top chamber of the moka pot, so I stopped my eavesdropping, went back over, and removed it from the heat. "Okay, so wasn't always, but He is now. He's a believer. What are you so afraid of?"

"Not recognizing him. I like my Frank as is, and all that talk about pruning...I heard God is a pruner."

"Yeah, but He doesn't over prune." I poured coffee into four tiny cups that I'd found at the thrift shop. "If anything, it's people who over prune…over prune other people. God is for growth, our growth. And He'll help us drop what needs dropping from our lives. He knows the differences between healthy and unhealthy, and isn't going to remove the healthy parts of any person."

Viv rolled her eyes. "Remember the old radios?"

"Yeah, what about them?"

"It's like there's a radio on, and everybody loves the station. Everybody is singing along but me. And since everybody loves it, I have to keep hearing the same type of songs again and again to where even when I'm alone, I still hear it."

"What do you hear?"

"All this stuff about God. It's in my mind now. I hear it in the breeze, even."

With an unreserved smile, my mind pulled out that memorized Psalm, "'Let the sea resound and everything in it, the world, and all who lives in it. Let the rivers clap their hands, let the mountains sing together for joy…'"

With time running out, I pulled from the console a vintage tablecloth I had found in the house when we first moved in, and after putting the coffees on a tray, I heralded everyone out onto the front porch. Peter took the tablecloth that was draped over my shoulder and spread it across the wicker table.

Viv sat down, then ran her hand back and forth across the arm of the old wicker chair "This chair reminds me of me, before I got certain things done to my face."

All of us looked at her like, *what a strange thing to admit.*

"You know how I feel about the natural patina of age," Frank said. "It only lends more charm."

"Bologna, bologna!" With feisty eyes, Viv leaned forward in her chair and pointed her finger at him. "Would you let the paint fade on your Bentley? You've had that thing for how many years now and there's not a doggone piece of chipped paint on it."

"I'm saying, darling, that in my opinion, even with a wrinkle or two— or three or four—I find you beautiful, I do!"

Viv relaxed back in her seat, softened her face, and we sipped our sweet as molasses café Cubanos. It didn't take long to finish the cups, and within seconds, Viv set hers down and stared at my front door with a brainstorming look in her eyes.

"Dark blue," she announced, like it was the password she had been working on all afternoon. "That's what you should paint your door! It would look great, and also, dark blue doors bring peace to a home."

"No offense," Peter blurted out, "but that's the goofiest thing I've ever heard, Vivienne. We don't need a blue door bringing us peace. We have enough peace here already."

I tapped Peter's foot. Viv was leaving soon and I wanted our time with her to wrap up smoothly. "I do like dark blue," I said diplomatically, "but it's a beach house so a more coastal color would be nice."

I wanted my comment to be the closing remarks on the subject, but then Frank chimed in. "Sorry, darling, but I can't keep my mouth shut here. For a while there, you were repainting our door every other month, it seemed, and I never said a word. But do you believe it's impolitic to put all your hope in the color of a door?" He threw his hands up in the air. "Who's even behind this? Who claims that if you paint your front door a certain color, certain things come your way? I'd rather put my hope in the Creator of the color blue, the creator of all the colors, the one who promises good things and whose promises are backed with evidence and testimonies."

After giving Frank's comments a respectful and deserving moment of silence, Viv let loose a laugh. "C'mon, you nincompoops, don't get so stony-faced on me. I'm having fun is all, lighten up." She looked at me. "We'll leave it at this, Addie. Of all the front doors you've had in your life, which was your favorite? Which door made your heart flutter and your insides sing? Which do you remember most adoringly?"

I put my empty cup to my lips, pretending to sip as I tried picturing in my mind the front door of our Michigan house. When I failed to recall even its color, I went instead to a verse I had memorized, one about Jesus knocking on the door of our hearts. There were other verses, too, and I was remembering them more than I was the old door. He *was* the door—into Eternity—and the only door I adored. He did more than make my heart flutter and my insides sing. Talk about the golden moments of life…I felt like a snowy egret, dancing across the water in golden slippers every time I praised Him.

"*Tick tock, tick tock,*" Viv urged me along. "I'm waiting."

"It's a no-brainer," Peter jumped in on my behalf. "Our old Michigan door, that was her favorite door. We lived in that house twenty years and never once painted the door."

Viv's mouth dropped open, as if us not painting our door was the most inconceivable thing she had ever heard. Then she looked at me. "You must have loved it. What color was it?"

"Oh, please," I said like none of it was important, when in reality I couldn't remember what it looked like.

"Think, Addie, think!"

I felt like a contestant on Viv's game show as I tried hard to remember the door I went in and out of a billion times, the door of the home I raised our children in. How could I forget its color? I put the cup down, then un-muted my thoughts, letting them hear as I worked out loud on the answer.

"Well, in the fall, I'd hang cinnamon-scented pinecones on it. The girls and I glued them together into a wreath, I remember that. And this time of year, I'd hang a set of silver jingle bells that jingled anytime anyone opened it." I closed my eyes. "I can still see the tulip door mat I'd put out in the spring."

By then, Frank was humming that old *Jeopardy* melody, and when Peter raised his hand, like he had the answer, Viv ignored him, keeping her attention on me. I didn't want to play the memory game. In the scratch pad of my mind, I abandoned all efforts to remember what the door looked like, the door my mother walked out of in the middle of the night, unable to return, unable to remember herself what it looked like or even which door was ours.

Like a form of Morse code, I clicked my eyes at Peter, expecting him to read the distress signal my blinks were giving off—*what if* what happened to Mom's brain was happening to mine, *what if* the protein fibers in my brain were twisting, tangling, and hard accumulations of proteins were building up?

"Slate black with a silver handle!" he blurted out, putting an end to the ridiculous game. "And there was a scratch of yellow on the right side, toward the top," he added. "The people who owned it before us must have had the door yellow at one point."

"Yellow doors are magnificent," Viv said. "They bring humor and merriment, mental clarity, too." She looked at me. "You could always paint your door yellow."

"Only fire hydrants should be yellow," Peter barked. "And there'd be strife, not peace in our house if you paint our door yellow, Adele."

The two of them continued their back-and-forth exchange of opinions until I let out a pathetic sigh. When Frank and Viv started going over their flight times, Peter leaned into me on the loveseat. "You're fine," he whispered into my ear.

"What if I'm not?"

"I'll say it again, you're fine. You were always walking in with kids, or bags of groceries, or trying to keep the dogs from running out. And you were tired from work, too tired to care about what color the door was."

When Viv overheard what he was saying, she jumped in. "Peter's right, Addie. I'm sorry I made a big deal of it. Not everybody appreciates their ex-doors the way I do, and once I get going, I don't stop. I should carry tape to put over my mouth, shut myself up."

We went on talking about pleasant things until Frank looked at his watch and stood up.

"Don't say the word," Viv insisted, then gripped Frank's arm and stood up. "I don't like the doggone, two-syllable word people say when they leave. I'm going to speed things up. I don't like these moments."

With that, I opened the screened door, then fast as a team picks up the greatest scoring athlete at the end of the game, Viv was in Frank and Peter's hands, hooting and hollering. Where Frank lacked in height, he made up for in strength, or love. He carried her down, proving love possessed a strength of its own, empowering the impossible.

Once she was seated in her chair, which they had parked there all along, I wanted to run down and give her a hug, but Viv didn't want that. Instead, I pushed my nose to the screen. "You better send me postcards… post cards from San Francisco!"

"From the Bay Area, sure. I'll send you postcards. I'll send you postcards of cable cars and Alcatraz, and even those sea lions I told you about, down by the wharf. Oh, and the Golden Gate Bridge, of course."

"Not until you walk it."

"I'll text you first…the bird with the golden slippers. But you have to text me, too. The moment you do something golden…anything…text me the same." Viv let out a sob, which all of us ignored. She couldn't help it and didn't want attention for it. "We're burning daylight," she managed to tell Frank, in-between more sobs. "Let's get this show on the road."

Peter waved, then escaped the scene, making it midway up the steps. I went out and stood with him as they went down our crunchy drive.

"Hope you sleep on the plane tonight," I called out.

She ordered Frank to perform a giant U-turn with her chair. "You know what I think you should do tonight?" she said, facing us. "Go to the beach…not at sunset, but in the middle of the night…if you can't sleep. Go in your pajamas. Make it like a pajama party, why not? Dance under the stars, do the rumba, or the tango. Just don't trip over sea turtles. Wish I could go with you. I'd bring my maracas."

Her departure was becoming too much. It was on the brink of a dragged-out, gushy good-bye. She signaled for Frank to continue. With that, the neighborhood friend I grew up with, went to college with, and lived next door to for a season on Sanibel—the lifelong friend who made me laugh like a fool and also bawl my eyes out—was off in a rip tide, going her own way.

Once she was out of sight, I thought for sure the good-bye scene was over. Peter and I were standing on the step, watching the osprey in its nest when from the road, Viv made a sound that set off the grand finale.

"*Honk!*"

"What was that?" Peter asked, and even the osprey turned its head, startled. "Sounded like a goose."

"*Honk!*" she called out again, egging me on.

Never mind Peter or the osprey. I elongated my neck and opened my mouth. Viv was expecting my usual quack, but I didn't feel like quacking, and instead let out a low, guttural sound that resembled the nasal bark of a mature roseate spoonbill.

"*Arf, arf, arf, arf!*"

My reply must have satisfied her. She didn't honk back.

"I will never understand you two." Peter shook his head. "I won't."

I laughed, not expecting him to understand us, or me, or why I made the sound that I did. He'd think me nutty if I told him that I used to quack back, but didn't want to quack back. I wanted a new sound for myself, and to sing a new song. Roseate spoonbills inspired me. They were stunning, ranging from pale pinks to bright magentas, and their pinkness intensified with age. The birds got pinker, brighter with maturity.

That evening, I was sitting at my desk with the rooster lamp, writing all about my God-given creativity becoming brighter, intensifying with age, when it hit me that other parts of me were dimming, becoming duller.

"Let me guess," Peter asked when I closed my laptop, turned the rooster lamp off, then sat there in the dark. "You're still worried that you can't remember the old door."

"Not just the door. I forgot my social security number last week. Oh, and I forgot to buy milk the other day when milk was the reason I went to the store. A couple days ago, I went outside to the driveway and forgot why I went out there in the first place."

"I was at the gas station," Peter said, "and punched in our old Michigan zip code. I couldn't remember our Sanibel one. It happens to us all, Adele. I wouldn't keep doing what you're doing, assuming early onset memory loss every time you forget something."

"Yeah, but why couldn't my brain remember the color of our old door? Yours did."

"Come here." He signaled me over. "You want to know my secret? I should have told you. When I was in Michigan this last time, I drove by the old house. No one was home, so I got out of the car…went up to the front door. I was missing the kids and our life together under one roof. I stood there, staring at the front door for so long, thinking how nice if I could go inside and savor an evening with all of you. So, there you have it. How's that make you feel?"

I could hardly talk. I had been missing them, too. I wanted to move back. "I'm missing them, too. What should we do?"

"I don't know. Why don't we get to bed, and tomorrow we'll paint the door, then go from there?"

FIFTY-FIVE

"In his pride, the wicked does not seek him; in
all his thoughts there is no room for God."
—Psalm 10:4

To the One Who Doesn't Mind Questions,

Here I am, my Lord, on this bench beneath the shade of a banyan tree on Periwinkle Way. Soon, I'll be flying home to where the benches are covered in snow, but it won't matter. I won't have time for sitting around. I'll be running around like a chicken with its head cut off, doing my best to keep up with life, and whatever the tide brings in.

I never want to forget, and hope my spirit retreats to this time I had sitting with You. The kids ask what I've been doing with my couple of hours alone each morning. When I tell them, they look at me like I'm from another planet. Or they probe further. "Isn't that boring, Ma? It's not like God talks, or anything, does He?"

Oh, such questions, and I'm glad they ask them. You don't mind questions, either. You want us being honest. I pray that throughout their lives, they seek answers through prayer, and in Your Word, and by going to a Bible-teaching church, or study group.

Nicodemus, the Pharisee and member of the powerful Jewish council the Sanhedrin, also had questions—for You, Jesus. He had questions regarding who You are. One night, in search of answers, he went to the steps outside the Jerusalem temple and waited around for You to come out.

Sure enough, when You were done teaching in the temple, You came outside and met up with Nicodemus on the steps. I thank You for meeting up with me like that, too. I've come to You with questions of my own. So many people have questions. Whether sitting alone in the dark outside of a church, or inside a church, I pray for those with questions. I pray they bring You their questions, and You show up to them…on a plane, or a beach, or wherever they happen to be. Please show up and answer their questions.

May You hear their seeking hearts and show up to them with the Truth of who You are, in a personal way. You showed up on the steps outside the temple and answered Nicodemus's questions, and Your answer is still true for us today.

The Light showed up to Nicodemus, and this is what He said:

> *"For God so loved the world that he gave his one and only Son, that whoever believes in him shall not perish but have eternal life. (17) For God did not send his Son into the world to condemn the world, but to save the world through him. (18) Whoever believes in him is not condemned, but whoever does not believe stands condemned already because he has not believed in the name of God's one and only Son. (19) This is the verdict: Light has come into the world, but men loved darkness instead of light because their deeds were evil. (20) Everyone who does evil hates the light, and will not come into the light for fear that his deeds will be exposed. (21) But whoever lives by the truth comes into the light, so that it may be seen plainly that what he has done has been done through God."*
>
> *—John 3:16–21*

Just like I've had questions for You, I have questions for myself, like why did it take me so long? When I was young and hyper, like a pup, I heard Your command—Love me, Finley. Love me with all your heart, soul, mind, and strength. *I didn't know how, but You taught me*—Come Finley, come to the cross. *I needed training with other things, too*—Bow in humility before me, Your Lord. *And sometimes, I just wanted treats. I yelped and begged and whined for treats, thinking I wanted treats more than I wanted You.*

It took me a while to learn I didn't need to spin around in circles and perform to impress You. The question I had for You when I first got to Sanibel— what now, what do You want me to do?

Sit, is what my heart heard. *Just sit with me.*

Whoever said an old dog can't learn new tricks didn't know what they were talking about. I'm learning new things, like sitting in Your presence... which I didn't do so much before. And playing dead to the way I thought my life should be, and alive to what You have in store for me. I'm no longer pulling away from You, like I did when I was younger. I'm content staying right here with You and following Your will for my life. Your presence alone has become my reward.

And still, You keep giving me more...joy, comfort, peace, wisdom.

After all of this, how can I not ask myself that question—why, Finley, why did it take you so long to savor sitting with your God?

Love,
The Bench Lady

FIFTY-SIX

Interior Design Tidbits

* * *

Once you make the slightest change to your house,
you'll only want more change.

* * *

It's the seemingly insignificant changes, one after the
next, that transform ordinary into extraordinary.

I painted our door aqua—like the super-bright salt-water taffy I ate as a kid. It had both curb and heart appeal, and before it even dried, I was out there dancing that sweet little dance I did at parties when I was younger.

"I'm not even going to ask," Peter said when he opened the front door and found me on the porch, turning myself around.

I put my right hand in, I put my left hand in, and I shook it all about. "Oh, come on, join me. If you love the color of this door as much as I do, join me!"

He didn't start shaking, but I could tell from his smile that he liked the color of the door, and so did the neotropical migratory songbirds in our yard. They were congregating nearby, singing louder than ever. "*That's what it's all about,*" I sang in tune with them, then let out a laugh.

Still in the doorway, Peter held up his keys. "I was coming out to ask if you wanted to go for coffee. You can finish the Hokey Pokey when we get home."

Peter wanting to go for coffee meant more than a plain old cup of Joe with skim milk. And sure enough, fifteen minutes later we were sitting on a bench outside the coffee shop sipping our iced gingerbread mochas topped with whipped cream and chocolate-covered espresso beans.

"So where are we at with the place?" he asked with agenda to his voice. "All the work we're doing…is there an end in sight…or is it safe to say, we're done for now?"

Painting the four-panel door had taken the better half of the weekend, and while freshening up the white trim, I had already found myself wanting a silver pineapple door knocker to go with it. As soon as I ordered the pineapple knocker online, I wanted seashell chimes to go with it. After buying the makings of seashell chimes at the local craft store, and hanging them on the porch near the door, I then wanted a lantern for over the door. And once I got the lantern…

I wanted a new door mat.

I tipped my head toward Peter. "Remember that book I used to read to the kids, *If You Give a Mouse a Cookie*?"

"Yup, I do. What about it?"

I took another sip, then licked my lips. "Well, in the book, once the mouse gets a cookie, it wants a glass of milk. Once it gets a glass of milk, it wants something else. It wants more and more and more. But in the end, all of its wants lead right back to its first want—a glass of milk."

Peter blinked his eyes at me. "You want a glass of milk?"

"No." I shook my head. He wasn't getting my point, that we'd never be done working on the house, that every time we fixed up one thing, it had me wanting to fix up something else, and there was no such thing as an end in sight. "If you get me milk, I'd want a biscotti to go with it. So no thank you, no milk."

Peter had whipped cream on the tip of his nose, and a secret in his eyes…something good. I had been married to him long enough to know when he was holding in a surprise. "Tell me," I insisted as I wiped the whipped cream off his nose with my finger. "What are you keeping from me?"

He turned to face me on the bench. "Alright, ready?"

"Yes, I'm ready. Tell me, for crying out loud," sounding like Viv.

"The kids," he started to say, but then paused, to hold me in suspense.

"The kids what?" I slapped his shoulder, to hurry him along.

"I know we were planning to spend Christmas in Michigan, but merry Christmas, the kids are coming. They're coming to Sanibel!"

It was a surprise like no other. The kids were coming, the kids were coming. Sound the alarm, prepare the harbor, precious cargo on its way—the kids were coming! Bells and whistles were ringing in my mind, and rounds of cannonballs going off in my gut, exploding further wants that I had for the house into oblivion. All I wanted was my family together, and my kids were coming, sailing into the harbor. I choked on my coffee.

"Um, are you alright? I knew you'd flip out."

I leaned forward on the bench, coughed into a napkin, then wiped my eyes. "When?" I gasped. "When are they coming?"

"Thursday."

I put my fingers up in a mathematical frenzy. One, two, three days from then…Lucy, Mallory, Charlie, and Henry! I had to sing, and out it came, "*I saw four ships come sailing in on Christmas Day in the morning.*"

"Three ships," Peter corrected me. "Three ships in the song."

"Yeah, yeah, I changed it…four kids."

"Okay, um, a long weekend, that's all we've got. But at least we've got that. We weren't going to tell you. I could have had them knocking on the aqua door, doing the Hokey Pokey, but I figured you'd rather know, right?"

Oh my goodness, prepare the nest, yes! I wiped my eyes, then jumped up and threw my arms around Peter's neck, letting my face brush against his whiskers. I caught whiff of the gingerbread mocha, and it smelled like Christmas. "I'm giddy. Beyond giddy."

"I know you are!"

"It's all I want. I want the kids here."

After all of that, we talked another hour, then Peter had errands to run. He invited me along, but I had things of my own to get done. And since we weren't that far from home, I walked. As I headed down Periwinkle Way, passing boutiques, I couldn't help but think how when the boys were toddlers, they didn't like when I changed my purse for the first time. They were used to Mom with her old, everyday purse, and didn't like the change. When I got my hair cut, they stared at me like I wasn't their mom. None of them wanted me trading in the minivan. They couldn't imagine Mom driving anything else and acted relieved when I came home with another one, exactly like it. I didn't like it when my mom changed, either.

Everything in life was constantly changing, so kids wanted their moms staying the same.

"What do I say to them?" I asked God as I walked. "If they notice anything different about me...if they catch me with my nose in the Bible...or wanting to say a prayer before we eat?"

If they were little, I'd tell them the story of how one day Mama Turtle was going along and heard Truth knocking on her shell, so she poked her head out to hear what Truth had to say to her. Once she heard a little of what Truth had to say to her, she only wanted more.

"And good for Mama Turtle," I declared as I turned onto our road, "not sampling but going all out...nose in the Bible, feasting on Truth!"

"What's that?" a voice from over near the trees said. "Are you talking to me?"

Embarrassed that someone heard me talking out loud to God as I walked, I pretended I didn't hear and kept going. But then to my horror, out from behind an overly pruned cabbage palm came *Ms. You Know Who*—the one notorious for tossing treasures out with trash. Her bones were thin as the upper branches of a tree, and her hair sparse with bits of pale scalp here and there showing through.

"Were you talking to me?" Her voice was brittle, her words cracking.

I went ahead and told her the truth. "I was praying, pouring my thoughts out to God." I let out an embarrassed laugh. "I guess I didn't realize I was doing so out loud. So, how are you today?"

She dropped her pruning weapon and came over to me on the road.

"Only because you asked," she said with a sunken face, "not so great. Good days and bad...today not so good." Her eyes were puffy and with hardly any white to them. "It has been a not-so-great year for me."

My lower lip stretched into a compassionate pout, offering my condolences for her not-so-great year.

"When I'm out pruning my trees," she folded her arms in a gripping way, holding herself up, "you don't see me, but I see you. I see you walking on by, always looking so happy. Why...why are you always happy?"

How could she have accused me of being happy all the time when that wasn't the case? I didn't want to be known as happy all the time. A person happy all the time wasn't experiencing the vast array of human emotions.

Even if she had meant it as a compliment, it wasn't true, and I wasn't going to play along, like a fake. Still, I had no scars to show, nothing to prove to her my battles with bouts of unhappiness.

All I could do was look her in the eyes, as if to say, *You have no idea how many boxes of tissues I've gone through, or tears I've cried into my pillowcase… the last couple of nights, at three o'clock in the morning, waking, missing my kids.*

"I'm definitely not always happy," I said.

"You look it to me. You look happy every time you walk on by."

At least she didn't tell me how happy I looked while confiscating her trash. I was about to shrug it off, be on my merry old way. But maybe *Ms. You Know Who* was beating around the bush, hinting for a morsel of Truth.

"If you really, really want to know. I like to walk and talk with God. Maybe that's what you're seeing on my face when I walk on by…me pouring everything out to Him, and finding comfort and joy in doing that."

"Good for you," she said in a snippety tone. "When I walk, I walk alone. I live alone, eat alone, watch TV, and go to bed alone. I used to have friends, used to be involved, but now I do everything alone." She glanced back at her house. "It's the loneliest place to be, but I'm moving out soon." She bent over and heaved, then stood upright again. "Moving out in the *big* way—the final move."

"Oh," I gasped, covering my mouth with my hand, as if I had no words good enough to say. The woman at the end of the road was dying, and that explained why she was getting rid of so much, unloading the treasures she couldn't take with.

"You think," she went on, bolder than before, "that God is here on this road with you, and you can just walk and talk with Him whenever you want?"

"He is. God is here, or I wouldn't be talking to Him." A verse I was memorizing—Matthew 2:20—came to mind, and though I couldn't fully remember it on the spot, I knew the gist of it. "Jesus told us He'd be with us always, and I believe Him. I believe His promises."

"Yeah, yeah, yeah," she said, like she had heard it before. "I've always had troubles with that…the whole Jesus thing…people claiming him to be the only way."

I was about to tell her people didn't claim it, He said it Himself. But then she launched into another coughing fit and was holding her ribs. "I have nothing to lose," she managed to say. "Pray for me, will you? When you go by my house, pray for me." She turned and headed for her house.

Of course I was going to pray for her! After I had shared with her that morsel of Truth, she wanted a prayer to wash it down, so the rest of my way home, I prayed for the woman at the end of our road. When I arrived at my aqua-colored door, I didn't feel like doing the Hokey Pokey. I felt bothered. The words on my brand-new doormat bothered me.

Unless barefoot,
you're overdressed.

I had laughed out loud at the store, then tossed the mat into my cart without second thought. But as I stood outside the door of Lovely Dwelling, after all the painstaking months I spent preparing the place, even polishing to perfection its wooden floors, I wished I had gone with the more adamantly stated mat: *Park your flip flops here!*

I did want people taking their shoes off, leaving them on the porch before coming in. But even if I had gone with the more adamantly stated doormat, my own kids weren't going to take it seriously. I had never cared before whether they took their shoes off or not. It wasn't until we put the old house up for sale that I became aware of how years of muddy, wet boots, dirty cleats, and roller skates wreaked havoc on its floors. I didn't want the new place looking like the old. I wanted it to be different, special.

I kicked off my flip flops and went inside, then spent the next three days spinning like a top, preparing my house for the kids. I set up a small Christmas tree, baked cookies, put sheets on the pullout sofa, and pumped air mattresses. I hung blue and white cabana-striped beach towels in the bathroom and set out seashell soaps. I even ran down to the yard and checked for fruit, wanting to surprise them with Grandma's famous Meyer lemon bars. When still no fruit, I bought fruit at the general store, and made several trips to and from. I shopped as if we were hunkering down for eternity, when it was only going to be a long weekend.

With bags of groceries dangling from my arms, every time I returned to the house with the aqua door, the words on that doormat troubled me.

"Hey," I called out to Peter when I came in for the umpteenth time and as always, there was sand on the floor, "you know it's no joke, right? I want us taking our shoes off before we come in. I mean it."

He must not have heard me. I put the bags down, then followed a fresh trail of sand from the door to the sofa, then all the way into our bedroom, to where the culprits—his sandy flip flops—were parked beside the bed. I picked them up and dangled them over his sleeping face. "Wake up, please. This isn't a dream. I'm not Mr. Sand Man."

With his eyes still closed, he sat up and brushed off his face. "What's wrong?"

"Obviously, you think I'm joking when I say I want shoes parked outside."

He opened one eye. "Relax. It's a beach house. Beach houses have sand. They do, and they're supposed to have sand."

I put my hands on my hips and looked down at the floor. "Yeah, but along with the sand comes other things...dust mites, fleas, and itchy nights." I left the bedroom, grabbed the broom, and swept the great room floor. All the while, the wording on the doormat bothered me.

Peter was right. It was a beach house and a few granules of sand didn't ruin what it was—a beach house. And the sand made it that much more of a beach house. It was like that with a lot of things...sea salt and dark chocolate. The two went well together, and the salt didn't ruin the chocolate. It made dark chocolate better. Regardless, my thoughts were swirling all over the place until soon they became like well-formed dust devils, organizing into a nice upward motion. I then understood what was troubling me.

If I allowed everyone to bring their dirty shoes into Lovely Dwelling, in no time, its floors would be like the floors of my old house in Michigan— filthy. And if God allowed me or anyone to track a single granule of sin into Heaven, it would ruin the atmosphere of Heaven. Heaven would no longer be Heaven. It would be like the world.

Although sand complemented a beach house, and sea salt complemented dark chocolate, that complementary combination didn't exist when it came to holiness and unholiness. The two weren't mixable, and even if they were, what if adding unholy to holy rendered the holy no longer holy, since by its nature holiness was pure?

If a person was allergic to nuts, would they allow nuts to be brought into their house? No, they'd bring chocolate in, but chocolate without nuts. God so loved the world. He loved us and wanted us in His holy presence and in His holy house. But a holy God couldn't tolerate sin. Holiness was pure. Adding sin to holiness would either dilute it, or change it to unholiness. But despite our sinful natures, and our unholiness, God loved us so much that He put outside of Heaven a way for us to be cleansed of our sin and made right with Him before entering His holy presence and holy house.

"Here I am, preparing my house for my kids," I muttered beneath my breath to God as I swept the floor of the great room, "and You're preparing Your house for us…for me, and for all Your sons and daughters." I held the broom still. "And Your home is holy because You are holy. Your presence fills Heaven with holiness, and there's nothing unfair about You wanting and needing our unholy sin left outside."

How could anyone look forward to Heaven if Heaven was a frightening place, evil and filthy like the world? I was glad it was holy, and that He made a way for me to be right with Him, despite my sinful nature. The lady at the end of the road didn't think it fair for anyone to believe that God put just one means—His only begotten Son—outside the door of Heaven for people to be cleansed of their gunk before going in.

But it was God's house, and His writing was on the mat, plain and simple. I wasn't going to argue with or rewrite the entry rules to Heaven just because I thought there should be a back door or another way of getting in like a broken side window to sneak through. Why, when God was waiting and welcoming us all with open arms? He was telling us in so many ways that Jesus was the door. The blood of Jesus was fully sufficient, all that was needed for me to be made righteous and to enter God's home, not just as a visitor but to live there eternally with Him.

I didn't know why cleaning did it to me, stirred up thoughts, but it did. A friend once told me a story, how after she gave birth to her first baby, not everyone saw the need to wash their hands before visiting. Hours after her daughter was born, a loved one came into the hospital room blowing their nose and coughing. Love happened to go well with a lot of things. It went well with speaking out, but also with turning a blind eye to things. Filled with love for the visitor, my friend turned a blind eye, and said nothing when the visitor sneezed into her hands, then without washing them, took the newborn into her contaminated hands. "I didn't want to offend her, this sweet person who came to visit," she had told me. But as a result, her baby got sick and ended up staying in the hospital six frightening days before coming home.

"I don't ever want to be that dear, sweet, ignorant person who thinks they can go barging into Your holy presence," I prayed as I poured the contents of the dustpan into the trash. "I get it, I do. We have to be cleansed of our sin first. We cannot do that ourselves."

I got down on my knees, then maneuvered the broom sideways under the sofa. "You sent—not a can of disinfectant or bottle of hand sanitizer—but Your only begotten Son to cleanse us of our sins, and make us righteous before You. Thanks to His cleansing blood, I can enter Your holy presence. It was out of love that You spoke out. You gave us Your Word, and made it so clear...Jesus was the way to enter and live in Your holy presence now and forever."

I wanted to live in God's presence not just after I died, but every day up until then, and it had me thinking of the words of David in yet another verse I had been memorizing:

> "One thing I ask of the Lord, this is what I seek: that I
> may dwell in the house of the Lord all the days of my life,
> to gaze upon the beauty of the Lord and to seek him in
> his temple."
> —Psalm 27:4

Still on my knees, I pulled out from under the sofa a small, dirty bowl with the remnants of guacamole gone bad. Peter must have slid it there during a game, then forgot about it. There was nothing more gross than guacamole gone bad, and I gagged.

"I'm sure there are things that make You want to gag, too, God...certain sins more deplorable than others. I also know from Your Word that sin is sin, and none...big or small...is allowed into Your holy presence. Jesus took them all on. He died for all sin, not some sin."

I brought the bowl with the disgusting guacamole to the sink and filled it with water, then went over and pulled from Mom's Bible, from the book of Isaiah, a piece of paper with another verse I was memorizing: "I have swept away your offenses like a cloud, your sins like the morning mist. Return to me, for I have redeemed you."

God's love…His housecleaning…it overwhelmed me.

I went out onto the front porch. Peter was still sleeping and wasn't going to see me. I knelt down on the doormat. "I know I'm dramatic," I prayed to Jesus. "But I can't help it. I chose this silly doormat for my house, and God chose You. You're the reason, the only reason I'm made right with God."

God did more than put a doormat out. He put His only begotten Son outside Heaven not just to wipe clean our feet, but to take our every granule of sin, big or little, and cleanse us so we could enter. "You are the way," I prayed. "The Door of Righteousness, leading into Your Father's holy kingdom. How can I not praise You!"

When I heard Peter moving around in the house, I ended my prayer and got up. I didn't want him opening the door, finding me on my knees, and thinking I had fallen while doing the Hokey Pokey.

Then again, I was fallen. We all were. And perhaps our fallenness was the main thing…and in some cases, the only thing…we all had in common. Jesus was there for us all…yet another thing. God put Him out there in the world for all of us, to take on our filth, cleanse us of our sin, so we could enter the presence of, and live eternally with our Holy God.

And that's what it's all about!

FIFTY-SEVEN

The moment I saw Lucy at the airport I feared something wrong. Her arms were crossed, and her eyes had a look to them, like she was coming down with the flu. Granted, it was late at night and she was tired, but the others were fine. Mallory sprinted toward us, tangling her arms around me, and Henry and Charlie came off the terminal in typical fashion, like a couple of boxers throwing practice punches at each other. But Lucy wasn't right.

"I've missed you so much." I took hold of her, pulling her close.

"Me too." Her words seemed few and faint.

I took a step back and studied her face. "You look tired. How was the flight?"

"Mom," she scolded. "I'm fine. Everything is fine."

I left it at that, not wanting to overdo it when she was exhausted and probably needed a beach day. Sunshine always worked wonders.

Peter put the top down on the Ford Mustang convertible, and the kids—our greatest treasures ever—climbed into the backseat. Soon, all of us except Lucy were laughing, talking up a storm, until talk shifted to politics, and it was like a hurricane forming. I predicted the conversation's trajectory to be heading nowhere good, and threatened two minutes of the silent game.

"But no quarters," Peter said. "Remember, your mother used to hand out quarters to the winners?"

"Can't just award the winners," Henry said. "You'd have to give us all quarters, for trying."

"Quiet," Lucy snapped. "No politics."

That launched more debate, but the moment Peter drove onto the Causeway Bridge, all talk broke apart and our voices hushed, as if we had entered a planetarium and the show featuring Florida's night sky was beginning. All eyes were looking up at the black expanse speckled with stars until a patch of clouds parted and the moon appeared, lighting up a panorama of the bay. With water on both sides, and how low the stretch of bridge was, it felt like we were crossing the bay in a boat, not a car.

I looked back at the kids. Henry's nose was up, catching its first ever whiff of mangroves. Charlie's lips were curved into a smile, and he was staring out at the bay with a daydream in his eyes—battling a twenty-foot tarpon, probably. Mallory's eyes were wide and alert, working, imagining all the luau-themed parties she could coordinate in such a setting.

Lucy, with her full lips, high cheek bones, and last-minute, but put-together braid looked like a spitting image of my mom. I didn't want to stare, didn't want her thinking I was still trying to figure out the burden in her eyes. If Mom was with us, Lucy would have told her right away what was wrong. The two of them had something special, and even when the forgetfulness was in full swing, Lucy would sit for hours in her grandma's bed, talking about who knew what.

On rare and curious occasions I put my ear to the door.

"Tell me," Lucy had asked her one night. "Who do you *think* you are?"

"FinFin," her grandma declared with gusto, even though she never went by that name before.

Lucy didn't question it. She just reassured her. "Aw, you know who you are, don't you...you're FinFin!" And when she shared the story with the others, the nickname stuck, and from then on, whenever the kids talked about her, they referred to her as grandma FinFin.

When a cluster of clouds moved in front of the moon and I could no longer see their faces, I turned back around.

"Now, listen up," Peter announced as we were just about over the bridge. "You're only here a few short days. Here's what we expect from you—"

"Uh oh," the boys said in unison.

"Refresh and refuel," Peter went on. "That's it. That's what your time here is all about, resting and refueling, you got that?"

No one objected, and perhaps they were feeling what I felt when I first arrived—a spirit of restoration in the air, and a desire to be a part of it. FinFin experienced it, too. Should I tell them? Sanibel wasn't just a vacation destination. It was the island their grandmother arrived to at full speed only to slow down and drop anchor—drift about with God in prayer—a couple of hours each day.

When we pulled into the drive, Lovely Dwelling was all lit up, glistening in the dark, and the *oohs* and *aahs* from the kids were delightful.

"Looks like a bed and breakfast," Mallory said.

"Why couldn't you guys have bought this place sooner," one of the boys said, hopping out of the car.

"Yeah, back when we were still living with you," the other agreed.

"Wish we could have lived here," Mallory said, and I wished that, too, wished all kinds of things—wished I could have raised them on an island, given them more, given them less, cracked down harder on certain things, less on others, and taught them how to walk and talk with God, and how to anchor a moment each day, sitting still in His presence.

Even as she toted her bags up the steps, Lucy was still playing the quiet game. But the moment she stepped foot on the porch, her silence ended. "Home sweet home," she declared. "I'm moving in, just saying, hope you don't mind, I really am."

Peter laughed. He thought she was joking, but when she and the others went to the far end of the porch in hopes of spotting a palm rat in the cabbage palms, I gripped Peter's arm. "She's serious, you know…serious about moving in with us."

"No," Peter said right away, confident we had defied the trend and raised our kids to be independent twenty-somethings like we were at their age—on our own in an apartment without furniture, working two jobs each, sharing one car, struggling to pay our bills and with a baby on the way.

But when I pressed my lips together in a know-it-all way, he raised his eyebrows. "You think it's Dirk…she's trying to get away from him?"

I wasn't sure what it was, but there was no time to answer. The kids spotted three palm rats poking out at them from the branches, and were roaring with laughter at their adorable Micky Mouse-like ears. When the osprey let out a slow, irritated succession of chirps from its nest, Peter opened the front door, encouraging our party inside.

"What if they all want to move in?" he whispered to me in the doorway. "Would we have enough energy for that...for all four to move in?"

"Remember the word I taught you?"

"What word...giddy?"

"No, you nut. Vim."

"Yeah, what about it?"

"It's not enough. If we want to be active participants in their young adulthood...fun, cool, attentive parents, then we need more than vim."

Peter peeked in at them swarming our hive. "What do we need?"

"Let me think about it," I yawned. "I'll let you know."

I went inside, thrilled to find them appreciating the picture gallery on the wall. I had put time and love into it, collecting coastal vintage frames, then picking out and printing enlarged black-and-white pictures featuring each of them, as well as extended family members. I put myself through great mathematical challenges, hanging them equidistant apart. There were no boring photos—no pictures of people formally posing or fake smiling. Every picture was of loved ones in the midst of "bird in the golden slipper" moments.

I joined the group, then stood there smiling at Charlie climbing his first tree, Henry hitting a homerun, Lucy singing on stage for the first time, and Mallory blowing out her sweet sixteen birthday candles. There was also my brother climbing Mount Kilimanjaro, Peter's sister skiing the Alps, the best man at our wedding white water rafting, and our niece zip-lining through North Carolina. There were even pictures of Viv in her younger years—a mini montage of her in faraway places, taking a t'ai chi class in Bangkok, riding an elephant in the Chiang Mai region, and holding a yoga pose in front of the Taj Mahal.

But of all the adventures captured and framed, it surprised me to hear the kids unanimously vote FinFin sitting on a bench beneath an oak tree as their favorite picture of all.

"It's the look on her face," Mallory said. "All she's doing is sitting on a bench, but look at the expression on her face!"

It looked like she was sitting on the top of a Ferris wheel with a view of the world below. If only they knew what their grandmother was doing on that bench…enjoying a golden moment, sitting alone with God.

By then, it was late. If Lovely Dwelling was a museum, it would have closed hours ago. The night shift security guards would have been struggling to stay awake. "We'll give you a better tour in the morning, but for now," I said, "beds are there, there, and there. Settle in and make yourselves cozy. We'll meet again for breakfast."

"Breakfast?" Henry griped. "What about dinner?"

"I hope you're joking," Peter said.

The room went quiet except for their stomachs growling, resembling prehistoric sounds. I peeked at the clock on the stove…just after midnight. "Okay, listen. The kitchen is open twenty-four-seven, but this chef is going to bed, so it's help yourselves." I pointed to the giant silver vault filled with goods.

"Don't let the food in there go bad," Peter added. "Your mother filled that thing with five-hundred and forty-eight dollars of food!"

Hearing that, the boys hooted and hollered and picked me up, as if I had scored the winning touchdown. I screamed and swatted, and when they put me down, I opened the freezer and pulled out four frozen pizzas.

Even though Peter and I had said we were going to bed, we kept catching second waves of energy. Hanging out with people their age was like tapping into another source, and we were on our ninth wave—in the midst of a pineapple-and-ham-pizza porch party surrounded by riled-up palm rats and osprey—when the words came to me.

"*Zing* and *zip*," I whispered to Peter.

"Huh?"

"*Zing* and *zip*…I thought of the words…for what we need. You need *zing* and I need *zip*."

"We're still up, so don't you think we already have them? Maybe they kick in for special occasions, like this. We've surpassed Charlie, even. I hope he found a bed."

"He didn't go to bed. He's in there playing his game," Henry said.

"Huh?" Peter and I said together.

"I'll bet a hundred bucks that's what he's doing. He's got the app on his phone now and he told me on the plane his new life plans…become a *Mamba Jamba* master."

"Say what?"

"Yeah, then get hired to create the sequel game. So far, there's only one other master in the world, this guy in China. That's why Charlie quit his job. He's been playing around the clock hoping to be the grand master."

Like a two-headed monster sitting on the wicker loveseat, Peter and I turned our peeved eyes toward each other.

"Did you know this?" I asked.

"No, did you?"

"No."

"Yeah. It'll take him a year to reach semi-master-level status, and another two years full-time after that to become a master," Henry said with expertise, "…if he's good enough…then another six months to be promoted to grand master."

Peter dropped his pie crust, then went inside. Henry and Mallory, drawn to whatever night life there was—the rats in our trees—went again to the far end of the porch to see what they could see.

I stayed put, with Lucy cuddled up beside me. My insides felt storm-tossed over Charlie quitting his job and aspiring to become a video game master. My self-blaming, tormenting mind went back to when he was younger, when his buddies were out there in the world, getting into all kinds of trouble. I had talked myself into believing it was less worrisome letting him stay locked up in his room than gallivanting around town. At least then I didn't catastrophize when I heard sirens down the road; I always knew it wasn't him.

Still, I should have pulled the plug on his *Mamba Jamba* game the summer before college. I assumed he was going to outgrow it, get bored by Level 400, and on his own accord—without mother's forcing—move on from the tedious game.

"Hey," I said when Charlie came out and plopped down on the other side of me.

"I lost round 888. And I needed to win it in order to move up a round. I've been on that round for three months and was hoping to move up to round 889."

My stomach churned with things I wanted to say that needed to come out. Since the others came over, though, I put it on hold for when Charlie and I were alone.

"I forgot to tell you, Mom," Mallory said. "I bumped into Mrs. P at the grocery store. She's going through a super hard time. Mr. P is sick and they don't know what's wrong with him, but he lost his job, and she's working two jobs...coming home at nine-thirty every night. Her face is grumpier than ever and if I were to guess, I think she's on the brink."

"On the brink?"

"Of a breakdown, yeah."

I didn't like hearing that my neighbor of twenty years was on the brink. I knew what the brink was—had been there myself. After Mom moved in, Peter and I weren't getting along. There were moments when we said things we shouldn't have, and to be honest, I didn't like him. We were running on exhaust fumes, both working overtime, managing Mom's needs, while trying to feed four hungry teenagers in a messy house. The brink was not a fun place to be.

"She asked all about you, Mom."

"Really?"

"Yeah, I told her I was coming to see you...said she missed you."

"Missed me? Oh, please."

"No, it's true...said she remembers you juggling so many things... wishes she had been more understanding when things dropped."

When things dropped! I wanted to be offended, but in reality, they had dropped. I wasn't good at juggling. "Well, if you happen to see her again, tell her I'll be praying for her, will you?"

Apparently, that was a strange and out-of-character thing for me to have said. Even Lucy woke up, and I got a different look from each of them—surprise, doubtful, satirical, and *are you serious, or just saying that to sound good?*

"I'm serious, tell her I'll be praying for her," I said again, trying to change those looks on my kids' faces. "I haven't always been a praying person, I admit. But something you kids don't know about me...for weeks, no, months now, I've been praying for each of you every single day."

I would have elaborated, if one of them had shown interest, but when Lucy, who had been scrunched up in the space next to me all that time, dropped her head back onto my shoulder, I decided it best we all get to sleep. Like a lifeguard, I stood up and announced everything closed…no more catching waves until morning.

"Hey," I whispered to Peter a short time later, as we climbed into bed. "We have to do something. I'm so angry at myself, angry at that game, how it crept into his life like that and now it rules him…all those hours he devotes to it, handing his life over to it!"

"A bit dramatic-sounding, Adele."

"Dramatic-sounding…are you kidding me?"

He rolled onto his side, facing me. "Sorry. I'm tired. I totally agree with you, but I'm already on it, planning to have a good talk with him tomorrow, alone, if I get the chance. But don't worry, I'm on it!"

"Good." I needed him to be on it. Him on it freed me up to be on top of whatever it was that was going on with Lucy. "So, what do you think… does Lucy seem okay to you?"

After a moment's pause, in which I assumed he was pondering, Peter let out a three-second, even-pitched, spooky trill that sounded like the Eastern screech owl. I smacked my lips together and made an annoyed clacking sound, waking him up again.

"What—" he said, "did you say something?"

"Never mind, I'll figure it out myself."

"Figure what out?"

"Stuff," I said. "Where is God in their lives? Do you think they even think about Him?"

"What do you mean?"

"Oh, you know what I mean…I wished we had taught them more, showed them that He's real and He cares and He loves them. I wished I did more of that."

When the silence in the room felt ominous, I assumed Peter was thinking through monumental stuff, taking his time to answer. But then he let out a two-second descending shrill. He had fallen asleep yet again.

I was glad when the cold front overtook the house. Peter liked recreating a wintry Midwestern feel by lowering the thermostat at bedtime to sixty-eight degrees, so he could sleep like a bear. Shivering, I reached for the comforter down near our feet, and pulled it up to my chin. The new light-blue comforter—hand-dyed and made of seventy-percent cotton and fifty-percent silk—comforted me physically, but emotionally brought me no comfort whatsoever.

No stores carried comforters that comforted the mind. I wanted my mind to rest. It was wide awake and thinking all kinds of things. What if I didn't say a word to the kids about my fresh love for God, other than tell them I was praying for them? Would they notice anything different about me? When a house was undergoing renovations, didn't the people living nearby hear construction? Then again, God's work produced a peaceful, gentle sound, which was nice. I didn't want to be a nuisance. I wanted my family to know what I was experiencing. It didn't seem right to keep it like a secret life I was living.

I wanted to fall asleep, but that what-if area of my brain was wide awake. What if one of life's storms showed up and tried knocking down the temple of the Holy Spirit within? What if a tsunami came and the overwhelming sense of God's presence in my life receded, pulling my re-claimed treasure chest of truths back out to sea? What if one day I looked back at this season on Sanibel and my hypersensitivity to God as no more than a fleeting phase, a temporary spiritual high? Highs always came down. And power walking…it burned people out. What if God became like a dear, long-lost friend to me, someone I once power walked with in a beautiful setting, but then lost touch with?

Fear had me all worked up. I kicked the comforter off my body, then climbed out of bed and went for my binder, ready to shred what I had written…write a fun romance instead. Did anyone care about the work I was doing in Lovely Dwelling, and the work God was doing in me?

"All these hours I'm putting into it," I mumbled as I clenched the binder by its spine. "The kids will think I'm a nutcase, or worse…a hippo!"

I was on the brink of letting my fears control me when I spotted Mom's Bible on my dresser. The moment I opened it, fear left.

FIFTY-EIGHT

* * *

"Praise be to the God and Father of our Lord Jesus Christ, the
Father of compassion and the God of all comfort, who comforts
us in all our troubles, so that we can comfort those in any
trouble with the comfort we ourselves have received from God."
—2 Corinthians 1:3–4

Dear Comforter,

*Good thing I keep finding in Your Word all these different names I can call
You because they describe for me who You are. Without them, I'd take my own
creative liberties, get to know You not for who You really are, but as a fabricated god character with traits and characteristics from my own imagination.
I don't want to know a caricature version of You, a god with unbalanced,
ill-proportioned features that I've drawn out myself. I want to know and love
who You really are!*

*I want to know my true self, too, not a caricature. But first I have to know
You, in order to better know myself. But knowing You also helps shape me. If I
didn't know You were a God of mercy and love, but knew You only as a God of
judgment, my lips might be too prim and proper, my eyes overly critical, and
I'd have exaggerated tendencies.*

*If I didn't personally know the fullness of Your grace, it would be easy for
me to shrink Your love down to where it's barely visible, while making Your
wrath larger than life. Or exaggerate Your mercy and grace, while erasing
completely Your holiness.*

*In other words, I so appreciate the names I keep finding for You in the
Bible. The names tell me more specifically who You are. And the way I view*

You alters how I view myself. If my view of You is off, I walk around discombobulated and look disproportionately at everything in the world, including myself. The more I get to know You for who You are, the less discombobulated I am as I walk through life.

God, Jesus, Holy Spirit.

The descriptive names I'm finding for each of the three distinct persons of the Trinity tell me not only who You are—God Almighty—but describe ways in which I can personally rely on You in my life. I've been keeping a running list of the names.

Father. Lord. Comforter.

Wow, not only are You God Almighty, but You're also my personal Comforter—way larger than a California King, large enough to cover all of my discomforts. By the way, it's three in the morning, so obviously, I'm not outside on a bench, but sitting up in bed, wrapped in Your cozy, larger-than-life presence.

My rock, my ransom, my redeemer. *No more than a heart's cry away, I don't have to wait until morning, or Sunday, but can call out to You anytime, twenty-four-seven, holidays and weekends. I'm reading the names over and over again—programming them into my heart—the contact names I've collected for You so far.* Savior, Living One, King of the Ages, King Eternal. *You are One God, with many names, and You meet all my needs.*

Light of the World, Lord.

Lord *is my favorite. I've experienced the bad kind of a lord, a slumlord, and it makes me appreciate You, a good Lord, that much more. Back home, every time an appliance breaks or the hot water doesn't work in the house I'm renting, my landlord bemoans me for calling, and makes me feel shame—like it's my fault or the kids' fault, and we're nothing but a bother. Before we left for Sanibel, the cheap washing machine wasn't working, and already I'm dreading telling her. She's going to blame and belittle me.*

When that happens, comfort me, please. But also, I'll praise You that much more, knowing You are my true Lord, and the opposite of a slumlord. You never make me feel unworthy of repair, and no matter what breaks in my life, or needs attention in me—even if the damage is my fault, which it usually is—You're waiting for my call, and to lend Your helping hand, or teach me a much-needed lesson.

Thank You. I feel like a prima donna so loved by You, and it's the best kind of prima donna to be, loved by the most decent, good, kind, nice, pleasant, reputable, respectable, honorable God Almighty. Thank You, my Lord, for telling me I'm so worthy of repair.

Wonderful Counselor, Lord of my Righteousness, King of Kings, Prince of Peace.

I have to go to sleep now, but the list of names for You goes on and on, reminding me of the full potential of our relationship, and who You are to me.

Love,

Finley (Your daughter through faith in Christ Jesus)

FIFTY-NINE

I woke the next morning with a craving to write. The world outside Lovely Dwelling was still black as ink, but I liked writing in the inky-black hours, the only one awake. Not wanting to disturb Charlie on the pullout sofa or Henry on the air mattress, I tiptoed into the kitchen to make coffee, then took it with me into the walk-in pantry. With nothing but built-in, floor-to-ceiling shelves stocked with food, plus a small counter and chair, the informality of it being a pantry and not an obvious writing space removed the pressure to write, and my writing flowed.

I wrote a review for the One who can do anything, and specifically His affinity for restoration projects.

The Father, Son, and Spirit are the ultimate and most influential restoration specialists of all time, and once I spent time collaborating with and getting to know the amazing God-in-three team, there was no denying their Heavenly craftsmanship, quality, and attention to detail. Customization is God's specialty, and so is demonstrating His love for people individually. Personally speaking, His renovation work on my heart and mind far exceeded my expectations.

And not just me. The testimonies are endless. For centuries, the members of the Trinity have been working together in harmony, maintaining their prominence as international leaders in the timeless design, refurbishment, and renovation of the individual's inner being. They have already proved and will continue to prove themselves as the trusted source for solutions by millions of discerning individuals worldwide.

God's entire kingdom of helping hands and feet have been working together, moving in the same direction to accomplish His purposes and deliver good news all over the world. He trains people to go the extra mile, and strategically places His Jesus-experienced design consultants everywhere on the globe, even in the most remote villages.

When I heard moving around in the kitchen, I stopped writing and poked my head out from the pantry. I saw a jar of peanut butter open on the counter, with a spoon sticking out, then Lucy. In the light of the refrigerator, her face was like a deer caught in headlights.

She pressed a piece of cheese into her mouth. "Hi, Mom," she mumbled.

"Peanut butter…cheese…so early in the morning. What's going on?"

She closed the refrigerator and the room went dark. "I don't want to make a big deal of it, but I'm pregnant."

I always heard that whatever words we once threw at our own mothers came back to us in roundabout ways. Lucy's words hit me like a boomerang. I reached for the light, but changed my mind and decided to keep the house dark. Sometimes my face did things that I didn't want it to do.

"I love you," I said automatically, knowing that the repetitive lyrics I recited to my daughters would one day roll off their tongues when talking to their daughters. "You know how much I love you, right? Now talk to me."

She told me everything. Dirk wanted nothing to do with her, and was already with another girl. In so many words, the dreams and goals she had for her life had vanished from the horizon. "I don't know what to do, Mom. I didn't want this for my life. I wanted more. I can hardly think straight. What do I do?"

That was the question, the monumental question minutes before sunrise, as I took my daughter's hand and together we walked out into the dark where the osprey, woodpeckers, and mourning doves were still sleeping soundly. There is something about the early-hour moments that allows a person to block out the noise and distractions of the world, and for things to become clear. Down the meandering path to the beach we went, her lips spilling forth plans to abort, and my lips moving without sound, privately, desperately praying to the One who makes things clear.

"I was in your shoes once, you know that. A long time ago, but it feels like yesterday." I choked at the thought of my life without Lucy, who started in me smaller than a granule of sand and turned into one of the greatest wonders of my world. And to think, I had once thought that little granule of sand in me was the worst-case scenario for my life. "I can't imagine my life without you." Struggling with my words, I squeezed her hand. "You say you want to end the pregnancy…what if I had done that to you?"

"Mom," was all she said, but with force to her voice, the same force she used as a teenager, right before slamming the door in my face.

"Okay, we don't have to talk. Let's just walk."

If only we had waited that extra ten minutes for dawn's true emergence, for the morning glories to unfurl, the carambola leaves to unfold, the spiders to pull back their webs, and the big brown bats to fall asleep. When we entered the dark trail at the end of the road, and Lucy tried getting me to promise that I wouldn't tell her father, the arching Australian pine branches looked like the arms of a monster reaching over us. The monster offered to swallow up her secret—hold it in its bowels, never let it out.

It was so dark I didn't know what to do except pray from within, the kind of prayer that required no lips, tongue, teeth, or mouth...just my heart speed-dialing names.

Counselor, Comforter, Savior!

"I wasn't going to tell you, Mom. I don't want it turning into a big deal, messing up my thought process and decision-making. But whatever I choose to do, other than you, no one else has to know."

Oh, the chipped and broken half-lies, half-truths, and misconceptions she had collected from the world. A life inside was always a big deal, and I wished I had better sorted through the contents of her bucket with her, filling it with more of God's Truths.

"You know, Lucy," I was unable to keep quiet, "since Dad and I moved out here to Sanibel, I've been walking a lot—and not just walking, but walking and talking with God."

"That's nice." Her tone was halfway between interested and disinterested.

I wanted to say more, share with her that I wasn't just walking and talking with God. I was combing the shore for shells, the pages of scripture for Truth, and filling myself chock-full of it. "Go to the One who loves you," I trod lightly. "Bring everything to Him. No matter what you're thinking, bring it all to the One who loves you, and is able. You're His child, you know."

"Yeah, I'm just not in touch."

"Well, I didn't help," I admitted. "I was no good at getting us to church, or talking about God. We were busy. I let things drop. But everything He has for us, it's here...up to us to pick it all up again. That's what

I've been doing…reclaiming my treasures. And I'm overwhelmed by it… God's love."

"That's great, Mom. I still want more, though, more for my life. What's wrong with wanting more?"

"I wanted more, too," I said to the daughter very much like me. "But fast forward and here I am…with more than I could have imagined, more of a different kind." Just as I wanted to say more—but didn't want to go overboard to where she would block me out—my foot brushed against a coil, sending it slithering into the shadowy preserve and me screaming like Peter, hopping on one foot like a yellow-crowned night heron. Lucy gripped my arm, and together we continued our jaunt in the direction of the whispering waves.

"I want to do things now," Lucy solemnly chanted. "Not eighteen years from now, like you and dad, finally doing something cool for yourselves, only because we're grown. I don't want to be in this situation. I don't want this for my life. I can't see a single thing good about it."

We had arrived at the beach, and I felt intense pressure to pray, *please, may her eyes dilate from the brightness of Truth.* As we stepped onto the silken sand, the Gulf of Mexico in front of us was pushing the sun into the world. Only the tip of it had appeared, but already the sky was reacting, decorating the morning in shades of pink. I had seen the birth of countless days, but no two were the same. Every day was new, fresh, different, ours to hold, and meant to be lived.

I would have given anything to go back to the moment Lucy was born, when I was handed her for the first time.

"Why are you looking at me, Mom?"

"Oh, because," I smiled. "You know what I think you should do?"

"What?"

"Go for a walk."

She looked at me oddly. "Didn't we do that…isn't that how we got here…we walked?"

"No, no, no, I don't mean a walk with me. With God…go for a walk and a talk with God. Trust me for once, I'm your mother."

She shook her head. "I wouldn't even know what to say to Him right now."

"Cry out to Him. There's something to it, and we're meant to do it."

She rolled her eyes. "What would I even cry out about?"

"Everything…in your life, and in your heart, and in your womb. He already knows the details, but cry out about everything, your entire situation."

I didn't want her believing she could throw life into the sea like a message in a bottle, sunken, forgotten, never to be read. There was no hiding anything from the One who knew everything…even what was on the floor of the ocean.

When she didn't answer, I refrained from saying more. But as we stood there taking our first breaths of morning, I detected it in her eyes. She was waking to fresh possibilities…the kind that came from starting days differently…starting them with the One who breathed fresh life into us. And that first cry.

The sea grape leaves were no longer hovering like spooky shadows, but hanging like works of art in hues of red, orange, and green. The heart-shaped leaflets of the common yellow wood sorrel, which creased at their center each night, were unfolding. Morning glories were opening, song-birds singing, and owls quieting. Every dune daisy was turned, tilting on its stem, facing the rising sun. Lucy's face was turned, too, her head tilting, and ears turning ever-so-slightly toward the Lord.

Daybreak was happening, and along with it, the promise that any-thing was possible with the One who loved us.

SIXTY

Lovely Dwelling was like a festival hall bustling with energy. The rhythm of us talking, along with the clanging of dishes and the smell of pancakes, filled the air, and in the midst of the hoopla, I wore a happy mask. But Lucy's secret was too weighty for me to hold, expanding within, like a hot air balloon, ready to burst at the seams.

"Don't say anything, Mom," she whispered as I heated the syrup. "Don't tell Dad. I don't want anyone to know right now, other than you, okay?"

Did she have any idea how hard that was for me? My happy mask was going to fall off, and her father was going to read my face. When the syrup bubbled, I removed the saucepan from the heat. "How are the pancakes coming along?" I asked Charlie, who was in charge of the griddle. But he was nowhere to be seen. Smoke rose from the pancakes. "Hey," I rushed to open the front door, letting air in, "where's Charlie? He's supposed to be flipping pancakes."

"He was up until four, playing his game," said Henry, who took over his brother's post, shoveling the burnt pancake off the griddle and into the garbage. "He went back to sleep."

"I'm on it," Peter whispered once the fire alarm stopped. "I'll talk to him today. I'll take him fishing, and have a good talk."

Oh, how much easier when they were in diapers, and Peter and I were running around searching for lost pacifiers. Their issues then were simple in comparison. It seemed like their current issues required more than Peter and I had to give. They required an entire task force of wise, diplomatic strategy experts trained in emergency response.

I was about to ask Peter if talking and fishing were going to do the trick, when Charlie came hurtling into the kitchen, disoriented, like he was late for work and about to get fired.

"I'm here, I'm here. Are they ready to be flipped? Where's my flipper?"

"Your brother flipped them for you." I handed him a cup of juice.

Relieved, he took a swig. "Hey, pretty good juice, Mom. Did you squeeze it yourself, from the trees out back?"

"I wish, but nope, store-bought. I keep waiting, trying to be patient, but still no signs of fruit in the yard."

"Hmmm." Charlie stared into his glass, contemplating the fruit trees having no fruit. He'd always loved trees, and when younger, if he wasn't swinging from a branch, or building a tree fort in the neighborhood, he was up in a branch, way too high. I missed little boy Charlie—that side to him that loved trees—and maybe I was reading into it, but his face let me know that he was missing it, too.

Falling out of a wonderful daydream, he blinked his eyes, downed his juice, then looked at me. "Are you positive there's no fruit? When was the last time you checked?"

"You don't want to know. Your crazy mother is out there every other day. One lemon and I'll be jumping up and down like a fool."

Mallory came into the kitchen and took her plate. "Why not clear out the trees and put in a pool instead? Imagine the pool parties you and Dad could have!"

Both Charlie and I nodded politely, but when she went to the table to eat, he whispered, "Don't give up on the trees, Mom. As long as they're good and healthy and growing, it's a matter of time. You'll get your fruit."

I put my arm around him and pulled him close for a hug. I prayed privately over him, that he would never stop thinking deeply, and that the One who gave strength would step in and help him keep his mind healthy and growing. His heart, too, because healthy hearts produced good fruit.

After breakfast, we changed into colorful bathing suits, and with teal-striped beach towels draped over our shoulders and beach bags stuffed like suitcases, we marched out the door. Our route was simple—down the front porch steps, and to the beach. With umbrellas on long poles and coolers on wheeled carts, we moved slow as a parade. Even the birds stepped aside to admire our pageantry, as spectacular as the Macy's Day Parade on television every year.

Halfway there, my steps turned into a somber death march. There was someone in Lucy with a reservation for life, and what if it got canceled? Did she know that sacrifice was a part of love, and one never went wrong when sacrificing for the sake of life and love itself?

On the beach, we claimed our spot, and with coolers parked, umbrella poles stuck into the ground, chairs unfolded, and blankets spread, we hunkered down. Time didn't matter, and we only knew of its passing when our first bottle of sun lotion was empty.

Every so often a combination of us went for a swim, or a walk, searched for shells, or worked on a sandcastle. At times we sat near the shore with our toes in the water...all of us but Charlie. There he was on the most beautiful beach in the world, with a towel over his head, blocking out the brightness to see his screen.

When Peter confiscated his phone, insisting he join us in the water, he dropped onto his back in the sand like a dying crab. Henry poked him, hollered for him to get up, but Charlie's body turned limp and remained that way until his brother grabbed and flipped him over. I was thrilled when in response, Charlie sprang up and clawed his brother back. Henry zoomed into Charlie, and the two of them dropped into the sand. It was how they used to play, like a couple of rambunctious ferrets.

Lucy wasn't entertained by her brothers' antics. She rolled onto her stomach and stayed put. Peter thought she was resting, but I knew otherwise. The weighty secret she was carrying had her feeling like a beached mammal, washed ashore.

I wanted to help, wanted to step in and rescue my daughter, send her back out to sea, and watch her live the life that she wanted to live, happy and carefree. But whoever claimed that happy and carefree was what life was all about? I wanted more for my kids than happy and carefree. I wanted them choosing what was right, even if it meant life didn't go the way they had wanted.

When the guys walked down the beach to go fishing, the girls and I found ourselves charmed by a plover standing at the water's edge, sporting a dramatic black belly. It was eyeing every cracker that made its way from the box into our mouths.

"What a handsome fellow," I said when it strutted over and stared at me.

The girls cracked up. "Your black and white bathing suit matches its feathers, Mom. It likes you. You should ask it to dance."

"Your dad would get jealous. And besides, all it wants is my food, which I will not share."

I loved sitting on the beach with my girls, and if only Mom was there, too. Never in a million years would she have imagined the family together on Sanibel. There was no better time to do what I had been wanting to do.

Whew, whew, whew. The plover cheered me on.

I crawled across the blanket and reached into my bag, pulling out one of her letters to God—the only letter left that I hadn't yet read. I had told the girls over the phone about FinFin's Bible, but it was time to share more. As I held the paper in my hand, I wanted them to know that FinFin wasn't the only one who loved the Bible. I loved it, too. I was getting to know better the One who loved me, and His Word was the definitive resource for everything related to the restoration of my heart, soul, and mind.

Whew, whew, whew.

I didn't know how to say that without sounding overly dramatic. It was more natural to talk about other things, like the living shoreline restoration in progress. Living shorelines were made of natural materials— plants, sand, rock. Then again, we were made of natural things, too… flesh, blood, and with hearts, souls, minds. And like the shoreline, we faced threats, too. Spiritual erosion happened. I experienced it myself… had broken away. Restoration was a very big deal, and I wanted to talk about it.

But I'd write about it later. Mangrove trees trapped sand and silt. But the One who wanted communication flowing, reached out His limb and made a place at the cross where our sin could be trapped, and our relationship restored.

Whew, whew, whew.

"Alright," I said to the girls, their eyes as attentive as the plover's, "are you ready to hear one of Grandma FinFin's letters to God?" It was emotional for me, and I took a deep breath. "If there's a viewing platform in Heaven, she's looking down, smiling, cheering us on. You know why?"

"Why?" Lucy rolled onto her side to face me, and Mallory settled onto her back with her hands clasped like a pillow behind her head.

"She'd want us knowing how she loved Him...and how He loved her...and loves us, too." Not wanting the breeze or the plover to snatch it, I gripped the piece of paper with both hands. "'To the Author of My Life,'" I read out loud.

Whew, whew, whew.

The plover winked its eye at me, then flew off.

SIXTY-ONE

To the Author of my Life,

I don't have to tell You it's my last day on Sanibel. You already know everything about me, and see the pages of my life before I even live them out. Still, You love when I share my thoughts with You, so here I go, not sitting on a bench this time, but on a blanket with my toes in the sand. And not under a cabana umbrella, but under my ginormous straw hat. There's no place I'd rather be, than sitting here with You!

Right before I left to come down here for my two hours alone, Adele had me playing her favorite game—"Mom, would you rather eat a peanut butter sandwich with worms in it, or a chocolate pie with dirt crust?" I chose the dirt pie because there was chocolate in it.

"A moldy donut, or a rotten pineapple?" I chose the donut.

"Would you rather live in a mud hut in the jungle if Daddy could still be alive, or in our old, beautiful house in Michigan, without Daddy?" I chose living in a mud hut with Daddy still alive.

Oh, dear God, may we never lose our silliness, and always play the games that make us laugh, and even cry. Adele likes to be the one asking the questions, and throws out a dozen a minute at me. Now that I have time to think, there's "would you rather" questions I'd like to ask her…when she's older.

*

*Would you rather spend an hour interviewing
your favorite author, or
spend an hour with the Author of Your life, Author of Salvation,
Author and Perfector of your faith?*

*

*Would you rather live twenty years on a tropical island,
or forever in paradise with God?*

*(I would choose both, but for the sake of the
game, it's about choosing one or the other)*

*

*Would you rather view yourself an aging woman of the world
with most of life behind you, or an age-defying
daughter of God with all of eternity ahead?*

*

*When you look in the mirror, would you rather see more of yourself,
or more of Christ—Light of the World—in you?*

*

*Would you rather walk around like a wilting hibiscus, or upright
and with purpose, fully confident you are the shoot God has
planted—the work of His hands for the display of His splendor?*

*

*Would you rather have the best wardrobe around,
or lay aside the robe of the world and put on
a new toga, clothed with Christ?*

*

*Would you rather live in a mansion overlooking the ocean,
or in a dive filled with God's presence?
(I'd choose both, but for the sake of the game)*

*

*Would you rather build your life upon
Christ, or build it on nothing?*

*

*Would you rather anti-aging be the ongoing battle within you, or
surrender to Eternity and let Eternity take its glorious reign in you?*

*

*When you notice your vibrancy fading, would
you rather mourn the formerly
vibrant you, or reclaim your vibrancy?*
Hint.
*Think of the seashells…how colorful they are when
submerged in water, but how chalky and uncolorful
they become over time when removed.*

Hint, hint.
True vibrancy comes from keeping yourself engulfed in Truth.

*

Would you rather think of yourself as old
through the eyes of the world,
or young in terms of everlasting life?

*

Would you rather notice wrinkles or wisdom?

*

Would you rather dress according to the trends of the world,
or let God, your Designer, dress you in garments of worth?

*

"I delight greatly in the Lord; my soul rejoices in my God. For
he has clothed me with garments of salvation and arrayed me
in a robe of righteousness, as a bridegroom adorns his head
like a priest, and as a bride adorns herself with jewels."
—Isaiah 61:10

*

Would you rather go to your favorite clothing
store, or make your way through the
lines of Ephesians, and be properly accessorized for the
walk from here into Eternity?
(Even though it's a book in the Bible, Ephesians sounds
like the name of a department store. It's where I've been
going for my protective spiritual accessories.)

*

Would you rather people ask where you got your cute beach cover-
up, or where you got that belt of truth that is buckled around
your waist, and the breastplate of righteousness that's in place?
Would you rather wear gorgeous shoes, or ugly
shoes knowing that your feet are fitted with the
readiness that comes from the gospel of peace?
Would you rather in a gust of wind lose your monstrous
floppy hat, or the helmet of salvation on your head?

*Would you rather go a single day on the beach
without sun lotion, or without your shield of faith
and the sword of the Spirit (Word of God)?*

*

*Would you rather dehydrate from gulping down lies of
the world, or hydrate your insides with Truth? Reading
God's Word is like sipping from Eternity's Fountain of
Youth.*
*(Please know, if circumstances allowed, I would say yes to all of the
below. It's always good, if presented the opportunity, to care for your
body, a temple of the Holy Spirit, but for the sake of the game...)*

*

*Would you rather get a deep-cleansing facial, or the
cleansing work of Christ in your life that produces radiance
in your skin and sparkle in your eyes—the kind that
comes from God's indwelling glory?*

*

*Would you rather get rid of the age spots on your skin,
or the sin spots in your heart?*

*

*Would you rather try out the claims on
expensive tubes of beauty cream,
or trust in the supernatural promises of eternal Truth?*

*

*Would you rather apply a rejuvenating serum, or feel
God's Truth penetrating your innermost layers?*

*

*Would you rather get a massage, or let the Holy Spirit's
nudging, softening, molding, and shaping be like a
much-needed spiritual deep-tissue massage?*

*

*Would you rather talk about the headline-making
superlatives—worst drought, biggest snowstorm, most
monstrous hurricane ever, fiercest wildfire, most formidable
flood, biggest volcano eruption—or about God?*

He's not the mightiest, most fear-inspiring, largest, most powerful, strongest, biggest, or even the greatest god out there. He's the one and only God Almighty, and needs no superlatives before His name!

Oh my, a second ago, there was this woman demolishing sandcastles up and down the beach, not far from where I'm sitting. No joke, she was kicking them down with her bare feet, one- after the next. I got up and was about to call her a meanie, but she told me she was a sea turtle volunteer, and that newly hatched sea turtles en route to the water can get stuck in the castles. I'm not sure if there's a relevant question to go along with that—would I rather go tell someone off, or hear them out first? Build a sandcastle, or save a baby sea turtle's life?

*

*Would you rather stay living in your current
body forever, away from God in Heaven,
or one day leave your body, and go to Heaven?*

*

"So we are always confident, even though we know that as long as we live in these bodies we are not at home with the Lord. That is why we live by believing and not by seeing. Yes, we are fully confident, and we would rather be away from these bodies, for then we will be at home with the Lord. So our aim is to please him always, whether we are here in this body or away from this body. For we must all stand before Christ to be judged. We will each receive whatever we deserve for the good or evil we have done in our bodies."
—2 Corinthians 5:6—10

*

*Would you rather rely on your own self-perceptions, or
look into God's Word as your mirror?
(I love how the Bible provides different
names for who we are as believers)*

*

*Would you rather be a temple of the Holy
Spirit, or some other kind of temple?*

I was reading in the book of Judges how long before Solomon built the temple in Jerusalem, there were other kinds of temples in the world—some built to Dagon, the chief god of the Philistines, and the god of grain and harvest. But worship in those pagan temples included human sacrifice. Since the temple roofs were flat, the townspeople climbed up and sat on the roofs and from there, witnessed the torture and humiliation of prisoners, and other horrible things going on in the courtyard of the pagan temples.

I don't even have to ask myself. There's no other temple I'd rather be than a temple of the Holy Spirit, one who walks in the light of Your presence, and with the Mind of the Lord, Breath of Life, Your Spirit of Creation and Renewal dwelling in me. And if someone were to climb up onto my roof (so to speak), and peek down into me, I'd rather they see an atmosphere of love, peace, and joy, than anger, hatred, and confusion.

And when I join with other believers, I'm a pillar in Your temple, a living stone, together with other stones, being built into a spiritual house, a dwelling in which You live by the Spirit of Christ, Your building, a holy temple of the Lord,

Love,
Finley

But I'm not just Finley. According to Your Word, I'm more: a child of the living God and of the Most High, a child of the promise, dearly beloved and longed for, someone who, thanks to Christ, can enter directly into Your presence, and live as a fellow citizen with the saints, and be Your heritage, like the other believers, heirs of God and co-heirs with Christ, heirs according to the hope of eternal life, heirs together of salvation, heirs together of the grace of life, an eternal excellency, Your treasured possession, Your chosen, apple of Your eye, Your turtledove, Your everlasting pride.

Would I rather be who others tell me I am, or walk out into the world knowing who You tell me I am? I'm a follower. Daughter of Yours through Faith in Jesus. She that has the mind of Christ. A woman who has tasted the heavenly gift and has tasted the goodness of the Word of God, and the powers of the coming age. Partaker in the glory that shall be revealed. One of Your very own. Servant of Christ. More than conqueror. Friend of Jesus. Warrior. One entrusted with the secret things of God. Your peculiar treasure. Aroma of

Christ. The Lord's portion. One who believes and knows the Truth. No longer will they call me Deserted but I will be called Hephzibah—the Lord's delight. Redeemed.

Wow, there's no one I'd rather be than all of that to You! Thank You, my father, for telling me who I am. And to think…Your Word even says we're like "letters from Christ, written not with ink but with the Spirit of the living God, not on tablets of stone but on tablets of human hearts."—2 Corinthians 3:2,3

P.S. It's my last day on Sanibel, but not my last day with You. Would I rather be like a snowbird, a winter visitor migrating to You only in the harsher seasons of my life, or be that year-round resident, living three hundred and sixty-five days a year in Your presence?

SIXTY-TWO

When I finished reading, both of my girls—even Lucy from beneath her giant floppy hat— had sweet looks of surprise on their faces, as if I had put pennies into a gumball machine for them, but giant, long-lasting jawbreakers dropped into their hands.

Mallory got up, stretched her legs, then walked over and stomped on the castle she had made earlier in the sand. "I'm saving a baby sea turtle," she declared. "Had no idea that maybe I was killing a baby sea turtle."

I applauded her, then turned my attention to Lucy who was wiping the corner of her eyes with her pinky.

"I want more," she said, and with her long hair flowing out from under her hat, she looked like my mother. "I really want more, Mom."

"More of what?"

"More of FinFin's letters to God."

"Me too," Mallory chimed in, and by then, she was standing at the foot of our blanket, staring up at the sky, with her arms stretched overhead, and her fingers wiggling. "I want more, too!"

Their voices reached my heart like two beautiful instruments in a wind ensemble, and I had to catch my breath. It wasn't often that my daughters wanted more of something that didn't cost money. I wanted to give them what they wanted, the encore they requested. And little did they know, they were going to be getting more of my prayers, too. Yes, their mother was going to pray and pray and pray for them.

I folded the prayer, then tucked it back into the zippered pouch of my beach bag. "As soon as I'm done with it, I'll send you Grandma's Bible with her scribbled down thoughts and prayers. You can each have a turn with it, keep it as long as you like. I'll get you your own Bibles, too. Read a little each day…self-care for your souls, break-through sunshine on a gloomy day."

"Sweet," Mallory said, "but I won't turn into one of those...I don't know how to say it. It's not stylish to be Christian, if you know what I mean. People think you're weird, and probably because Christians can be weird." She shook her head. "Ah, forget it, I don't know what I'm trying to say."

Lucy nodded stoically, and I wasn't sure if she agreed with what her sister was trying to say, or was nodding stoically for some other reason. Whatever the case, she got up from the sand and stretched her legs. "I'm going for a walk."

"Let's all go," Mallory said right away.

"No, I need to go alone."

"Are you sure?"

"Yeah." She looked at me and winked. She wasn't just going for a walk but a walk and talk with the One who knows how every story ends.

Whew, whew, whew.

Our plover friend was back, meandering along behind her. And it had friends, legions of plovers, wading in the water at low tide.

"What do you say," I said to Mallory, "should we go looking for shells?"

"Mom!" she burst out. "You've got baskets of them in every room. They're up and down your porch steps, in buckets, filled to the brim. Don't you think you have enough?"

"No, no, no," I gasped, then got up and pulled her up, too. "Two things in life we can never have enough of...seashells and—"

"Chocolate?"

"No, seashells and Truth, Mallory. You can never have enough seashells and Truth."

I handed her a mesh bag and soon we were both stooped over, our fingers digging through the sand. With every lapping wave, brightly colored mollusk homes surfaced for split seconds, then slid back under the sand. If their doors were closed, we left them alone. But if their doors were opened and the homes abandoned, we scooped them into our hands, adding them to our collection. The shore was carpeted with miniature coquinas, but we only took the unoccupied ones, spread open like butterfly wings.

A good hour into it, Mallory found a tangerine-colored shell shaped like a fig, and a creamy white bittersweet clam. But nothing thrilled me more than when I found an elaborately etched, snowy white bivalve shell—both sides still attached.

"I can't believe it...a *Cyrtopleura costata!*"

"A cyrto...what?" Mallory came to see.

"*Cyrtopleura costata.*" I was pleased with myself for having learned its scientific name, but holding one in my hands was more exciting than reading about it in a book. "Also called an angelwing clam. Looks like a set of angel wings, doesn't it?"

"I don't know. I've never seen an angel, but yes, that's what I picture angel wings to look like."

No shell would compare after that, and my back was aching from having remained so long in the "Sanibel stoop." I declared my shell-searching done for the day. As I stood there stretching my back, holding in my hand the *Cyrtopleura costata*—a good brain activity, learning and memorizing scientific names—I spotted Lucy with that whopping hat of hers, a long way down the beach. She was talking with someone, but not just talking...walking and talking...and I would have curiously stared longer, but the sky was preparing for sunset, and it was too bright for me to stare.

"I caught a six-foot fish," Henry announced, as they approached from the other direction.

"No, you didn't." Charlie punched him in the arm. "I'm the one who caught it."

Their boisterous tones, and the look in Peter's eyes when he saw me, told me that neither of them caught fish worth bragging about.

"All you caught was a pufferfish," Charlie teased.

"A puffer?" Mallory crinkled up her nose, like she didn't believe it existed, like it was some fabricated creature he'd put into one of the stories he loved writing for us as a boy. "You're lying, Charlie. I've never heard of a pufferfish."

"You would have loved it. It was like a super ball with eyes. It had porcupine-like quills. The thing inflated...blew up into the size of a basketball...and the moment it happened, our bro Henry here, well, he screamed like a girl, and a fisherman had to come help unhook his catch for the day."

"You should be a writer," Henry told him. "Seriously, dude, everything you say is like fiction…science fiction. Tell 'em the truth, Dad. Charlie was the one who caught the puffer, not me."

Peter didn't have a chance to answer; Lucy returned. "Hi, Dad," she kissed him on his cheek. "Hi, Charlie. Hi, Henry. Hi, Mom, and Mallory. Sit down. I need to tell you all something."

My insides swirled about. I dropped down onto the blanket. Lucy pulled the floppy hat off her head, then cradled it in her arms, while waiting for the others. The boys plopped down, and when Peter took the open spot on one side of me, I patted the empty spot on my other side. "Why don't you sit down, too."

"No, I'm fine. I don't want to sit." She handed me her hat, then picked up my mesh bag.

"You didn't take live shells, Mom…did you?"

"Nope."

She looked at her sister. "Did you?"

"I don't think so." Mallory shrugged her shoulders. "No, I wouldn't do that."

"So, what's this about?" Peter said.

"Well, I crossed paths with this sweet old lady on the beach. Her nose was super red because she forgot her sunscreen. I told her she could walk with me, under the shade of my enormous hat. So, there we were, walking and talking. She told me how she has tons of kids, grown up, of course."

"Is there a point to this story," Henry sighed. "Hint, hint…can you get to it quicker, please?"

"Hold your horses," Lucy snapped. "So, as I was saying, the lady was telling me about this piece of land she wanted to buy on Sanibel years ago. There happened to be a bald eagle nest smack in the middle of it, meaning she wasn't allowed to build on it."

"Just move the nest."

"No, it's protected by law. She also told me it's against the law here to collect live shells." She looked at me. "A live shell is defined by any specimen containing an inhabitant."

"Should we be taking notes?" Charlie said.

"Hush," Peter insisted, "let her finish."

"So even if a mollusk doesn't seem like a living thing, if there's a mollusk inside a shell, it's wrong to pull that shell from the water. Sea stars, sand dollars, and sea urchins are also protected by law."

"So," I said to my daughter turning sensitive, like me, to everything on the island from the sea stars to the eagle nests having life lessons to share, "what's your point here, in telling us all of this?"

Lucy pressed her lips together, shook her head, and glanced at the water behind her, then back at us. "There's more laws protecting a slimy mollusk than there are protecting the life in my womb."

Peter choked. He choked and choked, as if swallowing a bug. Mallory pushed her neck back, like the birds did when they were swallowing down fish too big for them. The boys, who usually lost interest in whatever their sister was saying, looked to be playing dead, but with their eyes wide open, staring her way.

I no longer felt seasick, and was reading my daughter's face. Written all over it was the start of a new story…a love story. The love was so powerful it was capable of changing the tides of her life, and the tides of someone else's, too. That someone was smaller than a mollusk, smaller than a granule of sand, and if the expressions on Lucy's face were to have been converted into words, they would have read: *I won't do it. I won't pull this life from its shell.*

Her unspoken words, together with the waves lapping the shore, reached my heart like a lullaby. The other reactions, or the "who, what, when, why, and where" details exchanged were a blur. The wall of sky behind Lucy, powdery blue all day, had turned pink, with hints of yellow here and there from where the sun had gone night-night. And fluffy clouds were scattered about like baby booties.

I looked at my daughter and saw more than a young woman standing on the beach. I saw a sanctuary, a refuge, a Lovely Dwelling, an intricate shell filled with life, smaller than a mollusk, but fully equipped with heart, soul, and mind. Only God knew them, but life lyrics were already written, and a voice being developed in that hidden place. *Lub-dub, lub-dub, lub-dub*, the valves of my own heart, one after the next, were clapping. Songs, heartbeats, and voices…no such thing as too many in the world.

Oh boy, oh girl, a baby was coming, a baby was coming. Precious cargo on its way.

Set up the cradle, prepare the nursery, a baby was coming!

I grabbed my thoughts, and slowed them down, then looked at Peter, who was still holding up the weight of the unexpected news. I worried it was triggering an unseen sinkhole in his heart. But then he went over and wrapped his arm around Lucy, who by then had sat down on a corner of the blanket.

I moved over a couple of inches and put my arm around the other side of her. Mallory and the boys came closer, too, and put their arms around us. We could have been in the wilderness. It didn't matter where we were. Our arms together formed a supportive shelter, a lean-to made not of branches and leaves, but love.

One side of us was open, and it was facing the water. But leaning on one another, our sheltering love formed a simple place…a place I could have stayed until the sun rose again the next day, and the next, and the next. To people walking by, we looked like a family of volunteers that had found a baby sea turtle and were insulating it.

Our huddling went on for a long time—longer than a time-out at a football game—and soon we were strategizing, motivating, and committing ourselves as a team to running alongside Lucy, celebrating and cheering her on as she carried new life.

"Now listen," Peter came through strong as the leader of our huddle, "let's each give our all, play our part, whatever we can do, whoever we need to be, you hear?"

Whew, whew, whew.

I wiped my eyes. Us together on the beach blanket reminded me of when our family was young and the kids climbed into bed with us on Saturday mornings. Everything I loved most in life was there on our king-sized blanket spread out across the sand. God's love was there, too, and it was big—big enough to cover us.

We stayed on the beach until the coolers were empty, our stomachs growled, and the conversations went to food, as they did when there was a pregnant woman in the midst.

"I wish you guys caught a real fish," Lucy told her brothers. "A snook would have been nice. Me and Dad would have grilled it up."

Henry pulled his brother up from the sand. "The only way Charlie is ever going to catch a fish is if a bird drops one and it falls on him."

"Oh, aren't you funny?" Charlie said. "Why do oysters go to the gym?" He held his bicep up and when none of us answered, he said with a grin, "It's good for the mussels."

Even as we packed up our camp site, there were more jokes…good and not so good, but laughter-inducing nonetheless. I stepped up to Peter, who was condensing the umbrellas, and whispered into his ear, "What did the girl octopus say to the boy octopus?"

He shrugged his shoulders.

"I wanna hold your hand, hand, hand, hand, hand, hand."

It wasn't that funny, but the two of us cracked up.

SIXTY-THREE

INTERIOR DESIGN TIDBITS

* * *

Closets aren't just for clothes. Turn yours into a momentous space.

* * *

Sort things into piles:
Keep, Donate, Dump.

* * *

Let your closet grow and change with you over
the years, and reflect who you are.

Sanibel offered nature preserves, gift shops, museums, theaters, and more, but the kids wanted one thing—the beach. Peter and I had no problems turning ourselves into beach bums, deserting the sand only to attend a beautiful Christmas Eve service celebrating the birth of Jesus—Son of Righteousness, Light of the World. Even though I had sung the same carols all my life, the lyrics struck my heart like never before. It was a hypersensitivity to Love's pure light so present within.

We kept it a gift-free holiday. Our family together on Sanibel was gift enough. Other than attending church and celebrating Light born into the world, we stayed put on the beach at the end of our road. There, we lounged around talking about whatever under the sun, and stayed put after it set each night, talking about everything under the twinkling little stars.

On our last full day together, they were in the water and I was resting on the blanket, listening to their laughter. I didn't want to think about saying good-bye and not seeing them for another six months. I wanted to shop for maternity clothes with Lucy, be there at her ultra-sound appointments, watch her tummy grow, and feel the baby kick. I wanted to be there for all the kids—be a part of their lives. It didn't matter what age they were. My kids still needed me. I wasn't Mommy or Mama, but I was still Ma, Mom, and on occasion, mother, as the boys liked to call me. My score for how needed I was may have dropped, but I'd step right in and hold up their lives with my own two hands, if they asked me to.

I wanted to be a matriarch, but knew that along with matriarch status came significant responsibilities. Matriarchs kept their tribes together. But also, matriarchs knew when their kids needed more than what they had to give. My kids needed more. They needed Christ—Redemption, Refuge, Righteous Branch, Ruler of God's Creation, Teacher. All throughout the Christmas season, I had been privately praying, warming up my matriarchal power, asking the all-knowing, ever-present Everything to break personally into each of their lives.

When they came out of the water, I wanted to let Peter how wrong I was in moving us so far away, and that I wanted to move back. Mallory could plan us a welcome home party, and we could get a hot tub for the yard.

"How's Captiva Island sound for dinner tonight?" Peter asked, and when we unanimously agreed, he and the guys offered to stay and pack up our stuff on the beach, giving us a head start in getting ready.

There was an enormous package waiting on the front porch when we got back. We tore off the brown protective wrap and went bananas over the chalky white seashell mirror I had bought online. Made in Key West, it was an elaborate piece of art, and Mallory and I dragged it inside, propping it against the hallway wall. "My friend Vivienne says we should put mirrors in every room," I told Mallory as she stood there in her bathing suit, staring into it. "To reflect beauty."

"Which room are you putting it in?"

"I don't know. What do you think?"

"I know," Lucy said, then signaled me into our master bathroom, with its vaulted ceiling, grass wallpaper, and freshly stained dark wooden hutch. "Put it in here, my favorite room. Makes me feel like a world traveler, like I'm in the West Indies every time I step foot in here."

I turned the bathtub water on, knowing she wanted to soak in the charming 1930s tub I had painted an icy, whitish blue. "Enjoy." I pulled a towel from the hutch and handed it to her.

I heard more water—Mallory, already confiscating the other bathroom. It was nothing new to me. I had learned not to stand around, but make the most of shower wait times. Although sandy from head to toe, I went into the kitchen and made three bowls of walnuts, raspberries, and goat cheese with raw honey drizzled on top. Lucy needed a bite before dinner. As I enjoyed mine, I stared out the kitchen window, nibbling along with the mockingbirds as they hopped from branch to branch, feasting on the yellow berries of a golden dewdrop shrub.

It wasn't until I turned from the window that from the corner of my eyes, I saw a woman—an intruder in my house—lurking in the front hall! The sight of her sent me into the same two-step hop and high-pitched scream I had been performing every time I came across huntsman spiders in the house. When I hunched over and stilled myself like that most famous ancient Greek statue, Praxiteles' Aphrodite, the woman crouched over, too. With our heads turned to the side, we stared into one another's vulnerable eyes.

I wrinkled my nose, and she wrinkled hers.

I was staring at myself.

It was me, my reflection in the mammoth seashell-encrusted mirror. Viv would have laughed her head off at my initial reaction, but all kidding aside, I wanted to find out if it was true or not what she had said about mirrors reflecting beauty in a room. With that in mind, I dared to step up close, and tried to see the beauty.

My skin was coated in layers of ghostly sun lotion, and my cheeks powdered with sand. There were lines delicately carved into my forehead, and more forming around the corners of my eyes. The matriarch-in-the-making wanted to appreciate the patina of age, but the signs of physical deterioration grieved me. I didn't want to mourn my bygone youth, or look critically at myself in the mirror. Like Mom wrote in her prayer, I wanted to thank God for my beauty, my invincible beauty enhanced, not harmed, by time.

"You're certainly no Aphrodite," I said to the woman in the mirror. "No goddess born from the sea." I let out a laugh, which softened my eyes. "But you are a work of art in progress, in the hands of the world's most skilled sculptor. And you're a masterpiece...made in the image of God, and made new by God."

I cringed at the sight of my hair, at the grey roots…a tangled mop of sea-weed from having swum in the Gulf. "But at least you swam," I said to myself, then reached down and scratched my itchy, sandy shins. "You didn't sit around on the blanket all day, watching everyone else swim. You got up with your kids, went right in, and had fun…even swallowed your first shot of salt water."

There was more I wanted to say to myself, but the guys were expected back soon, and I needed a shower.

"Mallory," I knocked on the bathroom door, "almost done in there?"

"About to get in, Mom."

"About to get in…what on earth!"

"Waiting for the water to warm up."

"The water to warm up…we're ten feet off the ground, in a bird house. Forget hot water!"

"Don't worry, I'll be quick." She cracked open the door and peeked out like a sea creature from its shell. "I love you, Mama. Do you have anything I can wear? I want to dress up fun tonight."

Oh, how I loved such moments, when I was still Mama, and needed. "Yes, let me go find you something. I'm sure I have something."

I went into my closet and pulled from the rack a slinky yellow sun-dress I wore once, years ago. If paired with the right flip flops, it was perfect for Mallory.

Still waiting for a shower, I sat down at the pencil-thin desk I had dragged into my closet one week prior. On the wall, I had hung a bulletin board on which I posted with seashell thumbtacks closet-related Bible verses.

If what Viv said was true—closets were momentous spaces—then I wanted to have a momentous experience in mine. I sat there looking up at the verses, hoping to experience a momentous closet moment.

> "But when you pray, go into your room, close the door
> and pray to your Father, who is unseen. Then your Father,
> who sees what is done in secret, will reward you."
> —Mathew 6:6

> "Therefore, as God's chosen people, holy and dearly loved,
> clothe yourselves with compassion, kindness, humility,

gentleness and patience. Bear with each other and forgive whatever grievances you may have against one another. Forgive as the Lord forgave you. And over all these virtues put on love, which binds them all together in perfect unity."
—Colossians 3: 12–14

"You were all baptized into Christ, and so you were clothed with Christ. This shows that you are all children of God."
—Galatians 3:26—27

I picked up my pen and wrote things I wished to tell my daughters, especially Mallory regarding what she had said on the beach earlier, about Christianity being unstylish.

Hello Beautifuls,

You think it's out of style to walk around wearing the Christian label, but once you spend time with the Designer of that label you won't care whether you match the trends of the world or not, or if others call you a fashion no-no. Once you start getting to know the Designer better, clothed with splendor and majesty, you'll appreciate more fully the materials Christianity is made of.

It might not fit the way the world thinks it should, but nothing fits around one's heart, soul, and mind more beautifully than Truth. The more you grow in Truth, and in Christ, the more you outgrow that which you didn't need anyway. Ask God to clothe You, and He'll clothe you in Christ.

If you're up for a closet experience like no other, get alone with the One who is not against you, but for you…and ask His help in unzipping your excuses, unbuttoning your ignorance, and righting inside-out thoughts you may have. I can think of no greater momentous closet experience than that.

Invite Him to help sort through things, keeping what needs to be kept, dumping what needs to be dumped, and giving away to others what others need from you. Sin can't be hidden from the One who ransomed us, so if there's sin unrepented for that you've stashed away in a box, high up on a shelf within yourself, so to speak, tell Him. He'll show you how to throw it into the dump pile and never wear it or the shame of it again.

You don't have to flaunt imposter goodie-two-shoes perfection to wear the Christian label. Walk humbly and with thanks to the Designer that, even though you don't deserve it, you're not permanently deep-dyed by the mistakes you've made. Ask for Truth to permeate your soul, and the blood of Christ to permeate those sin spots in your life.

God doesn't care only about the big stuff. He cares about the small-as-lint stuff in your life, too. Maybe He doesn't care about the visible accumulation of fibers on your clothing, but He does the innermost fibers of your heart, soul, and mind. He cares when they become detached or jostled out of the weave from which they were originally a part.

Always understand a thousand good deeds make you a better person and the world a better place, but your good deeds don't make you righteous. Rather than masquerading in self-made, look-a-like costumes of righteousness, why not wear the real thing—long-lasting garments of righteousness hand-crafted by God Himself.

Oh, and like the unattractive, saggy harem pants my friend Viv and I wore back in college, there are spiritual fads, too. If garments of salvation and robes of righteousness don't have Jesus written all over them, they weren't woven from the thread of the Bible, so don't try them on.

Finally, like a crab going into its protective shell, go into your closet and pray, knowing that when You come out, the presence of the living Christ is still with you wherever you go. If you don't have a walk-in closet, don't worry. There are closets—private, quiet moments to be had with God—everywhere, even in bed at night. Pull the blankies up, and enjoy the quiet time alone with the One who wants to hear your voice.

When I heard the tub draining, I got up from my writing desk and kneeled down in front of the five-tier wooden rack stocked full as a department store with flip flops in every color, style, and fabric. With so much inventory, I could have opened to the public—a flip flop shop. But who could have blamed me for having a flip flop fetish after decades of wearing suffocating socks and claustrophobic-inducing closed-toed shoes tied shut with laces! Moving to Florida had set my feet free, and wherever I went, my toes were wiggling like never before.

I didn't need jewelry. Flip flops were accessories enough, altering whatever I wore, transforming even my leggings from plain-old workout leggings into something more. Pairing flip flops with outfits was like pairing fruit with cheese, there was so much to it.

"Hmmm, which would look best with the yellow dress?"

I was in my own world, looking back and forth at the yellow dress and flip flops when the closet door opened. I didn't mean to, but my automatic reaction had me throwing a light blue, diamond-studded flip flop at Peter.

"Ouch, what was that for?"

"You scared me. I'm in deep concentration mode, picking out shoes for Mallory. It's taking way too long."

"Well, that's what happens when you have too much of something."

"What on earth," I gasped. "No such thing. Flip flops, seashells, and Truth…no such thing as having too much of!"

I decided on a silver pair for Mallory, and when I missed my turn for the bathroom—Lucy came out, and Peter snuck in—I sat back down at my desk, adding more to what I wished to tell my girls, and myself.

According to the Bible, there's a time for every activity under the sun. Maybe there's also a pair of flip flops to go along with every activity under the sun. Whether out in the yard planting or uprooting, killing poisonous spiders or healing, tearing down or building, weeping or laughing, mourning or dancing, scattering stones or gathering them, embracing or refraining, searching or giving up, keeping or throwing away, tearing or mending, there are (in my closet) matching flip flops for it all. Well, except for wintertime in Michigan. No flip flops for that.

I held my pen still and wiggled my sandy toes. Yes, I missed my kids, but did I want to return to a place where flip flops were worn only a couple of months a year? No, and I didn't want to wear snow boots again, either. Maybe I wasn't ready for my season on Sanibel to end, my walking in flip flops, talking with God, working on whatever it was I was writing.

When Peter announced that the bathroom was free, I put my moving-back-to-Michigan idea into the undecided pile. I didn't want to do anything without first consulting the One who knew what was best, and needed to go back into my closet to pray about it.

SIXTY-FOUR

In the slinky yellow dress with its playful ruffled hem, Mallory pranced in silver flip flops down the front porch steps and across the yard to where Lucy and I stood waiting under the Carissa shrub. The two of us had on lightweight casual skirts with tropical-colored tank tops, but were nowhere near as festive as Mallory, who looked like a flamenco dancer ready to take to the stage.

"Look at you," Lucy said to her. "You're not just a party planner. You're the life of the party, aren't you!"

I pulled a star-shaped white flower off the shrub and rubbed its fragrance across Mallory's wrist, then Lucy's wrist, and behind my own ears. "Nature's perfume…smells like intense jasmine mixed with gardenia."

I could still smell the fragrance when the six of us took off in the convertible down the bumpy drive, although really, there were seven of us counting the new life in Lucy. As Peter drove west into the blinding sun, I turned for relief, looking behind me at the row of sun-bronzed faces in the backseat. I wasn't going to mention that in a few days their scorched skin would peel off like the bark of the gumbo-limbo trees. Instead, I laughed at Mallory's long hair blowing wildly in the breeze, and at Henry batting it out of his face.

As we arrived on Captiva—the sister island that holds hands with Sanibel by way of a small bridge—Peter pulled off to the side of the road at a spot called Blind Pass. How could he not with the hot-pink beach ball of a sun dropping into the Gulf of Mexico. We didn't plan to get out of the car, but taking after me, the girls flung the door open, and dashed out.

"Girls!" Peter called after them. "You've been at the beach all day. I was pulling over for a minute."

"Aw, Dad," they looked back with giant smiles, "tomorrow we'll be in snow. A few minutes, pretty please?"

Without bothering to open the doors, the boys, who also got their beach-related impetuousness from me, jumped out like a couple of wild mustangs, galloping toward the sand.

It was Peter and me alone in the car, like a date at a drive-in movie. Playing on the screen of a sky in front of us was the longest-running, most beloved masterpiece of all time, starring the sun and the sea.

I didn't want it to end, but if I made a big deal of my homesickness, mentioned it to Peter and he felt the same, then Sanibel and the little house on stilts would be no more than a movie we once enjoyed together. That troubled me. Peter remembered everything about movies, even lines word-for-word. I didn't remember the names of the movies, let alone who starred in them. Granted, I fell asleep on the couch ten minutes into them. Regardless, I never wanted to forget the details of us living in our house on stilts, fixing it up as we did, while working on our marriage and relationship with God.

Then again, God was also in Michigan, and there were sunsets there, too. It set right behind Mrs. P's house every night, bounced off her garage roof. Did she know it was there? She usually worked until long after sunset, but I wished I had pointed it out to her once, watched it with her.

"You're quiet," Peter said.

"Am I?"

"Yeah, what's going on in that mind of yours?"

"Just wishing I could freeze all of this." The sky was the color of orange and pink sherbet, and melting quickly. "I don't want it to be like a dream. I want to remember it."

"Oh, stop. Tell me you're not stressing yourself again, about forgetting stuff." He turned from the scene in front of us and looked at me like I was a cuckoo bird sitting next to him.

"What? I can't help it. I want to stay awake. I'm awake, aren't I?"

"Of course, you're awake. You're fully awake. Your eyes are wide open."

"Good," I smiled. "Years from now, when you talk about this particular sunset, I want to talk about it, too—and how we watched it on Captiva, the movie with our kids on the beach and the sun setting behind them. I don't want to be asleep on the couch right now."

He reached over and pinched my arm.

"Ouch!"

"You're awake, Adele, fully awake." He took my hand. "We need more of this, just the two of us—" he started to say, but stopped when the boys began to show signs of ferret behavior. "Guys!" he yelled at the top of his lungs, "we're going for dinner. Don't get sandy!" He shook his head and looked at me. "Sorry, what was I saying?"

"I don't remember…something along the lines of needing more of this, just the two of us. It does feel good, talking in complete sentences again." I looked out at our kids, who for most of our married life were like choo-choo trains, crashing into our sentences, derailing our words the moment they left our mouths, turning the conversations we tried having with each other into detached phrases and run-away clauses.

I appreciated time alone with Peter, but the homesickness for my kids freighted my mind, and I couldn't hold it back. "I still want choo-choo trains in our life. Don't you, Peter?"

"Choo-choo trains…what are you talking about?" He tilted his head in the direction of the kids. "Them…they're locomotives!"

"True," I said with a laugh. "I was just so busy when they were little, overwhelmed." I paused. "I know the kind of grandma I want to be, that's all."

"Aha, I see what's going on. You're worried you can't be the kind of grandma you want to be if we're here, and they're there."

"Yep."

"Well, don't you worry about that. Presents, we'll send lots of presents. You of all people know how it works…one click of the mouse, and cha-ching—teddy bear on its way, making you the best grandma in the world! Oh, and twice a year, Grandpa sends airline tickets."

"Here they come," I said as the four of them approached.

"Really quick," Peter said at accelerated speed. "I tried, but didn't get through to Charlie about the video game. Seize the moment, if you can, if you have wisdom to share with—" And like our conversations used to go, Peter's sentence ran off in a different direction. "Very nice sunset for your last night here, wasn't it?"

"I don't think the guys even saw the sunset," I said at the sight of their heads coated in sand.

We continued along a road lined with sea oats. Blame it on my wild imagination, but the sea oats were standing tall and majestic like royal guards on duty, pleased that a breeze was carrying sand from the boys' hair back to the beach, where it belonged.

I stared out at the beach. Peter wanted me to share wisdom with our son. Well, if only wisdom was like granules of sand—when the beaches eroded, they brought in more of it by the truckload, and planted sea oats to protect it. All I knew about wisdom was that it came from life experiences, and was also a gift from God. I had a few granules in me, but prayed for truckloads more.

Captiva was an enchanting island, and according to history, the place where pirates once gallivanted, conquistadors explored, and Calusa Indians declared home. After reserving a table at a festive outdoor eatery with live music, we stood waiting under a mahogany tree with silver roots and orchids yellow and ruffled.

Three girls, no bigger than five years old, hiding behind the tree trunk, kept poking their faces out, giggling and pointing at Mallory.

"What is it?" She tossed her hands up. "Is there something wrong with me?"

Charlie raised a brow. "Look at you. Your bright yellow dress and silver shoes match the tree. You look like the tree!"

All of us glanced back and forth at Mallory's outfit and the tree, and laughed so hard. When the girls poked their faces out again, Mallory did a cha-cha-cha as Peter took her picture.

"Quick," I whispered to Peter. "Take a picture of Charlie, too." I couldn't help but notice him studying the tree with wonder on his face. I wanted to remember the look of wonder on his face, as much as I did the sunset. Probably, the tree was reminding him of childhood, of his years of climbing through branches, building forts up high, and pondering life from his tire swing.

The girls wandered into a gift shop, while Peter and Henry stayed put by the band playing in the courtyard. Charlie remained in a world of his own, with his head held back, staring upward at the leaves, like he used to do until the old tire swing broke.

The restaurant was crowded, and we had to wait. I wanted to make the most of our wait time. Glancing back and forth at my son and a nearby mango tree with shimmering purple fruit peeking out from within the dense branches, I tried coming up with a reason to steal a moment alone with Charlie.

I had spent more one-on-one time with the girls the last few days than I had with the boys. It didn't bother them. Charlie wasn't standing around wishing he got more personal time with Mom. It was me who wanted more time with him.

"What?" he said, creeped out by my staring at him.

"Oh, nothing." I switched my stare back to the mango tree.

"No, really, Mom. It looked like you were thinking."

I let out a laugh. "I'm always thinking, Charlie. I don't know how to stop thinking, do you?"

He raised a brow and grinned. "Not sure, I'd have to think about it."

I went over and put my arm around him. "Hey, it's going to be another fifteen minutes before we get a table, and I left something in the car. Come with me for the walk, will you?"

I didn't leave anything in the car, but hopefully God didn't mind the white lie of a mother wanting a moment with her kid. We did whatever it took, just as Charlie in kindergarten white lied about being sick when he wanted to spend the day at home with me. When he was still faking sick in first grade, I insisted he use honesty instead. Second-grade Charlie got right to the point, begging me to take him on days out. I managed a few but wished I did more. Before I knew it, middle-schooler Charlie no longer cared to be seen with me, and even lied that he was busy when I asked him out for ice cream.

Leaving the festive strip behind, we wandered down a side street lined with trees. The branches were strung with white bulbs, and glistening.

"So, what'd you forget in the car, Mom?"

I stopped, then squeezed his arm. "Sorry," I said with a shameful grin. "I didn't really forget anything."

"Okaaaaaay."

"I wanted a little time alone with you." I put my bottom lip out and made a silly pout.

"I get it, I get it. So, where are we walking to, Mom?"

"Oh, I don't know. I don't care. I love walking. You always loved walking, too. Remember how'd you'd walk to the park every day after school, but instead of playing on the slide and stuff, you played in that patch of trees?"

He hesitated. "I don't really think about it."

Oh, please, where were the fluctuations in his voice, and the sappiness in his eyes—did he not remember the patch of trees? He was always talking about it as a kid, although it wasn't a patch of trees to him, but a kingdom! I didn't want to say too much, make him wish he was alone in his room, playing his game, instead of walking with his ridiculous mother.

"I love walking," I said, stalling…stalling for wisdom to show up. Did the truck transporting it from Heaven get sidetracked on another mission? "You know what I love so much about walking?"

"What?"

"It's something we can do all through our lives, no matter our age. Around your age, when I was in college, I was always taking walks. I used to read a lot, too, and I'd take lines from the novels I was reading with me in my mind…Henry David Thoreau."

"I liked him, too…back in high school…thought-provoking. So, what's one of his quotes that you liked so much?"

Oh my, I gasped, but didn't need to gasp. As we were putting one step in front of the other, one word after the next of my favorite Thoreau quote came to me, and I recited it to my son.

"'He who sits still in a house all the time may be the greatest vagrant of all; but the saunterer, in the good sense, is no more vagrant than the meandering river, which is all the while sedulously seeking the shortest course to the sea.'"

The moment I finished, it was like someone blew a whistle for a race to begin. Charlie took off in a short sprint—one, two, three steps he took, then jumped high enough to clear a hurdle. Still at the starting point, I studied the ground for whatever triggered him. Sure enough, on the road near my feet was what looked like a pair of nude-colored pantyhose.

"You get that from your father, you know," I called down the road to him. "But don't worry. It's a snake skin."

He cautiously walked back. "No snake, are you sure?"

"No snake, just the skin, I promise."

Charlie shook his head. "Dad and I took off sprinting after seeing one just like it yesterday. The day before, too. We're getting in shape, but what's with the snake skins? They're all over the place."

"'Tis the season, I guess, the season for shedding." I hooked arms with him as we walked, leaving the skin behind. I couldn't help but think, *everything in creation has a relevant life lesson of its own waiting to be appreciated.* "How about you, Charlie? Have you been shedding?"

"What are you talking about, Mom? People don't shed."

"Sure, they do." *Those who grow in Christ undergo a natural shedding. In the process of being renewed in the knowledge of the Creator's image, they naturally drop certain things that no longer fit,* I thought but didn't say. I didn't want to overdo it. "You know what I sometimes do?"

"What?"

"I look back at where I've walked, at the path I've come down. What have I shed? What have I left behind? If there's nothing lying on the ground behind me—no old skin, so to speak—am I growing?"

"Unique of you, Mother."

"Thank you," I laughed. "I'll take that as a compliment. But you have a special way of seeing things, too…that patch of trees!"

"It was a long time ago," he said, monotone. "I see nothing but trees now."

"You still take walks, don't you?"

"Not really, no."

"Oh, Charlie, you should. You loved walking in nature. Never forget how much you loved that."

We came to another spectacular tree, perfectly situated to be used for God's majestic purposes. "Look at that royal poinciana tree!"

"What's so royal about it?" Charlie said. "It doesn't have leaves. Are you sure it's not dead?"

"Dormant phase," I said. "Mallory thought the plumeria tree in our yard was dead. But it's in its dormant phase, too, and soon, that plumeria, like this here royal poinciana, will grab the attention of every person walking by."

He went up to the leafless, dead-looking tree. "You think you're overly optimistic?"

"Nope. I'll come out here in a few months and take pictures...text them to you. I've seen it in books, but can't wait to see it, with my own two eyes, explode in vibrant orange petals. It'll stop people in their tracks, and they'll ooh and ahh over it, as if watching fireworks."

"Really?"

"Yep, but guess what?"

"What?" His back was to me, and his face to the tree.

"In order for that to happen, it first had to let go of its leaves. I'm sounding like a writer who should be putting this stuff on paper instead. But I'm also your mother. I can't help it."

"Let me guess. I have to drop the video game in order for new things to break through."

"Oh Charlie, you're so in-depth, *you* should be the writer! But for the trees, dropping stuff is simple. They don't have to think. It just happens. Us, on the other hand, or for me, it's never that simple. I don't like to drop things. And even when I do, nothing exciting happens right away. I've learned to appreciate the dormant phase."

"Where are you learning your tree facts, Mom?"

"Nature books," I said as we continued walking. "I'm also reading Grandma FinFin's Bible, and taking lots of walks. I like to pray when I walk. Daddy doesn't like me getting overly dramatic, but God is everywhere I put my eyes. Even in the tree branches, there's evidence of His wisdom."

"What about that tree?" He pointed. "I know you're dying to tell me about it."

"A gumbo-limbo tree."

He stepped up to the fifty-foot tree with twisted limbs and rubbed his fingers along its thin, peeling trunk. "So, what's the lesson here?"

Beneath its reddish rough bark, there was a smooth green under-bark. "Only because you asked...God doesn't just see our rough, messy exterior. He sees the smoothness hidden underneath. It's a process, but He helps us peel away the bark."

"That's all? What else?"

I looked up at the leaves. "It's deciduous. You know what that means, right?"

"Yeah, but tell me anyway."

"Deciduous trees already start their sprouting while the old leaves are still dropping."

He made a face, like he didn't understand the significance, or the lesson I had in mind.

"We don't always have to wait, Charlie. The moment we drop things, we already get to experience new things sprouting."

He raised a brow, like I was reaching too far. "We're people, not trees. For the trees, everything is easy. For us, nothing is."

"So true, my son. It's hard letting go of certain things…easier holding on." I shook my head. "But we don't have to let go alone. They probably taught you back in Sunday school…it's like a game of catch with God. You throw it not once, but a hundred times, not because He doesn't catch it, but that's what playing catch with your Father is all about. It's a daily thing, and you get better and better at it, while spending time together and building that relationship."

Charlie walked off, and I followed him over to the dark, slender trunk of a twenty-foot lush and leafy tree that in the moonlight was bursting with intense purple flowers.

"So, what's with this tree?"

"A purple glory tree in full bloom…pruned today, in fact." I pointed to a pile of droppings on the side of the road.

"But it's in full bloom. Why would it need pruning when it's already blooming?"

"Oh, I don't know…for enhancement purposes."

Only because he was staring at me like it was still my turn, I said more. "I'm no expert, but when things are going well—blooming in some area of my life—that's when I feel God's pruning hand the most, you know. So yes, even though the purple glory tree is in full bloom, it still underwent pruning. I don't think God's pruning is only corrective. It's progressive, too. But regardless, it's always with great purpose."

I never enjoyed waiting for a table as much as I did then, and could have gone on walking from tree to tree across the entire island, playing our game until morning. We didn't want the others to wait on us, though, and headed back to the sound of distant music.

"So," Charlie said as we turned down the street that the restaurant was on, "I do sometimes think about that patch of trees at the park."

I smiled that the child in him was coming out.

"When you were working, Grandma FinFin didn't like me going to the park alone, so she'd follow me there and sit on that bench. Sometimes I'd sit with her, and she'd tell me everything she knew about the Kingdom of God. I'd listen for a while, then run off into the trees...the kingdom, and there I'd talk with the king." He laughed self-consciously.

"Let me guess. Was the oak tree the king?"

He made a face, like I shouldn't have asked such a thing. "No, Jesus. Jesus was the King."

My heart skipped a beat. "What about the girls, and Henry, did they sit on the bench with FinFin...and hear about the kingdom?"

"The girls didn't go much to the park. And Henry, he went, but was obsessed with the monkey bars. We couldn't get him off. But yeah, once Grandma FinFin started bringing treats, he'd sit long enough to eat and listen. He believed in the Kingdom, too. Grandma FinFin made sure."

"What do you mean—she made sure?"

"She made sure we knew the basics—that He died for us, was buried, and rose, and that those who believe are a part of the Kingdom. She introduced us to Jesus on that bench, but after that, she told us it was up to us to accept Him into our hearts or not, and we did. Henry, too."

I didn't know what to say, but glanced up at the sky, hoping Mom was looking out at us through a window in Heaven. I wanted to thank her. When I was in the hustling, bustling phase, trying to get it all done, she was in the sitting, resting stage, and happening upon little ears that were hungry for Truth.

"To be honest, Mom," by then we had reached the hostess stand as the others were sitting down, "I do miss it. I do."

"It's still there, Charlie. You know that, right? It's with you, in you."

"I know," he nodded. "I know."

We sat down, and the waiter poured my water, although I could have filled it to the brim with tears of joy. I held those tears in, however, for another time...closet time alone with the One who promised good things.

Instead, I talked, laughed, and savored our outdoor family dinner, and afterward, our ride home in the moonlight.

Oh Lord, I pray for those who believed as children—who entered Your Kingdom long ago, but for all sorts of reasons, never grew up, maturing in faith. When a royal poinciana tree has no leaves, it's still a royal poinciana. They're still Your children, but I pray they learn to walk with You, and talk with You, and grow in their relationship with You. Meet them wherever they are, and may the dormancy end. Cut them loose from the snares so they blossom, and not just blossom but reveal to the world Your royal and majestic presence in their lives.

SIXTY-FIVE

INTERIOR DESIGN TIDBIT

* * *

Undress your windows. Pull down cumbersome window treatments.
The view out your window is more important than what you try
dressing it up with.

"And, they're off," Peter said like a sports announcer, his hands in the air, as we watched their plane leaving down the runway. "There they go, just like that…can't even see them anymore."

I didn't want to worry, but worst-case scenarios played in my mind. What if there's a mechanical problem, a lightning storm, a lunatic on board, a sick person coughing on the plane?

"Birds of the air," I mumbled beneath my breath. "Think birds of the air, and stop worrying."

But a few short months from then, the birds of the air would be taking off, too. It was almost time for the ospreys to abandon their big stick nest outside our front door, leave on their own extraordinary flight north for the summer.

Peter knew the look on my face. "They'll be back before you know it," he put his arm around me, nudging me away from the window, "and probably this fall."

Who—the kids or the birds—and what if they didn't make it back come fall? What if the dangers, the difficulties of this world got in their way, altering, delaying, preventing them from returning to the tropics and to me on my front porch, nose to the screen, watching the skies, waiting?

Is this how You feel, I privately prayed as Peter and I walked arm-in-arm through the airport. *When Your children take off, do You weep and long for their hearts' return?*

Usually, it was me who liked checking out the gift shops, but Peter pulled me over to a magazine rack. "Check this out!" He pointed to a do-it-yourself outdoor shower featured on the cover. "What do you think, should we make it our next project?"

I knew what he was up to. He wanted to get me distracted with a new project, so I wouldn't want to move back to Michigan. But as much as I loved Sanibel, I wanted to be gone come summer, like the ospreys, and still gone in the fall when they returned. I didn't want to hear the cries of the hatchlings while missing the cries of my grand-chick up north.

"What do you say?" Peter flipped open the magazine to a two-page spread featuring a variety of outdoor rinsing areas. "We can work on it together, start it today. You like these?"

"Nah, I'm not feeling it." I wrinkled my nose then spotted a rack of infant onesies.

Peter flipped open to more do-it-yourself outdoor rinsing areas. "It's too early for baby clothes. C'mon, this is the perfect project for us. Which one do you like here?"

I stared at the pictures for a good three seconds. "This one is nice. But why not use a hose...park a bench in the hose area, sit down and rinse our legs that way?"

But as he was about to put the magazine down, I saw it in his eyes. He wanted more...more time alone with me. After sharing me with four others for two decades, I couldn't blame him for wanting more.

"Okay, I'm in. Let's do it. Let's go home and build us an outdoor shower."

We left the airport and went straight to the home improvement store, and in record time hauled to the register two shopping carts filled with supplies, including three small outdoor benches. As Peter watched the dollar amount going up with each scanned item, he was probably wishing he had asked me out on a dinner date instead.

When his face turned red as a tomato, I removed the handheld sprayer from the pile. "We don't need this."

"You're right. We can use the garden hose."

Once home, we arranged the three wooden benches into an incomplete square, then filled the middle ground with stones smooth to the feet. While whistling in a distinctive, high-pitched, two-tone sound, like the fulvous whistling duck, Peter hammered wooden posts into the backs of the benches, then hoisted the garden hose down the wooden piling. I hung a line from the frame.

"We could have gone without the curtain, too," Peter said as I pulled the weather-proof turquoise curtain from the bag. "We could always return it. Do we need a shower curtain? We're going to have bathing suits on."

"Showers and curtains…the two go together, they do. Of course, we need it, and besides, the cabana stripes give it that resort feeling."

The magazine claimed it was a one-day project. After the curtain was hung, we kept going, making trips to and from the car, pulling out large seashell-shaped stepping stones, arranging them in a path leading to the shower area. The magazine also claimed that outdoor showers needed signs. I painted the word *shower* on an arrow-shaped wooden board.

"Great," Peter laughed when he saw it. "Now beach bums will be showing up at our place to clean off."

But we weren't done yet. I hung silver pineapple towel hooks on one of the wooden posts, while he attached an adjustable mirror on another.

"Project complete," I declared, hoping Peter had forgotten about the one last item still in the trunk.

"Hey, what about my clock? Let's not forget the clock."

The handsome, large, copper-framed clock was the one and only item we bought that wasn't on the pages of the magazine, and the only item he picked out for himself. But even as we hung it, it bothered me. The loud ticking was going to clash with the cacophony of the tree frogs, lizards, and crickets by night, and the euphony of the birds by day. Then again maybe, just maybe, it would stop Peter from whistling.

Once the clock was hung, we took several steps back to admire our project complete from afar.

"Do you love it?" Peter put his arm around me.

"Yep, love it!"

"Good, it cost a fortune. Let's hope I get my bonus."

I gasped. "Well, it was your idea. And we didn't need the clock."

"I know, I know. I take full responsibility. The whole thing was my idea. Just saying, things are expensive. Nothing's for free, that's all."

We stood there—*tick, tick, tick*—another minute and counting, and I liked the outdoor rinsing area, except for that clock. We lived on an island—*tick, tick, tick*—who cared about time? It meant we were getting older—*tick, tick, tick*—did we want to hear the seconds of our lives ticking by?

The next day, Peter had reports due by noon. I went down with binder and pen, and sat on the bench of the outdoor rinsing area. My feet weren't sandy but I turned the hose on, letting the water refresh my legs. The morning sun was shining on a nearby low-growing, ever-blooming shrub with seven-sided stems and one-inch thorns. I had looked it up in my nature book, and it was called crown of thorns—*Euphorbia milii.* I also happened to read about another crown of thorns…in the Bible.

> "They stripped him and put a scarlet robe on him, and then twisted together a crown of thorns and set it on his head. They put a staff in his right hand and knelt in front of him and mocked him. 'Hail, king of the Jews!' they said."
> —Matthew 27:28—29

I had never taken a trip to the Holy Land, never stepped foot in Israel, but the barbed succulent got me thinking. And even though I had to block out the noise and distraction of the irksome ticking clock, soon I went there, heart and mind, to the crown of thorns pricking into Jesus' head. Time was irrelevant. I closed my eyes and was there with Him, walking the hill on the outskirts of Jerusalem, toting my sin and burdens along.

Tick, tick, tick. "Two more reports to submit and we're beachward bound," Peter called down from the porch. "Just know I'm hurrying."

"No worries, I'm good."

I was better than good—going somewhere special, going to the cross. It wasn't my first time. I went when I was younger, back when I confessed with my lips, and believed in my heart. And I returned home with a souvenir…the gift of salvation.

But who said the cross was a one-time visit? It was like going to the beach. I went to Lake Michigan as a girl and couldn't wait to go back, and so I did all through my life, every summer, several times a summer. I went to the beach last week, in fact, and again a day ago, because what beach lover said, "I stood at the shore once, breathing its air, letting its droplets splash and refresh me. But once was enough. I'm never going to the beach again."

Never heard a beach lover say that, nor a Jesus lover say, "I kneeled at the foot of the cross once, breathing in eternal life, while letting the cleansing blood of Jesus wash over me. But once was enough. I'm never going to the cross again."

It was my third, fourth, fifth time visiting a place, or while reading about it again and again that I learned more facts, appreciating details I hadn't before. I opened my eyes and looked over at the crown-of-thorns shrub in my yard. Every time I read the gospel, I learned and appreciated new things. If I was a student, and the cross a field trip, and the teacher asked me one take-home message, it was that no matter how undeserving I was, I was loved. Thanks to God's love and Jesus dying for my sins, I didn't have to go through everyday life far away from God.

I turned the water off, and with my legs drying in the sun, scribbled out a summary of what I had been reading and appreciating in the Bible —how our access to God changed from Old Testament to New, thanks to Jesus.

The temple in Jerusalem had three special parts: the courts where all the people were allowed; the Holy Place, where only priests could enter; and the Most Holy Place, a small room where God's presence was.

The Most Holy Place was the most sacred spot on Earth for the Jews. But only the high priest alone could enter it. The other priests and people were forbidden to enter this small room in the temple where God's presence was.

It contained the Ark of the Covenant—a gold-covered chest containing the original stone tablets on which the Ten Commandments were written, a jar of manna, and Aaron's staff.

"Thank you, Jesus," I said out loud. "I don't have to know God from the outer courts of my life. It's like the Most Holy Place is in me, where the Holy Spirit lives."

"Are you talking to me?" Peter said down from the porch.

"No."

"Okay, well, I'm on my final report. Be thinking about the next project you want us working on…we can start it today, after the beach."

My mind went to curtains, and not the musty ones long since pulled off the windows of Lovely Dwelling, but a certain curtain that hung in the

Jerusalem temple. *Cumbersome curtains must come down*, Viv insisted in one of her tidbits. If only she knew what happened to the curtain in the temple the moment Jesus died on the cross.

Writing helped me process things. I jotted down a summary of what I had been learning about that curtain in the temple.

A heavy curtain hung across the entrance from the Holy Place to the Most Holy Place. Once a year, the high priest was allowed to cross to the other side of this curtain and enter the room with God's presence. Offering a sacrifice, he would use the animal's blood to atone first for his own sins and then for the sins of the people.

I held my pen still and stared at the turquoise cabana curtain. Peter was right when he said things were expensive, but not so right when he said nothing was for free. Jesus, sacrificing His life to atone for my sins, didn't cost me a dime. And even though it sounded too good to be true, especially in a culture where money was always involved and there were hidden costs to everything, God's love was true. So true that He sent us His Son, who paid the price in full. I wanted to call up to Peter, tell him, yes, the work on the house was costing money. But there wasn't going to be an invoice for the work God was doing in us.

It would cost money for us to visit Michigan, and the kids to visit Florida, but we didn't need expensive plane tickets to reach Golgotha, or a time machine to experience that moment when Jesus was crucified. No matter if I was washing dishes, walking along the shore, sitting in the yard staring at that crown-of-thorns shrub—the cross was within reach, although often it entailed a walk, a personal walk leading to it.

> "In about the sixth hour, darkness came over the whole land until the ninth hour, for the sun stopped shining. And the curtain of the temple was torn in two. Jesus called out with a loud voice, 'Father, into your hands I commit my spirit.' When he had said this, he breathed his last."
> —Luke 23:44-46

In that moment, when He took on my sin and the sins of the world, He Himself had to be separated from God.

I got up and closed the blue cabana-striped curtain around me. I didn't want Peter or the mail delivery person to find me on my knees. I didn't want anyone but the flock of birds congregating in the yard to see me with Jesus at His darkest moment on Earth—that moment when He took on my filth and the filth of the world…and because of it, was disconnected temporarily from His Holy Father. It was hard for me to imagine His pain. I imagined His love instead…His love for His father and His love for me.

The outdoor clock chimed. Jesus died at three. I heard the flapping of wings as the birds in my yard took flight. The curtain in the temple was torn. And so was the barrier of sin that separated me from God, dropped like a branch from a tree, heavy from the weight of my sin. God's love wasn't a forbidden, off-limits thing, kept hidden behind a curtain. Our Holy God made a way for us, and it was Jesus—Branch of Righteousness.

Three days later He rose from the dead. I chose long ago which side I was on, but it sure felt good to re-declare my allegiance to God's only begotten Son. I was on the side of the risen Christ in all His glory, who was face-to-face with His father on the other side of death. One day, I'd be face-to-face with them both.

Tears poured, putting my garden hose to shame. I opened the curtain and stepped out into the yard. Someone was watching me. I glanced up at the upper window next door, and sure enough, there was a set of eyes. Whoever it was—a person from the bank, or a real estate agent—must have looked down into the roofless shower and seen me kneeling, crying.

Trying to act normal, I left the shower area and wandered over to the fruit section. Mangoes galore were growing, but not on my property. I didn't let it get me down and was content with other things happening in my yard. But then, an object glistening in the sun, dangling on a nearby branch caught my eye. My salivary glands kicked into overdrive and my mouth puckered…a lemon! I didn't care who was watching. I did a lousy cartwheel. My toes weren't pointed, but it was fun.

I looked over at the window next door, and wouldn't have minded them seeing me so happy, celebrating fruit in my yard. I would have invited them over for lemonade, or better yet, homemade lemon bars. But the eyes were gone.

SIXTY-SIX

Interior Design Tidbits

* * *

*Hide treasures in the guest room—in dresser drawers, under
the bed, in the closet—for your guests to stumble upon.*

* * *

Name your guest room.

* * *

*To perk up a room and add impact, paint
one wall a special accent color.*

* * *

Put a guest book in the guest room.

In the months that followed, I didn't need the laser-cut Roman numerals of the outdoor clock reminding me of time's constant passing. It was spring when the ospreys were noisy as tea kettles, and summer when our yard went quiet, and fall when they returned, and I heard the cries of the hatchlings in the nest outside our front door.

There were cries from within Lovely Dwelling, too. Around the time the ospreys hatched, and not long after the plumeria tree in our yard was blooming pink, our first grandbaby was born in town, in the City of Palms, right over the Causeway Bridge. Peter and I had invited Lucy to spend her first year of motherhood on Sanibel, and she moved into the guest room weeks before the birth.

Although a precious year, it went by too quickly, and I wanted to fist fight against time—grab hold of its hands, pulling them back far as I could. But clocks were adjustable, time was not, and all the meddling in the world wasn't going to stop it. Even if I pulled the batteries from the clock, my foe marched forward without regard. I didn't want to sit around grieving moments gone by, but it had snuck by so quickly when my kids were little. I had to make peace with that, and all I could think of was to appreciate the outstretched moments in front of me, and see time in a different light, against the backdrop of Eternity.

Every morning I made sure to give Lucy an hour to herself. I didn't push it, but was delighted when she asked for her grandma's Bible. I then offered her two hours to herself, and as she read down on the hammock, I gave baby Laura her morning baths on the screened porch. The chicks watched from their nests and ruffled their feathers as I filled the tub with water, placed it in a sunbeam, and put Laura in. Soon, Laura mimicked the hunger cries of the ospreys, and Lucy, satisfied from having foraged on the Word of God, came back up to nurse. They were some of the best mornings of my life, but I let time fool me into thinking it had reached a glorious standstill.

"Don't bother," I told Peter, when the batteries of the outdoor clock drained. "Please don't replace them."

I preferred mornings to announce themselves with *goo goo's*, *gaga's*, and birdsong. And to know it was late afternoon as Lucy and I pushed Laura in her stroller, and saw blue herons foraging at the mangrove edges. I liked recognizing night by the scent of baby lotion filling our house, along with the fragrance of the blooming angel's trumpet drifting in through my bedroom window.

Around the time when the ospreys tried out their wings, Laura learned to crawl. It was spring, and I got all worked up when Mama, baby Laura, and the ospreys—all of them at once, it seemed—left their cozy nests tucked within the branches of the banyan tree on their flights back north.

"They'll return," Peter said when he found me out on the front porch my first morning without them, a slobbering mess, wiping my eyes, blowing my nose, and trying to sip coffee all at the same time. "They needed to leave, fly on their own, but they'll be back. You know they will."

Like that day at the airport when all four of them left at once, he urged me to start up a new project. And since we longed for more friends and family to come visit, I took his advice, making major changes to Lovely Dwelling's guest room. For starters, I hired contractors who did their thing, making it larger.

"I'm going to have fun," I said to Peter when he found me in the near-finished guest room, roller in hand, ready to paint over the baby-girl pink after its year as a nursery, "nothing but fun with this one wall!"

He looked into the open can of paint, then puckered. "*Yellow?*"

"Yep, like the lemons in our yard, only this wall."

It stayed yellow for a year. After that, I made it my tradition to paint that wall a new color every single fall, and we came to know fall by its changing color. Mallory, Charlie, and Henry all came for visits of their own, and every spring through fall, we welcomed a steady stream of friends and family. My brother and his wife were a great surprise. And old Mrs. P, who after the passing of Mr. P, took me up on the offer and came for a week.

I kept the Bible, along with Grandma FinFin's letters to God in the drawers of the old changing table converted back into a desk. It added significant impact to the room, and when my guests stumbled upon such treasures in the drawers, it sparked spirited conversations about things we normally wouldn't have talked about. Something I never knew about Mrs. P, for instance, was that she was a closet Christian. She came out openly while visiting, told me she had fallen away for years, but returned herself to the Lord, to the One who eagerly awaits our returns.

On top of the desk, I kept a guest book that I called *Seasons on Sanibel*, and invited everyone who stayed with us to write about their time on the island. Maybe in the winter they found themselves at the refuge, standing a foot away from a hooded merganser, or spotting an elusive mangrove, peeking down at them from an overhead branch. Or in the spring, got a kick out of watching a black-necked stilt flaunting its bright pink legs.

I loved reading what they wrote in that guest book. One person wrote how they came to the island to get away from it all, and ended up encountering God—and the Holy Spirit wasn't as elusive as they had thought. Perhaps in response to it, my next guest, however, wrote how they sat on a bench in the summer, staring into nothing but a stagnant swamp.

I prayed for my guests before they checked in, and after they checked out. For that person who saw nothing but a stagnant swamp, I knew their history, and prayed for their return to that season in their life when they walked and talked with God. *Fly birdie, fly, to the Branch of Righteousness, like a great blue heron returning to the refuge in the fall.*

"It's that time of year again, isn't it?" Peter came into the room and found me spreading a protective tarp over my two-tone white-and-cherry desk with turned legs. "So, what's it going to be this year? Would you like me to try and guess?"

"You wouldn't in a million years, Peter."

"How about a hint or two?"

"Vivienne."

"Uh oh, should I be nervous?" He gave me a silly grin, then left the room, choosing to be surprised instead.

When I removed the lid from the can of paint, I gasped at how dramatic the color was. But there was a story behind it, which I couldn't wait to share. As I stirred it with the wooden stick, round and round, I gave glory to God for the story. I poured a fair amount of the bold-colored paint into the pan, then dipped the roller in. It looked spectacular on the wall, and since my zing, my zestfulness wasn't what it once was, this would be the last time I painted the guest room wall.

But what a brilliant color!

I held the paint roller still. The magnitude of the story behind the color sent tremors up and down my spine. Long story short, I had sent Viv my finished manuscript. For the longest time, I waited and waited, but never heard back. Until one day, postcards from San Francisco—of cable cars, and Grace Cathedral, Alcatraz, and the wharf—one after the next, arrived in my mailbox. And then, I got it. I got the text: *The bird with the golden slippers.*

It had me speed dialing her number, heading down the front porch steps, then strolling for hours up and down the road, phone to my ear. Her postcards only gave so much detail, and I needed to know more. The way she described things on the phone with me, I felt like I was there with her as she rode those cable cars up and down the steep hills in pursuit of God, then heard Him whispering in her ear how much He loved her as she walked the labyrinth on the floor of Grace Cathedral, and sat crying out with the sea lions at the wharf, and dropping to her knees in a solitary confinement cell at Alcatraz.

"Would you mind if I kept your postcards in a desk drawer in my guest room...treasures for my guests to find?"

"Desk drawer! The stuff I wrote on those postcards is the stuff novels are made of. Start a new book, and make me another one of your characters! I don't care how you do it, just let your readers know I found what I was searching for, and no exaggeration, He's real. I swear that God is real!"

I ran right up into the house, into Villa FinFin. No one was visiting. I sat down at the desk and wrote it all down. In my own words, but using Viv's voice to the best of my ability, I wrote all that she shared with me about transformational encounters she'd had in San Francisco with God's presence, Truth, and love. Who knew if it was going to turn into anything or not, but it sure was fun to write!

When the wall was done, I was out of breath. I put the roller down, then walked over to the desk and pulled off the protective tarp. Opening the drawer with Viv's postcards, I pulled one out and held it up to the freshly painted wall. The colors were exact!

SIXTY-SEVEN

* * *

"You are the light of the world. A city on a hill cannot be hidden. Neither do people light a lamp and put it under a bowl. Instead they put it on its stand, and it gives light to everyone in the house. In the same way, let your light shine before men, that they may see your good deeds and praise your Father in Heaven."
—Matthew 5:14-16

Hi Addie,

Here's the postcard I promised to send. As you know from my text, I did it. I walked the Golden Gate Bridge all the way across, and I kid you not, it was a golden-slippered, snowy egret moment for me!

You love details, so here it goes. It was late when I got to the bridge. The sun was diving ridiculously fast into the Pacific, and the city skyline flickering behind me. Good thing I stepped foot onto its eastern walkway right before they closed it to pedestrians for the night.

In case it shows up in a game of trivia, orange vermillion is the color of the bridge. International Orange, the paint is called. No one ever intended to paint the Golden Gate Bridge its reddish orange. It was meant to be the sealant until everybody went bonkers over it, unanimously preferring it over the boring old silver or gray they were planning.

And to think, the Navy had suggested it be painted black with yellow stripes. Can you imagine the Golden Gate Bridge in black and yellow stripes? God did better than good when He picked that combination for the bumblebees, but I wouldn't want to see it on a bridge.

Sorry for my color tangent, but hear me out. Regarding that guest room of yours, if you add hints of icy blue to the room, the bold and vibrant color of the Golden Gate Bridge would look spectacular on one of its walls. I'd go for it if I were you. Be a daredevil. But tell Peter it's the color of the royal poinciana flowers, so he doesn't get mad at me. Nah, don't lie. If Peter doesn't like it, let me know and I'll send him a box of Ghirardelli chocolates.

So, where was I? Oh yeah, walking heel-to-toe, for real, the bridge that in my recurrent dream I never made it across. The sun was dropping, and so was the temperature of the ocean air. Gusts of wind were slapping me in the face. One foot in front of the other, I was doing it, though. I was walking the 1.7-mile bridge that stretched from the northern tip of the San Francisco Peninsula to Marin County, which they say is about 8,981 feet.

But then a telephone caught my eye. I was halfway across when the sight of it sent chills up my spine. More people die by suicide at the Golden Gate Bridge than any other site in the world. The phone was part of a suicide prevention initiative. It was in my dream, too. I never told you this, but it was the point where I'd always wake up, and from there, spend hours contemplating whether or not I even wanted to continue my walk through this scary, crazy world.

You know that list you sent me a while back—the descriptive names for the Father, Son, and Holy Spirit—I call on them twenty-four-seven.

But I already wrote to you about all of that in the postcard and letter leading up to this one, so back to my "bird in the golden slippers" moment on the bridge. There, at the halfway mark, I went to the railing and looked out at the bay. There were sailboats anchoring for the night, and a large container ship passing under, heading into the Pacific. I didn't want to look straight down, but I did. To jump from where I was would have been fatal, and I already knew what it was like to hit that hard place in life, sinking way down into the dark phases of spiritual hypothermia with numbness toward God.

As I stared down at the water, which was nearly 245 feet below, it made the deck of the bridge I was standing on feel oh-so high! I looked back and forth at where I had come from and where I was going, and the 1.7-mile bridge seemed so long. I peeked up at its two towers rocketing 746 feet into the sky above me, and it was all so lofty. Turning my back to the bay, I let my eyes travel the six lanes to the ocean side, 90 feet wide from here to there. The bridge was so wide!

I took a deep breath, trying to wrap my mind around just how wide and long and high and deep the love of Christ is, but there are no dimensions by which to measure His uncontainable love!

It's ENORMOUS. God's love is wide enough to cover the breadth of our experiences, long enough to span the length of our lives, high enough to rise to the elevated heights of all our celebrations, and deep enough to reach us at our depths of despair.

I glanced over at that phone. Thank you, Savior, Lord, King of Kings, Lamb of God, Life, Light of the World, Living One, Refuge, Jesus. You heard my crisis call!

You already know, Addie, about the encounter I had during my tour of Alcatraz, but as I stood on the bridge, looking out at the federal penitentiary on its own island in the bay, all I could do was praise my Savior for what He did. The currents in my life had washed me so far out, to where I was getting blown about by this wave and that. But God heard the foghorn going off in my heart, and dispatched His only begotten Son, sending Him to span the distance from Heaven all the way down to the lowest place on Earth, reaching me personally.

Remember our walks around campus, and our old favorite St. Augustine phrase—
Solvitur ambulando.
It is solved by walking.
Funny how we added two words of our own:
It is solved by walking…**and talking**.
I've come to appreciate it with yet two more words added:
It is solved by walking…**and talking with God**.
While walking the bridge, I kept hearing it in my mind, one of God's great restoration tidbits:

> "If my people, which are called by my name, shall humble themselves, pray and seek my face and turn from their wicked ways, then I will hear from heaven, and will heal their land."
> —2 Chronicles 7:14

Long story short, I'm seeing certain things in my own life solved by walking and talking with God, humbling myself, praying, seeking His face, and turning from my wicked ways. It works.

I don't want to bore you, but just as you love your Sanibel nature, I love my City by the Bay, and all of its details. Everything I look at—the dimensions of the bridge, even—has been turning my thoughts to God, the God of Restoration, who loves His people, and wants to return things not to how they used to be, but to even greater glory than before.

The older I get, the more I appreciate history (lol), so bear with me, please.

Before the bridge was built, the only practical route between the city of San Francisco and what is now Marin County was by boat across a section of the bay, until the ferry service began in the early 1820s.

And before Jesus came to Earth, the only route to God (after the fall) was through obeying His laws.

People could hardly imagine it possible that a bridge could be built across the 6,700-foot strait that connects the San Francisco Bay with the Pacific Ocean. It was too full of swirling tides, scary currents, ferocious winds, and blinding fog.

And who could have imagined the miracle of God sending His Eternal Word all the way from Heaven to Earth!

The bridge faced opposition, including litigation from several sources. The Department of War was concerned the bridge would interfere with ship traffic. The Navy feared that a ship collision or sabotage to the bridge could block the entrance to one of its main harbors. Unions demanded guarantees that local workers would be favored for construction jobs. And Southern Pacific Railroad—one of the most powerful business interests in California—opposed the bridge as competition to its ferry fleet. They filed a lawsuit against the project.

God's own solution—Jesus as the bridge intimately linking us to Him— faced opposition, too. God moved forward with His plan, anyway, and His plan was perfectly accomplished.

As I picked up pace, power walking the rest of the way across, I prayed that just as the bridge was declared by so many a modern wonder of the world, that in our hearts Jesus would be declared the greatest wonder of the universe, and recognized as God's solution for restoration.

You say you want to visit me in California, and I hope you do. In the meantime, like a tour guide, I'll keep filling you in on all the amazing details, so you feel like you're here.

Upon the bridge's 1937 completion, it was declared a miraculous engineering achievement. They did it. And it's no small thing to be walking with my own two feet on the internationally recognized symbol of San Francisco—the bridge that so many didn't believe possible.

My own efforts could never span long enough, wide enough, or high enough to get me across to the other side, from this world into Heaven. Realizing the depths of my sin has helped me appreciate the depths of God's love within me.

If some were to read this, I'd sound like a nutcase. No offense, but I used to think you were a nutcase, my friend, talking the way you did at times. But now I get it, and it's nice to know I can be as dramatic as I want with you. Both of us get it.

I looked up at the cables running between the two anchorages, and at the vertical wire cables spanning the length of the bridge. They were suspending the deck on which I was crossing, and were under constant tension. But the weight they were bearing was evenly distributed, thanks to the bridge's amazingly engineered design. The main cables passing over the towers were stretched, but they were built to absorb tension forces, and the suspender cables were spaced out so that no one cable was ever under enough stress to snap free.

Religions and bridges, there's all different types in the world. Talking about the major ones, there's beam bridges, cantilever bridges, arch bridges, truss bridges, cable-stayed bridges. I'm walking the suspension bridge.

And how amazing is the symmetry of the suspension bridge, with all its details working together to create its internal balance. If one part is compromised, the entire structure fails.

It's what I love most about the design of Christianity—the members of the Trinity all working together. Each plays a different role in bearing my weight, and holding me up as I walk through this frigid world so full of swirling currents, whipping winds, and blinding fog.

When I was almost there, about to reach the other side, and right before I texted you, the bird with the golden slippers, *I did something kind of wild, something I could see us doing together. I stopped walking, and with the city sparkling behind me, I reached my arms high over my head, then clasped my hands together. People walking by probably thought it was a yoga pose, but it wasn't. Pointing my fingers upward like a steeple, I closed my eyes and marveled.*

Why did I marvel?

I'll tell you why.

There's a universe
and within that universe,
are billions of galaxies,
one being the Milky Way.
Within that galaxy are planets, like Earth.
And on that planet are continents, such as North America.
Within that continent are countries, like America.
And within that country are states like Florida and California.
And within those states are cities like Sanibel and San Francisco.
And within those cities are women who love to walk and talk.
But within those walking, talking women
is something larger than the universe,
more energetic than the spinning galaxies,
and more radiant than the galactic stars.
Something more brilliant than the planets,
more glistening than the oceans surrounding North America,
more liberating than the freedoms of America,
more beautiful than the royal poinciana flowers on Sanibel
and the poppies of California,
more golden even than the bridge of San Francisco,
or the feet of the snowy egret.
Within them dwells the Spirit of Christ!
And wherever they go,
the Spirit is at home in them, and they are at home in Him.
They are walking temples of the Holy Spirit.

SIXTY-EIGHT

"For we know that when this earthly tent we live in is
taken down—when we die and leave these bodies—
we will have a home in Heaven, an eternal body made
for us by God himself and not by human hands."
—2 Corinthians 5:1

I was standing like Viv with my eyes closed, arms stretched overhead, palms together, fingers pointing upward like a steeple, when Peter came into the room.

"Wow," he said of the freshly painted wall behind me. "And what's with you...trying yoga?"

I let out a never-mind laugh and brought my arms down. "It's the color of the Golden Gate Bridge, and if you don't like it, Viv will send you chocolates."

He turned the overhead fan on, then took a few steps back. "I like it, but tell her I'll still take the chocolates."

We let the room dry overnight and the next morning, after pushing the furniture back into place, Peter and I left for the beach. Before turning onto the road at the end of our drive, I glanced back at Lovely Dwelling and let out an exhausted sigh.

"What's wrong?"

"Oh nothing, just all the never-ending effort and upkeep we've put into this place."

"Yeah, but we've enjoyed it, for the most part."

"True, but look at it," I said of its aged patina. The front porch steps needed replacing, as did the roof, and the peeling front door was begging for a paint job…again. "It always needs work. It's never done. And the things we've already done, they need doing again."

"Tug-o-war," Peter said, taking my hand. "Aren't you the one who always says that so much of life is a continuous game of tug-o-war?"

I nodded. He was right, I did always say that. It was with restoration on one side, deterioration on the other.

As always, when we arrived at the beach, we slipped our flip flops off, then headed to the shore, stepping ankle-deep into the Gulf of Mexico. If it weren't for the invisible biting bugs, it would have been close to perfect, but it wasn't perfect. Nothing was perfect. Homes falling apart, blood-sucking midges, plastic littering the beaches, red tide, fungus on the trees, white powdery mildew all over my cape honeysuckle shrub, and more than anything, the bodies of people deteriorating, and departing from the world.

"I know You never promised things on Earth would be perfect," I mumbled beneath my breath to God, hoping to get out of my deteriorating mood. "But You promised other things…good things!"

"Talking to me?" Peter said, a few feet away.

I shook my head with a laugh.

"I don't mean to interrupt if you're talking to God, but look what I found—your favorite shell."

I went over, and as he put it in my hand, I hid my disappointment that one of its wings was broken off and the other one chipped. "What's the name of this shell?"

"It's your favorite," he said again, like I should have known. "An angel wing."

"I meant its scientific name."

Peter shrugged his shoulders. "You know I don't know the scientific names of any of the shells."

"Yeah, but I usually do, especially this one. Let me think." I held it in the palm of my hand, staring at the elaborately etched, artistic masterpiece that looked dropped down from Heaven. "I can't believe I don't remember…I don't remember its scientific name!"

"Call it an angel wing. No big deal, it's an angel wing."

I wanted to believe that he was right, and it was no big deal. Whether I knew its scientific name or not, I could appreciate it the same. I slipped it into my pocket, even though I already had lots of them at home. It didn't matter that the blue canning jars on my windowsills were filled to the brim with shells, as were the woven seagrass baskets beside the sofa, and the silver pails on our front porch. There was no such thing as having too many seashells!

Peter and I walked out, shin deep.

"Too many" only became a problem when the vessels were no longer able to contain the increasing treasures, or when the vessels themselves corroded. I didn't like that everything from the silver pails I kept my shells in, to the wooden porch steps of our house on stilts, to the bodies that housed us all, eventually corroded, or eroded, or deteriorated.

I took hold of Peter's hand and we went further out, knee deep into the water. Nothing obtained in life lasted longer than righteousness. God was His Word and His Word was within me. Like the silver pail holding my shells, my body was the earthly container holding my God-given treasures. I just didn't like that the pail and my body were already corroding.

But God promised a new and everlasting body that would forever hold my contents. And promises from scriptures were etched across the surface of my soul like the markings on a shell, not to be rubbed off or faded by the elements or the harshness of time.

Still, how did God do it? How, at the hour of my death, was He going to ever-so-gently transfer the nature of Christ deposited within me, and the essence of my being, into an everlasting body that would never corrode? I was about to ask Peter if he knew, but as quickly as I had thought to ask him, I forgot what it was I was even wondering about.

"Hate to say it, it's about that time." Peter looked up at the sky. He knew time by the whereabouts of the sun. "We need to head back now, don't want to be late for your appointment."

I blew a kiss across the Gulf of Mexico. "See you later, Gulf of Mexico. If I don't remember your name the next time I see you, can I call you Sea instead?"

"You're fine," Peter said to my melodramatic side. "I keep telling you, you're fine!"

He was probably right, and I should have stopped talking the way that I was. But people did that when they got older—they thought about and talked more matter-of-factly about death, as if planning their retirement.

I didn't want to retire from the world, but like it or not that type of retirement was coming for us all one day.

"Does it ever scare you, Peter?"

"What?"

"Unloading your freight, disembarking from the world."

"No, I try not to think about it. What good does it do, thinking about such things?"

I didn't answer right away. But if at my appointment in town, science was going to tell me there was no stopping or reversing my disease, and that I was reaching the end of the railroad, then I was going to want to talk about it.

"Do me a favor, Peter."

"What?"

"When the day comes, and I'm nearing the end, keep reminding me, will you? In case I forget, keep reminding me."

"Remind you of what?"

"Not to be afraid. That of all the stops, it's the depot where I meet Jesus face-to-face. Keep telling me that, will you?"

Peter nodded. "Are you sure you want to go through with this, do you even want to know the results, Adele?"

How could he ask such a thing? Of course I wanted to know! I needed to know why for the life of me I couldn't remember the scientific name for my favorite shell, or where I had left my flip flops in the sand, how in the last couple of weeks, I had lost three pairs. And what was happening to my thoughts? It was like they congregated as words on the tip of my tongue, ready to leap out into the world, only to suddenly go missing. Were those thoughts and words still in me, or abducted by the same predator that took Mom's memory?

"Yes, I want to know. I want to know what I'm up against, so I can team up with doctors, science, and treatments. Pull, pull, pull, right Peter? In the never-ending game of tug-o-war, give it your all, pulling for dear life on the side of restoration."

We were about to step into the tunnel of trees when from the corner of my eye I spotted something wrong. "Oh, no," I grabbed Peter's arm, and when he saw it, too—a bird alone and languishing with a limp near the line of sea oats, its wing a bloody mess and hanging low—he gasped along with me.

I pulled out my cell phone and called the local wildlife rehabilitation hospital, and when the volunteer answered, I told her our exact where-abouts, and how the bird could hardly hold its head up. "It's not even blinking. My husband is down on his knees in the sand, talking to it, trying to comfort it the best he can."

"We'll send someone right away. What kind of bird is it?"

I didn't answer. I wanted to, but couldn't.

"Do you happen to know what kind of bird it is?" she asked again.

"Yes." I dug my toes in the comfortably familiar sand. "Um." I put my hands in my pockets, and felt the calcium carbonate formed into a shell. "Ahh." I looked away from the bird, over at the tall, subtropical grass, at its large, golden brown seed heads blowing in the breeze, then back at the bird I'd watched dance in the shallows a million times.

"Tell her it's the bird with black legs," Peter, who never knew bird names to begin with, said, "and bright yellow feet."

"Duh, the bird with the golden slippers," I said into my phone.

"Aw, a snowy egret. We'll be there as soon as we can."

I sat down in the sand near the bird, trying to convince myself that, just like the scientific name of a shell, forgetting the name of a bird was no big deal. It was another senior moment, like when I forgot the keys to the house the week before and had to squeeze myself into the unlocked kitchen window, drop down into the deep copper basin farm sink like a big old plump turkey ready for its bath.

"Hello, snowy egret," I whispered when it opened its yellow eyes and looked at me. "I know you don't want to be sitting here all alone, hurting. You'd rather be flaunting your elegant plumes, dancing in the shallows on those long black legs and golden slippers of yours."

The bird inched toward me, then opened its long, slender beak. If only I had food, or we spoke the same language, I could have comforted it with words.

"*Croaa,*" I shrieked, "*Rassssps.*"

Peter looked at me like I was the strangest person on Earth.

I ignored him, and let out a raspy, nasal squawk.

"Are you alright?"

"Fine, making the sounds I've heard snowy egrets making."

"I would never make those sounds again, if I were you. You'll terrify the poor thing, and we don't want it flying off with that bloody wing. Why not just talk to it?"

"If you want me to, sure. You don't have to listen, though. I'd prefer you not."

"I want to, alright…not something I'd miss."

"You," I looked into its partially opened eyes, "you and all the other Sanibel birdies, you've been nothing but joy to me. You did your best, reminding me not to worry, inspiring me to perch and dance and fly instead. In the midst of the hurricane, fly, fly, fly to the center of the storm, which for me is God….my go-to calm in the midst of the storms."

"That's beautiful, darling," Peter said. "Too bad there's not a translator present, turn that into chirps."

I ignored Peter and kept going. There were words on my tongue and I wanted them to make it out into the world. "This sure makes for a beautiful habitat!" I glanced up and down the beach, miles and miles of coastland, then back at the bird. "But Planet Earth is a far cry from a perfect home for any of us. It's a scary, scary world, that's for sure! You birds, and us…we face harsh and unpredictable environments, poor water quality, declining habitat—"

"Don't forget human disturbances," Peter said. "Other than all the dangers, anything else you want to say to the snowy egret?"

"There's always more, Peter. There's always more I want to say, you know that."

"The mic is yours. Me and the bird…we're all ears, continue."

I looked at the snowy egret, which at sunrise had been living the good life, dancing in the water. Yet by sunset, might not be around to see another day. Did any of us know whether we'd be around for another sunset, sunrise, or to see the white pelicans returning in the fall? Or the abundance of shorebirds in the winter, or the mating plumage of the birds come spring? Would we be here for the arrival of the warblers before summer?

"I know what I can do," I said of my impromptu moment, in which Peter had given me the mic and, without admitting it, wanted more. "How about I recite something?"

"Sure, what do you want to recite?"

"A Bible verse…one I've been memorizing for months now. You're going to like it. It's strangely relevant. Then again, aren't they all?"

He went from a sitting position down onto his back in the sand, hands behind his head. "Go ahead." He closed his eyes.

"Okay, then," I looked up at a cloud thinly stretched across half the sky, "words from the Apostle Paul's letter to the Corinthians—

"'We grow weary in our present bodies, and we long for the day when we will put on our heavenly bodies like new clothing. For we will not be spirits without bodies, but we will put on our new heavenly bodies. Our dying bodies make us groan and sigh, but it's not that we want to die and have no bodies at all. We want to slip into our new bodies so that these dying bodies will be swallowed up by everlasting life. God himself has prepared us for this, and as a guarantee he puts His Spirit in us.'"

SIXTY-NINE

If I didn't have a doctor's appointment in town, and one that took months to get, Peter and I would have taken a nap with our birdie friend in the sand. But we did have to go, and all we could do was take the snowy egret with us in our thoughts until later that day when the wildlife rehabilitation hospital called and gave us the news.

Its wing was broken, there was sand in its mouth, and it was dehydrated…past the point of rehabilitation.

"We had no choice," the volunteer said with passion in her voice, as if it was the one and only bird she tried, but couldn't save. "We had to put it out of its misery."

After such news, and the news we got in town, I was trying to get on with my day, trying to make Peter homemade Meyer lemon bars. The fruit trees in our yard were producing, and I was making lemon bars all too often, giving plates of them to friends. I didn't want to waste a single piece of fruit in our yard.

I mixed flour, sea salt, confectioners' sugar, and baking powder together in a bowl, then put it all into the food processor and added chunks of cold butter, vanilla, and lemon zest. But when Peter came into the kitchen and found me cutting into a deeply yellow lemon with a hue of orange, the two of us broke down.

Watching that bird suffer had been reason enough to cry, but we were crying over more than a bird. I didn't know all the reasons for Peter's tears, but I was crying about evil things happening in the news, and the human suffering all over the world, and for the hurting individuals wandering off in isolation, far from the crowded seashore, stepping on burr after burr, limping their way unseen through the sea oats, hearing from afar the distant laughter of others making their way through the same difficult world, but doing so while holding hands and finding joy and leaping over the waves of God's presence.

Peter used his arm like a windshield wiper, and cleared the tears from his face.

"We don't have to cry like this," I said, wanting to be strong. "That treatment sounds great, and it's going to help me. The doctor was optimistic. I just don't want to forget the names of our grandkids."

"Names, Adele, that's all they are—names. You can still love and enjoy them even if you forget a name or two, or three, or…"

"Seven, Peter. We have seven grandchildren."

But whether seven or a hundred, their names were important. And so were the names on the list I kept in the desk drawer—names for the Father, Son, and Spirit. I never wanted to forget who God was, or who I was to Him. I also kept a list of names I found in the Bible for who I, as a believer, was to God. And I read them often.

After blowing our noses and pulling ourselves together, I went about pressing the dough into the bottom of a lightly oiled baking dish. Once it was in the oven, I started on the filling, beating eggs and yolk together for about two minutes, then whisking white sugar, flour, and baking powder until smooth. I added lemon juice and zest, and by the time I poured it into the partially baked crust, I was already feeling better.

In some ways, Peter was right. A name was just a name.

There was joy in watching the small, white shorebirds gregariously chasing waves up and back, regardless of my knowing they were called sanderlings. The tree with the vibrantly blooming, frilly orange petals was always going to stop me in my tracks, whether I knew it was called a royal poinciana, or not. And the tall, silvery grass was still going to rustle for me in the breeze, even if I hadn't a clue that what I was hearing was called bushy broom grass.

I made the glaze, and when it was finished, dipped my finger in for a taste. Yes, I'd rather have experienced things and *not* known their names than to have known their names but not experienced them. The eight tablespoons of lemon juice and half a cup of confectioners' sugar mixed together was delicious, regardless of my knowing it was called glaze.

When I peeked into the oven, the custard had a thin, white, sugary look. I pulled it out, then drizzled glaze over the warm custard top. Once it cooled, I cut it into sixteen squares, and while dusting it with confectioners' sugar, Peter came back into the kitchen holding our favorite board game.

"Again?" I asked. "You want to play it again?"

"You know me, I'm always in the mood for SCRABBLE. Won't you play with me?"

I didn't need to answer. The smile on my face was yes enough, although I knew what he was doing…making sure I got my daily dose of a stimulating brain game.

He took a lemon bar with him as he went onto the porch to set things up. A few seconds later, as I was finishing up in the kitchen, I got a text from him: *The bird with the golden slippers.*

"That's how I felt when I took my first bite," he told me when I joined him at the round teak café table where we always played. "Scrumptious bars, perfectly golden crust."

The porch turned quiet as we picked our seven letters, setting them up on the wooden racks. The palm rats weren't up yet, and neither were the frogs. Well into our game, a spring breeze blew through the trees, waking the night critters. Things got noisy then. Peter and I were making a ruckus, discussing all kinds of words, because every word we put down seemed to warrant dictionary confirmations and debate.

Peter placed tiles that formed a big word—*SANCTIFICATION.* "Wow, did I spell that right?"

I adjusted my reading glasses on my nose, then studied the word. Sure enough, flowing in a row from left to right, he correctly spelled the fourteen-letter word. "You did indeed. Congratulations, Peter—you won!"

"I shouldn't admit this." He scratched his head.

"What?

"I have no idea what that word even means."

I gave him a look, like *no big deal.* He didn't know what *atonement* meant, either, but had experienced years earlier the overwhelming need to have his sins forgiven, and to be made right before God. *Reconciliation* was another one. He didn't know back when he declared with his mouth and believed in his heart that Jesus was Lord, raised from the dead, that reconciliation was the word for the special thing happening between him and God, but he experienced it nonetheless.

I handed my sins to Jesus back when I didn't even know the term *re-demption*. The assurance was there in my heart that I would live eternally with God in Heaven whether I knew the word *salvation* or not. I became spiritually alive, bursting at the seams with new, Christ-given life, but never thought to call myself that two-word-says-all, *born again*.

"*Sanctification*—" I said while Peter and I picked up the letters and dropped them into the velvet drawstring pouch "—working intimately together with the Holy Spirit as He transforms our inner selves. That's what *sanctification* means. You might not know all the big words, but to your point earlier, you can still know the experience."

He grinned, like he always did right before he was about to say something clever. "If you say so, I'll just have to take your *word* for it." He pulled the pencil from behind his ear and tossed it into the box, right before I put the lid on it.

SEVENTY

* * *

"The law of the Lord is perfect, reviving the soul. The statues
of the Lord are trustworthy, making wise the simple. The
precepts of the Lord are right, giving joy to the heart. The
commands of the Lord are radiant, giving light to the eyes.
The fear of the Lord is pure, enduring forever. The ordinances
of the Lord are sure, and altogether righteous. They are more
precious than gold, than much pure gold; they are sweeter
than honey, than honey from the comb. By them is your
servant warned: in keeping them there is great reward."
—Psalm 19:7—11

"How much longer until they hatch?"
"Mere days," I'd answered countless times.

To people walking by, I looked like a wildlife volunteer sitting in the
sand, keeping watch over a nesting site. But eggs or no eggs, I was sitting
on my rump in my favorite patch of sand, where I sat pretty much every single morning…just past the *do-not* sign, and several yards from the
staked-off snowy plover nesting site.

"Wow, three mornings in a row," a gal with a camera said to me. "You
must not want to miss it."

I didn't want to miss it, but was doing more than sitting around, waiting for eggs to hatch. Surrounded by bright yellow dune daisies, ablaze
from the sun, I was enjoying a golden moment alone with God, praying
for the snowy plovers, that they might never be driven into extinction.
And praying, too, for God's people, that they continue in ever-increasing
numbers on Earth.

I loved sitting with God in my own staked-off section of each day. Although a far cry from a newly hatched follower of Christ, mature ones needed to protect daily alone time with God as much as newer ones did.

I was glad the gal taking pictures stayed behind the string, with no parts of her body, camera, or lens crossing the line. The sign said *do not step closer than three hundred feet from any nest on the beach*, and I applauded—*whew, whew, whew*—whoever it was that put the protective *do-nots* in place. Obviously, they cared about the survival of the snowy plovers.

Still, there were always those who ignored the *do-nots*—*Do not pester the birds. Do not litter. Do not let your dog off its leash.* If only they understood the reasoning behind the *do-nots*, that doing them might lead to the death of a bird or a turtle. The *do-nots* were posted out of love—love for nature, love for life, and the preservation of the two. They weren't meant to ruin anyone's fun.

"Out of protective love for us, You posted *do-nots*, too," I murmured to the One who revived my soul and brought joy to my heart. "Thank you for caring…You've always cared about the preservation of Your people. And when Your people fell short in following Your law, You sent us Jesus to follow instead." I dug my toes in the sand. "Look where following Him has led me…sitting in Your presence."

Although the world had always been a threatening place, it was getting more so by the day. Ignorance and fearlessness were letting wickedness run leash-less and wild. Ignorance was oblivious, and fearlessness arrogant to the protective measures, the standards of living written in the light of protective love that God had taken all throughout history to preserve His people.

Ignorance hadn't a care in the world, and fearlessness feared the destruction of the world, but had no fear for the One who made the world. If ignorance knew, and fearlessness feared the Holy One, then both would have listened to what Earth's creator was telling us to do…humble ourselves, pray, seek His face, and turn from wickedness. Then, God would heal our land.

Stewards of the planet—I appreciated environmental efforts, but when it came to preservation, all I knew for sure was that self-preservation was futile. "For that, I need you, Christ, my Savior—the greatest preservationist of all times!" My insides applauded Jesus' efforts on Earth. Satan didn't stand a chance at putting God's people into extinction! *Whew, whew, whew.*

"Well, I sure got great pictures of the eggs." The gal with the camera walked over to me. "Would you mind if I took a picture of you, too? I read your book, and well, people told me you sit here in the mornings."

"Go ahead," I smiled warmly. "You're more than welcome to sit and chat for a moment, if you want." I always enjoyed connecting with my readers.

"Oh, I wish. But I have a plane to catch. Mind if I ask you a question, though?"

"Sure, go ahead."

"I read it once, and couldn't help but think how unrealistic it was that a long-lost friend just so happened to be living right next door to her on the island. But then I read it a second time, wondering if all the Vivienne parts were really just Adele sitting down to write her novel...pretending that her childhood friend was living next door. My book club is split in half on this. I'd love to go back and tell them I asked you." She looked at me challengingly. "Did her friend really live next door...I mean, it really was too unbelievable of a coincidence. Just curious."

It wasn't the first time I'd been asked that. "Here's what I'll tell you," I said. "I had a really good friend...and well, let's just say nothing was ever easy for her. From childhood on, it was one thing after the next, and it seemed like she was constantly in this never-ending dark place. As close as we were all the way through college, not once did I invite her to church with me, or even mention so much as a single word about God and how He loved the world so much—her included! We lost touch, although I knew she was working as an interior designer in northern California. But when I heard through the social media grapevine that she had tried taking her own life, I was beside myself. Why had I never said anything back when I had the chance...where was my voice for God, and why had I never used it before?" I pulled my glasses off and looked her in the eyes. "I'll let you wonder the rest, but one more thing...the world spinning out of control really did bother me, and I was doing nothing about it. Annoyed with my muted voice...living as if my words were in lockdown...I went to God about it, and He helped me...transformed me from worrywart into warrior. Praying and writing were my weapons. I wanted to use my writing for something good, help even just one person."

"Has she read your novel?"

"Oh yes. And we're not friends anymore."

"That's terrible."

"No, no, no." I squinted from the brightness. "We're more than friends...sisters in Christ now. She lives in San Francisco, and we talk all the time. In fact, I've already written that glistening chapter of her life and maybe I'll put it out there, I'm not sure. She wants me to. But regarding the novel, and what's real and true...well, my love for seashells, and for Sanibel, and for God is real and true. And so is His love for us."

She glanced at her watch. "Thank you. Thank you so much for answering that. I wish I didn't have to go...wish I could miss my flight, but I can't. Don't sit here too long. Your nose might burn."

I waved her off, like she didn't need to worry about that. Then, after watching her shrink down the beach, I stood up and reached my arms overhead, like Viv had on the Golden Gate Bridge that day. I clasped my hands together, and pointed my fingers upward like the steeple of a chapel...a chapel by the sea. Closing my eyes, I marveled. Why did I marvel? Let me tell you.

There is a sea and in that sea are islands,
sanctuary islands like Sanibel.
And on that sanctuary island are birds
fallen, rehabilitated, released from the clutches of death.
And there are people, too,
fallen, rehabilitated, released from the clutches of death,
whose refuge is God,
and who dwell in the shelter of the Most High.
I am one of them,
and in me is something larger than the universe,
gentler than the morning doves, more consuming than the sea,
more lasting than the memory of any bird
in the shallows of my mind,
more golden than the snowy egret slippers,
or the dune daisies in the sun,
more precious and purposeful than crude oil
in the Gulf of Mexico, even.

In me is the oil of gladness, and the eternal well,
more quenching than the juice of the freshest squeezed citrus,
and more fragrant than the ylang-ylang flowers.
Moving throughout me
is an irresistible wind
more constructive than a breeze to a tree,
helping the dead fronds drop.
In me
is the Spirit of Christ.
Whew, whew, whew.
I am a living, breathing sanctuary,
a walking temple of the Holy Spirit.

"Hi Grams, are you stretching?"

I opened my eyes, and there she was—no bigger than a mollusk her first time on Sanibel—my towering, grown-up beauty of a granddaughter standing in front of me, out of breath from her morning jog.

"Why hello, Miss Royal Palm." I had called her that for years, because every spring when she came to visit, her legs were an inch taller from the year before. "Yes, I was stretching." Stretching my hands toward Heaven. "How was your jog…did you make it farther than yesterday?"

"Yep, by an extra mile." She pulled her sunglasses off, then picked up a pen shell and drew a giant heart in the sand.

We both stepped into it, then sat down. Sitting in a heart drawn in the sand was our own special thing. We established it when she was little, and every time she visited, whenever she etched one, it meant she was craving a heart-to-heart talk. We spent many hours all through the years laughing, talking, crying together in hearts that she or I had drawn in the sand.

"I'm glad it's only day two." She leaned into me. "I have five more days with you on Sanibel."

"What's on your mind?" One of our rules for sitting in the heart was to skip the small talk, the beating around the bush, and get straight to the heart of whatever was on our minds.

"I've been crazy busy. I keep saying again and again that after this week, things will slow down, and they never do. I'm trying to keep up. But is that all there is to life…keeping my head above water? I don't enjoy my days. I dread my alarm going off. I'm tired…tired of constantly trying to get everything done. I'm more than tired, Grams."

"When was the last time you closed your eyes and went there?"

"Where?"

"You know, to God…in prayer?"

She tucked her hair behind her ears. "I don't know, sitting here in the heart with you last year. But it's not because I don't want to. I do. It's just all this stuff I have to get done is always right here, smack in my face, and overwhelming."

"And you feel like God is far away?"

She nodded, and I shifted my positioning, so instead of looking at the Gulf of Mexico in front of me, I was facing her. "I don't want to sound overly intense in what I'm about to say…"

"We're in the heart, Grams. You can be as intense as you want…say whatever you need to say in the heart."

"Okay then." I picked up a handful of sand, letting it slip through my fingers. "It's a fast-paced world, and there's always going to be something encroaching upon your precious time. See those strings put up over there, to protect the eggs?" I pointed to the snowy plover nesting site. "We have to take measures, too…mark out and protect our daily alone time with God. Even waking fifteen minutes early, reading a verse from the Bible, and sitting quietly, having coffee with Him in your kitchen—" I hesitated. "Have you been going to church at all?"

"No, Grams. Sunday mornings are the only mornings I get to sleep in, and stay in my pajamas a little longer."

"There's eleven o'clock services, you know."

"Yeah," she nodded. "I do want more God in my life, I'm just so tired."

I licked my lips. "You want more God in your life…a good want to have, and it's God-given. You're internally wired to want more of Him… deep within the infrastructure of your being, He has wired you that way."

"Yes, I do believe that."

"Then do not," I said, looking her in the eyes, "do not let the harassing distractions of this world, or any person intrude upon those precious wants, you hear me? Don't let anything destroy your wanting to be close with God...even your own hecticness. Take whatever protective measures are necessary...stake off your own undisturbed moments to read His Word, pray, and connect with others who believe."

She was quiet and her eyes contemplative. She rolled down onto her stomach and rested her chin in cupped hands. "Have you ever seen Him, Grams? Have you ever seen God?"

"No," I said as I looked out at the Gulf. "But I've seen His craftsmanship, His handiwork, His greatness, and who hasn't? Evidence of Him is everywhere...in the rising and setting of the sun, and everything in between. Would you believe I just memorized a verse relevant to what you asked me?"

"Let me hear it, Grams."

I closed my eyes and retrieved Psalm nineteen from the special place in my mind. "'The heavens declare the glory of God; the skies proclaim the work of his hands. Day after day they pour forth speech; night after night they display knowledge. There is no speech or language where their voice is not heard. Their voice goes out into all the earth, their words to the end of the world.'"

"Good for you, memorizing as you are! You keep at it."

I opened my eyes and looked at her intently.

"What?" she asked.

"I can see a glimpse of Him in your eyes, even."

"My eyes?" She squinted. "What do you mean?"

"You're a child of God. The light of God's glory, it's in your eyes. You accepted Him into your heart, remember?"

"Of course."

"Well, that light is in you." I hesitated, wondering how dramatic I wanted to be, then went for it. "You're my granddaughter, and you know I love you. But Your God's child, His royalty, heir to the kingdom. It's beyond what you can imagine, the inheritance He has for you. So, what are you waiting for?" I thought of the King David verse that once did its thing in me. "Go where your heart and soul are yearning...to the courts of your Lord, return to His presence, daughter of God!"

She rolled onto her back and put her hands behind her head. "Thank you, Grams."

"For what?"

"Reminding me who I am."

"You're a masterpiece in the making," I went on, "God's work in progress, a walking temple…restoration underway."

"It's so easy to forget all of that, and I don't want to. I want to remember."

"Then I'll give you a copy of the list…the list of names of who we as believers are to God…so you never forget. And if I forget, read them to me when you visit, will you? I keep it in the desk drawer of the guest room."

She smiled. "Anything else you want to say before our skin burns? I feel my nose burning, and yours is turning pink."

I looked up at the sky. There was always more…more I wanted to say. "Fly birdie, fly, return to your Refuge, your special go-to place. It's not far. The Branch of Righteousness is always within reach, so perch in God's presence…His real, not imaginary presence. And may He be your peace, your calm, your center in this unstable world."

Whew, whew, whew.

"Aw, Grams, I love sitting in the heart with you. I love that we can talk like this."

"It's good to talk like this…good to be dramatic, right? When I look back on my life…my goodness, it was my life…if anything I wasn't dramatic enough!"

THE END

OR MAYBE JUST

SEE YOU LATER ALLIGATOR…SEE YOU IN A WHILE, CROCODILE,

 **CHRISTINE LEMMON** grew up in Saugatuck, Michigan, in a house attached to her family's ice-cream shop and bed & breakfast. From childhood on, she wrote feverishly in her diaries. After graduating from Hope College, she moved around the country writing for radio, newspaper, television, and magazines. She also worked as a publicist for a nonfiction publishing house in northern California.

As well as writing novels, she enjoys taking walks through nature preserves, and boating with friends and family along Florida's Gulf Coast. Not only is Sanibel the setting for her novels, it was the setting for her life for nearly two decades, and she is incredibly thankful to have raised her family in the close-knit island community.

Christine is the author of the novels *Sanibel Scribbles*, *Portion of the Sea*, *Sand in My Eyes*, and *Steps to the Beach*; and the gift book *Whisper from the Ocean*. She speaks at events, including book clubs, and loves connecting with her readers. Visit her online at www.ChristineLemmon.com.

Made in the USA
Columbia, SC
14 May 2023

16548612R10280